The Soul
of a Stranger

Dana Abbott Celich

WESTBOW
PRESS®
A DIVISION OF THOMAS NELSON
& ZONDERVAN

Scripture quotations have been taken from the Christian Standard Bible®, Copyright © 2017 by Holman Bible Publishers. Used by permission. Christian Standard Bible® and CSB® are federally registered trademarks of Holman Bible Publishers.

WestBow Press books may be ordered through booksellers or by contacting:

WestBow Press
A Division of Thomas Nelson & Zondervan
1663 Liberty Drive
Bloomington, IN 47403
www.westbowpress.com
1 (866) 928-1240

ISBN: 978-1-9736-0083-1 (sc)
ISBN: 978-1-9736-0082-4 (hc)
ISBN: 978-1-9736-0084-8 (e)

Library of Congress Control Number: 2017913283

Print information available on the last page.

WestBow Press rev. date: 12/4/2017

Acknowledgements

I owe deep and heartfelt thanks to everyone who has encouraged me in my authorial pursuits. These dear people include:

LifePointe Alliance Church, Mars, Pennsylvania
Sue Stevenson, Heidi Burford, Marilyn Potter, Diann Coppock, and the Tuesday morning Bible Study ladies

Friends
Dwain and Nancy Howell, Bob and Gail Anderson, Ed and Anne Ludwig, Heidi Cox, Mike and Jill Cary, Gail Suhr

Co-workers at MSA—The Safety Company
Christy Weishorn, Dana Crano, Trish Luedtke, Emily Vukson, Tim Carrera, Todd Hagerich, Mark Hall, and Steve Grasha

In-Laws
Mildred Celich
The Stricklings, the DiCiccos, the Celiches

And especial love and thanks to:

My Parents
William and Barbara Abbott

My Daughter
Charis Celich

My Husband
Stephen Celich

Chapter 1

Miserable. That was undeniably the proper word for the weather on this gloomy spring afternoon—depressingly wet, unseasonably cool, and definitely miserable. But, after all, this was England, and, more to the point, it was a funeral.

Blunted raindrops—all but invisible against hard, gray church stones and sodden, black cloaks—battered the mourners as Henry Devreux, the third Earl of Hartwell, was laid to rest. Quite a few men had braved the downpour to be present at the cemetery, for Hartwell had always commanded the respect of people from all walks of life. Although he had been rigid in his opinions and reserved in his demeanor, he had lived an honorable and upright life. He was even rumored to have been strictly faithful to his wife of twenty-eight years.

It was rather an accomplishment for one of the aristocracy.

Standing well in the background on the fringes of the grieving crowd, William Devreux, the fourth Earl of Hartwell, watched his father's lifeless body carried by pallbearers into the family mausoleum. As the heir, he should have insisted on serving as his father's chief mourner, but to the outrage of many he had refused to do the job. His half-sister's husband had stepped in on his behalf.

Will had also declined to carry an umbrella, and now the cold spring rain was soaking him to the bone. He welcomed the wetness on his face, however, because the drops falling off the brim of his hat masked the tears upon which Society frowned. These would be his only tears, he vowed.

He had admired the calm assurance his stepmother had shown in public throughout this whole ordeal, but he was glad women weren't permitted here at the graveside. The Dowager Lady Hartwell had kept the vigil beside her husband's body at the house and had been able to say her private goodbyes there. Will alone had seen her savage grief, by accident, when he had gone down to the drawing room in the middle of the night to offer to relieve her watch. Deep, aching sobs had stopped him in his tracks. Afraid she would see him and be embarrassed by the interruption, he had hurried back upstairs.

If only he hadn't insisted on coming to Ashbourne Park in the first place! Would that he could turn back time, reset the clock, change his selfish decision. His father had written to him, suggesting that he postpone his visit, but he had been rather keen to avoid a certain angry gentleman from whom he had won two hundred pounds in a shady betting game. So he had made his way to the estate in the throes of a short-lived but nasty sickness.

That had been five days ago. He felt much better now, but the Earl had contracted the illness soon after his son's arrival. The older man's weak lungs had been unable to stand the strain of the virulent infection, and it had all been over in a matter of fewer than twenty-four hours.

Will's stepmother had been remarkably kind, but he had hated that. He wished she had railed at him in front of everyone, accusing him of killing her beloved husband as surely as if he had plunged a knife into the Earl's heart. After all, Will accused himself, he deserved her indignation. And although such a scene would have been ugly, he would have preferred her disdain to her soft tears and her attempt at hugging him, which she abandoned when it became clear that he would not under any circumstances put his own arms around her.

He had to get away from Ashbourne Park. The sooner the better.

He shivered underneath his cloak, resenting the cold air made raw by the unrelenting deluge. The interment was almost over, thank heavens. His father was now resting beside the mother he couldn't remember and the half-brother he remembered too well. A triumvirate of the righteous dead.

So where could he go when he put Ashbourne Park behind him? *Not to London*, he thought irritably. As his expensive Hessian boots squished in the mud on his way back to the family carriage—in which he had insisted upon riding alone for the funeral procession—he ruled out returning to his town house. Although the idea of living out the next few months in a drunken stupor had a certain appeal, for the first time in his life the thought of it also strangely repelled him. He grudgingly conceded to himself that the pain of his guilt and grief would only be dulled temporarily, and he might do something grossly stupid in the meantime. Furthermore, the season was underway in London with its crush of parties, balls, and entertainments; solitude was a complete impossibility.

Better to take a journey far, far away. But where should he go?

He could ride to Southampton or Bournemouth and take a ship from there to some remote destination. Not to France, naturally, which like much of Europe lay in the grip of Bonaparte's rule, but perhaps he could go to Sicily. Or, farther away still, he could even travel across the seas to North America or the West Indies. But what would he do in any of those places? The same things he would have done in London: drinking, betting, and other assorted forms of debauchery. He might as well go back to carousing with the Prince of Wales, he grunted with distaste, recalling what he considered to be the heir to the throne's tedious company.

He stared out of the window as rain-carved ruts rocked the coach uncomfortably from side to side. Who would welcome his presence and yet leave him to his own devices? Not his aunts and uncles or cousins; they would interfere, ask questions, write to his stepmother or half-sister, and generally make nuisances of themselves.

What about friends? Not that he had any real friends, he admitted to himself bleakly. The men with whom he surrounded himself were more like partners in crime, if his late father's opinions were correct. No, he didn't want to see any of their dissipated faces.

But another face rose up in his mind's eye, taking him by surprise. Now there was a fellow Will hadn't thought of in many years: *Barney!* Or—more precisely—Mr. Barnabas Worthington, now the squire of some undistinguished place in a far-off corner of Cheshire. They had been companions during their Oxford days, when Will's courtesy title of Viscount Disborough had not yet become synonymous with fast living.

3

Nonetheless, Will had been well on his way to garnering that reputation. He had been sent down for most of Trinity term his second year as punishment for a series of ill-considered juvenile pranks. Unfortunately, when he returned to the university for Michaelmas term, Barney had graduated. They had seen one another rarely after that, and it had been eight or nine years since Will had even written to the man, but now he recalled him fondly. Barney had not been above raising a rumpus on occasion, like any of the students, but he had been blessed with a steady temperament, and he had faced every day with good humor.

Yes, Will decided as the carriage came to a stop in front of the grand house at Ashbourne Park, he would search out Barney.

His stepmother was dismayed when he told her he was going away. "You are Lord Hartwell now," she scolded him. "Your duty lies here. What makes you think that you have the luxury to go off and mourn somewhere by yourself?"

"Mama, you have Esmé and John right here should you need anything. They're planning to stay at Ashbourne for several weeks." *Another good reason to flee*, Will thought. "And this way you need not feel that you must move out of the main house and down to the dower house straightaway. It will give you more time to organize your things, to adjust to the situation."

Her face fell. "Yes, that's true. I am tired."

"You see? It's for the best that I leave." He wanted to put his hand on her shoulder, but he resisted the urge.

She raised her eyes to his. "Won't you at least tell me where you're planning to go?"

"No. I don't want anyone chasing after me, hunting me down like a wounded animal."

"They won't. I'll see to it. I won't tell anyone where you are."

"They'll weasel it out of you, and you won't be able to stop them from tracking me down."

She sighed in acknowledgement of the truth of his claim and gave up. "Please take care of yourself."

He couldn't promise that, but he lied easily enough. "Of course I will. I'll come home eventually."

There was a long silence, and neither of them moved. Then she whispered, "I don't blame you for his death, Will."

His throat closed up, and the tears he had vowed he would not shed again threatened to storm out of his eyes. He took a few steps backward. "Perhaps not," he spat out, his voice cracking. "But *I do!*"

He whirled around on his heel and charged out of the room, slamming the door behind him with such fury that a maid walking in the hall jumped out of his way with a squeak of alarm. He stomped up to his bedroom, marched into the adjacent dressing room, and began to throw a few necessities into a satchel.

His valet came running into the chamber. "May I assist you, my lord…?" he started to say, but Will cut him off abruptly.

"I am going away for a while. Alone."

"But, my lord…"

"I shan't need you, Dibbs. Just stay here and—oh, I don't care—see that my entire wardrobe is cleaned and pressed, or something."

"But, my lord…"

Will closed the satchel and fastened it. "Do as I say. Be of assistance to the Dowager Countess whilst I am gone."

"Of course, my lord, but…"

Satchel in hand, Will pushed his way past the dismayed man. It was almost as though he were being compelled by an unseen force to rush out of the walls of his childhood home and into the darkness.

He avoided saying goodbye to his sister and her husband and went directly to the stables. There he mounted not his usual steed, but one of the estate's horses—an older, reliable stallion named Prometheus. Without even a clear idea of where he would sleep, he rode out into the dismal, wet night.

Chapter 2

Several days later Will found himself not far from where he'd calculated the Worthington estate should be. He'd spent a few sorry nights in unappealing inns drowning his sorrows in the company of colorful locals, but now he sat straight up in the saddle as he rode, anxious to be reunited with his old friend. It never occurred to him a surprise visit might not be the wisest of ventures.

When he reached a tiny village a few miles into the county of Cheshire, he suspected he was close to his destination. Satisfaction rose up inside him as he trotted Prometheus down the one and only street. Upon spotting a small public house, he decided here would be the best place to find out the exact route to the Worthington estate.

As he entered the humble establishment, its patrons stared at him in sudden, silent curiosity. The publican, recognizable by his leather apron and towel in hand, spoke up. "An' how may I help ye, sir?"

"I am looking for the residence of Mr. Barnabas Worthington. Could you be so kind as to direct me there?"

The man's eyes narrowed slightly. "An' what would ye be wanting with Mr. Worthington?"

"Only the pleasure of his company, I assure you," Will answered readily. "I am an old friend."

"Ye can't be too close of a friend, or ye'd know that Mr. and Mrs. Worthington have been gone for almost a year."

"What?" Will asked in dismay.

"Mrs. Worthington came down wi' consumption, so the squire

took her t' Italy last June." The publican picked up a mug and wiped it with his towel. "So I'm right sorry to tell ye the house is empty. Sad and lifeless, it is now."

This unwelcome information took him by complete surprise. What a fool he was—his only hope of a friend was not even in the country! Sad and lifeless, indeed.

"Ah," he mumbled, not meeting the publican's gaze. Humiliated, he sped out of the building and remounted Prometheus. Spurring the horse into a gallop, he rode as far as he could until he came to a moderately sized town, where he proceeded to buy enough horrible-tasting ale to drink himself into a stupor. He spent the next day in bed with a monstrous headache, but the day after that he was on the road again, even though he felt strangely lightheaded. He began to experience chills off and on, and as he steered his horse up onto a road that led over a steep hill, he realized that he was perspiring, although the afternoon was not warm.

It would serve him right, he thought, if he died of some unknown disease out in the middle of nowhere. He had thought he'd shaken off the sickness that killed his father, but here he was falling ill again just a week later, this time alone and far from any help.

And—as if it mirrored his tormented soul—thunder rolled along the edge of the sky. Wind began to blow in his face. Dark clouds overtook him, pelting him with merciless rain, and the road dissolved into a quagmire. But there was no available shelter of any kind, and he pressed on, the road narrowing dangerously as it wound along a steep slope.

He hunched over the saddle and kept Prometheus at a walk, but soon his thoughts became disjointed. Was that someone in the shadows following him? No, it was just an oddly shaped tree. A flash of lightning jolted the landscape into sinister relief for a fraction of a second, and Prometheus, sensing his rider's unease, broke into a run.

Will tried to hold on to the reins, but his brain felt woolly; he couldn't figure out what he should be doing with the two leather things in his hands. And as the progressively louder booms of thunder threatened to split his head in two, his horse galloped faster, now completely out of control.

Maybe a figure *was* pursuing them—could it be a monster or a demon? Will moaned as another bolt of lightning blinded him for an instant. Clutching at the horse's neck, he heard someone scream—and realized it was himself—as Prometheus tripped over a rock, slipped, and hurtled with his rider headlong over the edge of the cliff.

Sometime later—how much later he had no idea—Will struggled up out of oblivion into a consciousness marred by searing pain. His head throbbed viciously, and his right leg felt as though someone had hewn it in half with an axe. It was also strangely heavy and stiff. What was going on? What had happened? Where was he?

He groaned out loud, and the sound of his own voice reverberated in his head, spinning the room nauseatingly even though his eyes were closed. He realized that he was wearing a nightshirt, lying on something soft, and covered by a blanket, but the comfortable bedding had no impact on the agony that gripped his entire body. His mind seemed to be filled with hot molten lead, his thoughts heavy and slow. He did notice a sudden flurry of footsteps close by, and voices, but he could only process a phrase or two.

"…very serious…"

"…nothing more you can do?" That was a woman speaking.

"…may not last the night."

May not last the night. Funny, but he didn't care at all. Not one bit. In fact, he hoped this was the end. With any luck, soon he would enter complete nothingness, and he wouldn't be a burden to anyone ever again. Yes, it was probably better this way.

Unless, of course, hell was real. Then he was in deep trouble.

I don't want to go to hell! Had he said those words out loud? How pathetic, because he deserved to burn in everlasting torment just as much as his father and mother and brother deserved to enjoy eternal bliss in the heavenly realms.

He moaned again, although this time whether from physical or spiritual anguish, it was difficult to tell. Blackness seemed to close in around him, and he felt himself slipping away, down, down, down…

The second time he regained consciousness the pain was still very real, but at least it did communicate to him that he was yet alive. He shifted ever so slightly on the mattress, and at once he heard someone come over to stand beside him. He opened his eyes as far as he could pry them apart and saw the hazy face of a woman gazing down at him. He tried to speak, but the words came out as an incomprehensible croak.

"Shh," she told him softly. "Here is some water."

He felt a wet cloth gently pressing down upon his lips, and he sucked the liquid in greedily. Then he coughed.

"Easy there," she said. "Slowly now." He sipped again, successfully this time, as her fingers soothed his brow; from her touch, he realized that he was drenched in sweat. After he had sucked in all the liquid he could bear, she took the cloth away, dipped it in a bowl of water she must have had close by, and rubbed it over his forehead. He sighed, too tired even to thank her, and simply allowed his mind to slip back into the waiting darkness.

Suddenly aware of himself again, Will felt as though his entire body lay in a furnace. Searing pain consumed him with its fire, and yet somehow in the midst of the physical torment, he recalled that he had been out of control—shrieking, falling over a cliff in the midst of a vicious storm. How in heaven's name could he still be alive? Would that he had died! Or perhaps… this was hell itself! He thrashed ferociously, emitting a parched and rasping scream.

A male voice called out something, and he felt strong hands subdue him. Instinctively, without thought, he fought against the interference. Opening his eyes in rage and terror, he looked into the face of a middle-aged man. There was a brief struggle, and he heard a female voice cry out in the background, but it was over as soon as it had begun. He fell back onto his pillow, utterly spent.

The man who had wrestled with him spoke again, sharply. "Don't, Charissa! Don't approach him. You see that he's dangerous!"

"No, Godfrey," the woman's voice insisted. "You know as well as I do his only hope is prayer. Dr. Shaw said as much."

"You can pray for him in the other room."

"Aunt Caroline and I have been. Now I must to pray for him here."

"The Almighty can hear you anywhere."

9

"Of course, but I feel strongly that I need to do so at his bedside. You may stay and join me, or you should leave," she added firmly.

After a short pause, the man replied, "Oh very well, but if he should attack you in his delirium, I won't hesitate to take drastic measures."

"He won't attack me," she maintained.

But Will was angry. *Don't pray!* The defiant words flooded his mind, but he couldn't articulate them. *No! No!* He thrashed about in a pitiful, exhausted effort to stave off the woman's ministrations, but as soon as he felt the pressure of her cool hands—one on his head and one on his shoulder—all of his strivings melted away. He caught a glimpse of her face, her deep blue eyes gazing at him intently, and he wondered if she were an angel. As his eyes fell shut in surrender, she began to speak.

"Dearest Heavenly Father," she whispered, "I lift before You this man, this stranger in our midst. I don't know his name, Lord, but You do. You know his needs, and only You can heal his body and his mind and his heart. Please, Lord, I ask that You touch him right now and take away his fever and reveal Yourself to him. Work a miracle in his life, for I ask it in the holy and precious Name of Your Son Jesus. Amen."

"Amen," agreed the man.

As soon as she began to pray, Will felt a tingling sensation at the tips of her fingers, but it was totally unlike the burning of the sickness which ravaged him. In his feverish brain, he likened it to the touch of starlight—cold heat, if there were such a thing. Slowly it grew stronger, piercing through the vise-like illness which had warped his body and his soul. A silvery light began to fill his mind's eye, enveloping him with a power unlike anything he had ever known—and then he lost consciousness again.

A cool breeze touched Will on his cheek. It felt like a caress, and his chest rose and fell as he took a slow, deep breath. Was that a bird singing outside the open window? His eyelids fluttered.

Where was he? Opening his eyes all the way, he looked around the room in which he found himself. It had likely been built two-and-a-half centuries ago, given its characteristic dark paneling and painted timber ceiling. Its diamond-mullioned windows were large, however, and the cheerful sunlight streaming in through them prevented the chamber from feeling oppressive. On the contrary, Will had the distinct sense that he had come home, although he knew he had never been here before.

Odd.

He remembered he had had some sort of riding accident, but the details of it were fuzzy. He did recall several people had taken care of him in his delirium, and he wondered who they were.

Feeling tired but so very much better, he sat up slowly, noticing he had on a splint. He must have broken the lower part of his right leg; no wonder it hurt so badly.

Next, he looked around the room for his clothes. They were nowhere to be seen, but he did notice an empty chair pulled up beside the bed. He recalled vaguely that a woman had been in the room with him. But his attention was drawn away from thoughts of her to a table beside the chair, because on it sat a cup and a jug filled with fresh, cool water. He realized that he was desperately thirsty. Leaning over, he poured some out for himself and drank it down greedily; he'd never had such a delicious cup of water in all his life.

After he had drunk his fill, he lay back down, worn out by the effort but pleased with himself. Thinking that in the not-too-distant future he might even like a bit of toast and tea, for the first time in years he fell asleep with a smile on his lips.

Chapter 3

Charissa Armitage opened the door to the sleeping stranger's room. Entering quietly, she sat down in the chair at his bedside, where she had already spent a number of hours keeping watch over him.

She gazed at the man's pale face, now so calm, and wondered—not for the first time—who he was. There had been no papers to indicate his identity tucked away in his well-tailored clothes, and he'd had no baggage with him, at least that they had found. He appeared to be about thirty years old, and while she and Sir Godfrey were sure he was a gentleman, they did not recognize him. He was, however, wealthy; they had found a substantial amount of money in his waistcoat.

He also seemed to be an angry person. This morning, when Dr. Shaw had informed them their patient was out of danger, he had said only a man with the strongest of constitutions could have fought off so severe an illness. Speculating that the gentleman's cantankerous nature had likely contributed to his cure, the physician had joked that his patient was just too ornery to die.

However, both Charissa and Sir Godfrey thought otherwise. "He was afraid of hell," Sir Godfrey had observed. "We both heard him cry out. I believe it is the Almighty who has given him a second chance—an opportunity to pursue righteousness instead of iniquity."

"The Lord heard my prayer for him," Charissa had whispered in amazement. "I can hardly believe it." Then she caught the irony of her own statement. "See how small my faith really is!"

Sir Godfrey had smiled at her fondly. "One only needs a mustard seed's worth of faith to move mountains, my dear."

Whatever the measure of her faith, she thought happily, God had heard all their prayers. The stranger was going to survive and return to his family for, she hoped, many more years of life.

Suddenly she drew in a breath, for she saw the man slowly open his eyes. They were beautiful, deep black eyes rimmed with dark lashes any woman would envy, and they turned to her in guarded curiosity.

She gave him a warm smile. "Welcome back to the land of the living, sir. We were afraid for a long while we had lost you. But here you are."

"Here I am," he rasped.

"You need some water," she said, pouring him a glass out of the jug on the table close by. Carefully, he sat up on one elbow and drank.

After he had had his fill, he lay back down, tired from the exertion. "Thank you," he said politely. "Miss… Mrs.….?"

"I am Miss Charissa Armitage."

Miss Armitage. She was quite pretty, he noted, even though she was past what was often referred to as the first blush of youth. But this observation was only of passing interest; he was much more concerned with his own story. "Miss Armitage, I remember nothing much beyond riding hard in a rainstorm. Would you mind telling me where I am? What happened to me?"

"You are at Silvercrosse Hall near the village of Murrington in northern Staffordshire."

Will stared up at the fanciful Tudor ceiling. He had never heard of the village of Murrington, and he suspected that he'd managed to lose himself quite far off the beaten track. Not a bad thing, that.

Charissa continued, "Of course, I don't know why you were traveling through these parts, since we're not on the main road to Stafford or Stoke-on-Trent. But anyway, several nights ago there was a terrible storm. It came up quickly, with an awful, howling wind and driving rain. Sir Godfrey and I rode out early the next morning to check on the pensioners who live near the river, to make sure that they hadn't been caught in a flood or suffered any other type of damage. Thank goodness, they were all fine, but when we returned home through a narrow part of the lower road—there is another path on the cliff above—I saw a figure lying way back in the bushes. It was you, sir."

"I do recall falling."

"You must have gone over the cliff. You were in terrible shape, all twisted up, bruised, and bloodied. Your horse lay next to you, but he was nearly dead. Sir Godfrey had to destroy him. I'm sorry," she sympathized sincerely.

"I'm sure it had to be done," Will said with a pang of grief; he had always cared for animals.

"Sir Godfrey regretted that such a course of action was necessary."

She had mention Sir Godfrey several times, and, curious, Will inquired about him.

"Godfrey is my cousin—my second half-cousin, really. Sir Godfrey Scrivener of Silvercrosse Hall. This is his estate. I live here with him and his aunt, Miss Caroline Scrivener."

"Well, I am deeply grateful to you and Sir Godfrey, Miss Armitage. I regret imposing upon you this way."

"Oh, it is no imposition. It is our Christian duty to care for you. But I'm afraid it will take a while for your broken leg to heal. It looked dreadful when I found you." She grimaced at the memory. "We sent for Mr. Rowley, the local surgeon. He set it when you were still unconscious."

"That at least is a mercy," Will commented wryly. He had seen a surgeon setting a man's leg before—a *conscious* man's leg. The patient's screams had given him nightmares.

Charissa nodded. "Mr. Rowley was pleased that he didn't have to enlist four or five strong men to hold you down whilst he put the bone back together. He said you broke your lower leg near the ankle, but it is a small, stable break, and he anticipates it should mend nicely. He is very good at his job, by the way. You may take comfort in that. And he doesn't believe you broke anything else, thank the Lord."

"How long until I'm able walk again?"

"It may be a month or two, I'm afraid. Mr. Rowley will be back soon to speak with you about it in more detail."

"Months?" Will grunted unhappily.

"Weeks, at any rate. But no doubt you'll be able to get about much sooner on crutches."

"I shall see to it," he replied with grim determination.

"Good," she said, encouraged by his fortitude. "Yet you must give yourself time to recover your strength, too. You not only broke your leg, but you also had a very high fever. The physician told us the chances of your survival were slim. But we prayed for you unceasingly."

Will felt uncomfortable. Why had she prayed for him, this woman who sounded so very *good?* He certainly hadn't wanted her to pray, nor did he deserve her petitions.

She saw him glance away, so she returned to practical rather than spiritual matters. "There is something else I must tell you. Sir Godfrey and I have discussed it, and we hope you will remain with us for as long as it takes you to recuperate."

He turned his attention back to her. "That is most charitable of you."

"We are pleased to be of help. As I said, we take our Christian duty seriously here at Silvercrosse Hall. So then, may I ask, sir, who you are? After all, if we are to care for you, we must know your name."

As Will's eyes met hers, so serious and so kind, he discovered that he did not want her to make the acquaintance of Lord William Devreux, who had been known for years as the worthless Viscount Disborough and who had now assumed the title Earl of Hartwell.

"I'm…" He stared up at the ceiling. Noticing a boss on one of the beams which was carved in the shape of a lion, he blurted out, "I'm William Lyon. Mr. William Lyon, from London." Yes, he liked the sound of that name. Valiant and honorable—completely unlike himself.

"Mr. Lyon," Charissa repeated thoughtfully. "Is there anyone to whom you wish to write, to reassure them that you are well—or that you will be well, at any rate?" She smiled. "Your family? Mrs. Lyon, perhaps?"

"There is no Mrs. Lyon. Nor any other Lyons I wish to notify, actually." That was true enough, since the Lyons were entirely fictional. "I am quite alone."

His confession tugged at Charissa's heartstrings. "I must disagree, sir," she contradicted him firmly. "You are most certainly not alone. You are welcome at Silvercrosse."

Will was warmed by her generosity. He had no choice but to accept her offer, of course, but yesterday he would never have allowed himself to be grateful for it. He would have berated himself for having had an accident and grumbled disagreeably about his situation. But it was different today; he merely said, "Thank you, Miss Armitage."

It was rather nice being Mr. William Lyon.

At that moment, the door to the room swung all the way open, and a man strode in. Handsome, in his early forties, he had sharp brown eyes and brown hair only just beginning to gray at the temples. He was dressed simply, but immaculately, and Will noticed that his cravat, while lacking in frills, was expertly tied. Unquestionably, this was the owner of the estate, Sir Godfrey Scrivener.

"Ah, my good man, I see you are awake and in your right mind at last," Sir Godfrey observed approvingly.

Will didn't have the strength to sit up, and he hoped Sir Godfrey would understand. "Forgive me for not rising," he said.

"Please, do not trouble yourself on my account," Sir Godfrey replied reasonably. "You must remain in bed. I have no intention of letting you negate all the good work that has been done to get you this far."

"I am much obliged," Will sighed, dejected by his uncharacteristic physical weakness.

Sir Godfrey inclined his head politely. "May I introduce myself? I am Sir Godfrey Scrivener of Silvercrosse Hall. And I see you have already met my cousin, Miss Armitage."

Will hesitated only a fraction of a second. "My name is Mr. William Lyon of London." The lie was distasteful, but Will had already chosen to hide his identity. No turning back now.

"He has no family, Godfrey," Charissa informed her cousin. "I've already asked him if there's anyone we should contact, but he has no one. So I reassured him he is welcome to stay with us until he is recovered."

"I am happy to open my home to you, Mr. Lyon," Sir Godfrey reiterated as he pulled an empty chair over to the bedside and sat on it, next to Charissa. He fixed Will with his penetrating gaze, the look in his eyes stern, and Will understood that Sir Godfrey expected nothing but the utmost moral rectitude in return for his hospitality.

"Thank you, sir. I shall trespass on your kindness only as long as it's truly necessary," Will said.

"It is no trespass. So tell me, Mr. Lyon, how did you come to be riding through Murrington in a torrential downpour?"

A fair question, Will acknowledged inwardly. He would answer it as closely to the truth as he could. "I came into these northern parts to visit an old friend. I recently lost my father," he explained, "and I was in need of a place that… that would not remind me of him.

"But when I arrived at my friend's home, I discovered he had taken his ailing wife to Italy almost a year ago. I had no choice but to return to London, and I was angry with myself for having made the trip for nothing. I admit I rode hard—too far, too long. I wasn't feeling well, and I assume I made a wrong turn at some point. I remember hearing thunder in the distance. Rain began to fall, but I was so ill by that point, I couldn't think straight. My horse must have slipped and fallen over a cliff, but I recall nothing else until I woke up in this room."

"I see. Well, you had no possessions with you," Sir Godfrey said, "except a wallet in your waistcoat. We have kept it safe for you, including its contents."

"Thank you. You did not find a satchel? There wasn't much in it except a change or two of clothes and a few odds and ends."

"No, I'm sorry, we didn't retrieve anything else. It must have been lost during the course of your journey," Charissa informed him. "And I'm afraid the clothes you were wearing were so hopelessly muddy and torn we had to throw them out. Would you like to send to your home for your wardrobe and anything else you'll need whilst you convalesce?"

Contact home? Absolutely not, thought Will. "Perhaps I could have some clothing made for me here instead of sending to London for my own," he suggested. "It would be simpler in the long run, I think, since nothing I have will fit well over this splint anyway. I won't need too many items—just the basics. Is there a clothier nearby whom you could recommend?"

"As long as you don't need the latest fashions, the local tailor should be able to accommodate you in the course of the next few days."

Will gave her a smile. "Excellent."

Sir Godfrey scooted his chair back and rose to his feet. "That's settled, then. Come, Charissa, let us leave Mr. Lyon. Dr. Shaw will visit him later today, and we want our patient rested when he arrives." He held out his hand to his cousin.

Charissa stood reluctantly; she had more questions she would have liked to ask the mysterious Mr. Lyon, but maybe it was better to postpone any more conversation. She could see that his eyes were heavy, and sleep would certainly do him good. "I'll come speak with you again soon, Mr. Lyon," she promised.

"I would like that, Miss Armitage," he replied.

Chapter 4

On Will's second day at Silvercrosse Hall, Sir Godfrey came to see him after the rest of the household had breakfasted downstairs. They spoke about horses and hunting and other manly interests. On the whole they got on rather well—except when Sir Godfrey decided to entertain his guest by reading out loud from an intimidating book of sermons by the late Bishop Joseph Butler. The particular passage he chose contained sentences such as: *God has constituted our nature, and the nature of society, after such a manner, that generally speaking, men cannot encourage or support themselves in wickedness upon the foot of there being no difference between right and wrong, or by a direct avowal of wrong; but by disguising it, and endeavouring to spread over it some colours of right.*

Will resented his host's moralizing; the last thing he desired was to be reminded of his myriad sins. Fortunately, however, Sir Godfrey was eventually called away, and, for the time being, Will was left to himself. Gratefully, he slept.

Later in the afternoon Miss Armitage, too, kept her promise and dropped by his room. Will was pleased. He had, in fact, thought her about quite a bit since he had seen her last. She was very attractive, although rather unlike the ubiquitous ladies of fashion who thronged the shops, parks, and drawing rooms of London. Her light brown hair was simply styled, and her gowns reflected restrained taste. Nevertheless, there was something uniquely captivating about her. Perhaps it was the effect of her brilliant blue eyes, he mused. If asked, he would have described them as luminous, yet not in a vacuous way. They shone with intelligence, making him curious to know more about her.

Neither was her Christian name conventional. *Charissa*. He had never heard it before, but he liked it. It was soft and feminine-sounding, yet it also hinted at strength of character. It seemed to suit her, so it was what he called her in the privacy of his own thoughts.

When the door opened to admit her entry into his room, he was surprised to see a white bundle of fur nestled in her arms. She smiled at him tentatively. "Mr. Lyon," she asked, "do you like dogs?"

How had she guessed? "I love dogs," he replied. He kept none in town and missed the many hunting dogs he had grown up with at Ashbourne Park.

"Well then," she said, sitting in the chair by his bedside and depositing the fluffy package next to him on the bed, "here is someone who would love to meet you." The little white ball unrolled itself and stared at Will with two large black eyes and a twitching black nose.

Will extended his right hand to the canine stranger, who sniffed it with interest. After a second or two, the dog confidently stuck out its pink tongue and began to lick the tantalizing fingers of his newly found friend. Will chuckled and watched with amusement as the dog rolled over onto its back and raised up its left front paw, exposing its furry chest.

"And that," Charissa informed Will, "is why I have nicknamed him Mr. Pettmee. He is pathetic, I admit, but he will stay right by your side if you rub his tummy."

Will ran his hand along Mr. Pettmee's soft underbelly. "What is his proper name?"

"Sprite," she told him. "He's a very naughty little boy. Especially where food is involved. Mrs. Harper has banned him from the kitchen." She ruffled his silky ears.

"I'll make sure to feed him a few scraps," Will said, "and thus cement our friendship."

"And when you're well enough, you can throw a ball for him to chase. He loves to play."

Will continued to stroke Sprite. "I should very much like to take

Mr. Pettmee out into the garden, and that will be as soon as possible, I trust."

"Sir Godfrey thinks you should keep to your bed for a long time."

"On the contrary, I am determined to be up and about before the week is out," Will countered. When she frowned, he gave her a grin. "I'll be careful—don't worry."

"Bullheaded, aren't you?"

"You have no idea."

"I suspect I'm about to find out."

"Don't say I haven't warned you." Will gave Sprite a pat on the head. "But you'll be impressed with the speed of my recovery, I promise you."

Charissa didn't doubt for a moment what he'd said was true. Mr. Lyon—her heart whispered—was clearly an extraordinary man.

As Will had predicted, his health improved rapidly. Over the course of the next few days, both the physician and the surgeon stopped by to examine him, and both of them gave him a good report. Dr. Shaw told him his color was good and his constitution was admirable. Mr. Rowley inspected the splint he had made and pronounced himself satisfied with his work. "The break is small, and I believe it will mend completely, Mr. Lyon," he declared. "You'll not even have a limp."

Encouraged by this, Will resolved to rise and walk, in spite of the pain. He'd worried Mr. Rowley would insist he lie immobile for weeks on end, but the surgeon—who had not long ago been honing his skills on the battlefields of the Iberian Peninsula—agreed careful movement would in fact help him heal. Will asked for crutches, and Sir Godfrey ordered a custom-made set from a local carpenter.

The tailor also visited, and Will ordered several suits of clothes. Mr. Pearce was a generously proportioned man, with tiny eyes and unusually large spectacles. His attempts to get Will's measurements proved to be awkward and—where the broken leg was concerned—excruciating. Will gritted his teeth, suspecting irritably that the quality of the final garments would not pass muster in London. In this he was proved correct when the first pair of breeches (not the more fashionable pantaloons), shirt, waistcoat, cravat, and coat arrived the very next day. But the clothier was obviously doing his best to speed the order on its way, having engaged several others to work overnight on the various items, and thus Will could not help but appreciate the service in spite of the provincial quality of the work.

All in all, Will found himself surprisingly content with his new and unfamiliar surroundings, notwithstanding the continuing pain in his leg. It was almost as if he were another person entirely.

The crutches were soon ready for use, and Will was as good as his word. After breakfast one morning, he insisted one of the footmen help him make his way to the ground floor in order to join Sir Godfrey, Charissa, and the elderly Aunt Caroline. It was slow going down the stairs, but well worth the effort—he hated being bedridden.

The three residents of Silvercrosse Hall looked up in surprise when he entered their informal sitting room. Sprite ran over and jumped up on Will's good leg. "Hello there, pup," Will greeted him, as both Sir Godfrey and Charissa cried out, "Down!" Sprite, however, ignored both of them and continued to celebrate Will's appearance.

Charissa ran over and scooped the enthusiastic dog up in her arms. "Come now, you little ragamuffin, let our guest alone." She smiled at Will. "Mr. Lyon, you are very brave to venture downstairs."

"I hope I'm not interrupting you, but I confess it's good to be up and out of the bedchamber."

Sir Godfrey rose graciously. "Do join us." Will obliged his host, grimacing slightly as he leaned the crutches against the wall and eased himself onto a chair.

Sir Godfrey formally introduced his elderly Aunt Caroline to Will, then took an unoccupied chair from the corner of the room and placed it underneath Will's injured leg. "Now you may raise and rest your limb, Mr. Lyon," he instructed as he resumed his own seat.

Once Will was settled, Charissa asked him if he were in pain.

"I am, as a matter of fact," he replied. "But as you see, it has not deterred me from seeking out the pleasure of your company."

Sir Godfrey was reminded of the time he had sprained his own ankle. "I, too, once had to learn to walk about with crutches," he began.

As he launched into the story of his long-ago misfortune, Charissa gazed across the room at Will. She admired the fighting spirit which had undoubtedly contributed to his survival. And she had to admit he was also remarkably handsome. Tall and well-built, he was likely what society called a *Corinthian*—an athletic gentleman who was good at everything. His manners, too, were flawless.

Suddenly, however, she realized she was mentally cataloging his attractions with vivid enthusiasm, and she became annoyed with herself. Goodness, but she was a rattlebrain to think of their guest in such an unspiritual way! She should know better than to imitate the vain and fatuous women of the *ton*. For while they might consider Mr. Lyon to be one sort of Corinthian, on the other hand he might just as easily be the type of Corinthian described in the Bible: prideful, carnal, worldly wise.

She deliberately gave Sir Godfrey an encouraging smile as he went on with his story. Her cousin had been such a help to her when she had first come to Silvercrosse Hall. He had provided a mature, steadying influence when her emotions had been careening out of control after her humiliation in London. She should remember his patient instruction and know better than to let her feelings run away with her. Indeed, she had spent six years training herself to keep romance strictly inside the world of fiction, where it belonged.

So she fixed her attention on Sir Godfrey's voice, but it was difficult not to glance over at the enigmatic Mr. Lyon every so often, especially after Sprite had jumped up onto his lap. She sighed, unable to deny that his presence at Silvercrosse Hall was by far the most interesting thing that had happened in the neighborhood for a very long time.

Finally, after Sir Godfrey had finished his tale and everyone had discussed it at suitable length, Charissa spoke again to Will. "Mr. Pettmee has taken a liking to you," she remarked. "Do you have any dogs of your own?"

Will almost blurted out he owned a number of hounds and spaniels at Ashbourne Park, but he caught himself just in time. "My family had several dogs when I was growing up in the country, but I don't keep any in London myself," he explained. "After all, there's not much for hunting dogs to do in Hyde Park, is there? However, after meeting Sprite here, I might just consider acquiring a lapdog." He scratched Sprite's ears, and the little dog bent his head down with a contented grunt.

"Whereabouts in London do you live, Mr. Lyon?" inquired Sir Godfrey.

"In the West End," hedged Will, knowing it was a ridiculous answer. What gentleman lived elsewhere? He was spared further elaboration, however, when a white dog looking like a larger version of Sprite walked into the room, attracting everyone's attention. It padded somberly over to Will and paused, staring up at him with huge dark eyes.

Will reached out the hand he was not using to pet Sprite and allowed the other dog to sniff it.

"This is Commodore," Charissa said by way of introduction. "He's Sprite's brother. His self-defined purpose in life is to guard Silvercrosse Hall, a job he takes very seriously. Mr. Lyon is a friend, Commodore," she told the animal.

Commodore agreed. After spending an absorbing few seconds analyzing Will's aroma, he wagged his tail and gave Will's fingers a lick. Satisfied, he walked across the room and lay down calmly at Aunt Caroline's feet.

"Good boy," Will said.

"You have been given the canine stamp of approval," Sir Godfrey observed. "Frankly, I am surprised Commodore bestowed it so quickly."

"He knows a good man when he meets one," Charissa declared, thinking once again that Mr. Lyon was perfectly amiable. And besides, who was she to argue with Sprite and Commodore?

Sir Godfrey furrowed his brows. "Charissa," he suggested, "why don't you read to us all from the Holy Scriptures? Something from the book of Proverbs might be duly edifying. *The fear of the Lord is the beginning of knowledge; fools despise wisdom and discipline.* Is that not a profound truth, Mr. Lyon?" Sir Godfrey stood and walked over to a table upon which sat a large leather-bound Bible. Picking it up, he took it over to Charissa and deposited it on her lap.

Will calmly tickled Sprite under the chin. "What do you think, Mr. Pettmee?" he queried. The dog perked up its ears and tilted its head, trying to understand. "Do you despise discipline," Will asked him, "or do you fear your master?"

Charissa opened the Bible. "I think Sprite's an example of both those things, depending on his mood. Unlike Commodore, who is eminently predictable."

"Commodore is obedient and faithful," Sir Godfrey emphasized.

"Yes, he is," Charissa said fondly. "And I love him for it."

"That is as it should be," Sir Godfrey affirmed, sitting back in his chair.

"Well, let's see now." Charissa looked down at the beautiful Bible in her hands and turned its pages thoughtfully. "I do always enjoy the Book of Proverbs, Godfrey, but Aunt Caroline and I have begun reading in the Gospel of St. Luke, so I think I'll continue with that."

"Very well, my dear," Sir Godfrey acquiesced graciously.

"We left off in chapter five, and I'll take up the narrative again at verse twelve: *While he was in one of the towns, a man was there who had leprosy all over him. He saw Jesus, fell facedown, and begged him: "Lord, if you are willing, you can make me clean." Reaching out his hand, Jesus touched him, saying, "I am willing; be made clean," and immediately the leprosy left him.*"

As Charissa read, Will found himself actually listening—an activity he had studiously avoided in the many dull church services he had been obliged to sit through during his lifetime. It must have been the pleasing quality of her voice that caught his attention, he figured, or the attractive way her eyes glowed. Why else would the stories seem to come alive?

He wasn't sure how much time had passed when a footman entered the sitting room, causing Charissa to look up from the pages of the Scriptures. "Excuse me, Sir Godfrey," the servant intoned, "Mr. Finney of Holly Farm has arrived."

"One of my tenants," Sir Godfrey said, rising to his feet. "Please excuse me, everyone. Charissa, perhaps this would be a good time for you to speak with Mrs. Harper about the menu for your birthday dinner next week."

Charissa shook her head. "We'll be meeting tomorrow to go over everything. There's no need to do so today."

"Oh. Well, that's good, then." Sir Godfrey left the room without further comment, followed by the footman.

Charissa closed the Bible and returned it to its hallowed spot on the table. "I do think that's enough for now." She looked over at Aunt Caroline, who had fallen asleep and was snoring gently. "She does that a lot these days," Charissa said softly. "I think she's fading, though I haven't spoken of it to Sir Godfrey."

Will shifted in his chair, and, startled, Sprite jumped off his lap in a hurry. "Should we leave her in peace?" he asked quietly, reaching for his crutches.

"I don't suppose we'd wake her if we stayed, but if you'd like, I can show you some more of the house. If you feel up to it, that is," she qualified.

"I should enjoy that."

"Here, let me help you," she offered, coming over to steady him as he brought the crutches awkwardly under his arms. He detected a light floral scent as she stood close to him; it was most appealing.

Once he was leaning securely on the crutches, Charissa stepped back. "This, of course, is the sitting room. The paneling is original to the house, but as you can see the furnishings are new. My favorite object in this room is the painting over the mantel. It is a Staffordshire landscape, and if you look at the hill in the background, you'll find Silvercrosse Hall set among the trees."

Will hopped a few steps toward the fireplace and scrutinized the scene. *Nicely done for an amateur*, he thought. "Ah yes, that must be the house there. Was the painting done by a local artist?"

"In a manner of speaking. Godfrey's wife painted it."

As Sir Godfrey had no wife at present, Lady Scrivener must have died sometime between now and then. "I take it Sir Godfrey is a widower," Will surmised.

"Sadly, yes. Lady Scrivener died two years ago. They had no children."

Will wondered briefly why Sir Godfrey hadn't married again, in order to father an heir if for no other reason, but he also knew it was none of his business. Anyway, he was more interested in hearing about the house itself than Sir Godfrey's personal history, so he followed Charissa into the next room, which turned out to be a music salon. It had a harp placed at one end and a pianoforte at the other.

"Tell me the story of Silvercrosse Hall," Will requested, making his way into the center of the chamber and putting his hand on the large carved mahogany mantelpiece which surrounded the fireplace. "It must date from Tudor times."

"Yes, it was built during the early years of Queen Elizabeth's reign by a man who rose to prominence in the royal household. He was well rewarded for his service and chose this spot upon which to construct his estate. An old chapel existed on the site, but it had been abandoned during the dissolution of the monasteries, so he had it torn down. However, when they were digging the foundation for the house, they discovered a small but very beautiful silver cross buried in the earth directly below where the altar of the chapel had stood. Hence the name of the manor: *Silvercrosse.*"

"Where is the cross now? Does it still exist? Have you seen it?"

"Sir Godfrey keeps it with the rest of the family silver. And now," she said, idly running her fingers over the pianoforte keys as she walked by the instrument, "let me show you an even more interesting room." She opened the door into the next apartment, which was revealed to be a much smaller chamber occupying the back right corner of the house, obviously used as a private parlor or study. The walls were covered with paintings featuring animals, mostly dogs and cats.

"Marvelous!" exclaimed Will sincerely. Some of the scenes were large and busy; others were small, intimate portraits. "It is an extraordinary collection."

"I agree. We call this the Menagerie Room. Some of the paintings were purchased, but most of them are original to the estate and depict former inhabitants with their pets—of the canine, feline, and equine variety."

"As well as avian," Will observed, nodding at the portrait of a seventeenth century boy holding a brilliantly colored parrot.

"Apparently his name was Ethelred, and he had a reputation for saying obnoxious things at the most inappropriate moments." Then Charissa laughed, realizing that her words could be interpreted two ways. "I'm talking about the bird, not the child," she clarified.

Will chuckled as he hobbled up to the picture. "Judging by the look in that young master's eyes, I'd say your description applies to both of them."

"Yes, you may be right. But I don't mind. I'm fond of mischievous creatures, as you may have guessed by my attachment to Sprite."

Will looked over at her earnest countenance. "I understand what you mean. There is an impish sort of bad behavior that is merely immature. It hurts no one, and I daresay sometimes can even be used for good. To deflate a prideful person perhaps, or to bring laughter where there is sorrow. However," he cautioned, shifting his gaze to the window behind her shoulder, "there is also a selfish sort of misconduct that is rooted something much less benign. Anger at the world, perhaps." His eyes narrowed.

Charissa, however, refused to allow the conversation to be pulled in such a gloomy direction. "I am aware that wickedness exists, Mr. Lyon, but I do not see it in this young man's face. I shall hope that when he grew up, he retained his lightheartedness as a weapon against the heaviness of the world—as a candle in the dark, so to speak."

Will's attention was drawn back to Charissa. He stared at her for a moment, then decided to accept her gentle rebuke. "You have put me firmly in my place, Miss Armitage. A thousand pardons for my pessimism. You are indeed correct: the portrait gives no hint of a descent into dissipation. I am pleased to think better things of this young man."

"Thank you for indulging me," she replied, gazing again at the picture and touching the frame lightly with her fingertips. "It's true that unless a person gives me cause to change my mind, I insist on thinking well of him. I'm not always practical, I fear."

Guilt and hope burned in Will's breast simultaneously, but he refused to consider why that would be so. Instead, he abruptly pointed out another painting on the opposite wall and turned the discussion toward the artist's use of light and shadow, concepts which were much easier to understand on canvas than inside the human heart.

Chapter 5

Sir Godfrey had suggested Will spend the next day off his feet, but, true to form, Will was more than ready to exercise. Therefore, in the late morning after he had finished the breakfast which had been brought up to him on a tray, he decided to venture out of his room again. Determined to visit the Menagerie Room, he descended the stairs one at a time, slowly and without assistance.

When he entered the room at last, he was gratified to discover Charissa sitting there alone, bent over a small desk. Guiding himself with his crutches, he limped over to her. "Good morning, Miss Armitage," he said. "I hope today finds you well."

"Very well, Mr. Lyon," she replied, looking up in surprise. "But the more pertinent question concerns *your* health. Don't tell me you came down the stairs alone?"

"It was nothing," he shrugged.

"You are an amazement. Not so very long ago, you were on your deathbed."

"And now I am tottering around at lightning speed. A true miracle! This morning, the ground floor—next week, London."

"You shouldn't jest about such a thing," Charissa reproved him good-naturedly. "You really are a miracle."

"With that in mind," he countered cheekily, "perhaps I should walk to Murrington today. It's only a little over a mile, so I hear. Would you like me to bring anything back for you?"

She laughed in spite of herself. "Well, if you insist, I've decided to have another gown made. You could bring me a few bolts of cloth so that I can select the fabric. Why don't you carry them on your head?" she suggested. "Like the women in Africa do."

"Certainly. And I expect you'll need a brand new ladies' hat with ostrich feathers galore and heaps of Alençon lace! Yes, I'll bring two or three bonnets so that you can decide between them. I'll balance them side by side on top of the cloth."

"Oh dear! I daresay you shouldn't subject yourself to such indignity."

He sighed dramatically. "Alas, I fear you are correct. It appears I shall be forced to visit Murrington another day."

"What a pity. But for now," she concluded hopefully, "you might keep me company here." She indicated a chair beside hers at the table and almost asked him if he needed help, but thought better of it.

To her satisfaction, he took a seat, and after he had made himself as comfortable as he could, he looked down at the table to see what it was she had been working on. It was a pencil sketch.

"Are you trying to draw one of the dogs?" he guessed.

"Yes, Commodore was in here with me before you came down. Usually I can get him to stay put for a while, but he must have heard a noise he didn't recognize in another part of the house, and he ran out to make sure that all is in order. I've been trying to sketch him, but I'm not a very good artist, I'm afraid."

Will assessed the drawing. "The muzzle is a little too short, too small for the rest of the body," he pointed out. "Here, let me try something." He picked up her pencil and began to sketch lightly. "Perhaps if you just pulled it out here… and made this part a little softer…"

Charissa watched in amazement as—in only a few minutes—he improved her work significantly. Instead of an odd-looking, dog-like sort of creature, Commodore himself began to take shape on the page.

Suddenly Will recalled where he was and what he was doing. He put down the pencil. "I'm sorry," he apologized. "I've done too much. Forgive my presumption."

She shook her head slowly, her eyes wide. "But it's wonderful! I don't think I could make it look that real if I worked on it all year." She stared at Will. "Are you an artist?"

Will's lips twisted into an ironic smile. "No. My father was adamantly opposed to it."

"That's a strange attitude, I must say. There are many respectable men who are painters. Some have even been knighted."

Will knew such arguments intimately for he had used them all, but they had availed him nothing. Such a pursuit might be worthy of a lowly member of the gentry, his father had scolded him, but was in no way suitable for Viscount Disborough, the future Earl of Hartwell.

Will could not explain his father's objection to Charissa without revealing his own identity, so he said bitterly, "My father and I rarely saw eye to eye."

"But you obeyed him by not pursuing a career in art."

"Yes." In spite of their quarrels, Will had never really considered that he'd had a choice in the matter. After all, what nobleman had a career?

"Then how did you learn to draw so well?" she asked, looking back down at the picture of Commodore.

Will lowered his voice. "The truth is that I obeyed him publically, but when I moved away from home and bought my own house in London, I took private lessons from one of the members of the Royal Academy." He paused. "I've never told anyone about it before."

She turned her head toward him and found his face only inches from hers. He did not move away, and she was intensely aware of his dark eyes boring deep into hers. Her heart made a few severe, rapid beats, then she caught her breath.

"Well, we'll have to do something about that, won't we?" She pulled away and, grabbing a sheet of paper and a pencil, held them out to him.

He sat back. "What's this?"

"This is your first commission, Mr. Lyon," she announced. "I should like you to draw me two pictures, one each of Sprite and Commodore. It will give you something purposeful to do during your convalescence."

Something purposeful to do. Had he ever done anything purposeful, he wondered? "I cannot guarantee the quality of my work," he said out loud, "but if you're willing to settle for uncertain results, I'll tackle the job. I owe you and Sir Godfrey more than I could ever repay, but maybe this can be a small token of my thanks. The first of many, I hope."

"You owe us nothing," Charissa said warmly. She shook the paper and pencil at him. "Please, take them."

"Very well. I admit that I shall enjoy undertaking such a project."

"And what have you roped the poor man into, Charissa?"

Both of them looked up to see Sir Godfrey enter the room. Charissa beamed at him. "Mr. Lyon has just agreed to sketch Sprite and Commodore for me."

"An admirable enterprise," Sir Godfrey allowed. "You are an artist, sir?"

"No," Will said.

"He is being humble, Godfrey. I can already tell that he is extremely good. Much better than I shall ever be. And I have always wanted a realistic picture of the dogs." She gazed at Will in admiration.

"I'll arrange for you to have a lap board so you can work whilst keeping to your bed upstairs," Sir Godfrey offered. "Such an arrangement will be much better for you than stumbling downstairs every day."

"I thought perhaps he could work in here," Charissa proposed. "Commodore and Sprite often keep me company when I write. And in this room he can select what he needs from my modest collection of inks and paints and pens and brushes."

"But we shouldn't tire him," Sir Godfrey pointed out. "I would suspect that your leg is paining you even now, is it not, Mr. Lyon?"

Will couldn't deny it; his lower right leg was still hurting quite a bit. He'd just forgotten about it while he had been talking with Charissa. "Yes, you're right. But perhaps when my bone has healed a bit more, I'll be able to come downstairs for longer periods of time."

"Would you like Jack to help you return to your room now?" Sir Godfrey asked, referring to the footman.

"That would probably be wise," Will answered regretfully.

"I'll bring up whatever supplies you need," Charissa stated. "And whichever one of the dogs I find first."

"Why don't you let Jack do that? I have need of you in the library," Sir Godfrey explained. "There are a few things I would like to discuss with you, since tomorrow we'll be spending the day at the Humphreys."

"Very well." Charissa stood up. "Good day, Mr. Lyon."

"Good day, Sir Godfrey, Miss Armitage," Will replied. *And thank you, Charissa*, he thought.

Will used his time the next day to begin the drawing of Commodore; the dog lay obligingly on the bed for a lengthy modeling session. Will's only other visitor was Mr. Rowley, who came to check on his leg. The surgeon pronounced his patient to be improving at an even more rapid pace than he had expected. He also encouraged Will to continue to move about, although not, of course, putting too much weight on the leg or overdoing his efforts.

Will spent the following morning on the picture of Commodore, but later in the day he decided to repeat his visit to the Menagerie Room. He carefully made his way to the ground floor, but as soon as he reached it, Sir Godfrey, who had just come out into the hall from the formal drawing room, spotted him.

"Ah, there you are Mr. Lyon," he said. "I was going to send for you. Neighbors of ours have come to call, and they have expressed a desire to meet you. Would you care to join us?"

Will felt a momentary frisson of fear. Who were these people who wanted to meet him? Would they know him for a fraud the moment they saw him? Forcing down his apprehension and affecting an affability he didn't feel, he consented to make the acquaintance of the neighbors.

But, to his immediate relief, he did not recognize either of them. They were both women, one of whom was seated on a chair and the other of whom had taken a spot on the settee next to Charissa. Sir Godfrey made the introductions, and Will discovered that the ladies were Miss Penelope St. Swythin and her sister Helen.

Penelope, on the settee, was the eldest of the two. Will guessed that she was in her early thirties, possibly a year or two older than himself. She was not what he would have called classically beautiful, and she was wearing a gown several years out of date. Nonetheless, her rich black hair and solemn green eyes lent her a natural elegance which Will found appealing. She gave him an appraising glance, taking in his appearance thoughtfully, but not unkindly.

The younger woman, Helen, had no great beauty despite her name. Her gown, like her sister's, boasted few embellishments and had seen better days, but Will noticed a lively gleam in her pale blue eyes as she gazed at him.

Penelope spoke first. "I'm so glad you survived your fall off the cliff road, Mr. Lyon. What a dreadful ordeal. It's a blessing Sir Godfrey and Charissa drove out that way first thing in the morning."

"I'm very thankful they found me," Will said. "Without them, I would be dead."

"Your being here with us now is a miracle, Mr. Lyon. You have been spared for a reason," Helen stated confidently. "Do you not agree with me, Sir Godfrey?" Without waiting for his reply, she went on, "I know you all will think me daft, but I must inform you of something very important. Two weeks ago, God revealed to me Mr. Lyon was coming!"

No one said anything in response to this peculiar pronouncement. Sir Godfrey pursed his lips impatiently, while Charissa exchanged a furtive glance with Penelope. Will couldn't decide whether the comment was humorous or bizarre.

Helen shook her head in a way that reminded Will of a teacher bemoaning particularly dimwitted students. "I had a dream the Friday before last," she told them. "I was standing in front of Silvercrosse Hall, and there was a terrible storm. The wind was blowing leaves across the road, and the rain had turned everything to mud. I looked down and saw my dress had been ruined. That's when I noticed a man walking up the road. He was soaking wet from the storm, but he stopped when he saw the house and smiled at me. He looked up at the sky, and the sun came out. That's all I remember," she said, turning to Will, "but the man looked just like you. He *was* you!"

Caught off guard, Will said nothing.

Dismayed that her guest had been embarrassed by her neighbor, Charissa opened her mouth to redirect the conversation, but before she could speak, distraction came in the form of two canine allies. Sprite roared into the room with something in his mouth, followed by Commodore, who was barking furiously. They careened around the chair where Aunt Caroline sat sleeping and dashed out of the room again like streaks of white lightning. Everyone burst into gales of laughter, waking up Aunt Caroline, who joined in the merriment although she had no idea what was so funny.

"Oh dear!" Charissa exclaimed. "Sprite has gotten into the kitchen and stolen a tidbit from right under Mrs. Harper's nose!"

Sir Godfrey groaned. "Not again."

"He's such a rascal," Penelope commented. "Haven't you tried to train him, Sir Godfrey?"

"Not consistently, I'm afraid," he conceded. "And without enforcement of the rules, his obedience is bound to be lacking at best."

"I expect as far as Mrs. Harper is concerned, he's a terror," said Helen.

"She says so, but I think that's an exaggeration. He's actually quite good most of the time," Charissa claimed. "It's not as though we allow him to rule the roost. If that were true, there'd be nothing left in the larder."

Sir Godfrey chuckled as he looked at his cousin. "You are perceiving the situation a bit too optimistically, my dear. We are both far too indulgent with the dogs. So much so, in fact, that I'm afraid they're ruining my reputation for running a model household."

Penelope disagreed. "Nonsense—nothing could be further from the truth. Your *modus vivendi* is highly esteemed by everyone who knows you, Sir Godfrey. And that reminds me, I've been meaning to ask you. How is your latest sermon coming along?"

Sir Godfrey looked pleased. "Quite well thank you, Miss St. Swythin. I finished a fine message yesterday drawn from Psalm 94:2: *Rise up, Judge of the earth; repay the proud what they deserve.*"

"I'm sure it's very inspiring," Penelope nodded, impressed.

Sir Godfrey opened his mouth to pontificate, but judgment was not a topic of interest to Will. "Sermon, Sir Godfrey?" he interrupted. "What connection do you have with the Church?"

The distraction worked. "Ah yes," Sir Godfrey said, "you don't know my background. I was a man of the cloth before I inherited my title twelve years ago—unexpectedly—from a distant relative. As a rector, I had always enjoyed crafting my Sunday messages, and I saw no reason not to continue to do so when I came to Silvercrosse Hall."

"Mr. Humphreys, our rector here in Murrington, reads Sir Godfrey's sermons in the pulpit from time to time," said Penelope, "for the edification of the entire congregation."

"I am honored that he should do so," Sir Godfrey acknowledged. "And soon, because of Charissa's encouragement, I am hoping to have them published."

"And well they should be," Penelope said encouragingly. "Have you written to your publisher in London yet, Charissa? What has he said?"

Publisher? That was strange, Will thought. What did it mean that she had a publisher?

Charissa gave Penelope a frustrated glance, "I haven't received a response from him yet," she replied flatly.

The other woman's face fell. "Oh, I am so sorry. I suppose your guest doesn't know."

"You need not reveal anything you would prefer not to, Miss Armitage," Will said quickly.

Charissa shrugged. "It's all right, Mr. Lyon. I'm not ashamed of my pastime, although I rarely refer to it in public. I am a writer."

"Her last novel was serialized in the *Lady's Magazine*," Penelope elaborated proudly. "Charissa writes wonderful, godly tales about men and women of character."

"And yet the stories are exciting enough to keep me reading late into the night," Helen explained, looking over at Will. "They are most *passionate*."

"Helen!" Charissa's face burned bright crimson. "You will give Mr. Lyon the wrong impression."

Miss Charissa Armitage was an author? It was an unanticipated development, but Will instantly decided that he considered writing novels a delightful pursuit. He was also surprised to discover that he profoundly hoped Charissa had never written anything beyond the bounds of good taste; he would have been keenly disappointed in her if she had. But he need not have worried.

"I have read all of her works at her request," Sir Godfrey put in swiftly, "and I can assure you that the stories are purposefully written to edify the heart and mind of every female reader."

"Thank you, Godfrey. I use a pen name, of course," she told Will. "*Mrs. A. Castlewood.*"

Will gave her a grin. "I'm sorry to say I've never read anything by Mrs. A. Castlewood, nor any Castlewood for that matter."

Charissa smiled. "I should be worried if you had."

"But perhaps Mr. Lyon's *chère-amie* has read them," Helen suggested, glancing at Will with what she seemed to think was flirtatious humor.

However, no one else was amused.

"Helen!" her sister gasped. Charissa's eyes widened, Will arched an eyebrow, and Sir Godfrey looked angry. The French term meant *dear friend*, but was often used as a euphemism for a paramour or kept woman. Of course, it was no secret that gentlemen of the *ton* often lived a double life, but it was a subject never even hinted at in mixed company, since respectable women were supposed to turn a blind eye to the existence of their fallen counterparts.

Helen blushed furiously. "I mean his dear *wife*, Penelope. Whom else would I mean?"

Will frowned impatiently. "I have neither wife nor *chère-amie*," he stated with annoyance. Not that it was anyone's business—but then again, at least in this he was not deceiving anyone. For quite a while now it had been true; he had no love interest.

In spite of the awkwardness of the moment, warmth filled Charissa's heart when she heard Will say he had no romantic entanglements. Grateful that Helen's socially unacceptable remark had revealed this agreeable fact, she found it easy to come to the other woman's rescue. "I hear that you have a lovely new bonnet, Helen," she said brightly, attempting to sidetrack the woman before the conversation deteriorated completely.

To everyone's acute relief, Helen took the bait. "Oh yes, did Penny tell you she finally gave in and let me buy it? It's perfectly adorable! I shall wear it for your party on Tuesday evening," she declared.

"I'm looking forward to celebrating your birthday, Charissa," Penelope said, glad to help steer the discussion in a safe direction. "And just think, it's also the sixth anniversary of your arrival in Murrington."

"It's hard to believe it was six years ago I came to Silvercrosse Hall, on the day before my birthday, no less. Godfrey and Dorcas made me feel welcome in my time of need," Charissa recalled. Turning to Will, she explained, "Sir Godfrey is my distant relative, but he was also one of my father's protégés. He and Lady Scrivener visited us many times when

I was young, before my father passed away. That's why I felt comfortable coming here to live with them."

"Will *you* be at the party, Mr. Lyon?" Helen inquired, since she knew all the particulars of Charissa's story and was much more interested in the newcomer. "Penelope and I are coming, as well as the Shaws and the Humphreys. Have you met them? Oh, I suppose you've met Dr. Shaw."

Will drew his eyebrows together. He'd only heard the party referred to once, and he suspected he was not invited.

"I haven't spoken to Mr. Lyon, yet," Charissa explained promptly, "but I'm so glad you brought it up, Helen." She turned to Will. "On Tuesday night, Godfrey is hosting a small birthday party for me, and I would be so pleased if you would consent to join us."

"Charissa, as I have said before, perhaps we shouldn't keep pushing Mr. Lyon into such tiring activities," Sir Godfrey objected.

"Please don't feel obligated, of course," amended Charissa.

Despite Sir Godfrey's concern, Will wouldn't have missed the party even had his leg been ten times more painful than it was. It had been a long time since he had been asked to a gathering merely for the pleasure of his company and not because of his social standing, his wealth, or his notoriety. "Every day I'm feeling stronger," he declared to the group, "and I would love to come. It is an honor to be included."

"It's settled then," Charissa said happily. She had been looking forward to her birthday as usual, but now the prospect of Mr. Lyon's presence added a fresh, new dimension to her anticipation.

Helen looked pleased. "I have something very special to give you, Charissa," she disclosed, looking around at the group. "I can hardly wait for Tuesday!"

A birthday gift for Charissa? Will's enthusiasm faltered instantly— it hadn't even crossed his mind that he ought to bring something to the party. As the rest of them continued the conversation around him, he struggled with his own frustrated thoughts. Everyone who came would be giving something to Charissa, however small. But he had nothing—he hardly had any of his own possessions with him, let alone something he could give as a gift. And he would certainly have neither the opportunity nor even the ability to go into town to purchase anything. He felt foolish, and he berated himself for accepting the invitation to join the celebration. He should have taken his cue from Sir Godfrey and kept to his room.

Although, upon reflection, it occurred to him that he could draw a picture for her—a simple, yet personal gift. *What subject would please her*, he wondered? His first thought was to sketch her dogs, but he was already working on that, of course. He supposed he should choose a flower or some other small and pretty thing to capture with his pen. Whatever he drew, it would have to be something exquisite.

The contemplation of a suitable subject occupied him for the rest of the day, long after the company had gone home. Just before he fell asleep that night, as his mind floated through a half-dreaming phase, he hit upon a solution for his dilemma at last. It hadn't really been such a difficult problem after all, he congratulated himself as he drifted off into full-fledged slumber. And as for the solution? Well—it was perfect.

Chapter 6

Sunday brought with it a soaking spring rain; nevertheless, Sir Godfrey, Charissa, and Aunt Caroline entered their carriage at precisely ten o'clock in order to brave the muddy roads and attend the parish church in Murrington. As always, Charissa was uplifted by the hymns, prayers, and communion, but on this particular day she found it harder than usual to concentrate on the sermon even though Mr. Humphreys expounded on his text in great detail. Her mind kept wandering, and when Sir Godfrey whispered to her concerning one of Mr. Humphreys' points—as he often did—she had to ask her cousin to repeat himself.

After the service, Mrs. Shaw and Mrs. Humphreys made a beeline for Charissa and caught up to her just as she was opening her umbrella in preparation to step out into the rain. Wrapping their hands firmly around her arms and lowering the umbrella in the process, they pulled her back inside the building.

"I had so been hoping your mysterious guest would attend attended the service today, Charissa dear," Mrs. Humphreys remarked, crestfallen.

"My husband has informed me that he is quite the gentleman," Mrs. Shaw added, not bothering to hide her excitement. She cast a glance over her shoulder at her oldest daughter, a comely young girl of nineteen who was chatting with her sisters.

Charissa's first thought was pity for the unsuspecting Mr. Lyon. "Yes, he is clearly a man of means, but Sir Godfrey and I actually know very little about him. Nothing more than we told you the other day, Mrs. Humphreys."

"But it has been almost two weeks since his unfortunate accident," Mrs. Humphreys commented. "Surely he is eager to make the acquaintance of the people of quality in Murrington."

"That may be a difficult prospect for him. Breaking a leg is a serious injury, Margaret," Mrs. Shaw informed the rector's wife expertly.

"I am aware of that, Catherine, but why should it deter him from getting about," demanded Mrs. Humphreys, "especially when there are new friends to be met?"

"Well, what I want to know," Mrs. Shaw went on, "is whether or not he will be making an appearance at your party tomorrow night, Charissa. Is he feeling well enough, do you think?"

When Charissa answered in the affirmative, both ladies nodded approvingly. "I should like to ask Mr. Lyon if he is related to the Lyons of Blackburn," Mrs. Humphreys remarked.

"And I should like to invite him to dine with us," Mrs. Shaw stated breathlessly.

Mrs. Humphreys snorted. "I thought you said that he is unable to do any such thing."

"But you have declared that his infirmity is no obstacle," Mrs. Shaw responded triumphantly. "Besides, we live close by Silvercrosse Hall, and we can easily send the carriage to fetch him. Since Mr. Lyon has already established a relationship with my husband, he will certainly be delighted to make the effort to come."

Mrs. Humphreys opened her mouth to reply, but, seeing an opportunity to jump in, Charissa said swiftly, "I'm afraid I must be on my way, but I am looking forward to seeing you both tomorrow night," she interrupted. "Good day, ladies." And with that, she hurried out into the deluge.

Although it was not a male custom to eat a meal in the middle of the day, both men saw fit that afternoon to join the ladies for luncheon. Will ate quietly, his thoughts elsewhere. On the other hand, Sir Godfrey took the opportunity to launch into a lively critique of the morning's sermon. While Charissa frequently took an active part in such discussions, today she was not in the state of mind to labor over the finer points of theology, and as soon as the last plate was cleared from the table, she gratefully escaped upstairs.

Now she rested at her window seat, which opened out over the garden behind the house. The rain had finally stopped, and a fresh, fragrant breeze played with the curls that framed her face.

As she stared out the window, to her surprise she saw the object of her thoughts appear on the lawn below, followed by a little white dog who splashed merrily in the puddles still covering the grass.

"What in the world? The garden is nothing but a bog!" she exclaimed under her breath. Predictably, Sprite was morphing into a raggedy wet mess, and the instigator of the expedition would soon follow suit if he weren't careful.

But the condition of the lawn didn't seem to bother Mr. Lyon at all. He had a rubber ball with him, and in spite of the inconvenience of his crutches, he threw it across the lawn for the excited dog to chase. Sprite ran right over the ball at first, but he circled around and caught it up in his teeth. He bounced back to Will, dropping the ball at his feet and barking at him to do it all over again.

It was a strange thing, Charissa pondered as she watched them play, how in such a short time her whole world had been rearranged.

Part of her mind scoffed at this hyperbole. A handsome man was merely convalescing in their household; soon he would be gone, and she would never see him again. It was that simple.

Or was it?

From the moment she had laid eyes on Mr. Lyon lying half-dead on the ground, something deep inside her heart had stirred, like a crocus pushing up against the frozen soil that had weighed it down all winter.

However—before she could analyze the intriguing metaphor—she heard the door to her room open, and she turned to see Sir Godfrey enter. She stood up a little too quickly and moved over to her dresser, staring absently into the looking glass hanging above it.

"You are as lovely as always, Charissa," he said, coming to stand behind her.

She contemplated her cousin's reflection. Good-looking and dressed as always like the quintessential country gentleman, she could see the light of admiration in his eyes. "You are so kind," she replied. "I'm sure I do not deserve your compliments."

He met her gaze in the mirror. "You know I neither lie nor exaggerate." Then he turned away, moving to the window. "Have the dogs gotten loose in the garden again?" he asked pleasantly. But when he looked down and saw the answer to his question, a shadow fell across his eyes.

Charissa felt her face become hot. "Sprite is going to be filthy," she noted, pitying the longsuffering footman whose responsibility it was to clean him. "Poor Jack."

But Sir Godfrey's attention was not diverted from the other participant in the muddy game. "Charissa, I must speak to you about your regard for Mr. Lyon."

She marched across the room and seated herself on one of two chairs next to the fireplace. "I can't imagine what you mean."

Sir Godfrey strode over to the chair opposite her and sat down stiffly. "I know you too well, my dear. Do not dissemble with me."

Charissa forced herself to fold her hands on her lap composedly. "There is nothing amiss."

"You are putting yourself at risk, Charissa."

"Mr. Lyon is an agreeable gentleman, and I admit I am curious about who he is. But that is all."

"Perhaps." Softening his tone, Sir Godfrey went on, "Nonetheless I feel I must remind you of what often happens when, in a crisis, a woman tends to the needs of a man. Infatuation is an ever-present danger."

Charissa's heart beat just the tiniest bit faster. "I assure you that is not the case."

Sir Godfrey said nothing.

His silence was deafening, and she stared down at her hands, unable to keep up the façade. "Well, maybe it is just a little bit the case."

"I refuse to see you hurt again." He leaned over and grasped her hands in his. "Mr. Lyon has secrets. I am sure of it. And even should he not, he is an unattached gentleman from London. How can you doubt that he is everything you despise?"

"He is perfectly amiable."

"And so was Sir Richard Lowell at first, was he not?"

Charissa tried to pull her hands away, but Sir Godfrey would not release her.

"Forgive me, darling, but I must say it. You must not allow yourself to be deceived! Keep your heart here at Silvercrosse where it belongs—where you are safe."

She nodded mutely. He was right, of course. After all, she had agreed with him for six years that her passionate nature was best indulged in writing inconsequential stories rather than in real-life romance. "I suppose it would be more prudent to let Helen St. Swythin chase after Mr. Lyon," she said, trying to lighten the atmosphere. "Or watch Mrs. Shaw parade her daughters by our door."

Sir Godfrey chuckled. "Best of luck to them."

"You have great wisdom, Godfrey," she told him sincerely, withdrawing her hands slowly from his.

"I cannot take all the credit, for you are a sensible woman. I have simply reminded you of what you already know." He returned to the window and closed it. "Ah, I see that the miscreants have finally gone inside. Heaven bless the servants who have to clean up after them." Turning around, he smiled at her. "But now, I am disposed to listen to music. Will you indulge my whim and play on the pianoforte and sing for me?"

"Certainly." She stood up, thankful for the distraction he was obviously providing. "I'll play out of the new hymnal you bought me last month."

"Excellent," he said approvingly, taking her arm.

However—despite Charissa's noble intentions the next morning in the Menagerie Room—Sir Godfrey's guidance of the previous day bore no fruit. Even a third cup of tea couldn't revive her ability to concentrate on her latest tale, and the blank page lay before her as empty of ink as when she'd begun.

Finally, she threw down the quill and rose to open one of the windows. Sunday's on-and-off rain had given way to an unseasonably chilly day, but she hoped letting in more of the coolness would invigorate her imagination—meaning her literary creativity, that is.

Her imaginings about Mr. Lyon were already quite invigorated, thank you very much.

A cold gust of wind blasted its way into the room, ruffling her hair and causing her to shiver.

"Miss Armitage, you should be wearing your shawl. And I suggest you shut the window."

Charissa whirled around to see Will limping into the chamber, a serious expression on his face.

"You sound like a fussy old granny," she quipped. Nevertheless, she took his advice and closed the window, happier to see him than she was willing to admit.

"You could catch a cold if you're not careful," he admonished her.

"There's no need to worry. I am quite well," she said, wondering if his own recent bout with a near-fatal illness had made him more apprehensive than he might otherwise have been. "I don't think I'm in any danger of dying before the party tomorrow night."

Will's final visit to his father's sickbed flashed though his mind, but he forced himself to smile. "Certainly not. Nevertheless, I suspect that you would not want to be blowing your nose or coughing and sneezing your way through the evening." Picking up a woolen shawl she had tossed on her chair the day before, he walked over to her and slipped it around her shoulders, his fingers brushing lightly against her bare skin. She felt a chill of a quite different sort.

"You conjure up a lovely image," she said, adjusting the wrap self-consciously and moving past him back to the table. "Me with a bright red nose and a pile of handkerchiefs at my side. Ugh."

"That is a sight neither of us would find appealing. So I am quite correct in encouraging you to avoid it at all possible costs."

"Yes, very well," she admitted. "But I am yielding to your request to wear my shawl less on account of my vanity and more for the sake of the dogs."

"Commodore and Sprite? What do you mean?"

"Well, if you must know, they like to steal used handkerchiefs and eat them. So it is a serious matter in more ways than one when anyone in this house becomes ill with a head cold."

"That's not a very charming picture," Will chuckled.

"True, but that's life with dogs," she retorted, her cheeks coloring faintly as she sat down again. "At Silvercrosse, we are singularly unable to transform our canines into acceptable members of society. They are far too cunning. I have given up."

"And there's no avoiding the use of handkerchiefs from time to time, alas."

"Unfortunately, we humans do seem to have our fair share of ailments now and then, however much we strive to avoid them. It is our common misfortune, but there is no shame in it. Unless, of course, we cannot keep our pets from ravaging our linens."

She had spoken lightheartedly, but something she said struck him powerfully nonetheless: *it is our common misfortune.* The topic of sickness had reminded Will of his father's death and had jolted him with the familiar guilty pangs. And yet for the first time he wondered if that final illness really had been his fault. After all, the earl had had a lingering cough for the last several months of his life that had grown steadily worse. And one or two of the servants in the house had been suffering with colds before Will had even arrived that fateful day. Disease was humanity's *common* misfortune; no one escaped it. Therefore, perhaps Will himself was not to blame for his father's demise—or at least only partly responsible for it—after all.

He looked at Charissa with wonder as the self-recrimination under which he had been laboring began to ease.

Charissa could not help but notice the changed expression that came over his face, although she had no idea why it had suddenly appeared. But she recognized that something good was happening inside him.

"Thank you for your concern for me, Mr. Lyon," she said with a smile, bending her head back down over her manuscript.

He watched her for a few seconds, surprised by the tenderness he felt. "It is my pleasure, Miss Armitage."

He left the room quietly, allowing her to return to her work in peace.

Chapter 7

The weather could not have been more idyllic as Charissa's birthday party arrived at last. Monday's brilliant sunshine had dried up Sunday's puddles, leaving the day cool but vibrant with the exuberant, well-washed hues of spring. Tuesday brought with it a warm, dry southwest wind, which induced everyone to spend time outdoors at last and experience the rich tapestry of renewed life. The happy result of all this natural beauty was that the guests coming to Silvercrosse Hall for the party were eager to enjoy themselves.

Weeks ago, Charissa had ordered a new gown from London, pale blue silk with tiny dark blue forget-me-nots embroidered on the hem and sleeves. She had been tempted to purchase a hat with blue feathers, but had settled for a matching blue hair ribbon which she decorated with real forget-me-nots from the garden. She was pleased with the effect, and she hoped—albeit guiltily—that Mr. Lyon would think her pretty.

When she descended the staircase in anticipation of the guests soon to arrive, Sir Godfrey was waiting for her. His double-breasted tail coat was dyed a deep plum, an uncharacteristically high-spirited color, and Charissa commended him on his choice. He returned the compliment, kissing her on the cheek. Just as he did so, Will appeared on the stairs, coming down by himself as he always insisted on doing.

"Good evening, Mr. Lyon," Charissa beamed.

"Good evening, Miss Armitage; good evening, Sir Godfrey. I do apologize," he said as he took each stair carefully, "for my lack of proper attire." He had had no evening kit made for him by Mr. Pearce, and so he was wearing his ordinary day clothes. He felt odd attending a social function garbed in such prosaic fashion. "It is a bit of an embarrassment, but it is also, no doubt, a much-needed exercise in humility."

"No one will think the worse of you, Mr. Lyon," Charissa reassured him. "They all understand your situation. Besides, no matter what you wear, your bearing and manners are so very elegant."

Sir Godfrey exhaled testily and muttered something Charissa could not quite hear. She flashed him an uncertain glance, but he was already turning towards the front door where Mr. and Mrs. Humphreys had just been admitted. "Welcome!" Sir Godfrey boomed.

Will and Charissa accompanied Sir Godfrey across the hall, and there followed the usual introductions and pleasantries. Mrs. Humphreys gazed at Will with interest, but before she could commence any conversation with him, Sir Godfrey gave her his arm and escorted her promptly in the direction of the drawing room. Mr. Humphreys did the same with Charissa, politely leaving Will to bring up the rear.

Will, however, did not mind the reversal of the precedence that—unbeknownst to them—he was entitled to as Lord Hartwell. The freedom of observing while not being observed was a novel treat, and he enjoyed it.

The other guests arrived soon afterward, and once they were all there, they moved into the dining room. Sir Godfrey presided at one end of the table, while Charissa, the hostess, sat at the other end. Will was seated equidistant from either end, between Penelope and Helen St. Swythin.

When everyone had been served, but before the meal began, Sir Godfrey rose to his feet to propose a toast. "Ladies and gentleman," he said with a gracious nod, "thank you for joining me this evening. As you all know, we are here to celebrate the birthday of Miss Charissa Armitage, my loveliest of cousins and dearest friend. We must also not forget that six years ago Charissa came to Silvercrosse Hall. She left the city of Babylon, as it were, for this ancient place of refuge and was thereby delivered from the schemes of evil men. I am blessed beyond all measure to count her among my family. How truly it is said that *a woman who fears the Lord will be praised.*" He raised his glass. "To Charissa!"

They all raised their glasses and echoed him. "Charissa!" It was the first time Will had said her Christian name out loud.

In response to this praise from her guests, Charissa thanked them all with genuine gratefulness. It was a heartwarming scene, one which made Will feel as though he were standing inside a painting of idealized domestic life. Strangely enough, though, it also felt real.

After the toast, congenial conversation characterized the rest of dinner, much of it directed by Mrs. Shaw and Mrs. Humphreys toward the newcomer. Will was easily able to deflect any attempt to identify his—nonexistent—Lyon relatives. When he was asked about his childhood home, he felt that he ought to tell them the correct county, but fortunately, when he informed them he had grown up in Dorset, none of them had either been there or knew anyone from there.

It was trickier to skate around his more recent history; however, his luck held. None of the other men present—Sir Godfrey, Mr. Humphreys, or Dr. Shaw—frequented London or belonged to any gentleman's clubs there, and all of their attempts to discover any acquaintances in common with Will came to naught.

So far so good. Mr. William Lyon was making quite a good impression.

As dinner progressed, Penelope, seated on his right, spoke to Will about safe, polite things, demonstrating that she was as refined as her sister was forward. On his left, Helen didn't ask him any questions that would have been difficult for him to answer, but she tended to try to draw him into private conversation, which was irksome. At one point, she placed her pale right hand over his left. He looked at her piercingly, taken aback by her boldness.

Immediately, she lifted her fingers, but floated her hand in his line of vision. "Do you like my ring?" she inquired *sotto voce*.

Will stared down at a small gold ring on her fourth finger in the shape of a serpent with its tail in its mouth. He knew that it was a popular symbol of eternal love. "It's very nice," he felt compelled to reply.

"It means a great deal to me," she said softly.

Ah, he surmised, she must have had a man in her life at some point. He wondered what had happened, if the man had died. Perhaps he had been a soldier. "I do not doubt it," he answered.

She pulled her hand back into her own lap. "I'll tell you why I wear it. I know this may sound strange, given that it is a snake, but it reminds me of God's mighty power."

So much for a romantic connection, Will thought, but he didn't quite follow her meaning. "I was under the impression that in the Bible the serpent is a symbol of Satan."

"It usually is. But haven't you read in the Old Testament where Moses lifted up a bronze serpent in the wilderness?"

"Not recently." It sounded vaguely familiar, but not particularly pleasant.

"Even though the faithless Israelites had been bitten by poisonous snakes, when they looked at the bronze serpent, they lived."

"So is your ring some kind of protective talisman?" Will asked.

"Don't let Sir Godfrey hear you say that! He would call such an idea a wicked superstition."

"I'd have to agree with him." Will took a bite of his food. "I don't hold to such things."

"Neither do I, of course," Helen affirmed. "My ring is nothing of the sort. As I said, it's a reminder to me that it is Almighty God who has power over life and death."

At that point, from across the table Dr. Shaw asked Will if he had ever been to Somerset House to see the Royal Academy of Art's annual exhibition. In spite of his father's opinion of his own artistic endeavors, Will went to the show every year, and he was happy to refocus the group's discussion onto familiar, vastly more agreeable territory.

After the meal, the party returned to the drawing room, where Sir Godfrey announced it was time for Charissa to open her gifts. This declaration was met with universal approval, and the guests fetched whatever box or bag they had brought with them.

Charissa seated herself on a settee, where the rays of the setting sun behind her blended with the glow of just-lit candles, glittering her hair with golden strands. Will deliberately moved near her, enjoying the sight.

The first package, set in Charissa's lap by Mrs. Shaw, was a soft bundle swathed in white linen. Charissa untied it carefully and discovered a delicate lace shawl. After thanking the Shaws, she accepted a box from the Humphreys, which contained a cut-glass bottle with an exotic-smelling perfume inside."

Aunt Caroline's offering was next and had been purchased on her behalf by Sir Godfrey. It was a lovely fan, silvery white with blue forget-me-nots painted on it. Charissa opened it and swished it back and forth. "It matches my gown," she exclaimed with delight, exchanging a look with Sir Godfrey. "Thank you, Aunt Caroline." The old lady nodded contentedly.

"I want to give Charissa my gift now," insisted Helen. She handed Charissa a flat package wrapped in brown paper tied with a pink lace ribbon, and she watched expectantly as her friend opened it.

"What is it?" Mrs. Shaw asked eagerly, craning her neck to see.

Charissa pulled a reddish brown book out of the paper and ran her hands over its decorative leather cover. There was no title embossed on it, but fancy gold scrollwork shaped like leaves decorated the corners. She opened it to examine the title page and was surprised to see inscribed there:

A Meditation on the Eyes of the Lord which Roam Throughout the Earth
by Sir Godfrey Scrivener
May 1806
"For the eyes of the Lord roam throughout the earth
to show himself strong for those who are wholeheartedly devoted to him."
2 Chronicles 16:9

"It's one of Sir Godfrey's sermons," Charissa explained to the curious onlookers, "made into a book." She carefully flipped through the pages and saw that someone had handwritten the entire discourse in neat, beautiful letters. The margins of every page were illustrated with flowering vines, which occasionally extended into the text and curled possessively around the words.

"Did you create this yourself, Helen?" Charissa asked.

"Yes, I wrote out every word and illustrated it, too!" Helen answered, her eyes aflame with the passion of her effort. "It's always been my favorite of Sir Godfrey's sermons. I asked him for it months ago."

"How did you manage to have it bound it so beautifully?" Dr. Shaw inquired. "Did you send it to London?"

"Oh no. I simply copied it onto the pages of a blank book. You see, before Papa died, he had empty pages bound into a number of separate volumes for me to drawn in or write on. I've filled many of them with my art, and I also keep a diary. But I still have several empty volumes to use as I wish."

"I write a diary as well," Mrs. Humphreys said approvingly. "It is an excellent way to focus one's thoughts. And my faith is encouraged when I look back at prayers I've written and realize that the Lord has answered them."

Helen nodded. "Yes. I have found great comfort in my journal."

Charissa continued to examine her gift. "You've painted the flowers so realistically, Helen—but then again I wouldn't expect anything else from you where plants are concerned."

"I couldn't bear it if they weren't absolutely perfect in every detail," Helen declared. "See," she pointed out, "here is a honeysuckle vine—*Lonicera periclymenum*—and this fluffy white blossom is *clematis vitalba*. Papa called it traveller's joy, although he used to say that traveller's joy does the devil's work because it overwhelms and chokes out other plants."

Penelope smiled as she listened to her sister. "As you might guess, Helen takes after our father," she told Will proudly. "He was an amateur botanist."

"I used to walk in the woods with him," Helen recalled wistfully. "He would talk about the plants and their properties and things like that, but he died when I was young. I do so wish I remembered more about what he taught me. But when I paint," she added, her tone suddenly fierce, "I am very careful to depict everything exactly as it is in nature."

Charissa touched the page admiringly. "No one can deny that, Helen. This volume is in every way a one-of-a-kind masterpiece. It reminds me of an illustrated medieval manuscript." She closed the book and handed it to Sir Godfrey so that he could admire it in turn.

Helen glowed as Sir Godfrey, too, complimented her work and remarked that he had had no idea of the use to which she was going to put his sermon. "I am most pleased," he told her as he gave the book to Will.

"What do you think of it, Mr. Lyon?" Helen prompted Will with transparent eagerness.

In order to assess the book fairly, Will took a few minutes to examine the quality of the lettering and the drawings. They were all really quite good, and the plants, especially, were indeed beautifully done. Relieved to be able to compliment Helen honestly, he sincerely—though not effusively—praised her work.

"Perhaps I could make something like it for you, Mr. Lyon," she breathed.

Will hoped not, but he replied politely, "You are too kind, Miss St. Swythin." He quickly held the book out to Penelope, who had seen it before and so took it over to Mr. Humphreys for his inspection.

"Now it's my turn to present my gift to you," Penelope smiled as she gave Charissa a wooden box. "I'm afraid it's neither original nor unique, but I hope that it will please you nonetheless."

It did please Charissa. Her friend had found a pen and ink set which featured a peacock feather quill and a bottle of expensive ink. "Oh," Charissa said, touched, "you shouldn't have." She worried that Penelope had spent more money than she could afford, for while the St. Swythin sisters were not exactly poverty-stricken, it was common knowledge that they had to keep a careful eye on their funds.

Penelope waved her concern away. "You've been generous to me over the past six years I've known you, and it's my chance to give a little something back."

Will sensed that Sir Godfrey wanted to be the last one to present Charissa with a gift, so he took his turn next. Reaching into his coat, he drew out a roll of paper tied with a lavender ribbon the housekeeper had scrounged up for him at his request. "Happy birthday, Miss Armitage," he said, handing it over to her.

Charissa attempted not to broadcast the anticipation she felt as she held the gift from Mr. Lyon in her fingers. What had he selected for her, she wondered? Surely it was but a small token of his esteem, nothing more.

On the other hand, as Charissa unrolled the thick piece of paper, Will watched nervously, second-guessing himself. Had he gone too far?

Had he presumed too much on this family's hospitality and considered himself a friend when he was, in fact, nothing but a stranger?

If so, it was too late now.

When Charissa saw what he had drawn on the paper she held, her heart skipped a beat, and her lips parted slightly. Nothing short of spectacular, it far eclipsed Helen's competent illustrations.

It was a remarkably lifelike portrait of Charissa herself, from the waist up, done first in ink then lightly tinted with color. About eight inches square, it could easily be framed to decorate any room in the house—and, amazingly, Will had managed to keep its creation a secret.

"Mr. Lyon," Charissa murmured, stunned. "I am truly astonished. It's wonderful."

She looked directly at him; their eyes met and held. Something meaningful passed between them—a mutual understanding, perhaps, or a sense of the possibilities inherent in exploring a deeper bond with one another. It lasted only a moment, but everyone in the room could sense their connection.

Sir Godfrey quickly intervened. "Charissa, darling" he said, "how nice that is. Here, let me take it from you, because there is one more very special gift for you to open this evening." Relieving her of the portrait, he rolled it up and set it aside, to the frustration of the others. But no one said anything as he fetched a small, plush box from the mantel and gave it to Charissa. "Happy birthday, my dear," he said.

She opened the box curiously. Inside, lying on silk, was an exquisite silver cross with a ruby at its heart, attached to a silver chain. "Oh my!" she exhaled. "Godfrey, is this what I think it is?"

He nodded. "Yes. It is the silver cross found below the old chapel on these grounds. The filigree work is so delicate and the ruby so valuable that I thought it might work as a pendant. I took it to a jeweler in London last autumn, and he agreed with me. So now, my dear, it is yours."

"Godfrey... I don't know what to say."

"You need not say anything." He took the box from her hands and carefully extracted the necklace. The cross's shape and style reflected its medieval origin, although its scrollwork had an unusual flame motif.

The ruby was irregularly shaped and opaque rather than clear, but it had been polished so that it glowed as if it were lit from within.

"Oh my," she whispered.

As Will watched Sir Godfrey place the chain around Charissa's neck, he suddenly realized something. Perhaps he should have guessed it from his first conscious moments in the house, but even though it had taken him time to come to the conclusion, he had no doubt whatsoever that his impression was correct: Sir Godfrey was in love with Charissa.

Will noticed how Sir Godfrey's fingers lingered ever so slightly on her neck as he fastened the latch, and how his eyes followed her intently around the room as she showed everyone else his precious gift. The silver cross itself, Will understood, symbolized Sir Godfrey's domain. Yes, there was no doubt about it—Sir Godfrey had every intention of making Charissa into Lady Scrivener of Silvercrosse Hall.

Will's insides twisted with fierce resistance, although such a reaction was entirely illogical. Why should he care? He barely knew Miss Armitage, and she had everything to gain by marrying her financially comfortable, God-fearing cousin. Sir Godfrey wasn't even her first cousin, but was more distantly related, so there was no concern on that score. And to think that she would consider Will anything other than a pleasant acquaintance was absurd.

And it was wholly unacceptable.

After Charissa had shown the cross to everyone else in the room, she approached Will. "This is the silver cross I was speaking of just the other day," she told him. "A hidden treasure brought to life again."

He glanced at it, but only briefly. He looked up into her face, and, again, their eyes met and held. "It suits you," he said softly. He did not mean by this statement to endorse Sir Godfrey's intention—far from it. Instead, he meant that her heart, like the cross, was a hidden treasure he wished to know better.

The flash of comprehension in her eyes and the tinge of pink in her cheeks told him she sensed the significance of his reply. She took a quick breath, then seemed to recall that there were others in the room besides themselves. "Thank you, Mr. Lyon," she replied, moving to stand beside Sir Godfrey. "And thank you everyone for your generosity and your kind words. You are truly the best friends any lady could ask for."

Chapter 8

Sir Godfrey was called away on estate business at daybreak the morning after the party, and Charissa spent the time until breakfast alone in the Menagerie Room, writing. Once again, she wasn't concentrating well on her novel. The description of the heroine's accidental meeting with the hero in a chapel by the sea felt dreadfully flat. Irritated, Charissa wadded up the sheets of paper she had used, one after the other. "A complete waste," she muttered, sweeping them across the table with her arm.

Inevitably, her thoughts flew to Mr. Lyon. She looked over at the place where he had sat when he'd joined her a few days ago—here, she had discovered his artistic abilities. She ran her fingers lightly over the spot on the table where he had helped her sketch Commodore. It delighted her to imagine him, sometime later, surreptitiously drawing her own likeness. She hadn't noticed anything out of the ordinary in his behavior, but he must have take the time to observe her carefully in order to capture her image so well. The very idea of such devoted attention to her person caused an odd sensation in the pit of her stomach.

Really, she admonished herself sternly, how could she be so flighty? It was this sort of romantic fascination which had devastated her in the past. She had trusted a charming gentleman, only to be humiliated by his lecherous behavior. True, she had not been physically harmed, but she had been scarred by her emotional wounds.

All of a sudden she felt vulnerable, as if she were an eighteen-year-old ingénue all over again. Sir Godfrey's admonitions rang in her ears.

She shouldn't allow her expectations to soar, only to the collapse in the end. Romance was a fantasy, nothing more.

And yet, for the first time since her long-ago disastrous foray into the marriage mart, she admitted to herself that, yes, she wanted to soften her heart. She was tired of living life vicariously through her novels. And no, she was not sorry Mr. Lyon had come to Silvercrosse Hall, no matter what Sir Godfrey said, she thought rebelliously.

She was not sorry at all!

She entered the dining room with Aunt Caroline for breakfast and was pleased to find Will already seated at the table. "You are looking well, Mr. Lyon," she commented cheerfully.

He looked up and—thinking how attractive Charissa was—automatically moved to stand in her presence. A sharp twinge in his leg forced him to grasp the table, and he grunted in frustration. "I am not as well as I would like to be," he acknowledged, retaking his seat, "but every day I see improvement. In fact, Miss Armitage" he went on, helping himself to toast and cheese, "I was wondering if it would be possible for me to go into town today or tomorrow."

"Really? Do you think you're strong enough to handle the exertion of a carriage ride?"

"I believe so. It's not far, and I want to purchase a hat in Murrington, as well as a cane. I'm very tired of crutches, and the last time Mr. Rowley was here to examine me, he approved of my suggestion that I try out a cane."

"I'm sure Sir Godfrey has one you could borrow," Charissa felt obliged to point out.

"I would prefer to buy one of my own."

"I understand. Happily, I have already planned to make a trip into Murrington this afternoon." Her eyes sparkled. "I propose that we go together."

"Splendid," he agreed.

"I need a new parasol, Charissa," Aunt Caroline piped up unexpectedly. "My old one is falling apart." She pointed at Will. "Ask your young man which one he thinks is the best, and that's the one I want."

Your young man? As he watched Charissa's eyes widen, Will chuckled to himself. The elderly woman had it wrong on both counts—he was neither young nor did he belong to Charissa. But he did not correct the old lady as Charissa replied self-consciously that they would purchase something nice for her. Surprisingly, Aunt Caroline seemed to approve of his accompanying Charissa to town alone, something he could not have gotten away with in the city. Sir Godfrey would not be pleased about it, but then again, Will told himself smugly, Sir Godfrey was not available to object.

So Will and Charissa took the tilbury—Charissa's own lightweight, one-horse gig—into the village. Charissa drove, and while Will appreciated her skill, he did not care for being the passenger; it didn't seem right. But this was the country, after all, and it wasn't as though she were attempting to drive through London streets in an effort to turn heads. He sat uncomfortably beside her, watching her dodge the largest ruts, but the unavoidable bumps still bothered his leg more than he wanted to admit.

Charissa saw him wince. "I'm sorry," she apologized. "There's nothing I can do about the state of the roads. Perhaps you shouldn't have come. Should I turn round and take you back to Silvercrosse?"

"Gracious no!" he retorted. "I can take a bit of discomfort. I'm desperate to do something."

"I'm sure you are. And I suppose you are good at everything you do, are you not?"

"Not everything."

She guided the horse to the left of a nasty pothole. "But I expect you're an expert driver."

He was. He had once won a race from London to Brighton—an irresponsible and dangerous undertaking. No need to mention that. "I've impressed my fair share of young bucks."

"I imagine so." She smiled at the thought. "Pray tell, what else do you do well?"

"Hmm." Most of what he had done with his life she would find less than admirable. But there was something he had accomplished of which he was rather proud, whether or not Charissa would be impressed. "I have had occasion to participate in a few boxing matches. And I am, in fact, undefeated. I train at Gentlemen John Jackson's Boxing Saloon in Bond Street." He'd better be careful, he told himself. A boxing reputation was something that could be investigated.

"I've heard some gentlemen are enamored of the sport, but I've never understood why." She drew her eyebrows together. "Why would pummeling another human being bring anyone satisfaction?"

"I'm not sure I can explain it—at least not to a woman. But to demonstrate superior physical prowess and to be victorious in athletic competition produces a very real sense of accomplishment in a man." Not to mention that it was a temporarily effective way to release pent-up emotions such as anger and guilt.

"Oh yes, I understand how competitive men are. Even Sir Godfrey lords it over me when he wins at battledore and shuttlecock. But he doesn't always win—I am a good player, I would have you know."

"Perhaps when my leg is healed, I can discover that for myself, Miss Armitage." Nothing like inviting himself to stay at Silvercrosse Hall for nigh on the whole summer, he thought.

She was amenable to the idea, however. "I should like very much to take you on in a match. Beware, I might best you! But I really wish you would consider giving up fighting, Mr. Lyon. Not that I begrudge you your manly pursuits, but I would hate for you to injure your hands. You are a truly gifted artist, and art is a far more enduring achievement than the glory of the boxing ring."

"You have a point there," he conceded.

"Which reminds me—I do want to thank you again for the drawing you gave me last evening. It is exquisite and was a truly thoughtful gift."

"I enjoyed creating it. You make a charming subject."

"You flatter me, sir."

"Not at all."

Charissa's heart fluttered deliciously. "How are you coming along with the pictures of Commodore and Sprite?"

"Very well. I am done with Commodore, who has been most obliging. Now I must try to keep Sprite by my side long enough to capture his likeness. Unfortunately, though, I cannot pet him and draw him at the same time."

"Just feed him, Mr. Lyon. Like any male, he responds favorably to the gratification of his stomach."

Will lifted an eyebrow. "First a condemnation of boxing and now a cynical comment about a man and his appetite."

She laughed. "It was just an observation. I didn't say there was anything wrong with such a characteristic."

"Surely you don't believe a side of beef cooked in burgundy and a slice of apple cake would make me yours forever?"

"Wouldn't it?"

He sighed mournfully. "Alas, no. I much prefer parsnips."

They exchanged an amused look as the tilbury rounded a bend and Murrington came into view.

Will observed that it was a charming, prosperous village, not a large town, but neither a small backwater. Charissa guided the vehicle over to the front of a store with two large bow windows on the ground floor and the word *Colley's* painted above the door. "Here we are," she stated. "I'm sure Mr. Colley will have a cane or two from which you may choose. Then we'll see about your hat—for, after all, what is a gentleman without one?"

"Hatless," Will quipped, descending from the tilbury by himself, with a bit of pain he did his best to hide.

Once inside the shop, they were greeted by Mr. Colley, a pudgy middle-aged man with thinning blond hair, huge green eyes, and an unusually wide mouth. He reminded Will of an enthusiastic frog. "Miss Armitage," the shop-owner beamed, "how delightful to see you today. And this must be your guest from London."

Charissa acknowledged it was and made the introductions. Before she was finished, a young woman rushed out into the front room from the back of the building. "Mary," said Mr. Colley, "here is the gentleman who is staying at Silvercrosse Hall. Mr. Lyon, this is my daughter Mary."

Mary curtseyed and stared at Will mutely.

"Well, she usually has plenty of things to say, but not today, I see," Mr. Colley chuckled. "What may I help you with, sir?"

As Will picked out a strong mahogany cane—the best in Mr. Colley's small inventory—Mary came up next to Charissa and murmured into her ear, "He's very handsome!"

"I cannot deny it," Charissa whispered back.

"I heard Sir Godfrey gave you a family heirloom for your birthday—the ancient silver cross on a chain. I thought you'd be wearing it the next time I saw you. Is it very pretty?"

News travels fast, thought Charissa. "Yes, it's beautiful. I shall wear it to church on Sunday."

"Oh, good. Will Mr. Lyon be in church as well?"

"I hope so."

Their conversation was interrupted when Will tried to enlist Charissa to help him pick out a parasol for Aunt Caroline, but Charissa shook her head. "She specifically wanted you to select it. I am merely an eyewitness."

Will obligingly chose one made of pale pink oiled silk with ivory-colored fringe, stretched over a carved whalebone frame. He insisted on paying for it himself, and Charissa was pleased to note his selection was in very good taste.

Afterwards, because Will was fairing quite well with the cane, they returned the crutches to the tilbury. They placed the wrapped parasol under the seat and went off next to see Mr. Pearce. The clothier proudly showed Will a selection of hats. As Will placed the best of them on his head and with his other hand leaned on his cane, he let out a victorious "Ha!"

"Feeling more like yourself?" Charissa asked.

"Indeed I am!" Well, perhaps he was not feeling precisely like *himself*, he mused, but he was certainly feeling more like Mr. William Lyon.

Charissa's own errands involved stopping at the chandler's and the post office. Once those tasks were completed, she asked Will if he wanted to return to Silvercrosse Hall. He replied in the negative, so they walked up and down the street together, slowly, looking in windows and chatting like old friends.

When they arrived at the parish church on the far edge of the green, Charissa suggested they go inside. Will looked at the ancient building, whose warm golden stones rose high above the rest of the village, and decided that a rest was not at all a bad idea.

Inside, the nave's whitewashed walls contrasted attractively with the dark wood pews and ceiling beams. Several wall plaques on both sides of the building memorialized Murrington's notable dead. A stained glass window above the altar had five lower sections, each depicting a saint, and several teardrop-shaped windows on the top which came together in a circle to form a rose.

Charissa and Will sat down in one of the back pews. "This is St. Mark's Church," she explained, pointing to the window, "so St. Mark is the figure in the middle. On his left is St. Barnabas, who was his champion when the Apostle Paul gave up on him. The other three windows depict the remaining gospel writers: St. Matthew, St. Luke, and St. John."

Will cocked his head slightly to one side. "St. Paul gave up on St. Mark?" The thought disturbed him.

"At one point, Paul thought Mark was untrustworthy because he left the missionaries and went back to his home in Jerusalem. But eventually Paul changed his mind. At the end of his life, when he was in prison and his death was imminent, he specifically asked for Mark to come to be with him."

Will felt absurdly relieved.

Glancing around the nave, Charissa continued, "The church is simply decorated inside, but I like it. Sometimes I make a special trip here just so I can pray alone. I also especially like it when Mr. Humphreys holds Evensong."

"You are happy here in Murrington."

Her face grew serious. "It has been a safe haven for me."

Here was her past again, casting a shadow—however faint—over her present life. He wanted to know exactly what had happened to her in London, but he dared not broach such a sensitive topic, so he asked about her childhood instead. "Where did you grow up, Miss Armitage?"

"For the first years of my life, I lived in Warwickshire, where Papa was the rector of a prominent church. He was one of the many grandsons of the Marquess of Danleigh, a fact which tends to impress people, of course, but I always inform them his congregation loved him because he was so wise and kind. My mother died when I was born, and so, sadly, I don't remember her at all. After Mama died, Papa never remarried; he was much older than she was. I was his only child, and he passed away when I was fifteen years old. Afterwards I lived with an elderly aunt until she died, and then Sir Godfrey and his wife invited me to come to Silvercrosse Hall."

"My mother also died when I was born," he said, his expression darkening.

"I'm sorry," Charissa replied sympathetically. "There's always an emptiness in your heart no one else can fill. I know."

Will's mouth felt dry. "It's hard to live with the knowledge that I killed my own mother," he spat out bitterly.

"What?" Charissa was taken aback. "That's what you think?"

"Well, she died giving birth to me. So it's true, isn't it?"

"My mother died the day after I was born, but Papa never allowed me to assume any guilt whatsoever for her death!"

"My father never said anything about my mother after she died. It was as if she'd never existed."

"Oh." Sadness welled up inside Charissa. "It was probably too painful for him."

"I suspect that he couldn't forgive me for being her murderer."

"No, I don't believe that!" She couldn't allow him to contemplate such a ridiculous notion. "That's what you assumed as a child, but such a proposition doesn't take into account your father's loss and how it affected him. Don't be so hard on yourself, Mr. Lyon. Neither you nor I are murderers. We are simply children who tragically lost one of our parents at birth, just as our fathers were simply husbands who tragically lost their wives."

Will stared at Charissa, trying to process what she had said—his mind was in a jumble. For the first time, someone had challenged his childish assumptions about his father's aloof behavior, and he realized with a shock that he had never thought about his father's grief in a mature way before. He felt confused. He wanted to believe Charissa, and yet it seemed too easy to jettison the guilt that had gnawed at him ever since he could remember.

Not knowing what else to do, he frowned.

"Your mother loved you, Mr. Lyon," Charissa stated gently, reiterating what her own father had told her many times. "She loved you more than she loved her own life and was happy to bring you into this world. I am sure the Lord gave her great peace, even at the end, assuring her He had created you for a special destiny no one else in this world can fulfill." Charissa put her hand over Will's, which lay on the pew in between them. "Such knowledge is a special blessing God gives to mothers."

Will was horrified to feel tears well up in his eyes. "I shall... I shall ponder your words," he said stiffly, staring down at her fingers covering his.

"I suppose that's all I can ask," she told him, "since I've already discovered you're at least as pig-headed as I am."

He grunted, and managed to reply flippantly, "Oh, I'm much worse."

She smiled. "Given what I have witnessed so far," she said, "that doesn't surprise me one bit."

Chapter 9

Predictably, Sir Godfrey was none too happy Will and Charissa had gone to Murrington unaccompanied. As soon as she made an appearance downstairs the next morning, Sir Godfrey invited her into his study, where he had a before-breakfast tray waiting for her.

"Dearest," he said as she sat down and poured herself a cup of tea, "it was unwise of you to go to town with only Mr. Lyon. You should have taken a groom or a maid with you."

Charissa, however, was prepared for this discussion. After taking a sip of the warm, comforting beverage, she replied, "But I had already planned to drive myself and had ordered the tilbury. It would have been rude to exclude Mr. Lyon. And he is so pleased to have purchased a cane—he greatly prefers it to the crutches."

"His pleasure means less to me than your safety and reputation."

"How can you possibly imagine that I endangered either my safety or my reputation? Mr. Lyon has been nothing but the perfect gentleman in every way."

"We know precious little about him." Sir Godfrey leaned over and vigorously speared a herring on the tray.

"We know he is grieving for his father, and he has no other family to speak of. He needs our compassion, not our mistrust."

Sir Godfrey put the herring back on its plate without having tasted it. "Charissa, I must be frank with you. Lonely gentlemen oftentimes run after the first pretty face they encounter to satisfy their own need for... for companionship."

Charissa sighed impatiently as she put down her cup. "Godfrey, how long have you known me? I am four-and-twenty, and not as naïve as I was six years ago. I am aware Mr. Lyon is lonely. He has engaged me in pleasant conversation, but he seems to be a confirmed bachelor. Not every man chooses to marry."

"It may not be marriage he wishes," Sir Godfrey growled.

"And would he attempt anything untoward with a broken leg? He cannot even walk unsupported."

"He still has his charm."

"And I still have my brains."

"Intelligence has nothing to do with it."

"It has quite a lot to do with my ability to see through the schemes of a would-be seducer," she disagreed. "In addition to that, you know quite well I have no intention of allowing myself to fall in love with anyone, as you have so sensibly advised me." This was no longer true, but she had said it so many times before, it seemed obligatory.

After a slight pause, Sir Godfrey said, "So you have often informed me."

"So you see, you have nothing to worry about," she declared, busying herself with her tea.

He acknowledged her point without enthusiasm. "Indeed."

Since there was still an hour before breakfast, Charissa decided to go for a walk. The sun was shining brilliantly, moderated by a mild breeze, and it was just too beautiful, she thought, to stay indoors. So she put on a pretty hat with a brim long enough to shield her face and ventured out onto the well-manicured grounds. Intending to take the path which would give her a delightful view of the countryside northwest of Silvercrosse Hall, she strolled alongside the house. Before she had gone very far, she realized she was passing next to the windows which opened into the Menagerie Room. Unable to help herself, she looked over at them, hoping to catch a glimpse of Will, and she felt a tremor of satisfaction when she saw him standing there, watching her.

She smiled jauntily and waved. He gave her a lopsided smile and a gesture of his hand in return. As she continued down the path, with her back to the house, she wondered if he were still observing her, but she didn't dare turn around and discover if that were so.

Will joined Charissa in the Menagerie Room once again for a few hours the following day. His plan was not to interrupt her, but simply to be in the same room with her while she wrote. They would work quietly on their own individual projects, he explained, and so, with her blessing, he began a portrait of Sprite standing in front of Silvercrosse Hall while she tackled the next chapter of her story.

At first Charissa feared Will's presence would be too distracting. But from the very first moment he had made himself comfortable in the chair opposite her—and showed no signs of departing—she had been pleasantly surprised. To be sure, she felt a glow deep down inside whenever he was near. But she also found that she was able to concentrate on her work better with him there; her thoughts wandered less. So she made excellent progress on her fanciful description of the old Welsh castle central to her story, and somehow the room seemed brighter as she gazed at the dramatic words neatly written on the paper.

This arrangement worked out so well that Will sought Charissa out the next day, and the day after that, and every day thereafter.

Naturally, Sir Godfrey begrudged their time together, even though the door to the Menagerie Room was always left open, and servants regularly went in and out. He did his best to keep them apart, but circumstances often conspired to hinder his efforts. Unwilling to resort to petulant displays of jealousy or temper, he found himself in the unenviable position of knowing that while he worked on his accounts in the library or made his daily rounds on the estate, Will and Charissa were enjoying each other's company.

As far as Will was concerned, life couldn't have been more satisfactory. He took pleasure in the camaraderie that grew each time he was with Charissa; she could warm him down to his toes with just a few insightful words and her intriguing smile. All in all, it was a happy situation that was, Will felt, well worth his host's disapproval.

He continued his portrait of Sprite, giving the pup treats to keep him content. He also allowed himself a glance now and then at Charissa as she worked, lost in her imaginings. He noticed how her hair sparkled with soft, shimmering highlights as the afternoon sun illuminated her corner of the room, and he suddenly decided he ought to assess her feelings for Sir Godfrey.

Was she aware that Sir Godfrey was in love with her and wanted to marry her? Had she understood the significance of his gift of the silver cross? Was a match with her cousin something Charissa herself desired? Was her kindness to Will merely plain Christian charity? If those were her true feelings, Will wanted to know. In the regrettable event that she had formed an attachment to Sir Godfrey, he would have to curtail his own esteem for her so as to avoid the hot, humiliating sting of her rejection, however gently she might offer it.

In order to evaluate her frame of mind, Will relied on his own powers of perception. Every time he saw Sir Godfrey and Charissa together, he paid diligent attention to her words and actions. Did anything she say or do reveal a hidden passion for the man? Did she cast yearning looks his way? Did she make a special effort to see to his pleasure and comfort? Did they share confidences as lovers do?

Right from the beginning, however, Will saw nothing to make him think Charissa knew—or at least wanted to know—that Sir Godfrey was enamored with her. He felt confident she was not in love with her cousin, and soon he was completely certain he was right. The results of his informal investigation were entirely to his liking: Charissa was unmoved by Sir Godfrey's subtle appeals because she had no romantic interest in him whatsoever. In fact, she likely thought of him as an older brother, or even, since he was seventeen years her senior, a beneficent uncle.

The only area in which Sir Godfrey seemed to have a special connection with Charissa was the religious one. In the evenings he often read from either the Bible or a book of sermons written by some renowned divine, and the ensuing conversation between him and Charissa lost Will in a sea of theological minutiae. Not that Will was incapable of rigorous intellectual discussion, but in the past he'd given Christianity as little thought as possible, even when he had attended Oxford. He was conversant with the concepts of the faith as expressed in the Church of England's obligatory rituals, of course, but he had always steered clear of the unbending personal religion demonstrated by his father.

However, whenever it was Charissa who read from the Scriptures, Will found himself listening. And when he finally agreed to go to church with the family, he felt an unanticipated sense of peace as he sat next to her in the sanctuary. The nicest part of the morning was hearing her sweet singing voice fill the nave with its fervent, pure sound. He could tell she wasn't just parroting Christian sentiments as she gave voice to the hymns; she was worshipping a God who was real to her.

Thus it was—even in spiritual matters—Will felt an ever increasing attachment to Charissa. Their friendship was radically different from anything he had ever experienced before. And to be honest, he wasn't quite sure what it meant. So while his competitive spirit made it easy to enjoy the unspoken contest with Sir Godfrey for Charissa's time and affection, he hesitated to pursue the explanation for just why he wanted to win that fight. It was something he was neither ready to acknowledge nor willing to put into words.

In addition to accompanying Charissa to St. Mark's Church, Will received an additional, unanticipated benefit from attending the Sunday service. After its conclusion, Mrs. Shaw cornered him in order to invite him to dine with her family the next evening. He accepted with pleasure, so Monday afternoon the Shaws duly sent their carriage to fetch him. The vehicle was a spacious landau Will could tell had seen a good deal of faithful service; it needed to be re-sprung rather desperately, he thought as he bounced along the road in it. Fortunately, Edgemoor—a rambling stone dwelling half-covered by an exuberant expanse of ivy—was only half a mile from Silvercrosse Hall.

As soon as he arrived, Will was welcomed by Dr. Shaw, Mrs. Shaw, and their seven stair-step children: Jane, Henrietta, Arabella, Judith, Thomas, Colin, and Sophie. At the dinner table, the younger ones peppered him with questions about London, which he answered to their obvious satisfaction, describing fine buildings and parks and shops in entertaining fashion. Eleven-year-old Thomas begged to hear all about Astley's Amphitheatre and its famous equestrian shows. Will obliged him by recalling a particularly daring feat performed by a young woman riding bareback and was amused to see more than one mouth hanging open around the table as he told the tale.

The older girls, however, were far more interested to know whether or not he had ever been to a ball at Almack's. When they discovered he had been welcomed there by Lady Jersey herself—the most discriminating of that establishment's patronesses—they sighed in awe.

"And is it true there is a new dance there, Mr. Lyon?" Arabella asked breathlessly. "The waltz? Is it true one has to be granted permission by one of the patronesses to dance it? Have you danced it yourself? With a beautiful young lady?"

"I must answer yes on all counts, Miss Arabella," Will informed her.

Jane sighed, while Arabella and Henrietta looked at each other and giggled. "Is the waltz very *romantic*, Mr. Lyon?" Henrietta inquired.

"Very romantic," he replied with a twinkle in his eye.

"We have not got nearly enough romance here in Murrington," mumbled Arabella, "and poor Jane cannot even go to London for the season. It is dreadfully unfair!"

"Bella," Dr. Shaw warned. The fifteen-year old quickly busied herself with the food on her plate, her cheeks crimson.

But Will understood her point. It was very expensive to participate in the season, a debutante's wardrobe alone requiring the outlay of a large number of pounds. Furthermore, if one were presented to the Queen, court dress—so impractical that it could never be worn elsewhere—cost an outrageous sum.

But in spite of Arabella's despair, as Will looked at the naïve and pretty Miss Jane Shaw, he felt glad the family had no connections and was too poor to go to the capital city to attempt to rub elbows with the *beau monde*. Jane would do much better to wed a kind, countrified gentleman who had not succumbed to the temptations of the larger world.

"I daresay if one looks hard enough, one might be able to find a little romance even here in Staffordshire," Will posited, hoping to cheer the girls.

"You mean like Sir Godfrey and Miss Armitage?" gushed twelve-year old Judith. "We are ever so hoping they get married soon. What a magnificent wedding that will be!"

"Judith!" exclaimed Mrs. Shaw.

"Honestly, Jude, you are off in the clouds again. You know Miss Armitage has said many times that she does not wish to marry," Henrietta blurted out, mistaking the meaning behind her mother's corrective tone.

"And Sir Godfrey's so very much older than she is," put in Arabella.

"Well, I think Miss Armitage will want to marry Sir Godfrey once she finally realizes how much he adores her!" Judith retorted.

"Girls!" Mrs. Shaw cried again, especially upset because Will was a houseguest of the very people about whom her daughters were gossiping. "We will not speculate on such matters! It is none of our business."

"If you are interested in romantic places, let me tell you about Vauxhall Gardens," Will put in swiftly, drawing everyone's attention away from the thorny subject of local love stories and earning him a grateful look from Dr. Shaw. "It is a wondrous venue, I assure you. At night, thousands of lights hang from the trees, and many times I have been privy to fireworks displays that would put a Chinese emperor to shame!"

He went on in this vein for some time and set the stage for the rest of the evening, during which the conversation flowed energetically but without any more awkward moments. The children kept him amused, and he enjoyed himself. It was only much later, as he sat alone in the carriage on the way back to Silvercrosse Hall, that he had the opportunity to ponder what the girls had said about Charissa and Sir Godfrey.

Apparently, everyone except Charissa herself was aware Sir Godfrey was in love with her. It was possible, of course, she was just pretending not to know. But Charissa did not strike Will as the type of female who would engage in such a coquettish game.

Besides, one of the Shaw girls—Henrietta, he recalled—had revealed something far more credible where Charissa's character was concerned: *Miss Armitage has said many times that she does not wish to marry.* At the time it was uttered, the statement had served to defend Charissa's character. But as he contemplated it further, it deflated his happy mood—although it really should accomplish no such thing. He might enjoy Charissa's company, he reprimanded himself, but her marriage plans should make no difference to him. After all, the fictitious Mr. William Lyon was in no position to acquire a wife.

A wife? He shifted uncomfortably in his seat, putting too much weight on his leg, and he groaned out loud. For heaven's sake, he wasn't the one who wanted to marry Charissa. Oh, to be sure, he dreamed of a stolen kiss—or two or three. But nothing more serious than that. Certainly not.

And yet he couldn't help wondering why Charissa herself should be so dead set against matrimony. All the respectable young women he knew—and their mothers on their behalf—pursued eligible men with a vengeance. Many of them had pursued *him.*

Why was Charissa different? It was because of whatever had happened to her in London, of course. The more he considered that unhappy circumstance, whatever it was, the more angry he became that she should have been so ill-used. In a flash of impetuous gallantry, he vowed to uncover the story. It was possible he might be able to win her confidence and discover the identity of the man who had hurt her. Furthermore, he had money; he had connections. Maybe he could do something, even this late in time, to put the whole miserable business to rights.

Chapter 10

That evening, while Will was visiting the Shaws, Charissa reminded Sir Godfrey that she and Penelope St. Swythin were planning to take food baskets around to some of the poorer village residents the next day. Sir Godfrey was pleased she and her friend would be undertaking this charitable endeavor, and he encouraged her to spend all day ministering to the needy souls of Murrington. He saw her off the next morning with a kiss on the cheek and a merry wave. Then he disappeared into the library, where he ordered toast, eggs, ham, and coffee to be brought into him for a solitary, peaceful meal.

Thus it happened that when Will came downstairs, he found no one in the breakfast room. He inquired after Charissa and felt a sense of disappointment when the butler told him she would be absent until evening. He chose to work in the Menagerie Room without her, even though it lacked the comfortable ambiance he felt when she was present.

The day did not improve when Sir Godfrey dropped by the room. He asked Will several questions about how his leg was doing now that it had been almost a month since the accident, and Will understood from this interrogation that Sir Godfrey was more than ready to see him depart for London. Will, however, was not at all disposed to go.

About an hour later, a visitor arrived at Silvercrosse Hall. Will was not aware of it until the footman informed him that Sir Godfrey had requested his presence in the drawing room. Will rose reluctantly, grabbed his cane, and made his way across the house. When he entered the drawing room to join Sir Godfrey and Aunt Caroline, who was sleeping soundly in her chair, he was surprised to see Helen St. Swythin.

She looked up at him from under her lashes as he gave her a courtesy. "Mr. Lyon, I am so glad to see you."

Sir Godfrey indicated with his hand that Will should take a seat. "Miss St. Swythin wishes to extend you an invitation," he said.

"And what invitation would that be?" Will asked politely as he sat down.

"Our garden is so lovely this time of the year, Penelope and I have decided to host an outdoor tea on Thursday, if the weather is fine," Helen told him. "Penny asked me to send you all a written invitation, but I decided to extend it in person. And I am most eager to have you accompany Sir Godfrey and his family to our home, Mr. Lyon. We rarely have guests, but this gathering is my idea, and I am very persuasive when I want to be. Penelope has given in to my earnest supplications. I reminded her repeatedly of what the Scriptures say—*do not neglect to show hospitality, for by doing this some have welcomed angels as guests without knowing it.*" She gazed at Will admiringly.

The irony of her likening his company to that of angels was not lost on him, but he was learning to expect grand pronouncements from Helen. "If Sir Godfrey, his aunt, and Miss Armitage are able to come, I shall most readily join them," he agreed.

Sir Godfrey confirmed he had accepted the invitation on behalf of Aunt Caroline, Charissa and himself, but then—to Will's dismay—he stood to his feet. "I pray you will excuse me, Miss St. Swythin, but I have important business I must attend to. I'll see you on Thursday afternoon. Good day to you." He nodded at both Helen and Will and departed, leaving Will alone in the room with Helen and the slumbering Aunt Caroline.

Annoyed, Will recognized Sir Godfrey had purposely abandoned him to this undesirable fate. He looked over at Helen sitting across from him, her expression resembling that of Sprite whenever Charissa slipped him a bit of food underneath the table.

"I'm pleased that you're coming, Mr. Lyon," she beamed. "I'd like to ask your opinion of my paintings."

"I'm hardly an expert, Miss St. Swythin."

"Charissa says you are. She says the portrait you drew of her is superb, although Sir Godfrey put it away before any of us could see it."

"It was a humble effort, although I am glad Miss Armitage approves of it."

"Poor Sir Godfrey. He was terribly jealous of it," Helen recalled with an unladylike smirk.

Will raised an eyebrow—trust Miss St. Swythin to articulate something no one else would dream of saying out loud. Nevertheless, she was informative. "I would say Sir Godfrey's gift to Miss Armitage was by far the most exquisite of the evening, although both yours and mine were unique as well," he responded.

"Yes, that's true. His gift was the most meaningful. I do so hope Charissa becomes Lady Scrivener soon. Sir Godfrey has been waiting for ever so long."

Will played dumb. "He wants to marry her?"

"Oh yes, can't you tell? He's been in love with her for ages. Ever since the very first day she came to Silvercrosse Hall."

"But wasn't Sir Godfrey's wife alive when Miss Armitage arrived? And for several years after that?"

Helen chuckled. "Well, yes, but the late Lady Scrivener was not exactly the sort of woman to keep a man on his toes. Actually, she was excruciatingly dull."

Will had no idea if Helen's claim were true or not, but even if it were, it was hard to imagine a man like Sir Godfrey falling for another woman while his wife was alive. "Sir Godfrey seems to me to be a pious and high-minded man."

"Well, of course he is!" Helen affirmed. "That's part of the reason why he's waited so long to propose to Charissa. He's been smitten with her for ages, but he couldn't even hint at his love while Lady Scrivener was alive. And after she died, he felt he had to show proper respect for his wife's memory. He's behaved faultlessly in every respect. So you see, Charissa is the ideal match for him. She's as pure as the first snowfall in winter, I can assure you. She deserves nothing but the kindest, most righteous, most God-fearing man in the kingdom! Everyone says so."

Such a sentiment was undoubtedly true, but Will resented it. "And does Miss Armitage reciprocate Sir Godfrey's regard?" he inquired, with convincing—though utterly fraudulent—indifference.

"Until recently, I would have said no. But I suspect her affections are beginning to move in that direction. She is already chatelaine of Silvercrosse Hall in all but name, and she wore the silver cross to church on Sunday for everyone to see. Besides, Sir Godfrey is a handsome, virile man. What woman would not find him romantic?"

When he heard Helen's answer, instead of losing hope, Will in fact felt better. He instantly dismissed as weak the evidence she had marshaled to support her contention that Charissa was falling for Sir Godfrey. To be sure, he agreed that Sir Godfrey had matrimonial intentions. However, Will's own, much more careful observation of Charissa's inclinations had convinced him she did not welcome her cousin's ardor, and he saw no compelling reason to change his mind.

He did not want Helen to guess his thoughts, however, so he shrugged politely. "You may be right—but it is none of my business."

Helen gave him a satisfied smile. "I suppose not. But if I were you, I would avoid making Sir Godfrey even more jealous."

Will smirked inwardly. Little did Helen guess that her advice was failing to produce its intended results—on the other hand, it was fanning the flames of Will's already burning competitive spirit. As far as he was concerned, the sanctimonious Sir Godfrey had no God-given right to Charissa's affections. He rather liked the idea of seeing the man taken down a peg or two.

But most of all, the anticipation of taking Charissa in his arms and feeling her sweet surrender to his embrace made every obstacle to that end seem insignificant indeed.

Will continued to think his own thoughts as Helen rattled on about the upcoming party. He would have liked to ask her about Charissa's past, but he knew such an inquiry would be unwelcome. He also didn't want her to suspect his intentions toward Charissa, especially when Helen herself seemed infatuated with him. The best thing to do, he decided, would be to end the interview.

"Miss St. Swythin," he said, "I am sorry to bring this delightful time to an end, but I must tell you that my leg is paining me, and I should go upstairs to rest. Will you forgive me?"

Helen's face fell, but she rallied quickly. "Of course, Mr. Lyon. I wouldn't dream of causing you any inconvenience. May I help you?" she asked eagerly as he began to rise to his feet.

He started to decline her request to assist him, but before he had even opened his mouth, she was next to him, her hands on his arm and waist. He put his weight onto his cane and took a swift step. "I'm fine, thank you," he insisted. "The footman will see you out."

She backed away, her cheeks tinged with scarlet. "Of course." She gave him a courtesy. "Until Thursday, Mr. Lyon."

He nodded his head. "Until then, Miss St. Swythin."

Charissa and Penelope always enjoyed the charity outings during which they visited Murrington's humbler families. Gradually they had developed a rapport with the women they called upon, and occasionally—without fanfare—Charissa had helped some of the families with unexpected expenses, such as the cost of a doctor's visit or the purchase of a new animal to replace one that had died. It pleased her to be able to assist them, for her parents had left her a substantial fortune, to which she now added her modest writing income. It seemed only right to use some of the money to bless others.

Between family visits, Charissa and Penelope made it a habit— weather permitting—to eat luncheon by a long, winding brook called the Ferne, which flowed through Murrington on its way to the River Trent. They always brought a basket with them for that purpose, and today was no exception. As they walked the short way out of the village, Penelope found the large, flat rock which served as their traditional picnic spot, and Charissa spread out a blanket for them to sit upon. They unpacked the basket in order to feast upon the spread Mrs. Harper had generously packed for them.

Penelope looked around at all the natural beauty. "It's a lovely day, with just the right number of clouds to help protect our faces from the sun. We don't even need our parasols."

"And the breeze is delightful. Here, Penny," Charissa said, passing a plate to her friend, "have some chicken."

Penelope took the dish and sampled some of its contents. "Delicious."

"I'm glad that young Jemima Roberts has recovered from the scarlet fever," remarked Charissa, thinking of the home they had just visited. "Her mother said that it wasn't a bad case, and none of the other children were stricken. What a mercy."

"Yes. They were fortunate. It is always so worrisome when little ones are ill."

"And Widow Greene was as fascinating as ever. She knows so much about the history of Murrington. I didn't realize that the Duke of Gloucester Inn was renamed in honor of King Richard III because he spent one night there before he went to London to usurp the throne. He stayed right here in little Murrington. Imagine that!"

"That's the story, anyway," Penelope acknowledged. "It may even be true." She glanced over at her friend, and her eyes fastened upon the necklace around Charissa's neck. "Mrs. Greene was also interested in the silver cross Sir Godfrey gave you."

"Yes," Charissa answered, fingering it briefly. "I wore it specifically because I knew she would want to see it, given its background."

Penelope hesitated. "It's a significant piece of jewelry. In more ways than one."

Charissa turned back toward the basket. "Have a slice of cake. It has strawberries in it."

"I'll have some, but don't change the subject just yet. There's something I want to ask you about the cross."

"There's nothing more to be said, surely," Charissa replied, busying herself with the cake. "It's a symbol of my home—a reminder of the romance of the house's ancient past."

"And, I daresay, a suggestion of its *future* romance."

Charissa had picked up a small knife and was holding it over the cake. "So what size piece would you like?"

"Charissa."

"What?"

"We both know what the gift of the cross means," Penelope said pointedly.

Charissa put down the knife. "Oh, Penny, must we discuss this?"

"I shan't force you to confide in me. But, dear, we've been friends a long time. You've cleverly managed to convince everyone else you are utterly unaware of Sir Godfrey's attachment to you, but I know better. You are neither naïve nor stupid."

A few seconds passed, in which the only sounds were the gurgle of the brook as it swirled around the rock and a pair of birds chirping in a tree close by. Then Charissa said softly, "Very well. You're right. I know perfectly well what Sir Godfrey is suggesting by giving me the cross. But you must believe me when I tell you that it never occurred to me for the longest time Sir Godfrey might care for me in that way. I still find it hard to believe. After all, for years he has encouraged me to forsake my romantic inclinations."

"And thus he has kept you from finding a husband," Penelope observed shrewdly, "until he is ready to ask you himself."

Charissa looked pained.

Penelope, however, briskly continued her interrogation. "So you have realized that he loves you. But how do you feel about him? Do you love him?"

"Of course I love him, but not in that way," Charissa responded quickly, shaking her head. "More like a brother or a dear friend. It's not that he's unattractive or wouldn't make someone a wonderful husband, but just not me."

"He *is* very attractive. And a good man."

"I know. And I love living at Silvercrosse. I would certainly prefer things to remain as they are, but I suppose if I did marry Sir Godfrey, I could be content. And that is a great deal to be thankful for, since many women—married or not—do not enjoy contentment in their circumstances."

After she spoke, Charissa felt a pang of guilt. Penelope, at four-and-thirty years of age without a husband, children, or the means to live alone comfortably, might well fall into that category.

But Penelope simply asked, "So will you wed Sir Godfrey?"

"Do you think I should?"

Penelope paused for a moment before she answered. "Only you can decide whether or not to marry. But it is important you seek the Lord's will and not simply make the determination on your own."

"I agree."

"Prayer is the first and most critical component of any good decision," Penelope continued. "Another important factor for a woman to consider when contemplating marriage is finances. Fortunately, Sir Godfrey is not a spendthrift, a gambler, or a fortune hunter, so you have no worries there."

"Yes, I recognize that, Penny."

"But there are other considerations, too. You must not only be aware of the sensibilities of the man involved, but you must also know your own mind. You have acknowledged Sir Godfrey wants to marry you. Yet I don't think you've admitted to yourself the yearnings of your own heart. In spite of what you've told everyone about the blessedness of spinsterhood, I have always believed you dream not just of marriage, but also of love."

Charissa regarded Penelope apprehensively, but said nothing.

"In spite of what Sir Godfrey believes, why else would you write your stories? The point I am trying to make, Charissa, is that I know you are head-over-heels in love—with *Mr. William Lyon*."

Charissa's eyes widened in surprise. "What? I merely find him interesting."

Penelope arched an eyebrow. "On the contrary, I saw the look you two exchanged at your birthday party. You each could have fallen into each other's eyes and joyfully drowned there."

"What muddle-headed rubbish!"

"You may argue the point, Charissa, but I can see it's not simply a question of liking or esteeming him—you are *in love* with him!"

"You are only partly correct, Penny. I confess I am *intrigued* with Mr. Lyon. What woman in this village is not? But I am not the starry-eyed fool you are implying. The hours I've spent with Mr. Lyon have been agreeable. However, that doesn't mean that I want to run off to London and marry him. For one thing, he lacks faith in God. I could never be one with a man whose heart does not follow after the Lord." But a pleading tone had crept into her voice, and she sighed in spite of herself.

"Nor could I," Penelope concurred. "But I feel that Mr. Lyon's case is not quite so cut-and-dried."

Charissa inhaled slowly. "What do you mean?"

"I made it a point to observe him in church, and he didn't appear to me to be the typical bored, cynical gentleman. He was attentive to Mr. Humphreys' message on the consolations of faith, which was, I thought, most appropriate for him to hear and reflect upon."

"You noticed his interest in the sermon? I did as well. Mr. Lyon did listen!"

"You need not try to convince me. He is plainly a man of intelligence and feeling."

Charissa leaned forward, unable to hide her rising enthusiasm. "He is indeed! I must tell you, Penny, that I believe Mr. Lyon is being drawn to the Truth. Am I daft? Mad as a hatter?"

"Not at all."

"And it is not only in a formal setting that he attends to religious things," Charissa explained. "He pays close attention when I read from the Bible in the evenings."

"Has he disclosed any of his thoughts concerning what he has heard?"

"He has asked me a few questions. But—most revealingly—once he even spoke to me about a painful memory from his childhood. I was able to help him see it in a new light, I think."

"That is encouraging. He clearly trusts you."

"Those are good signs, but on the other hand, I know next to nothing about him or his history." She frowned. "Sir Godfrey insists his interest in me is less than benign."

"What do *you* think?"

"Honestly?" Charissa forced herself to say the unpleasant truth out loud. "I expect a man like Mr. Lyon is experienced when it comes to women. If he wanted a wife, he'd have one by now. And although he has always been honorable in his dealings with me, I don't know what he wants from our relationship. Surely I shouldn't expect more from him than he is able to give."

"No, you are right to be careful. Whether or not he has marriage on his mind, who can say? But since you are attracted to him—*intrigued* by him—you should take care how you treat Sir Godfrey." Penelope's eyes flashed suddenly. "Your cousin deserves the utmost respect."

"Of course he deserves respect," Charissa repeated, puzzled by her friend's vehemence.

"You must be mindful of that when he proposes to you. You *can't* marry him just because you don't want to hurt him. You *can't* marry him if you're in love with someone else. You simply mustn't!"

Charissa was tempted to remind Penelope women married solely for security, comfort, and other practical matters all the time. However, even pushing the thorny issue of romantic sensibilities aside, the truth was she wasn't comfortable with the idea of wedding her cousin just because it was the path of least resistance. Penelope had a point.

However, it really was too soon to think of marriage. "You need not worry about Godfrey's feelings just yet, Penny," Charissa said comfortingly. "Your analysis is based solely upon an assumption: that he will ask me to be his wife. But he hasn't yet. Maybe he never will. Maybe he is just as happy with the way things are as I am. And in that case, I shall never have to refuse him!"

Penelope gave her a half-smile. "Perhaps that's true."

"And at any rate," Charissa said earnestly, "for now, it is incumbent upon us to do our best to guide Mr. Lyon to faith. Do you not agree?"

Penelope approved wholeheartedly. "Yes, indeed, I do."

"Although, I'm afraid, directing our attention toward Mr. Lyon will put us in direct competition with the indefatigable Helen."

Penelope shook her head in frustration. "I know it all too well. Once my sister thinks she knows God's mind, there's nothing I can say to make her regard anything differently. She perceives reality the way she wants it to be. She always has."

"It's a fascinating state of affairs," Charissa commented, picking up the knife again and eyeing the cake. "Murrington has never been so fraught with intrigue. And just think, Penny—poor, unsuspecting Mr. Lyon rode over a cliff in a thunderstorm and became the impetus for it all!"

Chapter 11

"Would you like another cup of tea, Mrs. Mainwood?" asked Penelope. "Or perhaps a bowl of sweet strawberries?"

"I do wish I had room for them, Miss St. Swythin, but I am satisfied for now." The older woman swished her fan contentedly as she and Penelope sat under one of several tall trees dotting the modest lawn beside Wisteria Cottage. "It's good to be back in Murrington. I've missed everyone."

Penelope inclined her head graciously. "We are all glad you're home. I trust your daughter and her new little one are well?"

"Oh, very well indeed. It was a joy to be of assistance to her, but I must confess I am getting too old for the hustle and bustle of a very full household. A small gathering—such as yours today—suits me better. And you have outdone yourself, my dear. Everything is delightful."

"Thank you—although I must credit Helen with the idea to host a garden party."

Mrs. Mainwood tut-tutted generously. "You mean she wouldn't leave you alone until you agreed to her wishes? Well, I think your patience with Helen is extraordinary. From what I hear, she's been attempting to monopolize the mysterious Mr. Lyon since the moment he arrived."

"You know as well as I do there is nothing I can do short of locking her in her room to stop her from doing exactly as she pleases."

"Ah well, as long as she doesn't make too much of a nuisance of herself, I suppose there's little harm in it. A seasoned gentleman like

Mr. Lyon is well able to take care of himself." She chuckled and looked across the lawn at Will, who was entertaining the other women at the party with witty repartee. "So far he is succeeding admirably."

Even as the words came out of her mouth, Mrs. Shaw, Mrs. Humphreys, Helen, Aunt Caroline, and Charissa—who surrounded Will—all laughed at once, confirming Mrs. Mainwood's observation.

Seated a few feet away from Penelope and Mrs. Mainwood, Sir Godfrey hadn't heard their assessment of Will's social skills. However, he sat back in his chair and grimaced as he watched Charissa enjoy Will's company. Too aggravated to concentrate on anything else, he tried to come up with something to interrupt them, and soon a marvelous idea—if he did say so himself—came into his head. He promptly rose to his feet.

"Someone once told me that, years ago, St. Swythin family gatherings were famous for their battledore and shuttlecock tournaments," he announced. "I should very much like to enjoy this beautiful day by challenging Dr. Shaw to a friendly match. Are you game, my friend?"

Everyone stopped chatting as they heard him make this proposition, and they all looked at Dr. Shaw expectantly.

"I am most willing to take you on, Sir Godfrey," Dr. Shaw replied good-naturedly. "And I'll make short work of you, I daresay." He turned to Penelope. "I trust you have the necessary accouterments?"

Penelope smiled. "I do indeed," she said. "My father loved to play. We still have his equipment. Shall I fetch it?"

"Indeed, Miss St. Swythin, please do," Sir Godfrey instructed her. "And bring what is needed for four players, since I intend to ask Miss Armitage to be my partner. With whom shall you pair up, Shaw?"

"Mrs. Shaw, of course," the physician answered.

Penelope stood up, went into the house, and returned in short order, her arms laden with a heap of battledores and several shuttlecocks. "As many as want to may play," she declared, depositing her load on one of the tables which had been set up on the lawn. "All at once. We can make a regular war of it! What do you all say to that?"

A chorus of agreement arose, and most of the guests willingly chose one of the battledores, which were small wooden frames crisscrossed with strips of animal gut. Only Aunt Caroline and Mrs. Humphreys wished to sit out the game. Charissa saw with dismay even Will had taken one of the battledores in hand.

"Mr. Lyon," she said quietly, coming to stand beside him, "Such exercise cannot be good for your injury. Please do sit this out. I should be distraught if you were to harm yourself."

"I cannot resist the chance to move," he told her firmly, leaning on his cane. "But rest assured—I'll not be careless. I'll stand still and only hit the shuttlecock if and when it comes close enough for me to swat at it easily. I'll be out of the game soon enough, but at least I shall have participated."

Because the game did not need a net, the ten players grouped themselves in a wide circle. Charissa stood to Will's right; predictably, Helen saw to it that she stood on his left.

"We'll begin with one shuttlecock," Sir Godfrey decided. "If we find that it's not challenging enough, we can add a second." He held up a piece of cork with a ring of red and yellow feathers fastened around its top. Then he threw it into the air and gracefully smashed it with his battledore.

It whizzed through the air toward Dr. Shaw, who took a step backward and swished his racket in a wide arc parallel with the ground. He hit the shuttlecock off-center and it flew wildly toward Penelope. She was ready for it, however, and when she hit it, it sailed smoothly back toward Sir Godfrey.

Sir Godfrey narrowed his eyes and gave it a mighty whack. Like a small, fluttering cannonball, it headed straight for Will's head.

But Will shifted his weight slightly, raised his left hand, and sent the shuttlecock deftly towards Mrs. Shaw. When it reached her, in spite of a valiant attempt on her part, it fell sadly to the ground. "Well played, Mr. Lyon!" she exclaimed in admiration. "Carry on, then." She set down her battledore and retired to watch the rest of the game.

After that, there were several long, complicated volleys but little by little the circle of players shrank. Soon Mrs. Mainwood, Penelope, Mr. Humphreys, and Will had joined Mrs. Shaw at the sidelines. Next Charissa missed a difficult shot that flew way over her head, leaving Sir Godfrey, Dr. Shaw, Colonel Mainwood, and Helen battling for the championship. The women all cheered for Helen, and the steely gleam in the younger St. Swythin sister's eyes reflected her desire to win.

But in the end, it was Sir Godfrey who vanquished all his foes. Everyone applauded graciously, and Penelope had a piece of cake specially brought out to him as a victory prize.

As Will grumpily watched Sir Godfrey enjoy his triumph, Helen came up beside him. "Sir Godfrey will likely organize another round of battledore and shuttlecock," she speculated. "But perhaps you would prefer to come into the parlor and take a look at a few of my paintings."

Will quickly decided to accompany Helen. He didn't mind viewing her artistic efforts, and, he reasoned, there was always the possibility she might tell him something interesting. It was better than being unable to rise to his usual level of athletic competence, which at another time and place would have allowed him to make short, satisfying work of Sir Godfrey's ostensible prowess.

"I promised I would do so, so let us go," he agreed. Helen's countenance shone, but her enthusiasm was promptly tempered. Mrs. Mainwood, standing within earshot, turned toward Helen and Will and said loudly, "My dear Helen, what a delightful idea. I shall come, too. You've been speaking of your latest works for a very long time, and now at last I'll be able to see them."

Mrs. Shaw chimed in, expressing an interest in Helen's pictures, and Penelope suggested Charissa join the group as well, earning a grateful glance from her friend and a glare from her sister. Thus Will went inside Wisteria Cottage with several admiring women at his side.

Such an occurrence had happened numerous times before over the course of Will's life, but—as so often the case in Murrington—today felt radically different from the past. In his former existence, he would have been bored with middle-aged matrons such as Mrs. Mainwood and Mrs. Shaw. Helen he would have forgotten the moment she was out of his sight, and Charissa… well, he didn't know what he would have thought about her. Would he have recognized her exceptional character underneath her external beauty? Valued her intelligence as much as her feminine figure?

Probably not.

However, today he admired Sarah Mainwood's cheerful

determination to enjoy the party. He appreciated Catherine Shaw's willingness to exert herself in a game of sport, and he even felt a bit sorry for strange, lonely Helen St. Swythin. But most of all he found himself grateful that Charissa Armitage liked being with him—she liked him for *himself.*

Once they were all inside the somewhat cramped parlor, Helen's guests saw several of her paintings hanging on the walls and two more placed on the room's only table. "I haven't seen these before," Charissa remarked as she examined a landscape above the unlit fireplace. "Did you put these up recently, Helen?"

"Yes." Helen touched Will on the sleeve and pulled him toward the far wall. "These are all mine. Every picture in this room. What do you think of them?"

Will took a deep breath and began the task of evaluating each of Helen's works. Fortunately, like Charissa's birthday book, they were well done for an amateur, and thus he could be honest with their creator. Most of them were botanical subjects, and Helen took pleasure in telling him which plant was which. "This hillside is covered in ling," she told him, pointing at a landscape rich in purple hues. "You probably call it heather. And these are wild pansies that grow among the limestone rocks. Their Latin name is *viola lutea.*"

The other women took their time admiring each of the paintings. After Charissa had done her duty, she sat down in a chair by the window and made it a point to observe Will as he carefully explained his thoughts to Helen. She knew from long experience how tedious it could be to feed Helen's need for appreciation, and she respected Will's ability to use his charm to make Helen happy, even when such a performance was undoubtedly irksome. He was neither condescending nor insincere, and as Charissa watched him, the glow in her heart grew just that much warmer.

Helen was now pointing out the last of the pictures. "I did this when I was in London in 1805," she stated. "It's one of the few cityscapes I've attempted, instead of painting the natural world. But I liked the challenge of capturing the feel of the fog as it swirled about, hiding and revealing things at will."

"I believe I know that street corner," Will said thoughtfully. It was a decent part of the city, yet close to several of the infamous gaming dens he had frequented over the course of the last decade.

"You recognize it?" asked Helen eagerly.

"Yes. In spite of the grayness of the fog, I can see just enough of the buildings to know the place," he confirmed, peering at the picture again. "And are those two faint figures in the mist?"

"Yes," she nodded happily. "A gentleman and a lady."

Behind the two of them, Mrs. Shaw and Mrs. Mainwood had followed Charissa's lead and taken a seat. "Mr. Lyon and Helen, why don't you both rest for a moment?" Mrs. Shaw requested. "The breeze in this room is delightful, and the shade even more so."

Will wasted no time seating himself next to Charissa. "This is a pleasant room," he commented noncommittally.

"It is now," Mrs. Mainwood remarked. "It used to be rather depressing in here. I do like your artwork on the walls, Helen. It cheers the place up."

Helen, who had reluctantly taken a chair on the opposite side of the room from Will, lifted her eyebrows as if hesitant to accept the compliment, but Charissa privately agreed with Mrs. Mainwood. The plain furnishings were well-cared for, yet inevitably worn in spots, so Helen's paintings—which had replaced some old, nondescript prints from the last century—made an obvious and welcome change in the decor.

"It's been a while since I've called on you and Penelope, or anyone in Murrington for that matter," Mrs. Mainwood went on, folding her hands on her lap. She looked at Will. "Quite a lot has happened since I've been gone."

"Mrs. Mainwood has been away from Murrington for several months," Charissa explained, "visiting her youngest daughter."

"Who just presented me with my seventeenth grandchild, a boy," Mrs. Mainwood said proudly. "They named him Samuel, after his grandfather and his uncle."

"Ah yes, that reminds me," said Mrs. Shaw, perking up, "how is your son Sam, the hero? Have you heard from him since I saw you last? Where is he now?"

Mrs. Mainwood beamed. "Oh, I'm not exactly sure where his

regiment is at this very moment, but he's somewhere in Europe fighting Old Boney, as he calls that French scoundrel."

This time Helen chimed in, bringing Will up to date on the conversation. "Colonel and Mrs. Mainwood's son Samuel is a captain in the army."

"The Twentieth Regiment of Light Dragoons," specified Mrs. Mainwood. "He has fought in South America, Egypt, and Portugal, among other places. And he received a commendation for his bravery at the Battle of Vimeiro from General Sir Arthur Wellesley himself."

Charissa and Penelope smiled as they listened to the familiar recitation of Captain Mainwood's accomplishments. But when Mrs. Mainwood, intending to describe her son's glorious achievement, asked Will if he were familiar with the battle, his response took them all by surprise. "Unfortunately, yes, I am. My half-brother was killed at Vimeiro," he told them flatly.

Charissa's smile faded at once. Here was another grief that had pierced Mr. Lyon's life, and she knew him well enough to know he must mourn his brother deeply. She decided at once to steer the conversation away from the intrusive questions that would inevitably follow his revelation, but Mrs. Shaw was already saying sympathetically, "You must miss him terribly, Mr. Lyon."

Mrs. Mainwood leaned forward in her chair. "Do you suppose he could have known Samuel?" she asked Will in a motherly tone. "What was your brother's name?"

The last thing Will wanted to do was discuss the late Honorable Lieutenant Edward Devreux. Not only did Edward's memory pain him severely, but revealing his brother's name would expose his own web of lies. Nevertheless, loath to act ungraciously, Will answered Mrs. Mainwood. "I doubt they knew one another. Edward was an officer in the infantry, not the cavalry."

"I see. But perhaps my husband knew of him. What was his rank? Who was his commanding officer?"

"Had he been in the army a long time?" put in Mrs. Shaw at the same time.

"No, not long," Will answered Mrs. Shaw, ignoring Mrs.

Mainwood's inquiries. In spite of his outward calm, a crease formed in his brow and a familiar ache filled his chest.

"You must have been so very attached to him," observed Helen feelingly, pressing her hands against her bosom. "How grievous it is to be separated from someone you love."

Charissa, however, was sure that Will did not want to discuss so personal a matter with these ladies. Taking advantage of a momentary lull, she stood up abruptly. "Mr. Lyon, I find that I am becoming thirsty. Would you be so kind as to escort me to the refreshment table under the trees?"

The others looked disappointed, but Will rose at once. "Certainly, Miss Armitage." He extended his arm to her, and she took it. Somehow, even through the sleeves of his shirt and coat, the pressure of her touch gave him the unfamiliar sense of not being alone.

Charissa allowed him to guide her outside onto the lawn, where yet another round of battledore and shuttlecock was underway. Neither of them spoke as he led her to the table where punch had been set out for the guests. He poured her a glass and handed it to her.

"Thank you," she said warmly.

"Thank *you*," he replied. Somehow, he thought with amazement, she had recognized his internal distress when Edward was mentioned. His gaze lingered on her sympathetic eyes and sweet lips, and he knew he needed a distraction—from both Edward's memory and Charissa's nearness. Out of the corner of his eye, he caught sight of Dr. Shaw missing the shuttlecock in spectacular fashion. "And now I would like to take the opportunity to speak with Dr. Shaw, if you will excuse me," he proposed, hoping she wouldn't protest his apparent rejection.

To his relief, she replied with a comforting smile, "Of course, Mr. Lyon." He bowed courteously and left her.

As Charissa watched him join the physician and begin an innocuous conversation, she felt disappointed that he had dismissed himself from her company, but she also understood his need for masculine companionship. More importantly, however, she knew now he had lost his brother in tragic circumstances—which meant she had one more thing to add to her ever-growing list of prayers for him. Reluctantly, but with determined resignation, she turned her back to him and gave in to

Sir Godfrey's encouragement to rejoin the battledore and shuttlecock game.

In the meantime, Will's inner struggles eased as he chatted with Dr. Shaw. The physician noticed no change in his demeanor one way or the other, as was frequently the case—Will's capacity to mask his feelings was one of the things that gave him an edge in manly pursuits, card games in particular. That, and his uncanny ability to remember and sort in his head every card he ever saw in any particular game, even when he was in his cups. He was known for winning—which had not exactly endeared him to a large crowd of resentful losers—but he also knew when to walk away from the table and cut his losses. At any rate, his aptitude for discretion continued to serve him well in Murrington, albeit for a different purpose entirely.

After a while, Mrs. Shaw summoned her husband away from Will, who gazed around the garden, concerned Helen might swoop in again in an attempt to corner him. But she was likely detained by someone else inside the house, because it was the other hostess who came to speak with him. Penelope St. Swythin, he noted as she took a seat beside him, had dressed carefully today in cool colors that suited her. He decided that upon further acquaintance she was really quite handsome.

"I hope you have been able to find a way to enjoy yourself this afternoon, Mr. Lyon," she said. "I know it must be difficult for someone as energetic as you are to sit and watch others participate in amusements."

"I would as soon be giving the shuttlecock a good drubbing as sitting on this chair," he confessed. "But, nonetheless, I am content."

Penelope saw his eyes linger on Charissa as she jumped into the air and swung her battledore. "Although you have been with us for only a few weeks, it seems as though you are already one of us," Penelope told him. "I hope you are planning to stay for a while yet."

"To tell you the truth, Murrington is such a nice place, I haven't thought much about going home," Will said. "But my leg is healing rapidly—and I know I'm wearing out my welcome with Sir Godfrey."

"Mm, I suppose you may be," Penelope replied astutely. "But Charissa will be sad to see you go."

"She has been kindness itself to me."

Penelope opened her fan and swished it softly. "I can see you two have become friends."

"Yes. We have."

After a brief pause, Penelope said, "You have been as much a blessing to her as she has been to you, you know."

"In what way?"

"Just recently, I've seen a side of Charissa that—in all the years I've known her—she's never shown me before. Oh, she's always been kind and full of good conversation, but since you arrived at Silvercrosse Hall there's been something new in her eyes, something different in the tone of her voice. You should know that when she first came to Murrington, she was reclusive and sad. I'm happy to say she did move beyond that particular grief, but until you came…." Penelope closed the fan. "Perhaps I'm saying too much. Forgive me."

At last, thought Will, here was a chance to learn more about Charissa's past. "What happened to Miss Armitage in London six years ago, Miss St. Swythin?" he asked bluntly.

Penelope gazed at him for a moment. "I cannot break a confidence, of course, but it is really no secret that her marriage engagement dissolved in a most humiliating fashion. The man involved deceived her with regard to his character, and when she discovered him in a compromising situation, she was heartbroken."

Will smiled grimly. Too many marriages contracted by the *beau monde* were not outstanding examples of either love or marital faithfulness. "At least they had not yet said their vows—although such a discovery will not necessarily prevent a wedding."

Penelope began to fan herself again. "You and I know that to be true, but Charissa insisted on holding out for something better. She had thought she found a good man in Sir… I mean, in her fiancé, but she was wrong. She quite properly rejected him."

"What was the fellow's name, did you say?" Will asked casually. It would be fun to track down the blackguard, challenge him to a boxing match, and knock him out cold for Charissa's sake.

Penelope shook her head. "I most certainly cannot tell you." She glanced over at the house and saw Helen coming out with Mrs. Humphreys. "Ah, here comes my sister. And I see the battledore and shuttlecock players have had enough of their game. It is time to move on to other diversions. Perhaps I can coax Helen and Charissa into serenading us with a few songs appropriate for springtime. Will you excuse me, Mr. Lyon?" She smiled at him. "I have enjoyed our little tête-à-tête."

Will pushed himself up on his cane as Penelope rose. "And I, too, Miss St. Swythin."

For the rest of the afternoon at Wisteria Cottage, Will sat quietly as several of the guests took turns entertaining the group. Charissa sang two lovely solos and one rather long duet with Helen. After the ladies were finished, Sir Godfrey read out of *The Pilgrim's Progress*, and although Will expected—and, in fact, wanted—to dislike it, he discovered he was actually interested in the tale.

Before the party came to a close, other guests who wished to do so performed one by one: Penelope read poetry, Dr. Shaw tried out an original song while accompanying himself on the mandolin, and Colonel Mainwood told an amusing story. And as Will watched them all display their talents—or lack thereof—while at the same time demonstrating their good humor and total absence of artifice, a thought occurred to him.

Certainly, he admitted to himself, none of the people gathered here reached the heights of perfection, and some of them were not remarkable by any worldly standard. And yet they all seemed to have something he did not. Or perhaps it was more accurate to say something was present in their midst with which he was not familiar. It was not a tangible thing, but it was authentic nonetheless.

And it was… good.

He had always been so afraid to hope that the beautiful things he longed for truly existed, but maybe—just maybe—his brother Edward had been right after all. Maybe there *was* more to life than finding ways to kill the pain—something more than fast horses, beautiful women, and success at games of chance.

Much, much more.

Chapter 12

The moon shone like a round, faceted jewel in the night sky, and a gusty wind forced scurrying clouds to dance in and around its light. Charissa, too, was bathed in its glow as she sat at her window, unable to sleep. She was contemplating that afternoon's garden party at Wisteria Cottage.

Today she had been given one more glimpse into Mr. Lyon's heart. Although she recognized there were still many things she did not know about him, he had revealed once more he was no stranger to grief, that he mourned not only a father and mother, but also a brother.

Surely, she thought, this information had been given to her so she could pray for him. But even after she had done so, her mind still could not rest. She rehearsed over and over again every word they had spoken to each other and every look they had exchanged. She knew the attraction between them was increasing, and her heart pounded as she pictured how he had appeared when he had looked at her so intently and thanked her. Had it been desire she had seen in his eyes?

Oh, how she had wanted him to kiss her!

But he had not. He had made his excuses and walked away.

She expelled a breath, impatient with her own folly. Of course he hadn't kissed her right out in public for everyone to see. Perhaps he didn't even think of her in that way at all. He might very well consider her only a friend.

And just what would a kiss from him mean? Usually—from a good man, anyway—a kiss signaled a far more serious intention.

She leaned her head against the partly open window pane, wondering who the women in his previous life had been. Had he ever considered marriage to some well-born society girl? Or were his loves more of the light-skirt kind? She hated to think the latter might be true, but it was all too possible. And yet it was hard to imagine Mr. Lyon satisfied with just a *bit of muslin*, as such women were sometimes euphemistically called.

Therefore, it was tempting to think that, even if in the past his tastes had run to opera dancers or actresses, he was presently hoping for something more. Would he ever see her—Miss Charissa Armitage—as something more?

There was no doubt she wanted it to be so. Did that really mean, as Penelope had declared, that she had fallen head-over-heels in love with him?

Outside, the wind had softened to a light, warm breeze, and Charissa discovered her mind was finally beginning to quiet as well; her thoughts were becoming pleasantly jumbled. Her eyelids suddenly heavy, she was dimly aware there was nothing to do but creep back into bed. Having found her way in between the crisp linen sheets, she lay her head on the pillow and tucked her knees up to her chest. Within a matter of seconds, she was fast asleep.

"Before you disappear into your world of fiction, my dear," Sir Godfrey said affably after breakfast the following day, "why don't you take a turn about the garden with me?" To his satisfaction, Will had gone out by himself and Aunt Caroline was napping in the sitting room.

Charissa nodded. "That would probably be a good thing. I need some time to ponder what will happen next in my novel. The hero is in a bit of trouble, and I haven't figured out exactly how to extricate him."

Sir Godfrey took her arm. "Fighting a dragon, is he?"

"No, he's imprisoned in an *oubliette*." An oubliette was a particularly horrible dungeon cell, used in medieval times, where hapless prisoners were left to die.

"It sounds most unpleasant. I hope the heroine has not forgotten him."

"Oh no. The Lord has promised her in a dream she and her sweetheart will conquer their enemies, and he will claim her with a kiss," she explained.

"I like the sound of that."

Charissa said nothing as they stepped out of the house into the sunshine.

"I'm sure I'll approve of how you resolve the plot," he reassured her, mistaking the reason for her silence.

"Oh yes, I'm sure you will." But Charissa didn't want to pursue this particular topic with her cousin. "I'll let you read the whole story as soon as I've finished it," she hedged.

"I shall look forward to it."

"I enjoyed playing battledore and shuttlecock at the party yesterday," she said, changing the subject. "I did very well, too, if I do say so myself."

"I was proud of you." They turned onto a gravel path flanked by several blossoming apple trees, whose white and pink petals scented the air deliciously. "Oh, by the way, Mrs. Shaw and Mrs. Mainwood were plotting yesterday whilst you were busy with the game. Before we left Wisteria Cottage, Mrs. Shaw took me aside and confided their scheme to me."

"Their scheme?"

"It is of a convivial nature, I assure you, and I'll let you in on the secret. The two of them are going to organize a dance in the assembly room above the Duke of Gloucester Inn. Imagine that! It's been too long since we've enjoyed such a thing in humble Murrington."

"We shall be almost as grand as London!" she exclaimed in delight.

"Well, not quite. But it will be a triumph, no doubt. The ladies are planning on inviting everyone they can think of for miles around. Our invitation will arrive soon."

"What is the date for the assembly? Do I have time to order a new gown?"

"Another new gown? My dear, you are becoming quite vain," he teased.

"Oh Godfrey, you don't really think that?"

"Of course not! You'll be the most beautiful woman in the place—I shall be proud to escort you. And to answer your other question, the assembly will take place two weeks from Friday."

Naturally, Sir Godfrey wanted to be by her side as her escort. Without realizing it, Charissa sighed. The truth was she had pictured herself leading out the first dance with Mr. Lyon. But in two weeks he still might not be able to dance—or, conversely, by then he might not even be in Murrington at all. The very thought crushed her.

Sir Godfrey stopped walking and turned to face her. He saw her downcast eyes and knew at once what she was thinking: she was dreaming of Mr. Lyon! A wave of anger pulsed through him—this madness had gone far enough. Charissa was his and no one else's! If she were going to dream of anyone, for mercy's sake, it ought to be none other than himself.

So when she looked up at him, he took definitive action. Taking her face in his hands, he shocked her to the core by placing his lips on hers and kissing her.

Her face flooded with color, and she stepped back with a gasp.

Sir Godfrey's eyes widened. What had he done? "Charissa… Forgive me. I…" The normally unflappable man stumbled over his words; it was a gut-wrenchingly awkward moment.

Just then Charissa noticed a flash of color out of the corner of her eye, and when she looked in that direction, she saw two figures standing on the gravel path. With a rush of relief, she recognized the St. Swythin sisters. Had they seen what had just happened? Judging by the looks on their faces, they had.

Penelope moved forward swiftly. "Good afternoon, Charissa, Sir Godfrey. The footman told us you were out back, and I can well understand why. How lovely this part of your garden is! It is like a corner of heaven itself." She reached up and touched one of the soft, fragrant apple blossoms.

Frowning, Helen followed her sister toward Sir Godfrey and Charissa. "Penelope, we should come back at another time. We still have to call on Mrs. Mainwood, as well as Mrs. Humphreys."

"We have plenty of time for all three visits," Penelope replied breezily. She took Charissa's arm and firmly guided her along the path. Helen and Sir Godfrey came along behind them, although neither of them looked as though they wanted to.

"The party at Wisteria Cottage yesterday was a great success," Penelope declared. "Do you not agree, Charissa?"

Charissa managed to find her voice. "Everything was delightful."

"You are too kind. But at least allow me to thank you for the loan of the punch bowl. I have returned it to your butler."

"You're quite welcome."

From behind, Helen interrupted them. "And where is Mr. Lyon today? I am surprised he would be indoors—unless he's under the weather." Her brow furrowed. "I do hope he is well."

"Indeed, he is quite well!" Sir Godfrey snapped before Charissa could reply. "Well enough to pack up all his belongings and go back to where he belongs!"

"He has returned to London?" Helen exclaimed, dismayed.

"No," Charissa replied. "He's still at Silvercrosse. Today he is merely enjoying some time alone outside."

Sir Godfrey snorted. "Nevertheless, that presumptuous cad has sponged off me long enough. He has taken advantage of my hospitality, and I am determined he will be gone by this week's end."

The three women turned to Sir Godfrey all at the same time. "Why, Sir Godfrey," Penelope said, raising her eyebrows, "surely you misread the situation. I cannot imagine he is strong enough to make such a long and exhausting journey."

"He'll need to stay a week or two more at least," admonished Helen.

"And anyone can see his leg still pains him," Penelope pointed out.

Sir Godfrey sniffed. "He takes long enough walks."

"He doesn't walk far," Charissa disagreed. "He takes a book or a sketchpad with him and sits for most of the time."

"And he still needs a cane for support," argued Helen. "It's not simply for show."

Sir Godfrey looked resentfully at the women so boldly contradicting him. *"Everything* that man does is for show! You ladies have somehow been bewitched by his charms, but that scoundrel is up to no good. Everything about him is a sham. He is a charlatan imposing himself upon us."

"He is not!" Charissa shot back. "You yourself said the Lord is giving him a second chance."

"Reprobates like Mr. Lyon never change—they are what they are," Sir Godfrey snarled. "He is after you for his own good pleasure, nothing more. When he's gotten what he wants, he'll leave Silvercrosse never to be seen or heard from again. Unless he marries you for your fortune, of course."

"Mr. Lyon has plenty of money, so he doesn't need mine. And the accident that brought him here was not part of some plot, as you seem to think. It was providence!"

"Charissa's right, Sir Godfrey!" Helen maintained, her supercilious tone setting Sir Godfrey's teeth on edge. "I saw Mr. Lyon in my dream. I've already told you. I even wrote about it in my journal."

Sir Godfrey's eyes flashed. "Keep out of this!" he ordered her angrily.

Realizing that the strained conversation was rapidly heating into an argument, Penelope stepped in, putting her arm around Charissa's waist. "Charissa, dear, enough of this unpleasantness. Why don't you come with Helen and me now to call on Mrs. Mainwood? She's promised to read us the latest letter from her son in Portugal. It should be most interesting."

"That sounds nice," Charissa responded, taking advantage of the deliverance Penelope and Helen were offering. "I shall come."

The three women turned to go, but before they had taken more than a few steps, Sir Godfrey spoke abruptly. "Miss St. Swythin—Miss Penelope St. Swythin—would you stay behind for a minute or two? I wish to speak with you."

Penelope face lighted with surprise, and she caught a quick breath. "Me?"

"Yes," Sir Godfrey affirmed. "I won't keep you long."

Penelope turned to Helen and Charissa. "I'll be along shortly. If you walk slowly, I'll catch up with you soon, I'm sure."

After Charissa and Helen had left the garden, Sir Godfrey's face fell. "I apologize for what you just witnessed, Miss St. Swythin."

Penelope wasn't sure whether he meant the fact that he'd lost his temper or that he'd kissed Charissa. Or both. "I'm sorry we disturbed you, Sir Godfrey."

There was a short silence, then he said, "You are a woman, Miss St. Swythin."

"Yes, as a matter of fact, I am."

"I have known you for a number of years now."

"You have."

"We are friends."

"Yes."

"Then perhaps you can help me unravel the mystery of a woman's heart, for I am certainly at a loss."

"Ah." She looked away. "You're not the only man to feel this way, you know. Men and women often do not understand one another."

"But men are logical. Women make no sense."

"And yet maybe it is men who cannot see past the end of their noses."

Sir Godfrey stared at her and waved his hand in the air. "You see what I mean? I don't know what you're talking about."

"No, I suppose you don't." She turned to him and smiled. "But I can be very sensible. Come, take a turn about the garden with me, and tell me what's troubling you. I shall endeavor to speak plainly—without feminine befuddlement."

"Very well." He fell into step beside her. "Surely you know—it must be obvious. I wish to make Charissa my wife, to honor her with the title of Lady Scrivener."

"It's not exactly a secret."

"But she resists me. *Why*, Miss St. Swythin?" He grunted in frustration. "She is a good woman; I am a godly man. She adores Silvercrosse Hall. Where else would she live? Am I so repulsive she will not respond to my kiss?"

Penelope did not answer for a moment. "I'm sorry," Sir Godfrey said heavily. "I have said too much. Forgive me."

"No," Penelope countered swiftly. "No, I am honored you would confide in me. After all, as you have said, we're friends, are we not?"

"We are."

"Sir Godfrey, no one can say why a man or a woman falls—or does not fall—in love. You are certainly... not repulsive. But I think the simplest answer to your conundrum is the correct one: Charissa does not welcome your attentions because her heart has been stirred by another man."

"It is ridiculous!" Sir Godfrey growled. "She was so hurt years ago by Sir Richard and his loathsome circle of acquaintances she vowed never to marry. I have been deliberately careful in order not to alienate her. I've waited for so long to reveal my intentions—and just when I plan to tell her of my affection for her, in comes this lying, flattering toad…"

"I hate to say it, but I must be honest. There is nothing you can do about the way Charissa and Mr. Lyon feel about each other. Even though you are furious about it, my advice is not to press your suit, so you don't push her even farther away."

"But you must have seen. I forgot myself with her just now, and it did not go well. Have I ruined my chances with her? What a fool I am!"

He looked so forlorn that, daringly, Penelope reached out and took his arm in hers. "Don't be so hard on yourself, Sir Godfrey. Take heart. I'm sure God has a plan. *But seek first the kingdom of God and his righteousness, and all these things will be provided for you.*"

He did not draw his arm back; on the contrary, he allowed her words to sink in. "A wholesome sentiment."

"God's ways are never our ways, nor are His thoughts the same as our own. But I daresay all is not lost."

Sir Godfrey found her words heartening, and he cheered up considerably. It had truly helped, he acknowledged, to ask a woman about these perplexing matters of the heart. "You have been a great help to me, Miss St. Swythin. Or, rather, may I address you as Penelope?"

Unconsciously, she tightened her grip on his arm. "You may, Sir Godfrey. After all, we have been friends for a long time."

"Yes, that is true. Penelope, thank you for your wise advice. I was sorely in need of it. Tell me, would you care to take tea with me and Aunt Caroline before you leave?"

Her cheeks as rosy as a young girl's, Penelope conveniently forgot she was expected at Mrs. Mainwood's house. "Why, thank you, Sir Godfrey, I would love to stay."

"Mrs. Harper has made some lemon biscuits you must try," he told her as he led her back to the house. "They are delicious."

Chapter 13

On Mr. Rowley's next visit, he finally removed the splint from Will's leg. Will asked if he could also get rid of the cane, but the surgeon discouraged him from doing so just yet. "I know the pain has subsided," the army veteran told him, "but you would still do well not to put too much weight on the limb until six weeks have gone by."

"Do you advise me not to ride to my home in the south?" Will asked. "Personally, I would prefer to remain at Silvercrosse Hall a little while longer, but I'm afraid I'm wearing out my welcome." As far as Sir Godfrey was concerned, that was rather an understatement.

"My professional opinion is you should forego the rigors of long-distance travel for another couple of weeks. Even a particularly long carriage ride could cause pain. If you like, I'll speak to Sir Godfrey," Mr. Rowley volunteered.

"That would be very helpful," Will said with satisfaction. Now, in spite of Sir Godfrey's rumblings, he wouldn't even have to think about leaving Charissa just yet.

But although he was making a concerted effort to enjoy each moment at Silvercrosse Hall and not worry about his future, over the next few days Will's spirits began to sag. By now, he had finished his drawings of the dogs as well as three sketches of Silvercrosse Hall itself. It was becoming harder to find things to do to occupy his time in the Menagerie Room.

Plus, he was growing ever more distracted by Charissa's presence. He found himself memorizing the shape of her nose, the exact color of her eyes, and the way she chewed on the top of her pen when she was frustrated with what she had written. He liked to hear her opinions about things, so he asked her questions even while she worked. She didn't seem to mind the interruptions, however, judging by the way she sparkled when he spoke to her.

The thought of a day without her was troublesome indeed.

But the most distressing development in his life was the resurgence of the nightmare. He had not had it for almost a year, but now it returned in full force. In it he saw Edward again—young and handsome in his scarlet uniform, quiet but cheerful, full of hope. The two of them were standing together on a vast plain, but—without warning—the sounds of war encircled them, and Will heard bombs and cannon fire and, worst of all, the screams of the dying. As always in the dream, Edward tried to speak to him, but Will could never hear him over the pandemonium of the battle raging around them. Then, before his eyes, his brother was hit with shrapnel and killed, as Will's cries of anguish mingled with those around him.

He began to suffer this agonizing dream every night, and each time he woke up in a sweat, moaning.

His normally easy manner deteriorated over the course of the following days. Charissa noticed it, but he brushed off her concern, claiming tiredness as an excuse for his lackluster disposition. In church on Sunday the sermon was drawn from Psalm One, and the verse Mr. Humphreys expounded on at length was: *For the* LORD *watches over the way of the righteous, but the way of the wicked leads to ruin.* The message deepened Will's misery, for he knew full well to which of those categories he belonged.

Mrs. Shaw tried to lift his spirits by inviting him to dinner at Edgemoor; however, he politely declined her offer. Helen St. Swythin came by three times in as many days under various pretexts in order to see him, but he successfully avoided her unwelcome ministrations.

One day, although it was mild and pleasant outside, the gloom inside Will's heart prevented him from appreciating the fine weather. Nevertheless, the best place to be alone was outdoors, so after breakfast he headed through the back door, past the garden gate, and into the woods that stretched out beyond the garden wall. Looking at him from a window, Charissa sighed, her own heart heavy. She caught a glimpse of Commodore trotting down the path behind him, and she was touched by the sight of the loyal canine. She watched Will ruffle the dog's fur, allowing the animal to accompany him.

Hoping that she—like Commodore—might be able to win Will's trust and cheer him up, she impulsively grabbed a hat, ran down the stairs, and left the house to find him. After she went through the gate, she followed the gravel path as it wound into a copse of oak trees. She knew that just beyond the trees flowed a section of the Ferne, next to which someone in the previous century had built a gazebo. Thinking Will might have headed for that lonely spot, she hoped to find him there.

She was right. When she emerged from the shelter of the oaks and followed the path around a sharp bend, she saw him inside the gazebo, sitting hunched over on a bench and holding Commodore close to his chest. Pleased to have found him, she took a few steps closer, only to come to a sudden halt. His face was twisted in grief, and when he glanced up at her, she colored with embarrassment.

She had trespassed on his privacy, she rebuked herself inwardly. She should never have come.

She whirled around, prepared to run back to the house as fast as she could, but his voice stopped her. "Miss Armitage."

"Mr. Lyon." She turned back around slowly. "Are you ill? Is it your leg? Should I get help?"

Will released Commodore, and the dog ran over to Charissa, greeting her with a wag of his tail. Then he trotted straight back to Will, who scratched the animal's ears. "I'm fine, thank you," Will lied.

With a surge of boldness, Charissa walked up to the gazebo's entrance. "No," she stated, "you are not fine."

Will opened his mouth to deny it, but abruptly changed his mind. He shrugged. "You're more right than you know."

Charissa entered the gazebo and sat down on the bench across from him. "If you want to, you can tell me what's wrong. It might make you feel better."

Will regarded her skeptically. "I doubt such a confession would make either of us feel better." He took a breath. "I am a wicked man, Miss Armitage."

"And who is not wicked, Mr. Lyon? This is a fallen world, and we are all fallen people."

"Oh yes," he said sardonically. "You are so *very* wicked. Depravity personified."

She was not put off. "How dare you assume that you know me! Sin comes in many shapes and sizes, not all of it obvious. But all of it offends God."

His sarcasm deepened. "Well, that's nice to know."

"And yet all of that iniquity is forgivable," she explained, her tone softening. "Every wicked deed, each evil thought—from the greatest sin to the least. In fact, they are already forgiven because of what Christ has done on the cross."

Caught off guard by what was to him a rather shocking statement, he said nothing.

"So tell me what it is you have done that gives you such great pain," she suggested, wondering if she'd pushed him too far and praying silently for wisdom. She half-expected him to order her to leave, but instead he pulled Commodore back up into his lap and held onto the uncomplaining canine.

"The worst of my sins," he said raggedly, "is what I did to my brother."

"Edward?" she said softy.

He nodded. "Edward."

"Tell me."

"He was my half-brother. My father married again not long after my mother died, and Edward was born a few years later. He was completely different from me—soft-spoken, happy-go-lucky. I couldn't stand him."

"I don't think it's unusual for brothers not to get along well."

"He always wanted to be like me when we were young. He adored me—I can't imagine why. He followed me around, copied what I did, that sort of thing. He was a nuisance, to be sure, until I chose a lifestyle he didn't approve of, after which he no longer kept company with me. But I was glad about it at the time, because I had despised him from the beginning."

"Did he have a good relationship with your father? Were you jealous of him?"

In the past Will would have scoffed at her question, but now he took a moment to consider it. "I'm not sure. His relationship with our father was the same as mine for the most part—not close. My father was an honorable man, devout, very loyal, but he didn't know how to show either of us that he loved us. And my stepmother treated us both fairly, so I can't accuse either of my parents of showing favoritism. But now you mention it, I did feel like the odd man out. I don't know why."

"Well, you believed you were responsible for your mother's death. Perhaps that misconception caused you to remain aloof from your family."

"It's possible." He smiled ruefully. "I admit I never liked either my brother or my sister."

"You had a sister, too? Has she passed away as well?"

"No, she's very much alive. But I don't see her at all. She's my half-sister."

"I see. So tell me what happened with your brother."

"It's a simple story, really. He had planned on a career in the church. He was like you, Charissa."

Will didn't even realize that he had called her by her Christian name, but she delighted in the sound of it on his lips. "Do you mean that your brother loved God?" she asked, heartened he had known someone whose faith was genuine.

"Yes. I wouldn't have put it that way back then—I would have just called him religious. But yes. That's exactly it. He loved God. You would have liked him, I'm certain. But one day we had an argument. A blazing row over things I can't even remember. It was as if everything I'd ever resented about him, all the grudges I'd held on to all those years came out all at once, like a raging, merciless fire that burned him all over. I mocked him. I scoffed at him. I belittled his manhood. I called him a coward."

"It must have been dreadful," she whispered, "for you both."

"Soon after, he enlisted in the army. I guess that's a way to prove your manhood, isn't it? But he was savagely killed in battle not long after arriving in Portugal." Will stood to his feet, forcing Commodore to jump down on the ground. "I... I..." But Charissa never knew what he was going to say, because it was lost in a strangled sob.

He moved away and, turning his back on her, grabbed the side of the gazebo. Racked with anguish, he began to weep—not with dainty tears the way a woman would cry, but with agonized groans.

Charissa couldn't bear it. Before she had even considered what she was doing, she leapt to her feet. Throwing her arms about him, she pressed herself against his back and held onto him with all her might.

When he felt her touch, Will, too, acted instinctively. He whirled around again and pulled her straight into his arms, holding her tightly against his chest as he wept. Nuzzling her hair with his face, he let himself go, allowing the reservoir of tears he had never shed to escape their captivity once and for all.

His outburst of grief lasted for several long minutes, but when his shuddering finally stopped and his breathing became more regular, he did not release Charissa; he continued to hold her the way a drowning man clutches a lifeline. He had never before exposed the nakedness of his soul to anyone, not even to himself. But now, for the first time— although thoughts of Edward continued to linger in his mind—the inner voices that had obscenely accused him for so long began to fade into the background. He felt his tension drain away as Charissa pressed against him, soft and warm.

He wanted to continue to hold her close, but reluctantly he loosened his embrace. She moved her head off his chest and raise her eyes to his. "William," she said gently.

He smiled—she had used his actual name! Suddenly he discovered that he resented Mr. Lyon, the impostor. "Call me Will," he told her.

"Will," she repeated lovingly.

This was the moment—at last! He bent his head down, fully intending to give in to his desire for that long-awaited kiss, when they both heard a shrill voice.

"Mr. Lyon, Charissa!"

The two of them stepped apart instantly, their communion broken. Up came Helen St. Swythin at a run, puffing as if she'd run all the way from Wisteria Cottage.

"Helen, what's going on? Is something the matter?" Charissa asked, trying to sound as matter-of-fact as possible. Helen had to have seen her in Will's arms, and Charissa knew her friend certainly wouldn't be pleased.

"Everything is perfectly fine," Helen replied crossly. "Why wouldn't it be? In fact, I was coming to Silvercrosse to tell you I've ordered a new gown for the assembly at the Duke of Gloucester."

She scowled at Charissa, but taking a deep breath, she addressed Will, suddenly all sweetness. "You are attending the assembly, Mr. Lyon, are you not? I've been dying to ask you about it. You are staying in Murrington long enough, I hope. Do you think you'll be able to dance? You're moving about so well now." She smiled up at him.

Will answered her politely. "I intend to be there, Miss St. Swythin. And you have reminded me I must order a set of evening clothes from Mr. Pearce."

Helen smirked. "You'll have to give them away to the poor when you return to London. They won't exactly measure up to your regular standards, will they?"

"True enough," responded Will, "but then again I have never been a particularly zealous devotee of the dandies. And now—having been the fortunate recipient of the gracious hospitality found in Murrington—I find I care even less about such things."

"Your valet will have something to say about that," Helen laughed.

Will raised an eyebrow. "Undoubtedly."

"I'm so glad you're to have a new gown, Helen. Do tell me all about it," Charissa requested, taking the other woman's arm and escorting her firmly down the path back toward the garden. Will followed a step or two behind them, Commodore at his side.

"Oh, it's simple, but very elegant," stated Helen, excited to talk about it now. "Since I'll be dancing as much as possible, it won't have a train, but it will be decorated with some exquisite lace Penelope found that belonged to our grandmother. Three rows of it at the bottom. The gown itself will be pale yellow satin, and it will have *puffed* sleeves," she finished triumphantly.

"It sounds splendid," Charissa agreed, glad the St. Swythins had somehow found the resources to splurge on Helen's new apparel. "My gown will be pearlescent rose-colored silk trimmed with silver cord."

"Ah, silver," Helen repeated knowingly. "The perfect complement for your silver cross necklace! Sir Godfrey will be so proud to stand at your side. He's such a wonderful dancer—you will make a brilliant couple."

"Penny told me that she has new dancing slippers," Charissa went on hastily. "Green, to match her gown. And her eyes."

As the ladies chatted about their preparations for the assembly, Will paid no attention to their discussion of lace, feathers, and gloves. He was still contemplating the scene at the gazebo.

What had really happened there, and what did it mean? His torrent of emotion had been unprecedented, while his fascination with Charissa had taken a deep and unanticipated turn.

But what struck him most forcefully as he strolled toward the house was the serenity he felt, perhaps more accurately described as the absence of his habitual self-incrimination. Had he merely experienced a catharsis as a result of his outburst?

Or was there more to it?

It seemed as though Charissa had been trying to tell him God could forgive him for his despicable cruelty to Edward. But what did he owe God in return for this absolution? It couldn't be free, the way Charissa made it sound. Could it? No, that just didn't make sense to Will. And yet the faint hope of mercy made his heart feel lighter all the same.

Speaking of his heart... he watched Charissa walk gracefully in front of him, her form pleasing in every respect. He had to admit that their embrace had been nothing like he'd ever experienced before. He'd always wanted to take her into his arms, of course, but the reality of it vastly exceeded his expectations. Or, more accurately, holding her close in a moment of vulnerability had radically altered his understanding of what it might mean to love a woman.

Love.

It was the first time he had allowed that particular word to enter his vocabulary when he thought of Charissa. But it was undeniable his interest in her had grown far beyond an agreeable game. It was turning into something else altogether.

Chapter 14

The three of them entered the house, and Charissa attempted to escort Helen to the front door, hoping she would take the hint and go home. But Helen asked instead where Sir Godfrey was. "Would you take me to him, Charissa?" she demanded, peering down the hallway. "I have something I would like to tell him."

"Of course," Charissa answered without enthusiasm. "He's probably in the library."

Helen turned to go, reaching out and putting her hand on Will's arm. "Are you aware of Colonel and Mrs. Mainwood's dinner party tomorrow, Mr. Lyon? I hope you're coming with Sir Godfrey and Charissa."

"I hadn't planned on going," he answered bluntly, staring with annoyance at her fingers pressing against his sleeve. "When I received my invitation yesterday, I wasn't feeling well, and so I sent my regrets. But," he added in a lighter tone, glancing at Charissa, "I am much better now. I think I shall attend after all, if it would not be too rude to change my mind."

Helen smiled. "Oh, they will be delighted, I'm sure. And I would have been dreadfully disappointed had you not come."

"I am glad not to have been the cause of any loss of pleasure for you, Miss St. Swythin."

Her cheeks flushing with color, she pulled back her hand and bobbed him a curtsey. "Good day to you, Mr. Lyon. Until tomorrow."

She whirled around and grabbed Charissa's elbow. "You may take me to the library now."

"Very well. This way." Charissa shot Will an apologetic look as Helen drew her down the hall.

When they knocked on the door to Sir Godfrey's sanctuary, he called out a testy, "Who's there?" But his expression lightened when he saw the two ladies peek inside, and, rising to his feet, he made them welcome and insisted that they sit down to take some tea with him. Charissa would have liked to leave in order to rejoin Will, but thanks to Helen and Sir Godfrey's efforts—in what seemed suspiciously like a conspiracy—she was detained in conversation for almost half an hour. By the time she escaped, leaving Helen alone with Sir Godfrey, Will was nowhere to be found.

So she went by herself to the Menagerie Room, where she found Sprite lazily stretched out on a soft cushion Will had bought especially for him. The little dog rolled over onto his back, and Charissa grinned at she rubbed his tummy. She picked him up to cuddle him and was rewarded with several sloppy licks.

"Well, Mr. Pettmee, I expect your brother is still with Mr. Lyon," she said, kissing the top of his white, fluffy head. "I mean, with *Will.*" Saying the name out loud was so exciting, she kissed Sprite again. "And do you know something, little boy?" The dog pricked his ears, listening intently. "It's something you and Commodore realized long ago. Mr. William Lyon arrived at Silvercrosse an unhappy stranger, it's true. But no more. He's a wonderful, wonderful man. He's become a dear friend. And not only that—oh, Sprite," she exclaimed burying her head in his fur. "Penelope was right after all. I truly do think that I love him!"

Back in the library—after Charissa had gone—Helen took the opportunity to speak her mind to Sir Godfrey. He was looking at her expectantly, hoping she would leave, but instead of bidding him goodbye, she sat down again.

"I shan't keep you," she told him, folding her hands in her lap. "But I want you to know God is working in all this. Do not be afraid," she intoned, staring at him intently.

Sir Godfrey managed to keep himself from rolling his eyes. Clearing his throat, he walked to the window and looked out onto the lawn. "You need not worry about me, Miss St. Swythin."

She leaned forward in her chair. "You will marry Charissa. I know it."

Startled, Sir Godfrey's eyes darted back towards her.

"God has told me so," she said confidently. "And I am going to marry Mr. Lyon."

Sir Godfrey frowned. "Miss St. Swythin, what makes you think that the Almighty has communicated His plans for my life to you?"

"His sheep hear His voice, Sir Godfrey," she responded patiently. "Is that not so?"

"Well, of course," he said disdainfully, "but we must be certain that it is His voice we follow and not the desires of our flesh. Remember what the prophet Jeremiah wrote: *The heart is more deceitful than anything else, and incurable; who can understand it?*"

Helen brushed off his admonishment. "Oh, Sir Godfrey," she laughed lightly, "you must have faith! I dreamed of Mr. Lyon before he even arrived. How can that be anything but God?"

Sir Godfrey shifted his weight uncomfortably. "How do I know you speak the truth?"

Helen gave him a long-suffering smile. "What benefit would it be to me if I lied to you? I would end up looking like a jingle-brain. No, Sir Godfrey—I am sure of what I saw."

"But how can you be certain of your dream's interpretation? Women are illogical and prone to fantasy."

"You would not say such a thing of Charissa, would you?" challenged Helen.

"I wouldn't have until Mr. Lyon arrived on the scene and addled her wits!"

"Yes, well, I see your point," Helen admitted. "The situation has admittedly gone downhill. Speaking of which… well, I'm sorry, but you ought to know. I saw Charissa and Mr. Lyon in each other's arms this afternoon."

The abhorrent image took immediate shape in Sir Godfrey's imagination. "You must be mistaken," he snarled.

"Oh no," replied Helen, her eyes narrowing. "He was about to kiss her. I interrupted them just in time."

Sir Godfrey's face reddened, and it took him a moment to control his outrage. When he trusted himself to speak calmly, he said, "I've been gravely concerned about such an eventuality for some time now, although I've hoped against hope it wouldn't come to this."

"We cannot allow Charissa to make such a dreadful mistake."

"And yet what can I do?" Sir Godfrey complained, wishing that he were having this conversation with Penelope, whom he trusted, rather than with Helen, whom he did not. "I cannot lock Charissa in her room as though I were her father. Furthermore, I had planned to evict Mr. Lyon from Silvercrosse days ago, but the surgeon has told me unequivocally he cannot travel long distances yet. I may not trust Mr. Lyon, but I am not so unchristian as to put an invalid out on the road."

"I could offer him a place at Wisteria Cottage," Helen suggested with poorly disguised eagerness.

Sir Godfrey was tempted to agree to her proposal; the idea of Mr. Lyon's being subjected to her infatuation day in and day out amused him. But, once again, he thought of Penelope. He didn't want the elder Miss St. Swythin to fall under the spell of Mr. Lyon's charms the way her sister and Charissa had. And besides, he acknowledged to himself, if Mr. Lyon removed to Wisteria Cottage, he—Sir Godfrey—would appear to be an ungracious host.

"That isn't necessary, although I thank you for your hospitality," he refused Helen regretfully. "I am quite capable of handling him here."

"Are you sure?"

"I am."

She stood to her feet, "I shall leave you to it. But rest assured that all is not lost. I am on your side."

Sir Godfrey was not comforted by this, but he ushered her out of the room politely in spite of his unsettled feelings. How disconcerting that—of all people—Helen St. Swythin had become his ally, he mused as he shut the door behind her.

After everyone at Silvercrosse Hall had retired at the end of the long, eventful day, Charissa quietly slipped out of her bedchamber and made her way downstairs to the library. She opened its stout wooden door slowly, grateful that the housemaid had recently oiled its centuries-old hinges. Although the sun's rays had not quite disappeared from the sky, she held a candle in her left hand. It flickered brightly as she moved through the room toward the several shelves Sir Godfrey had reserved for her own books. Putting the candle on a table, she climbed up a step ladder in order to reach a high shelf, where she carefully retrieved a heavy, leather-bound Bible. It was one of her two personal Bibles; she used her father's for her everyday devotions, while this one had belonged to her elderly aunt.

She ran a finger gently over its gold-embossed cover, then descended the ladder.

Setting the Bible on the table next to the candle, she opened it to a particular psalm she had been thinking of all day. She had brought with her from her chamber two red ribbons, and she put one of ribbons in between the leaves of the open book. Next, she turned to another passage—this time in the New Testament—and placed the second ribbon there. When she was done, Bible in hand, she slipped out of the doorway into the hall and retreated upstairs.

Her bedroom was on the southern side of the house, but she softly made her way to the northern side. The hallway was not straight; it had a little jog in it, so that some rooms upstairs had doors hidden from the others. She was grateful Sir Godfrey could not see her stop at the door to Will's bedroom and knock softly.

The younger footman, Alfred, who was acting as Will's valet, opened the door. His jaw dropped. "Miss Armitage?"

"It's all right, Alf," she said reassuringly. "I'd like to speak briefly with Mr. Lyon. Is he available?"

"I'll ask him…" the servant began, but Will came up behind him as soon as he heard Charissa's voice.

"Miss Armitage!" Will said in surprise.

Charissa's heart thumped violently. Will already had doffed his coat and waistcoat and was standing before her in only his shirt and breeches. "Forgive my intrusion," she said quickly. "I just have something I wanted to give you. After our conversation this afternoon, I thought it might be an encouragement to you."

With a movement of his head, Will signaled Alfred to retreat into the room, while he himself came out into the hall, closing the door most of the way behind him. "What did you bring me, Charissa?" he asked.

Her hands trembling slightly, she held the Bible up in the dim light. "I meant what I said about forgiveness this afternoon. I figured that it would be best for you to read God's own words on the matter, so I marked a couple of passages that have meant a lot to me. But there are many, many more. So many people think the Scriptures are about law and judgment, and though that is certainly true, they are also full of mercy and grace." She put the book in his hand and looked directly into his eyes. "As the book of James says, *mercy triumphs over judgment.*"

He took the Bible and pressed it to his chest. "Thank you," he whispered. He smiled in such a way that her heart did somersaults, and leaning over, he gently placed his lips on top of hers in a soft kiss, literally stealing her breath away. "Good night, sweetheart," he murmured as he drew back.

She thought she would faint, but amazingly she was able to reply coherently, her face glowing. "Good night, Will," she whispered. Then she hurried back down the hall to her own bedchamber.

Will's heart raced as fast as Charissa's as he shut the door to his room. He had done it—he had kissed her for the first time! And it was nothing like he had anticipated, but it had been more satisfying than he had ever thought a chaste kiss could be. And Charissa herself had blossomed before his very eyes. *Please God*, he prayed, *let this be a portent of magnificent things to come.*

Please God. The phrase caused him to remember the Bible he held. He walked back over to where Alfred stood, ready to complete his evening toilette. After a moment's thought, he instructed the young man to leave him for the night.

"Are you certain, sir?" Alfred asked with a worried furrow in his brow.

"Yes. I think I'll be up for a while. I want do some reading. Don't worry," he added, seeing the servant's unease, "I'll just fold up the clothes myself when I'm ready for bed. I don't mind. You can deal with them in the morning."

Dibbs would have been horrified, but Alfred looked relieved. "Yes, sir. Good night, sir."

Will thanked him, and, alone at last, he sat down in a chair by the window, where a fat candle burned brightly. He set the Bible on his lap and noticed Charissa had marked two places with ribbons. Curious, he opened to the first one, near the middle of the book, and when he removed the ribbon, he saw the passage's heading: *Psalm Fifty-One.*

He saw that it was a prayer of confession, written by King David, and as he read the heart-wrenching words of repentance written by a profoundly guilty man, Will could identify with the king's grief—although not with his faith that God would forgive. But towards the end of the psalm, a line captured Will's attention, and he paused, reading it several times. As the meaning of the words sank into his brain, a burning feeling arose inside his chest, not so much a physical sensation but one of spiritual awareness, an anticipation of something important about to happen.

The sacrifice pleasing to God is a broken spirit. You will not despise a broken and humbled heart, God.

It was as though a fog lifted inside Will's mind; his confusion melted away. This passage said plainly that it wasn't attendance at worship services or doing good works that God wanted from him, although certainly those things were proper expressions of religious devotion.

What God really desired was his *heart.*

Will sat for a long time just contemplating this implausible thought, but he couldn't argue it away. What a holy God would want with him he couldn't fathom, but for the first time, the idea it was a man's *faith* that pleased the Lord made sense to him.

He wasn't sure he was ready to turn away from his place in the Old Testament, but he wanted to know which New Testament passage Charissa had thought he should read. So he flipped to the second ribbon.

It lay toward the front of the Book of Romans. Will started at the beginning of chapter four, and he didn't have to go far before he found another verse that seemed to leap off the page: *But to the one who does not work, but believes on him who declares the ungodly to be righteous, his faith is credited for righteousness.*

116

Will stared at the page, his heart beating rapidly again as he digested the meaning of the Scripture. In order to be right with God, he didn't—indeed, he shouldn't—try to impress the Almighty with great and abundant acts of piety. Even if he were the most diligent man on earth, he could never, ever do enough! On the contrary, he needed only to truly believe in Jesus Christ—and His sacrifice on the cross as sufficient payment for his sins—and God would count that faith as righteousness. He would be forgiven.

It was as simple as that.

Will expelled a long breath and felt himself relax; it had all—finally—fallen into place.

Why in the world had he never figured this out before? Was it the Church of England's fault or his own? Probably a mixture of both, he guessed. Many Church leaders had sought their positions because a religious career was socially acceptable, not because they cared one whit for spiritual things. They cared more about appearances than about truth.

But Will admitted that he'd been part of the problem, too. He had ignored the humble, God-fearing people in his life just as stubbornly as he had rejected the hypocritical blowhards. He'd been too determined to fight against a God he'd assumed didn't care about anything but judging his sins. A God who had rejected him.

And yet now it turned out that God hadn't rejected him at all. Instead, in His mercy, He had already provided for those sins—at His own infinite cost. Forgiveness and restoration were free for the asking. Will sat quietly, contemplating this undeserved invitation, and he sensed that heaven itself was eagerly anticipating his adoption into the divine family as a beloved son.

He looked up from the Bible in his lap and out the open window. A lone radiant star shone in the night sky as the whole universe held its breath. A single tear coursed down Will's cheek. "I believe, Lord," he whispered at last. "I believe."

Chapter 15

Will overslept the next morning, waking too late even for breakfast, but he felt more rested than he had in years. Perhaps ever. After he dressed, he grabbed his cane and headed straight for the Menagerie Room.

Charissa glanced up when he came in, her expression moving from one of deep concentration to happy welcome. "Will," she smiled. "You're finally up and about."

"I slept well last night," he said, sitting down in his customary place. "No nightmares."

"Nightmares?" she asked, a shadow of concern falling over her brow.

He'd forgotten she didn't know. Funny how he assumed she would have. "Ever since my brother died two years ago, I've occasionally had an unpleasant recurring dream about him. It surfaced again after the party at Wisteria Cottage—but not last night." Warmth filled him as he remembered how he had finally made his peace with God.

From across the table, Charissa noticed a difference in his expression and in his tone of voice. He appeared less defensive, more at ease. Hope rose in her heart, but she dared not press him. "I'm very glad to hear it. Indeed, you look well," she said kindly, "but I expect you are hungry. Shall I send for some tea and muffins?"

"And bacon as well if you please. I am ravenous," he stated. "When I'm finished, why don't we take the dogs out in the garden, and throw a ball for them to chase. I should like to steal you from your work—I admit it."

Charissa wanted nothing more than to be stolen; the imaginary romance of her characters had paled in comparison to her own sweet kiss the night before. "Please do," she replied.

Therefore, after food had been brought in for Will—which he ate heartily while they chatted about inconsequential things—they went out into the garden with the dogs at their heels. Sprite and Commodore both enjoyed chasing the ball, although long before Sprite was ready to stop the game Commodore wandered off in order to do some serious sniffing around the premises. But at last Sprite, too, decided that he would rather join Commodore on patrol duty. So, leaving the dogs to their own devices, Will and Charissa began to stroll together, walking by unspoken mutual consent down a tree-lined path from which they were not visible to the house.

"Thank you for the loan of the Bible," Will said.

"Oh, it wasn't a loan," Charissa answered impulsively. "You may keep it."

"Are you sure?" he asked, genuinely surprised. "I would not want to leave you bereft of such a valuable book."

"I have another that I use for my own study. And Sir Godfrey possesses several more. Please, Will, I want you to have it."

"I accept," he replied, "with many thanks."

"Did you enjoyed reading it?" she asked.

"Very much." He wanted to tell her of his spiritual awakening, although he wasn't sure how to put his thoughts into words without sounding mawkish—and his experience last night had been anything but.

"Both of the passages you marked were uncannily pertinent to my train of thought," he began. "And in the course of pondering those two pieces of Scripture, I understood something for the first time. I've always known what a sinful man I am, but I thought it was up to me to make myself good. An impossible task!" he declared with just a hint of disgust. He cleared his throat. "Well, it's impossible for me, but it's not impossible for God."

"For you are saved by grace through faith, and this is not from yourselves; it is God's gift—not from works, so that no one can boast," she quoted.

"Exactly," he said, finally daring to gaze into her eyes. "And I, of all men, have nothing to boast of. So consequently, I have accepted the gift."

"Dearest Will!" Charissa reached out instinctively and grabbed his hand. "You were brought to Silvercrosse Hall for a reason—that you might be drawn to Christ. Oh, I am so happy for you! I have prayed so earnestly for this!"

"Thank you, my dear," he said quietly, clasping her hands between both of his and smiling into her admiring eyes. He ached to pull her towards him and kiss her again, but he forced himself not to indulge his desire. After all, they were discussing spiritual matters, not amorous ones, and he did not wish to confuse the two. Rather than complicate things, he stated, "I think we ought to go back to the Menagerie Room now, my darling."

"Must we?" she asked plaintively.

"I think so. Otherwise I might be tempted to carry you off into the sunset, as in one of your novels."

She laughed. "Shall we escape to a wind-swept moor or a stormy cliff beside an angry sea?"

"Neither, I think," he chuckled, taking her arm in his and leading her along the path back to the house. "But I do regret Ashbourne Park isn't a wild and dreary castle to which I can bring you as a kidnap victim."

She looked at him curiously; he had just let slip a rare tidbit of personal information. "Ashbourne Park. Is that where you grew up? Is it very far from here? It must be yours now your father has passed away."

Will wanted to kick himself. This was his first gaffe—but fortunately it seemed as though she did not know of the place and who lived there. However, he was inwardly convicted of his deception about his identity. He should probably tell her the truth, but he ignored this uncomfortable suggestion.

"I did grow up there. It's a pleasant little place," he answered instead. His reply was only partly true, for while Ashbourne was indeed pleasant, it was not at all little.

Charissa opened her mouth to question him further, but just then Sprite ran up from behind one of the trees and started dancing on his hind legs in front of her, eager to play. She bent down and picked him up. He licked her nose, and she giggled. He barked sharply. "All right," she acquiesced, letting him flop back down onto the ground so he could run ahead of her.

Sprite's interruption spoiled Charissa's opportunity to follow up on the information Mr. Lyon had just revealed. She was disappointed, to be sure, but she enjoyed watching Will withdraw the ball from his pocket and throw it again for Sprite to chase.

"Go get it!" Will called, purposefully focusing all of his attention on the game.

The excited pup roared ahead of them, his eyes fixed intently on the ball. He swiftly turned back toward Will, his prize captured and held securely in his teeth. "Good boy," said Will, taking the ball and throwing it again.

Sir Godfrey had been out all day, but he came home in time for dinner. The atmosphere was strained, at least on his part. He could see the undercurrent of deepening affection between Charissa and Will, and he barely tasted the savory food set in front of him. It also didn't help that Aunt Caroline chose this particular moment to be awake and alert, conversing with Mr. Lyon.

"You have been full of good spirits today," the elderly lady observed.

"I must say that I am, Miss Scrivener," Will replied. "It was another beautiful day without rain."

"There is more than agreeable weather bringing light to your eyes," she guessed.

He did not contradict her. "Indeed, there are many particularly lovely things at Silvercrosse Hall which brighten my days."

Sir Godfrey mumbled something indistinct under his breath, while Charissa happily busied herself with her ham.

When they rose from the table, Sir Godfrey dourly requested that Charissa join him in the library. Sensing an impending confrontation, she was reluctant to go, but she could think of no credible reason to refuse him.

She entered the room and walked over to his globe, spinning it with her fingers and watching the continents fly around in a blurry whirl. She heard him close the library door a bit more firmly than he was wont to, and she girded herself for the onslaught.

"Charissa, I am most distressed and deeply concerned," he began heatedly. "Your infatuation with Mr. Lyon may be understandable from a woman's point of view, but it is a dangerous connection you are pursuing."

She turned around and glared at him. "I do not appreciate your tone, Godfrey. Please make an effort to treat me with respect."

"I would like to, but I confess I am disappointed in you. You were always a woman of sense—until this charismatic deceiver managed to bewitch you!"

"I am not bewitched. Mr. Lyon is outwardly attractive, yes, but he has depth of character as well."

Sir Godfrey snorted derisively. "You should know better than to attach yourself to an unbeliever."

"For your information, Mr. Lyon has just made a profession of faith. If you weren't so busy trying to find things to criticize, you might have been able to see the change in him. Aunt Caroline even noticed it."

"I expect his happy demeanor has more to do with the fact that you have fallen so far under his spell you have allowed him to take liberties with you."

She flushed scarlet with anger. "Just what do you mean by that accusation?"

"Don't bother to deny it," he spat out. "Helen St. Swythin saw you in Lyon's arms!"

"It's too bad she didn't know the rest of the story," Charissa retorted. "Mr. Lyon was expressing his grief over the death of his brother."

"How convenient that it led to an embrace with his targeted victim," Sir Godfrey shot back cynically. "I never thought I'd say it, but you are acting like a brainless ninny!"

"Will is not trying to seduce me!" Charissa exclaimed hotly. "You are just filled to the brim with self-righteousness and jealousy! Where is your vaunted Christian charity?"

"And where is your vaunted Christian wisdom? All it took was one handsome stranger paying attention to you, and you forgot every lesson you learned over the past six years!"

The two of them stood at opposite ends of the room looking daggers at each other. Then, abruptly, at the same moment, both of them deflated, losing their anger.

"I'm sorry, Godfrey," Charissa said dejectedly. "I didn't try to fall in love with Mr. Lyon—it just happened. It's not that I don't care deeply for you, but…"

"You need not elaborate," Sir Godfrey broke in huskily.

After a short silence, however, Charissa admitted, "You are partially right, though. I don't know as much about Mr. Lyon as I wish I did."

Sir Godfrey gave her a penetrating glance, then walked to the chair behind his desk, and sat down. "You won't take it amiss, then, if I research the man's background? You're aware I wrote to a few friends in London when he first arrived, and no one was acquainted with him, but I intend now to make some more detailed enquiries. It is the prudent thing to do. Mr. Lyon has not been very forthcoming."

Charissa nodded reluctantly. "He is a bit of a mystery—he's a very private person. But here's one thing I've learned: he grew up on an estate called Ashbourne Park. It must be in Dorset."

"Ashbourne Park," repeated Sir Godfrey thoughtfully. "Dorset." He took a pen, dipped it in the inkwell, and wrote the name of the estate down on a piece of paper.

"And he has a married half-sister with whom he is not on friendly terms. I'm not sure if his stepmother is alive or not, I'm afraid."

"Unfortunately, those facts are so vague that they're not helpful," Sir Godfrey commented, writing them down anyway. "And you must realize this means he was lying the day we first spoke to him, when he informed us that he had no family."

"And why should he have told us anything else? He is obviously not on good terms with them, which would have been awkward to explain at the time."

Sir Godfrey looked dubious.

"You'll undoubtedly find he has a checkered past," Charissa went on. "But that doesn't mean that he is insincere in his conversion. Promise me you will at least open your mind to the possibility he has truly given his heart to Christ."

"I suppose it's possible," Sir Godfrey said grudgingly, putting down the pen. "But I doubt it."

"You're wrong," she replied. "Just wait until you realize Mr. Lyon is a *new creation*, Godfrey, just as the Scripture describes." When he looked at her skeptically, she smiled. "You'll see."

Chapter 16

"Welcome," Mrs. Mainwood said warmly, after her manservant had shown the Silvercrosse Hall residents into her parlor later the same day. "I know it's a bit early for an evening gathering, even for the country," she apologized to Will, "but the Colonel prefers to retire early because he rises with the sun, even in the summertime."

"I am not at all inconvenienced," Will replied cordially.

"Splendid," she answered. "It will surely be a merry party. The St. Swythin sisters are here, and the Humphreys, as you see, but I do regret to inform you that since several of the Shaws are under the weather, none of them are able to come."

"We're delighted to be here," Charissa said, taking her seat. Will placed himself on her right side, while Sir Godfrey sat protectively on her left. "Although I am sorry to tell you," she continued apologetically, "that Aunt Caroline has stayed at Silvercrosse. She is not unwell, but merely tired. On the other hand, I do hope the Shaws have contracted no serious illness."

"Oh no, it's just a severe cold making the rounds in their family," Mrs. Mainwood assured her. "I remember what that was like when all my children were home. First one was sneezing and hacking and blowing his nose, then the other, then the next and the next... and a sorry lot we were indeed. Just what the Shaws are experiencing now, alas."

"It is fortunate the Shaws possess only cats and not hungry dogs," Will said waggishly, looking at Charissa out of the corner of his eye.

He was remembering how Sprite and Commodore loved to gobble up used handkerchiefs, and she stifled a laugh, while the others looked confused.

"How many children do you have, Mrs. Mainwood?" Will continued politely.

"Five," Mrs. Mainwood replied, her eyes brightening. "Three boys and two girls. You know about Samuel, our eldest, who followed his father into the army. The other three are well married and diligently providing me with grandchildren—except my youngest son George, who lives in Stoke-On-Trent. Hopefully, however, he will soon be following suit."

"George is very charming," Charissa recalled. "Is he contemplating marriage to the young woman you were telling me about?"

"Yes," Mrs. Mainwood said with satisfaction. "In fact, the Colonel is leaving tomorrow to visit him. Hurry him along a little bit, you know."

"I intend to do no such thing," Colonel Mainwood retorted, although the corners of his eyes crinkled just enough to reveal his amusement. "I am going to town on business and not to meddle in my son's affairs."

"It isn't meddling to give him a gentle but firm push in the right direction, Sam," his wife maintained. "Miss Arbuckle is the perfect match for him."

Colonel Mainwood looked at Sir Godfrey with a mournful expression. "I never fancied, when I retired from a career in which I risked life and limb for king and country, that I would be forced to undertake as hideous a task as this."

"My deepest sympathies," Sir Godfrey chuckled, as Mrs. Mainwood gave her husband a withering glance.

But before poor George's matrimonial prospects could be dissected at length, the butler announced that dinner was served, and everyone cheerfully entered the dining room.

After a tasty meal—during which Will managed to dodge several personal questions from Mrs. Humphreys and Mrs. Mainwood—Colonel Mainwood suggested that his guests might enjoy visiting the small lake that lay behind their house. "We are undertaking quite a number of improvements," he explained proudly. "I've hired two extra gardeners to assist with the landscaping, and I've added yet another skiff to our little fleet."

"It's lovely down there at this time of the early evening—when the sun is still in the sky, but it's not as hot as the midafternoon," Mrs. Mainwood said enthusiastically. "Shall we go?"

Everyone agreed, so they walked together across the lawn and down a gentle slope toward the lake. Will—who, typically, found himself surrounded by the ladies—paused and turned back toward the house. It was built in the elegant style so popular in the previous century, and although it was not particularly large, it sat proudly on a small rise overlooking the lake. "It is a very pleasant prospect," he commented, smiling at Mrs. Mainwood. Looking beyond the women at the Colonel, he added, "I can see that you have brought a touch of the wildness of nature back into what was once a very rigid tableau. Nicely done."

Colonel Mainwood nodded. "I am honored that you approve, sir."

"And yet it is wildness bound by aesthetic sensibilities," Sir Godfrey observed. "The effect is neither artificial nor undisciplined." He glanced sharply at Will.

"I agree," Mr. Humphreys chimed in. "It is both a feast for the eyes and a balm for the spirit."

"Well, I for one," Charissa proposed, "would love to go out on the water in one of the boats. Is anyone else up for an adventure?"

She looked hopefully at Will, but before he could respond, Colonel Mainwood offered to row her, along with his wife, across the lake. Not willing to be outdone, Mr. Humphreys volunteered to captain a boat for his own wife and Penelope. That left Sir Godfrey and Will in the last skiff with Helen, which to both men's minds was not exactly a jolly undertaking.

"I must confess my leg has been aching a bit today," Will said hastily. It was, in fact, true. "Please, Sir Godfrey, I insist you take the remaining vessel. I'm sure Miss St. Swythin will appreciate your sophisticated analysis of the placement of every rock and fern along the shoreline." He smiled pleasantly at Sir Godfrey.

"Oh no, Sir Godfrey," Helen countered with a sigh. "I'm rather afraid of the water. I'll just stay here with Mr. Lyon."

Sir Godfrey smiled victoriously at Will. "Of course, Miss St.

Swythin. Not for a moment would I wish to make you uncomfortable. And I'm sure as you spend time with Mr. Lyon, you'll come to appreciate his sparkling wit. But beware—I should not be surprised if he were a proficient breaker of hearts."

Will calmly raised an eyebrow. "Perhaps you would rather remain on shore with us, Sir Godfrey, in order to protect this sweet creature from my devastating worldly charms?"

Standing in between Will and Sir Godfrey, Charissa wanted to suggest that she stay behind with Will and Helen. But she realized that since she had been the one to recommend the journey across the lake, it would be impolite to desert the Mainwoods. And because she certainly didn't want to join Sir Godfrey alone in his boat, she looked apologetically at Will, but said nothing.

It was Penelope who resolved the impasse. "I'll go with you in your boat, Sir Godfrey," she said swiftly, "if the Humphreys don't mind, of course."

Sir Godfrey had wanted to ask Charissa to come with him, but at least she wasn't with his rival, and he acknowledged to himself Penelope would be pleasant company. "That would be delightful, Miss St. Swythin," he allowed graciously, as the Humphreys agreed.

With the ridership issues solved, the eight sailors carefully stepped into the three skiffs. When they were all seated, the men rowed out onto the calm waters, where the long, golden light of early evening surrounded them with its lingering embrace. Penelope trailed her hand in the cold, refreshing water, gazing happily at Sir Godfrey as he masterfully pulled at the oars. In the second boat, Mr. Humphreys quoted a psalm praising the Creator, while in the third boat Mrs. Mainwood sang a song about spring. Charissa joined in, although she couldn't help a glance or two backward towards the bank, where Will stood stiffly next to a triumphant Helen.

Helen waved breezily across the water at Charissa. "I concur with you, Mr. Lyon," she remarked as she lowered her arm. "About gardens, I mean. I prefer landscapes that are lush and free. Strict adherence to convention does nothing to elevate the soul. Those of us with eyes to see—we artists—perceive things more deeply, I believe. We are more spiritual."

Will stepped away from her, using his cane for support. "That depends, I think, on how one defines the word *spiritual*. I think of it differently than I did not so very long ago."

"Oh?" She closed the gap between them, stepping up onto small boulders artistically placed by the side of the lake.

"I used to think of spirituality as either a religious duty or the stirring of one's emotions. Now, however, I understand that—without the proper context—those things only serve to feed one's vanity. Real spiritual life must have its roots in Christ Himself."

Helen regarded him with wide, puppy dog eyes.

"In the same way," he continued, formulating his ideas as he spoke, "beauty must be fastened to truth, which is itself found in the character of God. But do not ask me to elaborate," he cautioned her sternly. "My thoughts on the matter are neither complete nor settled."

"Your thoughts are very profound," she said admiringly, leaning even closer to him.

"Do not praise *me*," he countered, backing away and carefully taking a few steps toward the lake. "It is the Almighty who is revolutionizing my thinking." He looked out over the waters at the Mainwoods' boat. "I must also credit Miss Armitage for the genuine spirituality she has consistently demonstrated to me."

Behind him, Helen scowled.

"She is an extraordinary woman," he went on, mostly to himself. "And I…"

But whatever he was going to say was lost by a frightened wail. He turned abruptly to see Helen on the ground, her foot caught between two of the rocks. "I fell!" she gasped. "Oh, my ankle!"

Will rushed over to her as fast as he could, given his own difficulty. "Allow me to assist you," he said as he reached out his hand. She took it, but as soon as she tried to move, she groaned.

Will readjusted his own position and bent down. With a little effort he managed to loosen one of the stones and free her foot. "Try again," he ordered, holding out his hand again.

She made another attempt to stand, but to no avail. "Oh, it hurts terribly as soon as I put any weight on it! Would you be so good as to ascertain if it is broken or merely sprained?" she asked plaintively.

"I'll try," he replied. He sat down carefully and took her ankle in his hands. "I don't think it's broken," he said after examining it. "Nor does it seem swollen." He lay it gently back down on the ground. "Fortunately, I believe it is not a severe injury, and your pain should subside momentarily."

"I hope you're right," she answered, "but I'd like to return to the house. Would you help me up again? And escort me back?"

Will sighed inwardly. "Of course, Miss St. Swythin." This time he managed to help her to her feet, although she cried out in pain and clutched at him for support. "Here," he said as he recovered his own balance, "as I cannot carry you, perhaps we can both lean on my cane."

She gazed at him tearfully. "You are a true gentleman, Mr. Lyon."

"We ought to call for your sister." The boats were all the way on the other side of the lake, but Will waved his free hand anyway.

"Don't disturb her, please!" Helen insisted. "Look, her boat is the farthest from shore. Let's just go to the house now, so we can ask the housekeeper if there's any ice left in the icehouse for my ankle. That will keep it from swelling."

"Very well." Will gave in, and the two of them slowly made their way up the lawn, Helen holding onto him as tightly as possible.

When they arrived at the terrace behind the house, Helen stopped just as they hobbled behind a large ornamental tree. Reaching out and steadying herself by holding onto his arms, she pulled her body against his before he realized what she was doing.

Looking up into his face, she whispered violently, "You were brought here for a reason, William! Don't fight against it. It's God's will that we should be together. I've waited for you so long. I love you! Say that you love me!" And she leaned upward, moving her lips towards his.

Horrified, Will pushed her away from him with both hands, although he didn't release her for fear she might fall. "Miss St. Swythin, you forget yourself!"

"We are meant to be together! You must feel it. Forget anyone else. You are *mine!*"

He shook her slightly. "Listen to yourself. This is unseemly."

"I love you, William!" she declared passionately, oblivious to his discomfort.

He realized that only boldness would break through her delusion, and he most certainly could not allow this farce to continue. He released her and said sternly, "Though I consider you an interesting person, Miss St. Swythin, I am most emphatically *not* in love with you. Please be so good as to believe me and cease this nonsense at once."

Her face fell, and her lower lip quivered. "Nonsense?" she repeated with a sob.

Gratefully, at that moment Will saw a manservant coming out onto the terrace. "You there!" he called. "Miss St. Swythin has injured her ankle. Would you be so good as to carry her into the house and see that she is attended to?"

"Yes, sir," the man replied, alarmed. "At once, sir!" He approached them hurriedly and swept the weeping Helen right up into his strong arms. He took her into the house, where the housekeeper ordered him to convey her upstairs to one of the bedrooms.

Somewhat dazed, Will stayed out on the terrace. He saw that the Mainwoods, recognizing something had happened, had already brought their boat ashore. Charissa was running up the lawn ahead of them, heading straight for the house. Mr. Humphreys was rowing diligently back to shore, as was Sir Godfrey, but they had not arrived yet.

Will gave a sigh of relief when Charissa reached him. "Will, what happened?" she asked anxiously. He looked almost as pale as he had when she had first seen him lying half dead on the ground.

"Miss St. Swythin has apparently sprained her ankle, although," he said pointedly, "I suspect that it is all a charade."

"A charade?" Charissa repeated, perplexed. "What do you mean?"

Will pulled Charissa closer to him and lowered his voice. "She just confessed her undying love for me and her conviction that a union between the two of us is nothing less than divine providence. She was completely unhinged. I believe she pretended to hurt herself in order to lure me into a solitary place."

"Oh no! You don't think she'll accuse you of any untoward behavior, do you?" It was not unheard of for a desperate woman to attempt to entrap a gentleman into marriage with false claims of seduction.

"I don't think so. We were unobservable for mere seconds until the Mainwoods' servant appeared on the terrace. But I told her in no uncertain terms that I do not love her."

"Poor Helen," Charissa murmured.

"Poor *Helen?*" Will exclaimed, his voice rising in disgust. "I think not! I've had my fair share of women throw themselves at me, but this was pathetic!"

"Precisely," replied Charissa softly. "Look, here come the Mainwoods. They will be solicitous for Helen, I'm sure."

"And Miss Penelope St. Swythin will be as well. She is a charming woman who has a lunatic for a sister."

"Will!" Charissa scolded him, in spite of the fact the same thought had crossed her own mind any number of times. She was relieved when Colonel and Mrs. Mainwood finally made their way up onto the terrace. Upon hearing the news of Helen's accident—though not of her heartbreak—they rushed inside to see to their distraught guest. Will and Charissa followed them, but stayed in the drawing room downstairs.

Soon the Humphreys, Sir Godfrey, and Penelope arrived. Penelope immediately went up to see her sister, and when she returned, she reported with relief that Helen's ankle did not seem to be swollen. Will and Charissa exchanged a look, but neither of them made any comment. Sir Godfrey offered to take Penelope and Helen home in his carriage, and Penelope gratefully accepted.

It was an awkward business during the ride. The three women, as was the custom, rode facing forward while the men sat opposite them. Helen had her bandaged foot up on Sir Godfrey's lap, and she chewed on her lip the entire way to Wisteria Cottage, periodically casting Will a mournful look. Will sat stiffly, ignoring her, while Sir Godfrey's embarrassment at having a female's foot resting on his person would have been funny had the tension in the coach not been quite so palpable. Charissa and Penelope carried on a pointless conversation about the new gown Mrs. Humphreys had worn that evening, a topic neither of them cared about but which, under the circumstances, was better than strained silence.

Needless to say, each of them was very glad to bid the others goodnight.

Chapter 17

"Tell me more about the St. Swythins," Will remarked to Charissa the next day as they sat in the Menagerie Room.

"Are you concerned about Helen?" Charissa inquired, putting down her quill.

"Not for her own sake, no. But I worry that she could make trouble," he acknowledged. "Not only is she obsessed with me, but she is clearly *non compos mentis*."

"She does behave strangely sometimes, but I honestly believe she is harmless," Charissa replied. "Nonetheless when we see her in church on Sunday, we'll be better able to assess her frame of mind. And I can always ask Penelope for advice."

"Although they are sisters, they are very unlike," he observed. "The same was true of Edward and me, but of course we were half siblings."

"Penelope and Helen are full-blooded sisters, but Penelope takes after her mother and Helen takes after her father, or so I am told. Everyone loved Mrs. St. Swythin, but they all say that Mr. St. Swythin was—how should I say it—eccentric, at the very least."

"I see. And the sisters are not well-situated financially, I take it?"

"Penelope is wise with their funds, so they are not insolvent. But they would be much better off had their brother not gambled away most of his inheritance after their father died."

It was a familiar story, one which Will had seen played out in the gaming dens of London. "What happened to the brother?"

"After he lost most of their money, he left the country. Mrs. St.

Swythin was forced to sell their estate and move to Wisteria Cottage. That was a long time ago, when Penelope was just set to make her come-out into society. Instead, she came back to Murrington to take care of her mother, who was crushed by her son's irresponsibility and his desertion of the family."

"How unfortunate." In spite of her lack of a fortune, Penelope would have made some discerning gentleman an excellent wife, Will thought.

"Later, with the help of generous relatives, Penelope managed to scrape up enough money for Helen to go to London for a few seasons. But, sadly, Helen had little with which to tempt an eligible bachelor to wed her." Charissa did not need to elaborate.

"So she returned to Wisteria Cottage?"

"Yes—although she's always claimed God has a husband set apart for her and that someday the chosen gentleman will find her. I never paid much attention to her pronouncements," Charissa confessed. "Perhaps I should have."

"Even if you did, it surely would change nothing. It seems as though she has decided this elect gentleman is none other than myself. But perhaps I have managed to disabuse her of the notion."

Charissa nodded, although she wondered what it would really take to dissuade someone as stubborn as Helen St. Swythin. "We'll soon see," she said, attempting to sound at least mildly optimistic.

"I most certainly hope she has given me up," Will murmured. After all, he thought as he looked at Charissa, even if Helen had been an appealing woman, his attention was otherwise occupied.

Nothing dramatic happened for the next few days. Will spent time reading Scripture, which he had always found dry and uninteresting before, but now the words rang true. Even when Sir Godfrey read one of his more lengthy sermons to everyone on Saturday night, Will understood the basic meaning of the passage and its application to daily life. Once he made an astute comment, which earned him a radiant smile from Charissa. She turned to her cousin with a look that plainly said, "I told you so." Sir Godfrey, however, refused to be impressed, and he continued reading with the barest nod of his head to acknowledge Will's point. Will, however, considered it a victory.

Will's other private triumphs were the moments he was able to spend alone with Charissa. Several times they met in the Menagerie Room; once they walked in the garden. However, he did not kiss her again, although he felt sure she would not have objected. This need to honor her and protect her virtue was something completely new to him in a romantic relationship, and he was amazed to discover such a noble sentiment in himself.

The only thing troubling him was a faint but disturbing insistence at the back of his mind that he should tell her who he really was. Part of him wanted to, but another part of him feared her response to his duplicity, even if he apologized and explained his reasons for the lie.

So he said nothing.

As for Charissa, she savored every moment with Will. Thoughts of marriage swirled in her mind and inspired her fantasies, but he seemed reluctant to make any definitive statement on either love or matrimony. It was hard for her to resist the temptation to push him in that direction, but nevertheless, with effort, she refrained.

Sunday provided Will with his first time in a worship service as a believer. Mr. Humphreys' text was Psalm 5:12: *For you, Lord, bless the righteous one; you surround him with favor like a shield.* For the first time, Will felt as though the words applied to him—not because he was righteous in and of himself, but because he was forgiven.

Both Will and Charissa had wondered how Helen would behave, and they were prepared for something outrageous. But as the three of them greeted one another outside the church after the service, Helen treated them with the one thing they had not anticipated: warm geniality. She even passed over the opportunity to point out that Charissa was wearing Sir Godfrey's silver cross, complimenting her instead on her hat. When Will inquired about Helen's injury, she thanked him cordially and insisted that she was in perfect health.

"In fact," she informed him, "I'm planning to go to Oxfordshire soon to visit a widowed cousin of mine. She's often begged me to come stay with her, so I've decided at last to take her up on the offer. Her brother has been visiting friends up north, and he has offered to come fetch me this week and escort me to his sister's home on his way back to London. I'm so terribly excited."

"How very nice for you," Will responded, musing that she seemed to have accepted his rejection of her profession of love. Perhaps she was the sort of person who moved easily from one romantic caprice to the next—he hoped so. It would certainly save everyone a great deal of trouble.

Sir Godfrey was far less willing than Helen to treat Will affably, his cool indifference towards his guest making it clear that Will's days at Silvercrosse Hall were numbered.

Will himself was well aware of his impending eviction. He had been recuperating for almost six weeks and by now was ready to put aside even the cane. This meant that he would be able to dance at the assembly with Charissa—but also that he had no excuse to remain in Murrington.

His inner urgency to reveal his identity to her grew stronger, but so did his fear that by doing so he would impact their relationship in a negative way. While his title commanded respect from most people—and evoked flattery from many—he cringed at the thought Charissa would see him differently than she did right now.

But he would have to confess his deception soon, since he wouldn't be able to maintain the fiction of Mr. Lyon beyond his stay at Silvercrosse Hall. And, truth be told, he was glad. He longed to be known and liked for himself. Even loved. Then he could take the final, irrevocable step of asking for Charissa's hand in marriage.

Yet the thought of matrimony daunted him. He certainly didn't have much experience in righteous living. Was he really so changed? He felt that way now, but maybe he was too dull in the things of faith to satisfy a woman like Charissa. Furthermore, it seemed entirely possible to him Charissa might suddenly realize she had always loved the meritorious Sir Godfrey and reject Will's suit. That he had been lying to her for over a month did nothing to boost his confidence.

And yet he wanted her for himself. She seemed like a part of him already, and he couldn't bear the thought of losing her.

He would have to tell her the truth.

But he would wait until after the assembly, he decided. No need to cause a kerfuffle which would overshadow the event and cause tongues to wag. Since the dance was on Friday, he would reveal himself to her as the Earl of Hartwell on Saturday. He would beg her forgiveness, express his devotion, and ask her to become his wife.

"I am going to take a walk without my cane today," Will announced Thursday morning as he finished breakfast. Demonstrating his newfound freedom, he pushed back his chair, stood up, and took a step away the table. "It has been exactly six weeks since my accident, and Mr. Rowley has given me permission to discard the dreadful thing at last!" he exclaimed.

Aunt Caroline nodded, and Charissa clapped her hands. Sir Godfrey was pleased, too, but for an entirely different reason. He decided then and there he would send Will on his way as soon as possible after the assembly on Friday. Since everyone would rise late Saturday and Sunday was out of the question, Monday morning would do nicely. He had not yet heard from his contacts in London about any secrets Mr. Lyon might be hiding, but it mattered less now. Once the unwelcome stranger had departed, Sir Godfrey believed, the scoundrel would lose his hold over Charissa's heart. Out of sight, out of mind.

As he watched Mr. Lyon prove his agility by walking around the table to Charissa's applause, it occurred to him perhaps the man had actually done him a favor. How? Mr. Lyon had jolted Charissa out of her romantic indifference, which, in some ways, had been Sir Godfrey's own fault. But now he himself would surely find her more open to his declaration of love. In the end, Sir Godfrey concluded, everything would work out in his own favor, which was only right and proper. The Almighty would see to it the blameless man was justly rewarded for his moral rectitude and longsuffering.

"That is excellent news, Mr. Lyon," was all he said out loud, however. "Enjoy your exercise" he added, smiling in anticipation of Will's removal from Silvercrosse Hall. He put his napkin on the plate, rose from the table, and headed for the door. As he strode down the hall to the library, he hummed the tune to one of his favorite hymns by Isaac Watts: *Let God arise in all His might, And put the troops of hell to flight, As smoke that sought to cloud the skies Before the rising tempest flies.*

Charissa, unaware of her cousin's thoughts, was thrilled at Will's pronouncement. "Mr. Rowley has given you very good news," she reiterated after Sir Godfrey departed. "May I accompany you on your walk? Or would you prefer to celebrate your newfound freedom on your own?"

To her delight, Will readily agreed that she come along. After they left the breakfast room and stepped out of the front door, he eyed the sky uncertainly. "It appears we shouldn't journey too far. The clouds could become rainclouds at any moment."

"I'll bring two umbrellas, so we can go as far as we dare." She ran back inside and came out again with the aforementioned raingear. "Hopefully, we won't need them, but better safe than bedraggled," she said, handing one of the umbrellas to Will.

He agreed, tucking it under his arm. "But you will notice I am not using it to support my weight. Where shall we be off to, then?"

"Why don't I just show you my favorite spot beside Ferne Brook? Penelope and I like to sit there. It's not terribly far."

"Very well, let's go."

Once they reached their destination, they sat on the big, flat rock next to the swift-flowing stream. Its fresh, clear water raced over smooth, smaller stones and emerald-green moss, sparkling in the sunshine that managed to peek out of the clouds every so often. Birds chirped back and forth to one another as they flew to and fro across the open spaces. It was an ideal place to glory in the delights of late spring.

They chatted about the drawings Will had done of Sprite and Commodore; Charissa had had the original two framed, and they now graced one of the walls in the Menagerie Room. "It makes me so happy to know the dogs will be a part of Silvercrosse forever," she said. "I wrote their names on the back of each of the pictures. Just think—one hundred, even two hundred years from now, the inhabitants of the house will know that they lived here, and that someone loved them."

"Are they your dogs or Sir Godfrey's?" Will asked. "If you left Silvercrosse Hall, would you take them with you?"

"I suppose that they're really Sir Godfrey's, although I was the one who brought them home as puppies. They were given to him by one of his tenant farmers. But I'm sure that if I asked, he would give them to me."

"You have Sir Godfrey wrapped around your little finger, don't you?"

"Well, I don't know if I'd go that far. But he's been good to me. He is very godly. That's the reason why—although he's always been kindness itself—he's never allowed me to sink too deeply into self-pity. I'm grateful, because that's probably exactly what I would have done if I'd been left to my own devices. Years ago I didn't have the maturity or the perspective to sort through my feelings, but Sir Godfrey did."

Will glanced at her; she was gazing out over the water. He felt a surge of jealousy over her intimacy with Sir Godfrey, but at the same time he was determined to learn more about what had happened to her. He still held out hope maybe there was something he could do to make it right.

"You've never told me the story," he said quietly. "And it seems only fair I should know one of your secrets. You know a lot of mine."

"You'll probably think me a simpleton," she warned.

"Impossible," he retorted with complete sincerity. "Maybe naïve or inexperienced, but never stupid."

"Thank you," she said, touched by his praise. "It's not a complicated story. I was making my come-out, and, as you know, my father had left me a generous legacy. I fell in love almost at once with a very handsome man who made it a point to charm me with his wit, his talent, and even his ability to quote Scripture. Little did I know he had recently gambled away most of his own inheritance—rather like Penelope and Helen St. Swythin's brother had done."

"I've seen it happen, I'm sorry to say." Not only had Will witnessed the recklessness of such young men, he had even upon occasion been the agent of their downfall.

"Of course, it was my money he loved, not me." Charissa had long ago overcome the pain of this realization, but it was still difficult to admit out loud.

"You ought not be embarrassed. We all know such a situation is common."

"But that's not the worst of it," she told him, her cheeks turning scarlet. "It's how I discovered his debased character—through a cruel practical joke."

A strange feeling suddenly overtook Will, a foreboding he couldn't quite put his finger on. "Remind me what year this was," he requested, for the first time trying to recall what he had been doing then.

"1804," she replied.

No, he thought apprehensively—it couldn't be! Could it? He tried to recall the woman's name, but wasn't able to dredge it up. It had been so long ago—and the whole thing had meant so little to him—he had completely forgotten her. Could the girl's name have been Miss Armitage?

He wasn't sure.

But there was one way to find out, so he asked, "And who was the man who betrayed you?"

"Sir Richard Lowell."

Will's stomach plummeted right down to the soles of his boots— this was a wretched development! How could it be that the young woman targeted in his disreputable scheme was his own Charissa?

How much did she know about what had happened? Surely not everything. Although he felt sick to his stomach, he hid his mortification and nodded sympathetically.

"Sir Richard asked me to marry him," she went on, unaware of his guilt-ridden thoughts, "and I accepted his proposal. I was thrilled to wed such a wonderful man—the man of my dreams. However, he hid from me his love of gambling, not to mention his other vices. I had no idea that just before we were engaged, he had lost an enormous sum to a conceited and cruel man—a viscount, the eldest son of an earl—who was famous for winning high stakes card games. Sir Richard insisted he was cheated, but others believed he lost fairly. Who knows? In any case, as I later learned, he was financially ruined."

"And so he courted you in an attempt to re-establish his fortune."

"Yes. But even so, he would not let go of his humiliation at the viscount's hands. His anger consumed him. Although not within my earshot, he continued to behave offensively toward the lord, unwisely insulting him, even goading him. Fortunately the quarrel didn't end in a duel, but Sir Richard was out of control and behaved abominably— completely past the boundaries of whatever it is that gentlemen feel is acceptable in such situations. And so at last the viscount had had enough. He decided to squash Sir Richard once and for all, and although he had never met me, he used my innocence as the instrument of his vengeance."

Charissa turned away from Will as she spoke, because the rest of the story was not really an appropriate one for a lady to tell a gentleman. And yet she wanted to share it, because it was a part of her past she felt Will ought to know.

"The whole thing was planned in advance," she explained. "It took place one evening when I went to Vauxhall Gardens with Sir Richard and his circle of friends. I was enchanted by the place, with its colonnade and maze of beautiful walkways. My party had reserved several boxes where we were served a light supper. After we had eaten, I found myself strolling through the gardens with three of Sir Richard's acquaintances. Unfortunately, these men had been instructed to separate me from the others and escort me to a certain spot in the Gardens at a precise time, specifically so that I would discover a scene instigated by the viscount himself."

"You're sure the viscount was behind it?"

"Oh, yes. It all came out in the end. He had plotted with the people involved—except, of course, Sir Richard, his victim."

"What happened?" As if Will didn't know all too well.

"My fiancé was nowhere to be found, and so I was all alone with Sir Richard's so-called friends. I remember that as we walked we came upon a quartet playing by a fountain. I sang a solo accompanied by the musicians, to great applause from my companions. Of course, they had all imbibed far too much of Vauxhall Gardens' famous arrack punch."

"It's very potent." Will knew such an intoxicant was useful when one wanted to encourage others to participate in irresponsible activities.

"But, foxed or not, they really weren't interested in the musicians or me. They were simply biding their time. At the set hour, they led me to a particularly far-off, sheltered corner of the Gardens." Will saw Charissa stiffen as she continued. "I was taken around a corner only to view a horrifying sight. A woman of low morals and my fiancé himself were engaged in…" Unable to find words modest enough to describe the scene, Charissa broke off the sentence.

"They were engaged in more than a flirtation," Will finished for her, his voice hollow.

She nodded, still facing away from him. Even now, the memory made her face burn. "Yes. I saw them. I learned later that the woman had willingly participated in the plot. As you may imagine, I was devastated, embarrassed, humiliated. While all the men laughed uproariously, I ran away in tears. I became lost on the paths and had to be escorted back to the box by strangers. Afterwards, not only did I break off the engagement, but I refused to see Sir Richard ever again. The episode became the scandal *du jour*—maybe even you heard about it, if you were in town at the time."

"I do remember the incident," Will murmured. "But I'd long ago forgotten the name of the young lady in question."

"Thank goodness," Charissa said softly. "Perhaps my identity wasn't very important to the gossips after all." She looked up at the sky, noting the clouds were thickening again. "At any rate, Sir Richard certainly became a laughing stock, but, far more seriously, his future prospects were decimated. No parents are keen on marrying their daughter to an indiscreet, penniless fool. He lost his best chance to acquire a wealthy bride. Quite the revenge for the viscount, wasn't it?"

"Effective, certainly," Will concurred.

"And that is when I decided romantic love was a mirage, a subject fit only for fiction." She took a breath, adding, "I left London as soon as I received Sir Godfrey and Lady Scrivener's invitation to live at Silvercrosse Hall."

"And you announced to the world that you would never marry," Will said.

"Yes." She couldn't meet his eyes. Did he realize how drastically her feelings had changed?

"And then," he continued, "you proceeded to write and publish stories about the marriage game using what I expect are the most felicitous of terms."

She cringed. "It sounds bizarre, I know. But somehow it helped me. I can't say why."

"But I understand, Charissa," he said kindly. "I've done something similar myself. When my brother died, I painted his portrait from memory. Not in his uniform, but as the happy young man I remembered. I lied to my father and concocted a convoluted story about how I had commissioned some else to paint it before he joined the army. My father hung the portrait in the drawing room at Hart…." Will caught himself just in time. "At his house in London."

Charissa turned to look at Will. "Painting your brother's likeness helped you work out your grief?"

"It was the only reason I survived," he answered grimly.

A roll of distant thunder caused them both to glance up at the clouds, which had darkened considerably. But neither of them wanted to leave just yet.

Taking advantage of the lull, Will turned the conversation back around to Charissa's story; there was something else he wanted—no, needed—to know. "My dear," he asked evenly, "do you know the name of the viscount your fiancé insulted?"

"Yes, of course I do," she replied, as a shadow of loathing touched her features. "He was Viscount Disborough—by all accounts, an unscrupulous, degenerate, self-consumed cad!"

Will's expression remained blank; her disgust hurt, especially because a good portion of it was deserved. "Ah," was all he said.

She noticed his tepid response. "Have you met him?" she asked sharply.

"Yes, I knew him," Will said bitterly. That he himself was the author of her tragedy made it infinitely more difficult to tell her the truth about himself. However, he would do it, he vowed—after the assembly.

As for now, a thought struck him, and he declared emphatically, "But, fortunately for us all, Disborough's dead." It was not a falsehood, at least spiritually speaking. He would explain what he really meant later.

"Oh." Charissa's eyes widened, and her voice lost its acerbity. "Dead?" She shook her head slowly. "Then he is to be pitied—for it seems he wasted his life in the pursuit of meaningless things and brought harm to others when he could have done much good. I am sorry for it."

"So am I," said Will—more sorry than she could possibly imagine. He lifted his hand and touched Charissa gently on the cheek, brushing it tenderly with his thumb. "Very sorry indeed."

Her expression softened. "Darling Will," she whispered, "let us no longer speak of him or of Sir Richard or of that dreadful time. It is over, and—truly—I am the better for it. But thank you for caring about my suffering."

Unable to find any words with which to express himself, Will simply leaned over and kissed her on the mouth. Although she couldn't know it, he silently begged for her forgiveness as his lips caressed hers. Sir Richard had certainly been a loud-mouthed bonehead, but he himself had been vindictive and in the process he had carelessly devastated the heart of a young woman who had done nothing to deserve such public shame. He would make up for that, now and forever, by loving her and protecting her every day of her life.

It was their second kiss, and even more wonderful than the first. Charissa thrilled to the warmth of his touch. No longer a woman rejected, she now belonged to the most wonderful man she'd ever met. William Lyon had resurrected her stone-dead heart at the same time as he himself had received both physical and spiritual new life. It was the perfect story, she thought—the true happy ending.

But before they could lose themselves in their passion, another clap of thunder shook the air and the rain that had been threatening all morning began to fall. Will and Charissa pulled apart at once, laughing as the drops multiplied, falling faster and faster. He opened one of the umbrellas they had brought with them and held it over her head.

"Thank you," she nodded, picking up the other umbrella and taking his arm. They both stood, and Will carefully guided her over the wet rocks to the path beside the stream. Without further conversation, they returned to the house together, both of them lost in their own thoughts of love and all its wondrous possibilities.

Chapter 18

"Simply glorious!" Charissa exclaimed as she entered the large upstairs assembly room at the Duke of Gloucester Inn the following evening. The room glowed with the light of at least a hundred candles, some of which had been paid for by Charissa herself, and when she saw their radiant effect, she was glad she had contributed them to the festive cause.

Aunt Caroline grasped her arm, scanning the premises for the most comfortable chair. "Everything is so nice. It reminds me of the dances we had here when I was young," she recalled. "We used to have such fun."

"And so we shall tonight!" Charissa replied, gazing around happily. She felt as though she had never looked prettier than she did this evening. Her rose-colored silk suited her coloring, and her hair had been curled and piled high in the latest fashion, with a tall pale-pink feather adding just the right amount of sophistication. She had seen admiration in both Will's and Sir Godfrey's expressions when she had come down the stairs at Silvercrosse, which had added to her satisfaction. The two men now stood behind her, both of them particularly handsome and dignified, Charissa thought with a thrill.

Charissa's excitement matched that of every other person in the room, which buzzed with animated voices talking and laughing in anticipation of a memorable evening. She saw Colonel and Mrs. Mainwood conversing with the Humphreys and, when she acknowledged them all with a nod of her head, both wives gave her a smile every bit as bright as those of the younger ladies in attendance.

Sir Godfrey escorted Aunt Caroline to her preferred seat, then came back to join Will and Charissa near one of the decorated tables. Charissa was telling Will that Mrs. Shaw and her girls had spent the afternoon beautifying the hall with garlands and flowers, lending the atmosphere a soft, colorful elegance. Just as she finished speaking, the objects of her story—Jane, Henrietta, and Arabella Shaw—dashed over to greet Charissa, Will, and Sir Godfrey and began chattering at once about their handiwork.

"I'm glad we are all well now. We worked for hours until we had to go home to dress for the dance," said Henrietta. "But I am not tired at all."

"Jane directed us, of course, since she has such good taste," Arabella informed them, as the oldest sister demurely cast her eyes down onto the floor. "She chose the color theme: pinks and purples, with just a few touches of yellow. Isn't it lovely?"

"You have done a marvelous job," Charissa complimented them. "And you yourselves look lovely, too."

"Thank you. We all have new gowns, of course." Arabella pirouetted gracefully. "Your gown is so very modish, Miss Armitage. And your silver cross with the ruby complements it perfectly."

"Indeed it does," Sir Godfrey, at Charissa's side, couldn't help adding.

"With whom are you opening the assembly, Miss Armitage?" asked Henrietta eagerly. "Mr. Robert Buckley has invited me."

"And I have him for the next dance," giggled Arabella.

The fresh-faced Mr. Buckley was clearly the gentleman of choice for Murrington's eligible young ladies, with the exception of nineteen-year old Jane. "Good evening, Mr. Lyon, Sir Godfrey," she said shyly, glancing at Will with rosy cheeks.

Charissa had already resolved the issue of her first dance. Sir Godfrey had insisted it was only right she partner with him, and she had consented. "I shall be standing up first with Sir Godfrey, and Mr. Lyon has requested my second dance," she told the girls.

"Of course," Jane answered hopefully, gripping her fan tightly. She looked sweet in her white muslin edged with scalloped lace.

Will felt a noble urge overtake him. "Miss Shaw," he said, "if you are not otherwise engaged, would you be so kind as to honor me with your first dance?"

Jane's eyes lit up with pleasure. "The honor is mine, sir," she replied.

A few minutes later, as musicians brought in from Stafford readied themselves to play the first tune, Charissa walked out onto the floor with Sir Godfrey. They took their places opposite each other, and she curtsied to him as the music began. At the same time, he bowed and, reaching out to her, took her gloved hands in his. They walked around each other in a circle, and he gave her a penetrating gaze signaling his intent to not give her up without a fight. She looked away from her cousin, unsure of how to respond.

The music continued, and she surreptitiously glanced at Will. In spite of the fact he was used to an environment far more refined than Murrington's, he looked superb and totally at ease. She wished she were the woman holding his hand right this very second, but she could see how thrilled Jane was to be paired with him, and she didn't begrudge the younger girl her delight.

As she and Sir Godfrey moved away from Will and Jane, she expanded her inspection to include the rest of the assembly room. Noting which of her friends were there and who was dancing with whom, she was surprised the St. Swythin sisters had not yet arrived. Surely they would appear soon.

Finally the opening number concluded, and the partners rearranged. Will came straight to Charissa and led her to the opposite side of the dance floor, far from Sir Godfrey. "I did quite well in spite of my injury," he boasted with a grin. "I would say I am hale and hearty at last. But I am keeping my capers to a minimum, just in case."

"You are the best dancer in the room," Charissa told him, her eyes twinkling, "but you must forget I mentioned it, otherwise excessive pride might cause you to stumble."

"How can I be anything other than well-pleased with myself when I am about to partner with the most stunning lady in Staffordshire, indeed in all of England?" he replied, bowing as the instruments began to play.

"Do you not remember I am immune to such flattery, sir?" she teased.

He took her hand, and they turned sideways, taking a few steps backwards then forwards. "My compliment was an awkward attempt to direct attention away from my own inexcusable self-conceit," he defended himself with a grin. As they came close together and faced one another, twirling about in a circle, his face grew thoughtful, and he said gravely, "But in all seriousness, Charissa, my love, you know full well that you hold my heart."

My love... *my love!* He had just used the sublime word! He'd confessed he loved her! She spun away from him, her emotions soaring. Everything seemed possible now. Life would never be the same— because Will loved her!

Towards the end of the dance, she looked over Will's shoulder and noticed Penelope and Helen St. Swythin had finally arrived. The sisters stood at the far end of the room with a finely dressed gentleman. Penelope lifted her head gracefully, searching for friends, while Helen whispered back and forth with their escort.

"The St. Swythins are finally here," Charissa informed Will, "with someone I've never met before. He must be the cousin from London escorting Helen to Oxfordshire."

Will turned to follow her gaze and saw the three of them close to the hall entrance. He froze momentarily.

"What is it?" Charissa asked him, pulling him back into the dance.

"I..." Will couldn't think of what to say.

"It isn't your injury, is it?"

"No, no. My leg is fine. It's that gentleman." He glanced at the St. Swythins again.

"The gentleman with Penny and Helen? Is he someone you know?"

"Yes."

"Could he cause trouble for you? He wouldn't realize that you've changed."

"No, he wouldn't."

"But, truly, what does it matter?" she pointed out. "You're a part of Murrington now. We know you."

"You don't know everything." A wave of panic crashed over Will—why in the world hadn't he told her who he really was when he'd had the chance? "Dearest, there's something I must tell you."

But it was too late. The music had stopped, and before the orchestra started to play once more, the unknown gentleman saw Will.

"Disborough!" the man said loudly. "What on earth are *you* doing here?" He strode across the room, Helen trotting after him. All eyes turned towards the stranger making his way to Will, who stood stock still, wishing he could vanish from sight. But there was nowhere to hide.

"Lord Disborough," the man said again, his nasal voice rising above the room's ambient noise. "Or I suppose I should say Lord Hartwell now, eh? What in heaven's name are you doing in this out-of-the-way spot?" He planted himself in front of Will, and the buzz of conversation around the room died down around them. The man turned his attention briefly to Charissa. "Luring the local lovelies into your arms, are you?" he sniffed. Then he glared at Will suddenly. "Or perhaps cheating at cards?"

"I never cheat, Duddridge," Will snapped.

"Disborough?" echoed Charissa at the same time, confused by the mention of that repugnant name.

Helen swept up beside the gentleman. "No, Edgar. Don't go off half-cocked. This is my friend Mr. William Lyon."

Edgar Duddridge began to laugh. "Is that what you're calling yourself here, Hartwell? I'm surprised you're not throwing your title around to impress the young ladies and their mothers." He winked at Charissa, who instinctively stepped backward.

"Title?" she responded dismissively. "You have confused Mr. Lyon with someone else."

"I think not," Edgar sneered. "Allow me, Miss, to present to you William Devreux, the former Viscount Disborough, now the Earl of Hartwell."

Charissa stood speechless, while a hum of shocked voices rose around them.

Sir Godfrey seemed to appear out of nowhere to stand next to Charissa. "Is this true, sir?" he demanded.

"Oh certainly," responded Edgar, plainly amused by it all.

"I wasn't speaking to you," Sir Godfrey said coldly. "I am addressing the man who has been enjoying my hospitality for the past seven weeks." He glowered at Will. "You will tell me the truth and nothing else. Who are you?"

There was nothing for it now but to reveal who he was. "I am William Devreux, Earl of Hartwell," Will stated.

Gasps could be heard around the hall.

Charissa's thoughts spun around madly inside her head; she couldn't believe what she was hearing, and she couldn't quite breathe. "You are... you are Lord *Disborough?* You said he was dead." None of it made any sense.

Will turned again to her. "Charissa, my darling," he said urgently, "Listen to me. The blackguard who was Lord Disborough is indeed dead. I am truly a new man!"

But Sir Godfrey let him speak no further. To the amazement of the fascinated crowd, he inserted himself physically in between Will and Charissa. His face, stained red with fury, was just inches from Will's. "You have lied to us!" he bellowed. "You have lied to me! You have lied to Charissa! No wonder you chose the name *Lyon.* Ha! What a disgusting play on words—a foul joke which has no doubt kept you laughing at us dupes all this while. But I've seen through your wicked deception right from the beginning."

"Your assumptions are erroneous," Will countered angrily, taking a step back from Sir Godfrey in an effort to keep himself from lashing out. "I am Lord Hartwell, but…"

However, Sir Godfrey cut him off again. "I care not one whit that you are a peer of the realm," he declared hotly. "You have entered my house like a serpent to seduce my bride and disgrace me, but I will allow it no longer! No, I will not!"

In his rage, Sir Godfrey raised his fist, clearly intending to strike Will. Helen shrieked. Charissa cried out, "Godfrey! No!"

But if he thought he could teach Will a lesson, Sir Godfrey had a lesson of his own coming, because he had forgotten his opponent's athleticism. Before Sir Godfrey could touch his rival, Will's trained boxer's instincts instantaneously took over. Not only did Will block Sir Godfrey's wild swing, but with a powerful punch to the jaw, he knocked the older man right to the ground.

"I've never harmed any of you!" Will shouted down at his stunned foe. "I didn't ask to be carried to your house and subjected to your pharisaical expectations. But you were never even willing to give me a chance! To you, I was always merely a vile sinner!"

Sir Godfrey gingerly touched his painful jaw, his humiliation and wrath boiling up into a rancor the likes of which he had never felt before. He looked up at Will and snarled, "Obviously, I was *right!*"

Sir Godfrey's final judgment flew like a poison-tipped arrow and hit its mark with deadly accuracy; Will felt the pain in his heart as surely as if he'd been pierced by it. Maybe Sir Godfrey was correct. Maybe William Devreux was a worthless human being after all.

Will whirled around, his eyes seeking out Charissa once more. She was staring at him, utterly shattered, and the guilt was more than he could bear. "I'm so sorry..." he began, but he couldn't continue. What could he say to her in front of these people that would explain anything?

"Oh, Will," she said miserably. He took a step towards her, but she backed away from him. "Go away," she groaned, and tears began to flow. She threw her hands over her face in despair. "Just go away!" She felt arms wrap around her and pull her close; it was Penelope.

"I think, Lord Hartwell, that you had better leave," Penelope said frostily, holding the now weeping Charissa in her arms. "Before there is even worse unpleasantness."

Sir Godfrey had recovered his composure and was now on his feet again. "You will not return to Silvercrosse Hall, Lord Hartwell. I forbid it." His voice was low and hard. "You will hire a horse from the inn and leave Murrington at once, this very hour. I shall have Jack pack up your things and send them to you. Ashbourne Park in Dorset, is it?"

Feeling like prey surrounded by predators, Will refused to display fear; instead, he took refuge behind his old devil-may-care façade. "You needn't bother sending the clothes," he replied, raising one eyebrow scornfully. "In fact, you needn't bother sending anything at all. You may even keep the money I left in my room—or, if you prefer to demonstrate your *Christian charity*," he said with heavy sarcasm, "give it to someone who could use it. It matters not to me." He then strode across the floor, the awe-struck observers parting the way for him as he went.

"Your lordship! Wait!" Helen called out, but he disregarded her. She ran over to Edgar and hissed at him words unintelligible to the rest of the crowd, but evidently what she said convinced him to reach into his waistcoat and hand her a small pouch. "Lord Hartwell!" she cried, following Will out of the hall entrance and down the stairs.

The stairwell was small and dark, but Helen put her hand out and managed to grab onto Will's coat. He whirled around abruptly, and she bumped into him. "What do you want, Miss St. Swythin?" he demanded, thrusting her back so that at least a few inches separated them.

"William," she said, her heart pounding, "you have no money to pay for your return home. Here, take this." She lifted up the soft doeskin purse.

Will's natural instinct was to reject her offering, although the truth was he had neither notes nor coins with him, and he did need cash to cover his travel expenses. But to receive money from Helen St. Swythin? He didn't want to be beholden to her for anything, ever, and furthermore, as far as he knew, she could not afford to part with a single penny. "I cannot accept it," he said brusquely, turning away.

"Please!" she insisted stubbornly, shoving it under his nose. "Don't consider it a gift, if that helps. You can pay it back if you want to."

He paused. "Very well. Thank you. I shall send back every farthing." He took the purse in his hand.

"But I don't care one way or another if you do," she claimed. "I love you, William. And I believe in you—no matter what you've said or done."

This unwelcome sentiment, on top of the pain already blistering his soul, was too much. "Goodbye, Miss St. Swythin," he said bitterly, pushing her out of his way and continuing down the stairs.

He rode out of the village on horseback a short time later, his jaw clenched and his expression hard, vowing he would never have anything to do with any of the residents of Murrington—or for that matter the whole of Staffordshire—ever again.

Chapter 19

Hartwell House, located in London's Mayfair neighborhood, felt empty and stifling— lifeless—when Will entered it after his long, ghastly journey from up north.

A fitting metaphor for himself, he thought darkly.

The skeleton staff hid their surprise at his unexpected arrival, springing into action to make the new earl as comfortable as possible. Although they capably saw to his needs, privately they worried over his appearance. He looked haggard and worn, the dark circles under his eyes giving away his lack of sleep for the past few days. Although it was early evening, he went straight upstairs to what had been his father's bedroom, undressed, and collapsed onto the bed, falling into an exhausted sleep.

The footman acting as his valet threw the almost unrecognizable evening kit he had been wearing into the dustbin.

When Will awoke the next morning, well after noon, he felt hot. No cool breeze came in the window, just the heat and noise of the city, which had long since begun its workday. No little white dogs barked outside, ready to play—there were only the yelps and growls of street mongrels fighting for their share of the refuse left behind by others.

And no sweet smile and ready laugh awaited him downstairs.

Charissa.

He groaned out loud and rolled over. The look in her eyes the last time he had seen her haunted him: confusion, betrayal, bitter disappointment.

He couldn't stand it. He couldn't stand himself.

He had to forget her; he had to numb the pain. But how?

He crawled out of bed and called for the valet. "I am going out tonight, and I need suitable clothes. Send for my things from the townhouse on Weymouth Street, since I will be selling it soon anyway."

"Yes, m'lord," the man replied, and by evening, Will was dressed acceptably and on the way to one of his clubs.

When he came home again, at dawn, he was three—maybe four—sheets to the wind. After spending some time being violently sick, he fell into bed again and slept until midafternoon. Then he repeated the sordid cycle, adding to his itinerary a visit to Gentleman John Jackson's, where he knocked senseless no less than three other would-be boxing champions.

And on it went.

However, a week later, when he woke up with the usual fierce headache, for some reason the thought of doing the same wretched thing again and again and again just plain revolted him.

There had to be more to life than this.

He lay on his back and stared up at the tawny yellow canopy arching over the enormous black lacquer bed.

God, create a clean heart for me.

Where had that thought come from? Will took a deep breath and remained quiet. From somewhere, a stream of cool air wafted over him gently.

God, create a clean heart for me and renew a steadfast spirit within me. Do not banish me from your presence or take your Holy Spirit from me. Restore the joy of your salvation to me, and sustain me by giving me a willing spirit.

Now Will remembered—those verses were from Psalm Fifty-One, one of the Scriptures he had read over and over since the night he'd told God he believed in Him. Read, that is, until his hasty departure from Silvercrosse Hall. Now, he didn't even know where a Bible was.

There must be one somewhere in the house, he surmised. He would have to try to find it. But he would do so later. Now he just wanted to savor the first moment of peace he'd had in a week. A long, grim week.

When he finally rose, he went down to the dining room for

something substantial to put in his stomach. He felt better after he ate, but as the day turned into evening, the inevitable frustrations of his lonely life conspired with his internal fragility to wear him down. In the end, he gave in again to the temptation to escape from his pain by losing himself in the world.

He went out into the night—and ended up winning, then losing, and at last winning a modest amount of money in a series of ignominious card games. After that, he met up with some of his former companions and together with them drank copious amounts of *blood and thunder*, which was a strong mixture of port wine and brandy.

As he sat listening to them tell crass—and mostly untrue—tales of their depravity, he felt disgusted by their idiocy, even as foxed as he was. He stared down at the reddish brown liquid in his glass and despised himself. *Help me*, his heart whispered. *Oh God, help me.*

Immediately, however, another voice jeered in the back of his mind, challenging the very assumption that God was there, and even if He were, that He would listen, that He cared. The Divine Puppeteer—this taunting interlocutor suggested—had amused Himself by dangling a remarkable woman in front of Will's eyes, only to withdraw her at the moment best calculated to rip his soul to shreds.

The Old Testament reading from the last Sunday in Murrington rose up in Will's memory as if to mock him: *For you, Lord, bless the righteous one; you surround him with favor like a shield.* Bless? Favor? Shield? Will tasted bile, and abruptly he picked up his drinking glass and threw it across the room. It shattered into a thousand satisfying shards, the liquor inside it staining the wall like blood. He stared at the mess with glazed-over eyes.

The other men started and swore at the unexpected sound. They began to a lively and detailed discussion of Will's wretchedness, deciding after some debate that the best solution for his bad attitude was a woman.

So without telling him what they were about, they dragged him up and out of the building, hiring a hackney coach once they were out on the street. The coach took them to the theatre district, but it didn't stop at one of the playhouses; instead, it rounded a corner and halted in front of an unobtrusive, well-kept house that looked just like any number of respectable dwellings in town.

Except this one was not at all respectable.

The men exited the hack and gave the cabbie a generous fare. Will, who was paying absolutely no attention to where he was being led, went with them up to the commonplace front door. But when they were ushered inside and shown into a gaudily appointed parlor, it suddenly occurred to him he just might want to inquire as to the nature of this establishment.

"Figured you hadn't been here before, Hartwell," chortled one of his sidekicks in answer to his question. "You've never come with us on these little jaunts."

"Fastidious prig," mumbled another.

It was true Will had never been able to stomach the idea of paying a woman for pleasure; the thought repelled him. He was ready to lurch toward the door and make his escape, when a lavishly dressed middle-aged madam entered, accompanied by several attractive younger women.

The older woman introduced her employees and departed. The other gentlemen paired off with the girls, leaving one of them for Will. She came over to him and smiled.

He gazed at her, his emotions raw. She looked nothing like Charissa, he thought dully; she was overly blonde, short, with large, pouty, unnaturally red lips. "Good evening," she said softly, prettily fluttering her eyelashes.

That nasty voice in his mind piped up again, urging him to take advantage of the situation. Surely he needed the physical indulgence she was offering him. Didn't he deserve a fleeting moment of exhilaration in the midst of his pointless existence?

"Let's go upstairs," the girl proposed, her fingers caressing his sleeve.

But another Voice spoke, to his heart this time—*Will.*

All he heard was his own name, yet it felt like a fresh wind blowing in his face or a cup of water on a hot day. He turned his head away from the girl, listening for the Voice, his soul hungry.

Will.

The lady-bird moved her body closer to his, whispering something suggestive. Her perfume was sultry, even intoxicating, but instead of enflaming his desire, it made him queasy. He put his hand on hers and lifted it up off of his person.

"Forgive me," he said firmly, releasing her. "I was brought here under false pretenses, and I have no intention of accepting your services." Even though he was still drunk, he was surprised how noble and resolute he sounded.

The girl was not pleased, however, and she reached out again to tantalize him with her touch and seductive words.

"No, miss," he repeated, taking a step away from her. His head ached, and his nausea deepened. "It's nothing personal, I assure you, but I shall be taking my leave."

Her sulky disappointment darkened her expression and motivated him to move as quickly as he could manage to the parlor door. He had one last glimpse of the girl stomping her foot petulantly as he turned the handle and stumbled out. He ran through the entry hall as if pursued by a monster and charged out of the house onto the street, where he was promptly sick to his stomach.

After he finished his violent retching, he stood up and wiped his mouth with his handkerchief, afterwards throwing the lacy bit of linen on the ground. He realized his new, expensive hat had fallen off his head as he'd bolted out of the call house, but nothing on earth could have persuaded him to reenter that obscene place. So he staggered down the road looking for a hackney to take him home, yet for some bizarre reason—considering there would be theatre patrons needing transportation soon—he couldn't find a single coach. He fell against a wall and closed his eyes, unable to move for several long minutes.

At last, he heard a few hackneys clip-clop by him, heading for the nearby theatres. He wanted to hail one, but he discovered that he wasn't physically capable of such vigorous movement; on the contrary, when he tried, he simply threw up again.

But he desperately wanted to get home, so after a minute or two, he forced himself to stagger around the nearest corner. He saw he was about a block from one of playhouses, which had just begun to release its audience after a show. Concerned some of the playgoers might recognize him, Will stayed well back in the shadows, leaning against a faux column attached to the stone edifice towering above him. When the crowd had dispersed, he reasoned, he would find an empty coach. He hoped in the meantime he wouldn't be noticed, and, fortunately, no one paid him any attention.

Until, that is, a nicely dressed couple walked by in search of a hackney.

Just as the pedestrian glanced at Will, Will turned his face toward the man. They locked eyes and instantly recognized each other.

"Diz!" exclaimed the man in disbelief. "Is that you?"

"Barney?" Will groaned in surprise; there weren't too many people who would call him by his old Oxford moniker. What was Barnabas Worthington doing here, of all people, of all places? Wasn't he supposed to be in Italy with his sick wife? Who was the healthy-looking woman on his arm?

Barnabas moved closer to Will. "What on earth happened to you? Do you need help?"

Thinking the answer to this was obvious, Will made a grunting noise and nodded.

Barnabas grabbed onto Will's arm and helped him stand straight. Will was able to remain upright as long as he kept his hand pressed onto the column, and with as much dignity as he could muster given his slightly slurred words, he asked, "Would you be so good as to hail me a hackney, old man?"

"I will," Barnabas said, taking in Will's sorry condition at a glance. "But we're coming with you to ensure you actually arrive at your destination in one piece."

Will flicked his eyes towards the woman, who had come up beside Barnabas. In outward appearance—strangely enough—she resembled the temptress whom Will had just avoided, blonde and petite. However, in every way that counted, she was completely unlike her fallen counterpart. In fact, something about her reminded him of Charissa. Perhaps it was her eyes.

"No need to inconvenience you, Barney," Will said, his fingers slipping on the column a little. "But if you will find a hack to drop me off at Hartwell House, I'd be much obliged."

"At Hartwell House?" the woman asked.

"Oh, pardon me, darling," Barnabas replied, as if they were in a ballroom and not on the streets. "I haven't made introductions. This is Viscount Disborough, eldest son of the Earl of Hartwell. Diz, this is my wife, Mrs. Susannah Worthington."

"Actually," Will corrected him, "my father died a couple of months ago. I'm Hartwell now."

"I'm sorry to hear it," Barnabas responded. "My deepest sympathies."

"And mine as well," Susannah added. "However, be that as it may, you are certainly…er…ill. I shall only consent to send you alone to your house, Lord Hartwell, if Lady Hartwell is there to receive you, and not just servants, however skilled and loyal they may be."

Will stared at her; even if he'd had a wife, he certainly wouldn't have presented himself to her in his current state. He felt another wave of sickness, although it was less severe than before. "I have no wife," he said weakly, closing his eyes.

"That settles it," declared Barnabas, glancing meaningfully at Susannah. "We are not dropping you off at Hartwell House. You are coming home with us." Will was in no condition to argue with his old friend, and therefore, without delay, Barnabas found a coach to take the three of them back to the Worthington residence.

They spoke little on the way, and Will was grateful. He was also able to repress his nausea, the contents of his stomach having long since been emptied. He was barely aware of their arrival at a nice house in a pleasant neighborhood, and of going upstairs, undressing, and falling into bed. As soon as his head hit the pillow, he fell into a very-much-needed long, sound sleep.

Chapter 20

When he awoke the next day, he had the expected headache, but he remembered the events of the previous evening quite clearly. It floored him he had run into the Worthingtons outside the theatre. What a strange coincidence.

And yet, perhaps it was not so coincidental after all. Had he not prayed for God to help him? True, the prayer hadn't been a formal supplication on his knees in a church—quite the opposite, in fact—but it had come from his heart. *The sacrifice pleasing to God is a broken spirit. You will not despise a broken and humbled heart, God.*

Slowly he rose and sat on the edge of the bed. Then he stood up gingerly and walked over to a washbasin sitting on a small table, where he splashed his face with cool water. Just as he was wondering what in the world he was going to wear, he heard the door to his room open and was surprised to see his valet from Hartwell House come in with a suit of his own clothes.

"Good afternoon, m'lord," the man said calmly. "Mr. Worthington sent for me and asked me to bring along whatever you might need."

So Will dressed and—looking almost unrecognizably better from the night before—went downstairs to search out his hosts. He found them together in a sitting room, where they made him welcome. He sat down opposite them in a comfortable chair.

"I hope you slept well, Diz," Barnabas said congenially. "I put you in the quietest room in the house, although it's smaller than the other guest rooms."

Barnabas' continued use of his university nickname amused Will, and he grinned. "A benevolence I don't deserve, Barney, but one for which I am nonetheless grateful," he replied truthfully.

"It seems you're feeling better, Lord Hartwell," Susannah observed. "I'm glad—I was worried about you."

"And I'm happy to see you well, Mrs. Worthington," Will answered. "I was told that you were very ill and had to be taken to Italy. Wherever you went, it must have been a salubrious place indeed."

She looked at him patiently. "I've never been out of England, I'm afraid. I am Barnabas' *second* wife."

Embarrassed by his ignorance, Will said, "A thousand pardons, ma'am."

Barnabas waved Will's shame away. "No need to apologize. How could you have known? You see, Phoebe died soon after we arrived in Sicily. I returned to England thereafter, and I only made it as far as London, for that is where I met the widowed Mrs. Susannah Elwood." He gave his wife a warm smile. "I married her straightaway, and we have been a great comfort to one another."

"My sincerest best wishes to both of you," Will said. But it hurt to see the obvious affection between them.

"God has been gracious to us," Susannah confirmed.

"For you, Lord, bless the righteous one; you surround him with favor like a shield." The words came out of Will's mouth before he thought. But why had he recalled that verse? He hated that verse, didn't he?

Barnabas gave Will a probing look. "Yes, exactly," he said.

"Are you a student of God's Word?" Susannah asked.

Wasn't the answer obvious? Will lowered his head. "No." There was a short silence, but instead of feeling unworthy, he sensed a wave of comfort flow all around him, encircling him like a warm cloak. Encouraged, he raised his eyes. "But I want to be."

"Truly?" his old friend inquired, not sure what to think.

"Yes. Yes, it's true." Will did not hesitate—he meant it with everything in him. "I want to know the Scriptures."

"I'm so pleased, Diz." Barnabas raised his fingers to his chin and stroked it thoughtfully. After a second or two, he exchanged a look with his wife, and both of them smiled.

"Well then," Barnabas addressed Will, "might I suggest you stay with us for a week or two? I can explain some important passages in the Bible and answer questions you may have about faith in Christ. Is that acceptable to you?"

"Most agreeable," Will replied, floored he would receive such an invitation.

"Excellent," Barnabas stated, pleased.

"I'm glad you'll be staying with us, Lord Hartwell," Susannah put in. "You will discover my husband is very knowledgeable about the things of the Lord. Yes, I can see that our encounter has been no accident. Barnabas and I rarely attend the theatre; we were given tickets for last night's performance of *Hamlet*. But more than entertainment was afoot—indeed, the three of us have experienced a divinely ordained appointment!"

Having succinctly summed up the whole situation, she smiled again at Will. "I shall go and make the necessary arrangements for your accommodations. And I must also look in on the children." She stood up and excused herself from the room, leaving Will and Barnabas to speak with each other privately.

"She brought three boys to our marriage," Barnabas explained. "Rather a challenge for me, as you might imagine, but they're dear little fellows. I also hope to have a few of my own someday. Susannah and I are working on that," he added with a wink.

But Will was unable to reciprocate his friend's good humor, and when Barnabas saw Will's pained expression, he leaned forward in his chair, concerned. "All right—enough chitchat. What happened to you?" he asked. "Why in the world were you out on the streets alone last night, as drunk as a wheelbarrow and indistinguishable from a derelict? A bad spot, even for you."

Will wanted to tell him, but his tongue felt as twisted as an old toad's.

"I know it's difficult to talk about the things deep down inside our souls, Diz," Barnabas said sympathetically. "We always think we have to appear strong and confident and above it all. I daresay that's true with the world at large, but I'm convinced it shouldn't be that way between friends."

Will nodded, but couldn't still couldn't broach the subject.

"Why don't I go first?" Barnabas proposed, sitting back again and crossing his legs at the knee. "My story will prove to you I'm a weak and sinful man, in need of God's grace every bit as much as anyone."

"What rot!" Will exclaimed. "You were always head-and-shoulders above the rest of us, Barney."

"That's not saying a great deal!" Barnabas laughed ruefully. "But you know nothing about my life over the past decade. Permit me to enlighten you."

Although Will couldn't imagine his old acquaintance had been so very bad, he agreed to listen to the story and was astonished as Barnabas openly confessed his struggles.

Barnabas' first wife had been a cold, standoffish woman with a large fortune; they had wed in an effort to please both their families. However, even though Barnabas had studied theology and made a public profession of faith, his deep unhappiness with the marriage led him into an extramarital affair. For a while he was able to justify his actions to himself, but when his wife became consumptive—and her condition worsened as a result of his neglect—he repented of his adultery and vowed to be a faithful, caring husband once more.

"After my wife died in Italy," he concluded, "I returned to England determined to live a life worthy of the Savior who had forgiven me. Miraculously, I met Susannah, whom I absolutely do not deserve, but a few months ago I married her anyway."

Will appreciated Barnabas' honesty, but, seeing his friend's contentment, he could not help an unpleasant twinge of jealousy. "At least your story has a happy ending."

"And yours does not, I take it?"

"'Tis a tragedy with a fool for a protagonist," Will said glumly.

"Tell me."

And Will did. Barnabas was a good listener—neither condemning nor patronizing—and he asked appropriate questions. When Will finished at last, he felt unexpectedly better. The hard knot inside his stomach had begun to unwind.

"I'm sorry," Barnabas said quietly. "Miss Armitage sounds like a lovely woman."

"She is," Will replied, then added bitterly, "and I ruined her life. Twice."

"I think *ruined* is too strong a word."

"I don't!"

"But you say that she is a woman of great faith. If that's so, her life is in hands far superior to your own."

"What do you mean?"

"You may rest assured that God has a plan to prosper her, even in her sorrow. As the psalmist wrote: *weeping may stay overnight, but there is joy in the morning.*"

Will remained silent, staring at the floor and trying to comprehend this novel idea.

"The best thing you can do is leave her in His care and concentrate on drawing close to Him yourself," Barnabas suggested. "Such a undertaking won't be as simple as I'm making it sound, of course, but you may just find life is still worth living."

In spite of everything, Will felt an upsurge of hope. He was certainly tired of feeling sorry for himself day in and day out. Perhaps Barnabas was right; perhaps there was a better way to live. Will lifted his head and declared boldly, "I'm ready to meet the challenge. Tell me where to begin."

Barnabas reached over and clasped Will's hand. "Let's begin with the Gospel of St. John," he said.

Will stayed with the Worthingtons for a little over two weeks and spent much of his time with Barnabas discussing spiritual matters. Susannah treated him graciously, and her young sons provided an entertaining distraction. They all went to church together on Sunday mornings and evenings; interestingly for Will, it was a nonconformist congregation. He missed the liturgy to which he was accustomed, but he liked what the minister had to say, and he felt welcomed by the parishioners, who came from all walks of life.

After he returned to Hartwell House, he continued to meet with Barnabas for fellowship and study. He also assiduously avoided his old haunts and the men lurking there who had pulled him back into his former lifestyle.

Moreover, he began a project which he kept secret from everyone but which gave him a surprising outlet for some of his still-raw emotions. When for the first time he entered the study which had been his father's, its wooden paneling and paintings of horses reminded him of the Menagerie Room at Silvercrosse Hall. Grief gripped his insides, and he sat down at the mahogany desk, resting his elbows on it and putting his head in his hands.

He didn't stay in this position for long, however; he pulled himself together and decided instead to open the desk drawers and examine their contents. In one drawer he found a thick stack of fine paper and in another several expensive quills and accompanying bottles of ink. Bringing them all out and setting them on top of the table, he automatically filled one of the pens and began to sketch.

First, he made a quick drawing of Sprite, labeling it *Mr. Pettmee.* Pleased with it, he added Commodore, whose soulful dark eyes stared unblinkingly up from the page.

He wondered if he could draw Charissa.

Yes, he remembered every detail of her face and form. He took out a new sheet of paper and refilled the pen. Quickly sketching, he saw her appear before his eyes, her soft wavy hair and her engaging smile flawlessly captured.

As he stared down at her lovely face, he remembered what she had said: *Painting your brother's likeness helped you to work out your grief.* Yes, it was true—not so very long ago he had been comforted by drawing the brother he'd lost. *How strange*, he mused once again, *that such an exercise lessens rather than increases the pain of one's loss.* Perhaps creating an extraordinary portrait of Charissa herself would bring him some measure of peace.

So that very day he went out and purchased an easel, a canvas, a wooden frame, pencils, brushes, and an assortment of high-quality oil paints. Thinking unrepentantly how shocked the late earl would have been, he set them up in the study and began to work. As he painted carefully hour by hour and day by day, he began to bring to life the woman he loved.

Perhaps, he thought as he applied himself to his task, this was his way not only to grieve but also to give Charissa over to God. He was not building an altar of stone and fire and blood, as found in the Old Testament, but one of texture and color and tears.

After another few weeks, Barnabas informed Will that he and his family would soon be making the journey to the Worthington estate in Cheshire. He had not been there for over a year, and, he pointed out unnecessarily, the London summer heat was now unbearable. Furthermore, he wanted the boys to enjoy more healthful pursuits in the countryside. Clearly, Will realized, the Worthingtons had stayed in the city far longer than they had wanted to in order to support him in his new Christian walk.

"Come up north with us," Barnabas requested at the last dinner they shared together, and Susannah echoed the invitation. "Do come," she repeated warmly. "I know the boys would enjoy your company as well as we would."

"No, I'm afraid I cannot, although I thank you from the bottom of my heart," Will declined, thinking he would rather not travel so close to Murrington. Anyway, he knew another journey was required of him. "I have suspected for a while now it is time to go home. To Ashbourne Park, I mean."

Barnabas nodded. "Yes, you are ready. I admit that I've been afraid to turn you back over the world—but you are growing so solidly in your faith, I trust you to be diligent to test all things and hold on to what is good."

"We can only hope so," Will said dryly, secretly gratified by his friend's encouragement.

A week later, Will found himself riding in his carriage up the long, majestic drive to his ancestral home. How life had changed since he had departed from this place in a whirlwind of self-condemnation and regret.

Or, more to the point, how he had changed.

The staff became noticeably energized the instant he walked in the door; the news he had returned spread throughout the estate like wildfire. The dignified Dibbs tried to contain his enthusiasm, but Will could tell the man was thrilled to have something to do at last.

The butler and housekeeper fussed over Will shamelessly—a situation which only months before would have annoyed him, but now made him smile to himself.

However, he had something else on his mind. "Where is the Dowager Countess?" he inquired. He had written to her once from London, but had said little in his note, and her reply to it had been a masterpiece of cautious understatement.

"She has removed to the dower house, my lord," the housekeeper informed him.

"Ah yes," responded Will, wishing that she had not. "I think I'll take a stroll down there to visit her."

"Very good, my lord," said the butler, who rushed to find Will's hat and hand it to him.

As Will made his way down the shady path to the substantial house built in the last century specifically for his widowed grandmother, he felt unsure of what he would say when he saw his stepmother. Had she changed her mind about not blaming him for his father's death? Would his presence remind her he lived, while her natural son—Edward—had died? Did she resent leaving her sumptuous home and exchanging it for a less exalted place?

When he was almost at his destination, he saw a figure coming toward him, moving swiftly up the gravel walkway. He stopped short; it was the Dowager Countess.

What was she doing? She must have been told immediately upon his arrival he was here. He watched in amazement as she ran up to him, breathless.

"Will!" she greeted him, forcing herself to behave with restraint. "Oh son, I'm so glad to see you." Her eyes were moist, her smile hesitant.

A tenderness he'd never allowed himself to feel before overtook him as he looked at the gracious lady standing in front of him—the only mother he'd ever known. The woman who had been unfailingly kind to him, even as he had pushed her away time and time again. "I've come home," he said, his voice cracking.

And he pulled her into his arms.

Chapter 21

Charissa sighed as the mail coach in which she was riding approached Murrington. True, part of her longed to return to Silvercrosse Hall—it had been months since she had slept in her own bed. The cooler winds of October were blowing, and she was weary of visiting a long succession of Mrs. Humphreys' family members and friends.

But coming home also meant she had to face Sir Godfrey—and give him an answer to the all-important question he had asked her before she had left.

After the dreadful night of the assembly, Sir Godfrey had tried to comfort her, but his angry humiliation had made the whole nightmare harder for her to bear. They had had a terrible argument about the dog pictures Will had drawn; Sir Godfrey had wanted to burn them, but Charissa had insisted on keeping them on the walls. Sir Godfrey finally relented because Sprite and Commodore were so dear to her, but he continued to fume. Indeed, the nasty bruise on his jaw paled in comparison to his wounded pride.

Charissa herself experienced a gamut of emotions: first, stunned disbelief that Will had deceived her so boldly; then acute sorrow; and, finally, fury that he had played her for a fool. How could she have been so stupid as to let the scenario from London happen all over again? She had thought herself steady and wise, when she was nothing but immature and gullible.

And the conclusion she drew from it all—again—was the obvious one: romance was a farce. She abandoned her writing for the time being, hoping that her publisher would forgive her. Putting away her notebooks, she told herself darkly if she wrote anything in her current frame of mind, she would probably leave her hero in the *oubliette* until he rotted.

Furthermore, although she kept the pictures of the dogs in the Menagerie Room, she removed from sight any other reminder of Will. The image he had drawn of her she stuffed beneath her pile of least favorite gloves. Perhaps one day she would frame it and give it to Sir Godfrey, but not any time soon. She also retrieved the Bible she had given Will, the one which had belonged to her aunt, and returned it to Sir Godfrey's library. After putting it up on the tallest, most hidden shelf, she had collapsed in a heap on the floor and cried until she'd had no more tears left to shed.

And, to top it all off, a letter had arrived for Sir Godfrey from London, informing him that Ashbourne Park in Dorset was the seat of the Earl of Hartwell. The current earl, Sir Godfrey's friend wrote, was known for his unsavory lifestyle.

It had been a very difficult time.

In a true act of mercy, Mrs. Humphreys came to her rescue. The rector's wife had been planning on visiting relatives in Yorkshire for the late summer and autumn, and she invited Charissa to join her as a travelling companion. Both Sir Godfrey and Penelope encouraged Charissa to go, and she accepted the distraction with thankfulness.

But not long into the trip—with a few weeks and many miles now between her and the catastrophic assembly—Charissa began to have second thoughts. She started to wonder if maybe, just maybe, she had misjudged Will. As she looked back on that painful evening, her shock and resentment began to subside, and she recalled Will's response to the situation more clearly. He had seemed sincere in the moments he had tried to explain himself, before he had transformed into a sardonic rogue she didn't recognize.

Perhaps the circumstances weren't as grim as she had imagined them to be. Perhaps Will was not the monster she had assumed he was. In spite of all her previous cynical thoughts, she indulged herself in a few days of hope—until she received Helen's letter.

From her cousin's home in Oxfordshire, Helen had written:

My dearest friend in all the world, Charissa,

I miss you so very, very much and wish you were with me enjoying the delights of this place. You would especially appreciate the extensive gardens, and the woodlands are lovely. As you might imagine, Agnes and I spend most of our days painting. She is undertaking a series of wildflower illustrations, whilst I have chosen mushrooms as my subjects. They have amusing names, like fool's webcap, jelly tooth, *and* soapy knight.

Penelope informed me you are now in Sheffield with Mrs. Humphreys, though I daresay you would rather be here commiserating with me after our frightful ordeal at the Murrington assembly. I could see how devastated you were. I am so glad I left the next morning, before I was forced to endure the inevitable wagging tongues discussing your humiliation ad nauseum. *I expect the whole village was talking about how you pinned your hopes on a lothario who wouldn't have married you.*

As for me, I am astonished that Mr. Lyon was really LORD DISBOROUGH (now Lord Hartwell)—the very same man whose scheme shamed you six years ago! You must surely be relieved to have disentangled yourself from that villain's clutches, and I have some news that will confirm your providential escape. My cousin Mr. Duddridge wrote to me from London, and he told me when Lord Hartwell returned to town, he straightaway took to carousing wildly, drinking, and fighting. Furthermore, although I am ashamed to even mention such a thing, he said that Lord Hartwell has been seen visiting a house of ill-repute! It is shameful, and goodness knows I am reluctant to write it down, yet I am convinced it is better for you to know the truth….

So much for the authenticity of Will's conversion. Charissa wept with disappointment and burned the letter. She determined once and for all to put the memory of Will clean out of her head. Forever.

And now, today, she had to put her money where her mouth was, so to speak; she had to give Sir Godfrey an answer. She shifted in her seat, and Mrs. Humphreys turned to her. "Almost there now," the older woman commented knowingly.

"Things are beginning to look familiar," Charissa agreed.

"Sir Godfrey will be so happy to see you."

"And I him." It was true she had missed him, even though she wasn't at all sure she was ready to take the next step.

But she had no doubt *he* was. Before she had left on her trip, Sir Godfrey had spoken to her privately. "Charissa," he said, "whilst you are away, I would ask you to consider something."

Her eyes were still as sad as they had been the day after that cursed assembly. "And what is that?"

His heart melted, but he steeled himself to appear dispassionate, calm, in control. "I shall speak to you plainly. I want you, my dearest, to marry me."

He watched in dismay as her eyes filled with tears. "Oh, Godfrey."

"You need say nothing now," he interrupted swiftly. "I know you are struggling with your emotions, as women are wont to do in such circumstances. But as you bring reason to bear upon this situation, you would do well to consider your future. I know you are not in financial need, but as my wife, you will have a godly and faithful husband to protect you as well as the security of a beautiful home. And someday, of course—God willing—children."

He was regarding her with particular intensity, and she felt confused. All those things were good; she desired them all. And yet...

He leaned closer to her. "You must know, my darling, that I love you deeply."

Charissa felt faint. "I...I must pray about this," she stammered.

He seized her hands. "I know well what the Lord would say to you. *It is not good for the man*—or the woman—*to be alone.*" He raised her fingers to his lips and kissed them. "We shall speak again when you return."

And so during the weeks of her absence from Silvercrosse Hall, Charissa had considered his proposal. True, her prayers seemed to bounce off the ceiling, and she received no divine revelation, but whenever she was afforded solitude, she took the opportunity to examine her heart and mind on the matter.

She cared for Sir Godfrey, of that she was certain. He was kind and sensible, and his faith was an important part of his life. He was a physically attractive man, and although he was quite a bit older than she was, such matches were not uncommon. That they were related posed no obstacle, because, to be precise, he was her second half-cousin, once removed; his grandfather had been the half brother of her great-grandmother. Most importantly, however, he was not merely a distant relative, but an old family friend.

And yet, try as she might, she had not been able to forget Will Devreux, Viscount Disborough, Earl of Hartwell. As angry as she was with him, he had left a gaping wound in her heart that still—against all odds—felt suspiciously like love. Several times she found herself praying for him when she should have been lifting up her prospective marriage to Sir Godfrey. Irritated with herself, she would resolve to put Will's memory aside, only to be reminded of their time together by some seemingly trivial sight, such as a little white dog or a gazebo.

And yet the reality was that he was gone, truly lost to her, never to be seen again. The man she loved didn't really exist.

So what would she say to Sir Godfrey? She still had no idea.

When the four-in-hand arrived in Murrington—right on time— Mr. Humphreys and Sir Godfrey were waiting at the inn, and as Charissa stepped out of the coach behind Mrs. Humphreys, Sir Godfrey greeted her with a large bouquet of deep-red hothouse roses in his hand. "Charissa!" he exclaimed with all the fervor of a devoted lover. "My darling, welcome home!" It was clear which answer to his proposal he expected her to give.

Mrs. Humphreys cast a glance their way even as she greeted her husband, and Charissa knew the village grapevine would be embellishing the scene before sunset. Everyone would be anticipating an announcement in the next day or two and the first of the banns to be read the very next Sunday.

After Charissa's trunk had been loaded onto Sir Godfrey's carriage, the two of them bade goodbye to the Humphreys and set out on the short drive to Silvercrosse Hall. Inside the coach, Sir Godfrey sat next to her instead of across from her, where the flowers now lay.

He took her hand in his. "Dearest, I have missed you so."

"I've missed you, too," she replied honestly. "Mrs. Humphreys is an amiable travelling companion, but I'm glad to be home."

"I was right to encourage you to take some time away."

She gave him a small smile. "You were."

"And have you given thought to my proposal?"

"A great deal of thought. And prayer."

Sir Godfrey said nothing. When she did not continue, he forged ahead. "I cannot wait one moment longer—I must speak now. You say you have considered the question I put to you before you left. That being the case, I now formally ask you to make me the happiest man in the world. Charissa, will you consent to be my bride?"

An image of Will flashed through her mind, but she consciously rejected it. In his place she concentrated on Sir Godfrey, who was so close that she could see his jaw tense in anticipation of her answer.

And what would that answer be? In the end, she knew, there was only one sensible reply, the one he assumed he would hear. "Yes," she said quietly, staring at his fingers, which had become entwined with hers. "I will marry you."

His face lit up with joy. Pulling her into his arms, even as the coach bumped along the road, he found her lips with his and kissed her. Finding the sensation pleasurable, she returned his demonstration of affection. It was not quite the way she had felt when Will kissed her—but, of course, Sir Godfrey didn't need to know that.

Chapter 22

Aunt Caroline lit up when Charissa and Sir Godfrey walked into the sitting room. "Oh Charissa, I am so glad to see you, dear! I've missed you—and I've missed that kind, handsome man who is so in love with you. Where is he?"

Charissa paled, but she kissed Aunt Caroline on the cheek.

Sir Godfrey frowned impatiently. "There is no such man. You remember, I'm sure," he prodded his aunt. "At the assembly a few months ago. We discovered he is a charlatan and a bounder. He is long gone, gratifying his lusts elsewhere."

Aunt Caroline shook her head. "I liked him," she retorted stubbornly. "And he loves Charissa."

"*I* love Charissa, Aunt Caroline," Sir Godfrey said crossly, "and she is going to be *my* wife! She has accepted my offer of marriage."

Aunt Caroline looked confused. "She has? I thought you were married to Dorcas."

Sir Godfrey's temper died away as quickly as it had come. "Dorcas has been dead for years," he said with a sigh. "Soon *Charissa* will be Lady Scrivener."

"Oh," murmured Aunt Caroline, closing her eyes.

Sir Godfrey moved away and put his hand on Charissa's waist. "Come, darling," he directed her, "let us take a turn about the garden."

Late summer had woven the outdoors into a beautiful tapestry of deep, rich hues, and now the glories of autumn crowned the year with scarlet, titian, and gold. It seemed to Charissa an eternity since spring;

so much had happened, and she herself had changed irrevocably. Like the colors of the seasons, she mused, her own life had moved from the pale white of winter to the light pastels of spring and finally to the more mature and darker—yet richer—tones of the harvest.

"Shall the first of the banns be read this Sunday?" she asked Sir Godfrey as they made their way together along the path, knowing he would be keen to get the process leading up to the wedding underway.

"Ordinarily, I would say yes," he replied. "But I have a proposal of another kind to make to you. It will delay the wedding a few weeks, but I hope you won't be too disappointed, darling. Of course, if you disapprove of my plan, I'll abandon it at once."

This was not the reply Charissa was expecting. "What is so important you would postpone the wedding?" she asked, more curious than upset.

Sir Godfrey lifted his chin just a bit higher into the air. "I have been asked to deliver a sermon in London at Grosvenor Chapel."

"Oh, Godfrey, that's wonderful!" she exclaimed. "How did this come about?"

"The answer to that question involves another bit of good news. Three weeks ago a letter was delivered here from Mr. Harold Morris of Morris and Sons Printing."

"From Mr. Morris? Why didn't you forward it me?"

He paused for dramatic effect. "The letter was addressed to me."

"Godfrey," she said, her eyes brightening, "are you saying what I think you are?"

"If you are thinking I am about to be a published author," Sir Godfrey beamed, "you are correct. Mr. Morris has agreed to print my sermons in a two-volume set!"

Thrilled, she looked up at him. "That's marvelous! I'm so proud of you—well done!"

"Thank you, my love."

"And how does this happy situation relate to your preaching at Grosvenor Chapel?"

"It so happens Mr. Morris also publishes the writings of a well-known scholar of divinity, the Reverend Dr. S. J. Seymour."

"Oh, yes." Charissa recognized the name.

"Dr. Seymour is to be the featured speaker for a four-day convocation entitled *The Greatest of These* which will be held at Grosvenor Chapel," Sir Godfrey explained. "He will instruct a smaller group of select participants during the daytime, but in the evenings he will preach for the general public. Each night there will also be an introductory sermon given by a guest speaker. These speakers were selected months ago, of course, but the scholar who had been scheduled to deliver the opening sermon on the final evening has fallen ill and will be unable to participate. Mr. Morris, who is on the committee responsible for the convocation, suggested I be asked to preach in his stead."

"And the committee agreed to invite you!"

"They did. Happily, another gentleman sponsoring the convocation—an old friend of mine from my Cambridge days—vouched for me as well."

"So when is this gathering?"

"In about two weeks. And my proposal to you is, of course, that you must come with me."

"I wouldn't miss it for the world!" Charissa declared.

"I thought as much," Sir Godfrey said with satisfaction. "And, as the Almighty would have it, the arrangements have fallen easily into place. Colonel and Mrs. Mainwood are leaving for London in a few days as the Colonel has business in town. They have invited Penelope and Helen St. Swythin to accompany them—or, rather, the Colonel confided to me Helen invited herself and he conceded to her wishes. But, at any rate, I suggested to them you and I come along as well, and, as you might imagine, both Colonel and Mrs. Mainwood were wholly amenable to the idea."

"But what about Aunt Caroline? Will she be watched over whilst we are gone?"

"I thought I'd ask one of the women from the village to come to Silvercrosse to be her nurse. I'll pay a generous wage, of course. I've assumed you would know a good candidate for the position."

"I do indeed." Charissa could think of one young woman in particular who would be both willing and able, and the extra money would be a blessing to her family. "Miss Nancy Roberts."

"So you see, I have thought of everything. The only drawback is the Mainwoods must leave London to return home the day after the last lecture. It will be tiring, but the benefit of departing directly is we'll return to Murrington in time to arrange for the first of the banns to be read on the following Sunday. The sooner, the better," he added fervently.

"It all sounds very exciting," Charissa agreed, although she would barely have enough time at home now to catch her breath, play with Sprite and Commodore, and visit her favorite haunts in Murrington before she would be on the road again. However, there would be plenty of time for all that later. A lifetime, in fact. As for now, the opportunity to visit London at her trustworthy fiancé's side and hear a famous inspirational speaker pleased her.

But another thought crossed her mind, and her eyelids fluttered down toward her feet. What if… what if Will were in London? That's where he had gone in June to dive headfirst back into his dissipated lifestyle. She couldn't bear the idea of seeing him even on the other side of the street let alone across a room. What if he were obscenely drunk or had a woman on his arm? She would rather die than witness such a thing.

Sir Godfrey noticed the sudden deflation of her spirits and guessed the reason. "I know what you're afraid of, my love," he said, "but I've made inquiries as to the Earl of Hartwell's whereabouts. He has not been in town for some time, and most people believe he is at his family seat in the country. It would be customary for him to remain there throughout the autumn season. We'll not encounter him."

She nodded; tears prickled her lashes but she blinked them away. Clearing her throat, she said determinedly, "You're so thoughtful, Godfrey. Yes, I'll enjoy the trip, especially the sermons." She gave him a sudden smile. "But I do believe I'll spend some time shopping for my trousseau. Which means that, as my husband-to-be, you cannot censure me for purchasing new gowns and hats and whatnot!" she teased.

"Indeed not," he laughed, his tension at the mention of Will ebbing away. "For it will be the last time I don't have to pay for it all myself!"

The Mainwood's roomy coach left Murrington four days later with six passengers on board. Helen sat in the middle, facing forward, with

Mrs. Mainwood on her left and Charissa on her right, while Colonel Mainwood and Sir Godfrey sat facing backward, with Penelope in between them. Charissa wore the silver cross around her neck, to Sir Godfrey's clear satisfaction. He was in very good spirits and spoke expansively about the upcoming convocation.

"I'm sure your message will be well received, Sir Godfrey," Penelope told him admiringly.

"You are most welcome to accompany Charissa to the evening sessions, Miss St. Swythin," he said.

"I shall be delighted to come," she replied. "I'm glad we're all travelling to London together. I've seen little of you recently—and of Charissa, too, since she's been away. She and I haven't even had a chance to catch up on all our news."

Helen chimed in. "Well, I should think her news is obvious—her engagement to Sir Godfrey, of course. It's so exciting!"

Penelope glanced away. "Yes. Very exciting."

"Well, *you* certainly need a holiday, Penelope dear," observed Mrs. Mainwood. "I'm beginning to be concerned about you. Why, yesterday in church you were the picture of gloom. Have you tried drinking jasmine tea? It always helps me when I feel blue."

Penelope flushed. "Have I really been such dreary company? I'm sorry."

"One would think you'd be happy, Penny, now that we know Hector is alive and well," Helen remarked.

Charissa had been gazing out the window, but she quickly turned toward both Penelope and Helen. "Oh yes, I've only heard the barest details about your brother's letter. Do fill me in."

Penelope obliged. "As you know, it's been years since he lost his inheritance and left England. But last week we finally received a letter from him! He is living in India and has married a merchant's daughter. I suppose her family has found a way to keep him in line," she added wryly.

"And he has invited us to visit him," put in Helen.

"Are you going to go?" Charissa asked.

"We cannot afford it," Helen said bluntly. "Don't look at me like that, Penny, everyone knows it's true. But perhaps Hector will send us passage to India."

Penelope looked down at her hands folded tightly on her lap. "I doubt it, Helen. But, frankly, I'm not particularly anxious to see India anyway."

"I would *love* to travel there," Helen disagreed vigorously, "just as I am thrilled to be on my way to London! Oh yes, I am convinced this trip will be a *wondrous* adventure!" She stared at everyone in that way she had when she was about to make an announcement. "In fact, the Lord has revealed to me that a treasure awaits me in London."

"A treasure?" Mrs. Mainwood asked, nonplussed. Colonel Mainwood grunted and looked intently out of the coach at nothing.

"Oh, I don't know *precisely* what it is yet, but I have written all about it in my journal, so when it comes to pass, I'll have proof of it. I am positively wild to uncover it!" Helen exclaimed.

"Undoubtedly," Mrs. Mainwood replied, raising a sharp eyebrow. Sir Godfrey coughed suspiciously. Penelope busied herself by digging into her reticule and handed him a small sweet, while Charissa managed to say, "How very intriguing."

If Helen noticed anything less than sincere in their responses, she didn't allow it to disturb her in the least. Anticipating a propitious future, she began to hum a little tune.

Charissa wondered what was going through Helen's mind. Was she just generally excited about the possibilities of good fortune awaiting her in London or did she have a specific outcome in mind? After all, she had invited herself on this trip. Curious, Charissa decided to pursue the subject. "Helen," she asked, "what are your plans when we get to town?"

Helen turned toward Charissa with a self-satisfied smile. "Well," she said, "my cousin Mr. Duddridge has been corresponding with me, as you must remember from the deplorable news I passed on to you in my letter." This reminded Charissa Helen had likely told everyone about Will's return to debauchery; the entire village of Murrington had no doubt picked apart every detail of the report.

Helen continued, "I have asked Edgar to show me around the city, and he has promised to be most accommodating. Penny has said she doesn't want to keep company with us, although I can't imagine why not because the Mainwoods will be spending time together, and Sir Godfrey will often be with you, Charissa. But Penny has insisted on leaving Edgar and me to ourselves."

Charissa met Penelope's eyes and sympathized. Together, the unpredictable Helen and insipid Edgar would be doubly tedious.

"He's going to take me to the Tower of London to see the Traitors' Gate and the crown jewels and the menagerie. And of course, I want to go to Vauxhall Gardens. I want to see the fireworks there and…"

"I am hoping Charissa will let me come with her to the couturier's shop," Penelope cut off her sister. "That will be great fun."

"Of course," Charissa replied.

"Naturally you'll enjoy taking your dear friend Miss St. Swythin with you," Sir Godfrey told Charissa encouragingly. He glanced over at Penelope. "Perhaps you could have something new made as well. You would look nice in emerald green. Such a color would highlight your eyes, which are quite lovely."

Penelope's face grew pink. "I'll certainly take your advice into consideration, Sir Godfrey."

What a nice idea, Charissa thought. She would offer to pay for a new ensemble for Penelope, although her friend might protest the expenditure. But, on the other hand, perhaps Penelope would accept the gift now Sir Godfrey had encouraged it. She had always set great store by Sir Godfrey's opinions.

And naturally—to be fair—Charissa realized she would have to purchase a new ensemble for Helen, too, complete with all the latest frills. She chuckled to herself, knowing the younger St. Swythin sister would certainly not object to that.

Chapter 23

The Queen Anne Hotel—the lodgings selected by the Mainwoods—stood serenely on a charming side street in Kensington. All of the travelers were glad to bid farewell to the inconveniences of the journey and, after a good night's sleep, were eager to be about their business.

Over the next few days, they went their separate ways and tended to their own affairs. Colonel and Mrs. Mainwood took care of whatever business had brought them to town. Charissa and Sir Godfrey met with Mr. Morris, and Sir Godfrey signed the contract with Morris and Sons. The publisher reluctantly agreed to a postponement of Charissa's next story, but Sir Godfrey assured the man that once he and Charissa were married, she would be writing with renewed enthusiasm. Afterwards he took her to Gunter's Tea Shop to celebrate his success with the rare and expensive treat of ice cream—practically unheard of in October.

Mr. Edgar Duddridge did indeed stop by to provide Helen St. Swythin with an escort to the many sights of the city as well as the parties to which they all were invited. Most of the *beau monde* were at their country estates, but there was no shortage of gatherings that welcomed the little group from Murrington.

Charissa found herself enjoying the city as the difficult memories of her time in London six and a half years ago faded. And when Sir Godfrey gazed at her with unabashed admiration, she could not help but feel beautiful. If, in the deepest recesses of her heart, she wished she were experiencing it all with Will, she refused to acknowledge it. After all, the man was fictional as her own novels.

Soon after they arrived, she and Penelope spent the entire day at a dressmaker's shop being measured, sorting through patterns, and selecting fabric for new clothes. Charissa insisted on buying an outfit for Penelope, and—keeping Sir Godfrey's suggestion in mind—they ordered for her a gown of fine white lawn complimented by a stunning emerald green spencer decorated with braids. A green striped hat with a large green bow would complete the ensemble, they decided, and so before they went home, they visited a milliner, taking with them green ribbon from the couturier's shop so the match would be perfect.

On their walk home together, they took the opportunity to sit on a bench in a small park which was tucked away between two buildings. "You'll look lovely in your new gown, Penny," Charissa remarked, as they rested from their labors. "I can't wait until it's delivered."

"I don't know about *lovely*," Penelope confessed, "but it's been so long since I've had stylish new clothes, I'm sure I shall feel almost pretty. Thank you, Charissa," she said, squeezing her friend's hand.

"What in the world do you mean—*almost* pretty?" Charissa argued. "You're a handsome woman, and I simply can't fathom why you wouldn't think so. Sir Godfrey considers you most attractive."

To Charissa's surprise, however, instead of being encouraged, Penelope stood up abruptly and walked a few steps away, her back to the bench. "I wouldn't know," she said sharply, wrapping her arms around her waist.

And it was then that Charissa finally understood something she had never perceived before—and she was deeply disappointed with herself. How self-consumed she was—she had spent years thinking only of her own hurts and disappointments! How could she have spent so much time with Penelope and missed her friend's deepest longing? How could she not have known that Penelope was in love with Sir Godfrey?

"Oh, Penny," she said sadly. "I am as dumb as an ox. Forgive me."

"Nothing's wrong," Penelope lied, still looking away from Charissa. "I just have something in my eye." She reached into her reticule and fished out a handkerchief.

"Rubbish!" Charissa exclaimed. How must it feel to go unnoticed by the man you loved, only to watch him fall in love another woman, who also happened to be your best friend? No wonder Penelope felt unattractive. "Listen to me, Penny," Charissa tried to comfort her. "You are beautiful inside and out, even if you don't believe it!"

"I know you mean well," Penelope said stiffly, "but, please, drop the subject."

Charissa rose to her feet. "It's true I've accepted Sir Godfrey's proposal of marriage, and he is dear to me. But, Penny, I've been so blind. I've never once suspected that you love him."

Penelope gave a strangled laugh. "Love him? How ridiculous! I don't love him in that way."

"Yes, you do. Please don't deny it. I'm so, so sorry for everything. I'm a poor sort of friend for not figuring it out before."

After a moment's pause, Penelope turned back to Charissa, who could now see the tears swimming her friend's eyes. Penelope shook her head. "Oh, it's true, Charissa. I wish it weren't so, but it is. I do care for Sir Godfrey. But it's not your fault you haven't known. I've done everything I could to hide my feelings. I would have been appalled if anyone had guessed my secret. Indeed, I'm appalled *now*!"

"Please don't be upset," Charissa begged. "Your feelings are reasonable, and you have handled yourself with remarkable grace. At this point, I'm surprised you would want to be my friend at all."

"Oh, I thought about hating you," Penelope said, half seriously, half in jest, "but I decided against it."

Charissa snorted with unladylike laughter. With a burst of deep affection, she ran to Penelope and threw her arms around her friend, who returned the gesture. They held onto each other for a while; no more words were necessary.

When they finally released each other, Penelope said composedly, "Let's go back to the house and tell Mrs. Mainwood and Helen about our purchases."

"We can return to the *modiste* tomorrow with Helen," Charissa resolved. "And she shall have new clothes, too."

"That is kind of you," Penelope replied as they headed back to the hotel arm-in-arm. "Now Edgar is taking her around town, she'll be happy to look the part."

"What do you think of Helen's relationship with Mr. Duddridge? Do you think there is any serious intention there?"

"I don't know. We've heard from him and his sister occasionally over the years. Frankly, I've never liked him, although she's tolerable enough. But why he and Helen have been drawn together at this particular time, I couldn't say. I hope something comes of it. Imagine if Helen were to be married!"

"That," Charissa said, "is certainly a most thought-provoking—and entirely welcome—prospect."

The next day Mrs. Mainwood suggested the ladies visit one of the lending libraries scattered throughout the city. "I don't know about you, but I need some good reading material," she asserted. So the four women bundled themselves into a hackney and had themselves driven to Hookham's Circulating Library, located on Bond Street in Mayfair.

Once inside, Helen searched for and found a copy of one of Charissa's novels. "Here it is!" she proclaimed triumphantly, waving it at Charissa, Penelope, Mrs. Mainwood, and even the library's other patrons. "I know Mrs. A. Castlewood personally," she told everyone gleefully, with a brazen wink at Charissa. "Here, young lady, check it out," she ordered, pushing the book into the hands of a bewildered girl who accepted it meekly. "It's simply marvelous. You won't be able to put it down."

Charissa and Penelope disappeared among the bookshelves, eager to escape Helen's strange spectacle. Mrs. Mainwood watched the scene with disapproval, distancing herself from Helen by asking one of the librarians a question. Fortunately, Helen herself soon began to look through the available titles, and peace reigned once more.

When the ladies reassembled after an enjoyable time browsing, they were all satisfied with their selections. Charissa had found a previously unread volume by one of her favorite authors and had also discovered a tome on medieval history which interested her. Penelope and Mrs. Mainwood had chosen several new novels to share, while Helen held in her arms what Charissa considered an especially dreadful gothic romance along with an illustrated botanical book titled *Fairy Rings of the Forest*.

"Last year I concentrated on drawing vines," Helen explained as she deposited *Fairy Rings* on the librarian's desk. "This year I'm focusing on fungi. Did you know that fairy ring mushrooms are edible, and that they're also called Scotch bonnets? Of course, if maggots infest them..."

"How very charming," Mrs. Mainwood cut in promptly, abbreviating Helen's fungus lesson. "But rather than discuss maggots and toadstools, I should very much like some edible refreshments."

"An excellent suggestion." Penelope turned to one of the librarians. "Excuse me, sir. Do you know of any coffee houses close by?"

"Yes, madam, I am aware of several nice places where you could get some coffee or tea and a bite to eat," the man said courteously. "There's a delightful one popular with ladies called Greene's Garden Gate. If you wish to leave your books here, I'll hold them for you until you return."

"That would be lovely, thank you," Charissa said, placing her books beside Helen's. "Where is it precisely?"

The man described how to walk there, then added for good measure, "It's across the street from Hartwell House."

Charissa froze, her hands gripping the desk. "Hartwell House?"

At the same time, Helen asked loudly, "The Earl of Hartwell's home?"

"Yes," the man answered, unsure as to why this information would be so startling.

"But Lord Hartwell is not in town," Penelope said sensibly. "It is no matter to us."

"Begging your pardon, madam, but Lord Hartwell arrived in town a day or two ago," the librarian told her.

"Are you sure?" exhaled Helen. When the man avowed the truth of his claim on the testimony of several witnesses, she turned to her sister. "Oh, Penny, we must go to Greene's Garden Gate now! We simply must."

"It is up to Charissa to decide," stated Penelope.

"Why should it be Charissa's decision? She may return to the hotel if she objects," Helen disagreed. "I, on the other hand, wish to go!"

Charissa felt as though she couldn't breathe. She willed her heart to beat at a normal rate, but it refused to obey. Her hands trembled slightly, and she felt faint. How stupid! How absurd! Will was a rake, a cheat, and a cad, and the two of them were worlds apart in everything that mattered. So what if he happened to be just around the corner? He might as well be in Zanzibar or Katmandu.

But she couldn't bear the thought of being so near him. "I'm sorry, Helen. I would prefer to go back to the Queen Anne," she said in a small voice.

"Of course, dearest. Your feelings are natural and understandable," Mrs. Mainwood proclaimed in a motherly tone. "We shall all accompany you back to Kensington. And that includes you, Helen," she said firmly.

Helen let out a huff of disgust, but Penelope—ignoring Helen's dramatic pout—picked up Charissa's books and put her other arm around her friend's waist. "Come," she said gently. "We'll find a coffee house in our own neighborhood and enjoy a delicious afternoon treat."

"I should like that," Charissa replied, forcing herself to sound as composed as she could.

But she was unable to go out for coffee; upon the ladies' return to the hotel, she went straight upstairs to her room, afflicted with a throbbing headache. Finally alone after her maid had brought her a tisane, she lay on her bed wide awake, watching the late afternoon spin shadows around the room and trying vainly to settle her mind.

The memories of her disgrace at the assembly taunted her, while at the same time her doubts about the fairness with which she had treated Will revived. She had been too wrapped up in herself to know even Penelope's heart, and perhaps she had misjudged Will's as well. Yet it was too late to undo any mistake she might have made, and even if she attempted to do so somehow, it wouldn't change the fact Will had returned to his sinful lifestyle.

And besides, she was engaged to Sir Godfrey—*Sir Godfrey!* She hadn't even thought of him until now. But she knew someone would tell him what had happened at the library, and she feared his response to the news of how she had behaved. How could she explain it to him? She wasn't even doing that well explaining it to herself.

Fortunately, however, Sir Godfrey did not seem disturbed by the incident, although he certainly knew about it. The next morning when everyone gathered for breakfast downstairs, he greeted her cheerfully and inquired about her health. When she assured him of her full recovery, he expressed pleasure.

As they sat down to begin the meal, Colonel Mainwood opened the conversation with an announcement. "Now that our entire party is here," he said, gazing at them all with anticipation, "I have an invitation to share with you all."

"An invitation?" Helen questioned eagerly.

"A most felicitous kindness has been extended to us. We have all been invited to dine on Wednesday night with General Zebulon Rutledge, my former comrade-at-arms. Of course, when I served with the old boy he hadn't yet been promoted to his present rank, but he's done well for himself, and he…"

"We know the party conflicts with the convocation that evening," Mrs. Mainwood interjected hastily, "but General and Mrs. Rutledge have declared whoever is able to come is more than welcome. You will find their company most stimulating, I assure you."

"You are correct, my dear," affirmed the Colonel. "So, who among us wishes to accept their invitation?"

"I shall be delighted to come," said Penelope.

"And I," added Helen. "Is Edgar invited?"

"Yes," answered Mrs. Mainwood politely, if not enthusiastically. "And what about you, Sir Godfrey, Charissa?"

"Alas, I am expected at the convocation," said Sir Godfrey, genuinely disappointed. "Please extend my regrets."

"More's the pity," commented the Colonel, "but quite understandable."

"I would like to go," Charissa spoke up, "that is, if you are not opposed to it, Godfrey. I know I've committed to go with you to Grosvenor Chapel every evening, but this is an opportunity I should be sorry to miss. And you won't be speaking until the next night, of course."

"I've no objection, darling," he answered congenially.

"Then it is settled," the Colonel said with satisfaction. "But we'll miss you, Sir Godfrey."

"I'm sorry not to accompany you," allowed Sir Godfrey, "but I confess I'm looking forward to the convocation. Its participants are truly second to none. What a privilege I've been given to speak to such an illustrious assemblage of godly men!"

"It is a superb honor," said Mrs. Mainwood generously.

"You will be pleased to hear, Sir Godfrey," the Colonel added, "that I have rearranged my schedule. Mrs. Mainwood and I will be able to attend this distinguished gathering on the night you preach."

"I am humbled you would come," replied Sir Godfrey, pleased.

"I wouldn't miss it for the world," Penelope told him admiringly.

Helen laughed. "I suppose I'll have to force Edgar to come to Grosvenor Chapel on Thursday, too. Religion isn't his cup of tea, I'm afraid, but I'm working on it. With some success, I might add."

"Ah, fortunate man," observed Colonel Mainwood under his breath.

"What are your plans for today, Sir Godfrey, since the convocation is yet a few days a away?" Mrs. Mainwood asked quickly.

"I am escorting Charissa and Miss Penelope St. Swythin to the Society of Arts exhibition."

"And Edgar is stopping by this afternoon," Helen informed them, "to take me to tea at Greene's Garden Gate. I also am planning on returning to Hookham's. May I pick up another book for anyone?"

Penelope looked at her sister suspiciously, since both Greene's Garden Gate and Hookham's were near Hartwell House.

Helen smiled sweetly. "Enjoy the paintings at the exhibition, Penny. They are very good. I've already been there with Edgar."

"I'm sure we'll have a marvelous time," Charissa replied crossly. The thought of Helen anywhere near Will vexed her.

Helen rose from the table. *"This is the day the Lord has made,"* she proclaimed smugly, gazing around at them all. *"Let us rejoice and be glad in it."*

Chapter 24

Will hadn't wanted to leave Ashbourne Park and return to London so soon, because the Dorset countryside was beautiful in autumn. Recently, he had joined his nearest neighbors on several hunts and thoroughly enjoyed himself. He had also taken a new interest in the running of the estate, and—to the shocked delight of the long-time estate manager—had undertaken to learn as much as he could as fast as he could. He had also chosen two puppies from a litter of retrievers born recently in the blacksmith's cottage and brought them into the house for companionship. On the human side of things, he was spending time with the Dowager Countess, hoping to ease her burden of solitude.

But when a letter from Barnabas had arrived, announcing a trip to London and suggesting the two find a way to meet there, Will had decided to take advantage of the opportunity to visit with his friend. Such occasions might not be as frequent in the future as they both would like—Susannah was expecting, Barnabas had written, clearly elated at the prospect. However, the downside to her condition was she did not want to travel. Furthermore, the boys loved the country so much that in all likelihood the Worthington family would be staying in Cheshire permanently.

But for the time being, not only did Barnabas have business in the city, he was also attending a convocation featuring one of his favorite theologians. Perhaps, he proposed, Will might want to come to the evening meetings, which were open to the public. Will agreed this would be edifying, and he suggested Barnabas stay with him at Hartwell

House for as long as they were both in town. Therefore, they planned that Will would arrive in the middle of the week, and Barnabas would come a few days later, just before the convocation opened.

Will's first morning at Hartwell House found him searching for something to do. He missed the people at Ashbourne Park, not to mention the dogs. He tried to read in the library, but discovered he just couldn't concentrate on his book. After taking a walk around the block and then eating breakfast alone, he eventually wandered into the study.

There on the easel sat his painting of Charissa, not quite finished. He realized with a pang that it was probably the best human figure he had ever painted. He had left it in London for both practical and emotional reasons, and he wondered if now he should put it away. But he couldn't bear to stuff it into a closet somewhere, so, against his better judgment, he decided to keep it right where it was.

One afternoon later in the week, before his friend's arrival, he was engrossed in his accounts, writing several generous checks to the charitable societies he had begun to support. The butler knocked on the door of the study and, after entering, announced, "There are a gentleman and lady here to see you, m'lord. Are you at home?" It was a standard convention to turn away unwanted callers with the polite fiction that the resident in question was not at home.

Will looked up impatiently. "Who are they?"

"Mr. Edgar Duddridge and Miss Helen St. Swythin," the butler answered, handing him two calling cards.

Shocked, Will put down his quill and glanced at the cards. What were these two unlikeable characters doing in town? Why did they want to visit him? He had returned the money Helen loaned him the night he had left Murrington forever, just as he had sent Sir Godfrey a sizable sum, not wishing to be in anyone's debt. And didn't Duddridge realize that Will would like nothing better than to rearrange the man's facial features?

He ought to send them away without a moment's thought, but—then again—Helen St. Swythin surely knew how Charissa was faring. "Tell them I shall see them," he instructed the butler.

"Yes, m'lord," the man nodded, closing the door behind him.

When Will went into the drawing room a few minutes later, Edgar and Helen gave him their courtesies. "Lord Hartwell!" Helen smiled. "You look well."

"As do you, Miss St. Swythin," Will replied, thinking she did in fact look tolerably well. She was wearing a striking new outfit, and her excitement at seeing him put roses in her cheeks and a sparkle in her eyes. Edgar, on the other hand, appeared as vapid as ever.

"Won't you sit down?" Will invited them. After they had settled into their seats, Helen began the conversation.

"Lord Hartwell, I pray you don't think me forward for calling on you today, but I owe you an apology, and when I discovered you were in town, I had to come straightaway to express my regret in person."

"You owe me no apology, Miss St. Swythin."

"But I do," she insisted. "It was I who brought Mr. Duddridge to the Murrington assembly without informing anyone. If I had not kept him secret, your true identity would not have been revealed. Well, at least it wouldn't have been such a hair-raising scene. I am truly sorry."

"It is not your fault. Why would you have notified me of his presence? Your visitors are none of my business."

"Well," she replied, looking humbly at the Turkey carpet beneath her feet, "I see what you mean, and you are very kind, but nonetheless it was all because of me you were subjected to such unpleasantness. And as I said, I am sorry for it."

"I, too," put in Edgar with a sniff. "Most dreadfully."

Will doubted the man's sincerity, but he saw no reason to challenge it. "Very well. I accept your apologies."

Helen looked up happily. "You are the soul of generosity! Perhaps we can make amends by inviting you to take refreshment with us at Greene's across the street?"

"Thank you, no," Will declined, having no desire to be seen in public socializing with them. Instead, to be polite, he invited them to have tea and cake at Hartwell House, and they promptly accepted.

As they sipped fine Indian black tea and nibbled on light and flakey pastries, Will questioned Edgar about his activities in town. The answer was a dull recitation of worldly pursuits that Will, for the most part, no longer enjoyed. After Edgar had concluded his discourse, Will asked Helen why she was in the city.

"I came at the generous invitation of the Mainwoods," she answered. "And my cousin here has introduced me to his circle of acquaintances, for which I am most grateful. I am returning the favor by encouraging him in his flirtation with a certain lovely young lady upon whom he has his eye," she chuckled. "Miss Mary Gowthorpe."

Edgar glared at her. Will, guessing that Helen had divulged this information in order to disavow any romantic connection between herself and her cousin, changed the subject. "Have you been drawing or painting lately, Miss St. Swythin?"

"You remembered!" she exclaimed. "Yes, I have been working industriously on my art. You know I specialize in botanical subjects— rare flowers and complex vines and other things one finds in the woods. Like *Phegopteris connectilis*, for example—beech ferns. I think they resemble fairy pavilions, don't you?"

Will rather admired her unusual imagination, but something about the way she stared at him made him uncomfortable. "Ah yes," he replied evasively.

"And I know something else that might amuse you," she went on enthusiastically. "There are *auricularia* mushrooms called wood ears that grow on logs, and that's exactly what they look like—ears on logs." She gazed at Will intently. "Sometimes I think they might truly be listening, and I wonder, what do they hear?"

He had no idea how to reply to this unlikely suggestion, but thankfully she did not seem to be looking for an answer. "I do so wish I had more information about all these fascinating varieties of plants," she sighed. "I want to be able to paint them just as they are in nature, and in order to do that I must know everything I can about them. Don't you agree?"

Will could sympathize with her thirst for knowledge much better than he could understand her fantastical reveries. "Yes," he replied, "I can appreciate the importance of being familiar with such details."

Helen smiled at him as she looked longingly at a long row of bookshelves at one end of the room. "I don't suppose you have any volumes on botany you could loan me whilst I am in London? No, how rude of me to ask. Never mind. It's not important."

Will understood if she borrowed a book she would probably come back to Hartwell House in person to return it, giving her another chance to solicit his company. The easiest, and most appealing, response to her presumptuous request would be for him to ignore it and move on to another topic of discussion. But, on the other hand, he did identify with her passion for improving her art. What could it hurt to lend her a book? Besides, he wasn't obligated to see her when she brought it back if he were not so inclined.

"Wait here," he said, rising to his feet. "I have a book in the library I think you'll find helpful in your study of plant life. I'll fetch it and bring it to you."

Helen glowed. "Oh, thank you, Lord Hartwell."

When he returned with it—an expensive volume featuring detailed drawings—she was standing in front of the fireplace staring at the portrait above the mantel. Hearing him enter, she asked, "Is this handsome man your brother?"

It was the posthumous painting Will had done of Edward, but he wasn't about to tell her it was his work. Although any mention of Edward had always been painful—and today was no exception—he answered her question honestly. "It is."

"You must miss him terribly," Helen responded sympathetically, her eyes fixed on the painting. "My brother Hector isn't dead, but he may as well be. I haven't seen him in years, although we did finally hear he is in India. He wants us to come visit, but Penny says we haven't got the funds to go. It is too bad, for it would be an amazing adventure, don't you think? Anyway, Hector is handsome, too, like your brother, and he always found himself in some kind of amusing scrape."

Will doubted the man's "scrapes" had been in any way amusing, given that they had destroyed the St. Swythin family. How unlike his own brother. "Edward was an honorable man blessed with many talents, whose life was tragically cut short," Will stated, unable to hide his bitterness.

"It is so sad,' Helen sighed. Without warning, she turned away from the painting and searched Will's face, as if trying to turn him inside out.

Disturbed again by the intensity of her stare, he held out the book he still carried, placing it strategically in between them. "Here is the volume I spoke of, Miss St. Swythin."

Fortunately, she was distracted. "Oh my!" she exclaimed as she took the book and sat down, placing it on her lap. For the next few minutes she leafed through it, completely absorbed in its pages. Edgar shifted in his seat several times, visibly bored, but Will went to stand by the window and made no effort to engage him in dialogue.

At last, however, after Will had allowed Helen to examine the illustrations for a while, he asked her what he really wanted to know. "And how are the other residents of Murrington faring these days?" he inquired casually.

She raised her eyes to his and gave him a broad smile. "The most exciting news is Sir Godfrey and Charissa are going to be married."

Married. The word hung in the air like a death sentence.

Well, of course they were getting married, Will chastised himself. *Of course* Sir Godfrey would waste no time. *Of course* Charissa would run straight into her cousin's arms. He should have expected it. So why did it feel as though Helen had wielded a sharp, unforgiving blade and cut out his heart?

"What happy news," he lied. He would have been better off not knowing; too late now.

"It is as I always believed," Helen said dreamily. "They are a match made in heaven."

She was correct, Will acknowledged to himself. It was laughable to ever have thought anything else. He moved to the door. "Thank you for calling today. Now if you will excuse me, I have business to attend to."

He left them without delay and let a footman show them out; he had had enough. *More* than enough. Rebelliously, he went into the study and slumped into a chair miserably, staring at Charissa's picture.

The thought came into his mind—he should go to his club on St. James Street, one of the establishments he'd been avoiding. Just to forget; he needed to forget. Who could blame him?

No, he told himself.

Perhaps a night of cards somewhere else, then. It always felt good to play the game, to exploit the weaknesses of others.

But was that the action of a man of God, the attitude of one saved by grace?

No.

How about boxing? Maybe he could release his anger if he just imagined Sir Godfrey's holier-than-thou face on his opponent.

This idea was too tempting to resist. Will jumped to his feet, ready to order a carriage to take him to Gentleman John Jackson's. But just as he rounded the corner into the front hall, he saw a footman opening the door, and there on the stoop stood Barnabas.

"Barney!" Will blurted out.

"Diz!" Barnabas said happily, moving past the footman into the house. "So sorry I'm arriving a whole day early. Susannah knew I was anxious to see you, and she literally pushed me out the door, bless her heart." He took a closer look at Will's expression, and lowered his voice. "You look upset. What's wrong?"

Everything, thought Will. *And yet perhaps not.* He relaxed suddenly, his face softening. "You've come exactly when I needed you, Barney."

"Have I?" replied Barnabas. "Well that, my good man, is what is commonly known as God's perfect timing."

Chapter 25

The opening day of the convocation finally arrived.

Charissa was looking forward to the evening, although when she realized Grosvenor Chapel was located in Mayfair, her insides twisted unpleasantly. But, of course, there was nothing to be done; she simply hoped the Chapel was nowhere near Hartwell House.

Sir Godfrey returned from Reverend Dr. Seymour's daytime teaching animated by the men he had met and the topics discussed. After an early dinner, he left with Charissa and Penelope to return to the Chapel for the public sermons. Penelope had asked to accompany them, although the rest of the group would not be attending until Thursday, when it was time for Sir Godfrey's debut in the pulpit.

Both Charissa and Penelope dressed smartly for the occasion in white lawn with colorful spencers, Penelope's her new emerald green and Charissa's a brilliant blue. Sir Godfrey enjoyed having the two attractive women at his side as they entered the Chapel; not a few of the mostly male attendees glanced their way. As the three of them walked to the pews down in front, greeting others as they went, he proudly presented Miss Armitage as his intended bride, while Miss St. Swythin, he explained, was one of their dearest friends.

Soon the Chapel was filled with people eager to be inspired and uplifted. The evening began with a hymn—*When I Survey the Wondrous Cross*—after which the first preacher spoke for an hour on the love of God shown to mankind through His creation. When he had concluded his message, it was announced there would be a fifteen minute interval before it was time for the renowned Reverend Dr. Seymour to enter the pulpit.

Penelope leaned over to ask Sir Godfrey a question, while Charissa stood to her feet and turned around, gazing at the back of the room. About two-thirds of the way back, on the opposite side of the aisle, a tall, well-built gentleman had his back to her and was chatting with a companion. But when she saw him, her heart began to beat wildly, and blood roared in her ears. No, surely, it couldn't be... but it was.

He turned and saw her. Their eyes met. Suddenly it was as though no one else existed in the whole, crowded room.

"Charissa. Charissa!"

She felt a hand tapping her arm, and realized Sir Godfrey was next to her, calling her name and asking her if she had enjoyed the message. "Oh, yes," she breathed. "I... yes, I did."

He gave her a curious look, but quickly turned around to greet a plump, balding gentleman who had come over to speak with him. Charissa flashed her eyes back to the place Will had been standing—however, he was gone. Had she imagined him? No, she was sure he had been real.

Will!

When Will entered Grosvenor Chapel with Barnabas, he felt uncharacteristically overwhelmed in the presence of so many dedicated believers who had walked for years in the Lord's footsteps. Most of them knew who he was, and he was the recipient of numerous glances—some welcoming, a few hostile, most merely curious.

There were some women in the sanctuary, but none of them were sitting near him, and those down in front were obscured from his view by taller men. As everyone rose to sing the hymn, he thought about how much Charissa would have loved a meeting like this. He would have given anything to have her standing next to him, her lovely voice giving life to the words, *Were the whole realm of nature mine, that were a present far too small; Love so amazing, so divine, demands my soul, my life, my all.*

The introductory sermon was quite good, he felt, although occasionally the speaker alluded to concepts that were over his head at the moment. He made mental notes of things to ask Barnabas later.

When it was over, he rose, anxious to move about. He informed Barnabas he was going to go outside for a moment, and as he turned around, out of the corner of his eye he saw an elegantly dressed young woman stand up in the second row. Casually, he glanced in her direction and received the shock of his life. It was Charissa—*his* Charissa—staring at him as though he were a ghost.

Rooted to the floor, his muscles frozen, Will felt his world turn upside down. She was in London? In the same room with him? His gaze locked with hers, and the connection that had once flourished between them burst into life in less time than it took for him to take a breath.

And then it all fell apart. Sir Godfrey was standing beside her—possessively close, Will fumed, until he remembered Sir Godfrey was her betrothed husband. And, yes, she was wearing the silver cross, the symbol of Sir Godfrey's dominion. His insides aching, Will whirled about on his heel and stalked down the aisle, striding through the front door with clenched fists.

Once outside, the cold late October wind did little to change the burning sensation in his chest. He wanted to rush into the night and walk somewhere—anywhere—but he couldn't just leave Barnabas without a word. "Oh God," he began to pray, bowing his head, but no other words came to his lips.

"Are you unwell?" It was the ever-patient Barnabas, who had seen him hurry out and had followed him onto the Chapel's front steps.

"No. Yes. No, not physically." Will paused until he had composed himself. "I saw Miss Armitage. She's here, inside."

Barnabas cocked his head in surprise. "Miss Armitage from Staffordshire? Miss Charissa Armitage, whose portrait sits in your study?"

"Yes. The very same."

"At Grosvenor Chapel?"

"Did I not just say so?" Will snapped. "Yes!"

Barnabas did not take offense. "Do you wish to leave? It is a short walk back to Hartwell House."

Will hesitated. To quit the premises had been his instinctive reaction, but—confound it—why should he run? He had done no wrong being here; he had nothing to hide. "No," he answered more sharply than he meant to. "I just needed a breath of fresh air."

"You're a braver man than I would be in your shoes," Barnabas admitted. "Shall we go back in? The Reverend Dr. Seymour will be speaking soon."

"Yes," replied Will resignedly, although he wasn't at all sure he was ready to hear a discourse on—of all things—love.

Holding a large Bible, the venerable theologian climbed into the pulpit. He placed it on the stand in front of him and opened to First Corinthians, chapter thirteen. Charissa, like many Christians throughout the ages, had long loved this beautiful portion of Scripture. But her mind could not focus on doctrine this particular night as she listened to the familiar words. Was Will still in the Chapel? Was he sitting behind her? Why was he here?

Love bears all things, believes all things, hopes all things, endures all things.

Dr. Seymour's rich baritone voice at last caught her attention as he began to expound upon verse seven, and her heart ached as she pondered what the Apostle Paul had written. The qualities of love the speaker had just read out loud—those were precisely how she had failed Will! She had neither borne with his weaknesses nor believed him when he had tried to tell her he was a changed man. She had not hoped with any faith-filled conviction that "Lord Disborough" was indeed dead, and she had not even been willing to endure Sir Godfrey's wrath in order to find out the truth.

Her love had turned out to be a pale, pitiful thing indeed—a romantic vapor easily dispersed by rejection and fear and lack of faith.

Have mercy on me, Lord, she prayed silently, closing her eyes. She had often thought of herself as a mature Christian woman setting an example of godliness to those around her, but the truth was less flattering. On the contrary, she had revealed herself to be quick to judge and so eager to protect herself that she had allowed lies to flourish rather than ask to hear the other side of the story. Will had wounded her pride, nothing more, but she had been too concerned with her own hurt to give him the benefit of the doubt until it was too late.

When the sermon was over, the congregation rose for the closing hymn. At its conclusion, Sir Godfrey bent over and spoke softly to Charissa. "What is wrong, sweetheart?" he asked. "You seemed tense during the message, and just now I could hardly hear you sing."

She contemplated tossing his question aside with a vague response, but she decided she would not lie to him. "Godfrey, you won't believe this, but Lord Hartwell was here tonight. Sitting behind us."

He stared at her, astounded. "What?"

She repeated herself, explaining what she had seen. Penelope heard her, too, and gasped. Sir Godfrey quickly surveyed the room and caught a glimpse of Will and Barnabas at the far end of the Chapel just as they exited. "That insolent wretch! He is a madman! He is *obsessed* with you!" Sir Godfrey exploded.

A few people standing close by turned and stared at them. Penelope's mouth fell open, but she closed it again quickly. "Sir Godfrey, it cannot be so."

"Please don't make a scene," pleaded Charissa, putting her hand on his arm. "Lord Hartwell has not spoken to me, nor even approached me. I'm all right. Truly."

Unfortunately, Sir Godfrey was convinced Will was stalking her as a wolf would hunt down its prey, but he calmed down enough to maintain proper decorum. The curious observers lost interest and went back to their own conversations.

"Don't be afraid, dearest," Sir Godfrey comforted her, pulling her arm close. "You'll be safe, I promise, for if Hartwell returns tomorrow— he shall have to answer to me!"

Chapter 26

Charissa tossed and turned much of night, for she had no answers to her questions. Why had Will been at the convocation? Was he there looking for her, as Sir Godfrey claimed? Such an interpretation of Will's motives lacked credibility for he had been as stunned to recognize her as she had been to see him.

What reason would he have to attend a religious meeting? True, the rumor mill had ground out the accusation Lord Hartwell had rushed headlong back into debauchery, but maybe it wasn't true. Maybe the scandalmongers were wrong.

Love bears all things, believes all things, hopes all things, endures all things.

The words of Scripture echoed in her mind, and the Holy Spirit's gentle conviction lingered. Thus it seemed to Charissa this time she should refuse to assume the worst of Will—not out of naïveté, but out of a willingness to let go of her preconceived notions. Instead, she acknowledged Will just might have come to the convocation because he was genuinely seeking God.

The idea brought tears to her eyes—tears of joy because it was everything she had prayed for, but also tears of sorrow because of what it meant she had lost.

When she rose the next day, Sir Godfrey had already gone to the Chapel, Helen was out with Edgar, as usual, and Colonel Mainwood had gone to meet a man about a pair of horses. But Mrs. Mainwood was still at the hotel, embroidering in the front parlor, where Penelope, her nose buried in a book, had joined her.

Charissa hoped Penelope hadn't told anyone about Will's presence at the convocation the night before, and when Mrs. Mainwood said nothing about it, she was relieved her friend had held her tongue. Frankly, Charissa didn't want to discuss the situation with anyone, even Penelope. Instead, she was in search of a distraction.

After chatting with Mrs. Mainwood about odds and ends for a while, Charissa decided to read. "I've finished my novel from Hookham's, and I'm just not in the mood for medieval history," she said. "Do either of you have anything you could let me borrow?"

Penelope looked up from her page. "Have you read *Memoirs of an Old Wig*? It was rather clever."

"No, I haven't."

"When I finished it, I gave it to Helen but I don't think she's had the inclination to begin it yet. It would be in her room, on the table or perhaps in her trunk. You may enter her room through mine—they're connected by a door which doesn't lock. Here is my key."

"Thank you, Penny," said Charissa, taking the room key after Penelope fetched it out of her reticule.

When Charissa entered Helen's room, she didn't see anything lying on the desk, so she opened the trunk Penelope had mentioned. There she saw a stack of books, including what she thought was probably Helen's journal, but no *Memoirs of an Old Wig*. She closed the trunk and scanned the room again, this time noticing a book which had fallen off the back of the desk and landed vertically between a desk leg and the wall. Happily, the volume was the novel she'd been looking for.

As she bent over to pick it up, she just happened to glance into the wastepaper basket beside the desk. Several crumpled up sheets had been tossed into the basket, and she noticed a bit of writing on one of the papers. She would never have given it a moment's thought had the visible word not been *Hartwell*.

Hartwell? She reached into the basket and pulled out the paper, opening it fully so that she could read it. To her surprise, she saw Helen had written out, over and over again in neat, flourished script, *Helen*

Devreux, Countess of Hartwell and *Lord and Lady Hartwell of Ashbourne Park* and *Lady Hartwell.*

Helen had been practicing her signature.

Charissa felt sorry for Helen. The discovery proved the eccentric woman—who had never had any real marriage prospects—was not pursuing an attachment with Mr. Duddridge. She was still deeply infatuated with Will, absurdly so.

Charissa folded the paper and tucked it into the pages of the book. Then she went downstairs.

Only Penelope sat in the front parlor when Charissa returned; Mrs. Mainwood had returned to her room. Penelope smiled when Charissa gave her the room key, noting her friend had found the book she was looking for, and started to go back to her reading. But Charissa took the sheet of paper out of the book and, unfolding it, held it out to Penelope. "You ought to take a look at this, Penny."

Penelope's eyes flitted over the carefully embellished signatures, and she understood immediately what they meant. "You found this in Helen's room?" she asked wearily, although she was well aware of the answer.

"Yes. I didn't intend to pry. I saw it by accident, but I couldn't ignore it once I saw what it said. I wonder if she's up to something. I'm afraid I don't trust her."

"Nor do I." Penelope handed the paper back to Charissa. "Perhaps she's just dreaming, as we all do. I don't suppose I should say anything to her."

"No, probably not. Even if she's trying to chase after Lord Hartwell somehow, it would do no good to confront her. She'd just become defensive."

"Surely the situation isn't that far gone," said Penelope, trying to convince herself that nothing was amiss. "I would hate for her to embarrass herself or Lord Hartwell—or us."

"I expect it's not that serious," Charissa echoed, though with far less confidence. "Besides, her bubble will burst soon enough."

Charissa's thoughts wandered for the rest of the day, with Lord Hartwell at the center of them. She tried to put all of her concerns aside without much success; Will's face continued to intrude upon her attempts to read, sew, or do just about anything. Penelope was content not to broach the subject of either Will or Sir Godfrey or Helen, for which Charissa was grateful—it was difficult enough to not obsess over the circumstances as it was. *What a tangled mess of affections,* Charissa mused more than once as she vainly attempted to sort through it all in her mind.

Her contemplations were no clearer as she sat in the hackney on the way to Grosvenor Chapel that evening. She was relieved Helen didn't know Will had attended the convocation the previous evening, because she would have insisted on coming with them. That would have been a nightmare for them all, Charissa was certain.

Of course, she couldn't predict whether or not Will would be at the convocation again. Yet she couldn't deny that she hoped to see him once more, and her imagination raced. Where would he be sitting? Would he see her? Would he speak to her? Would he even *want* to speak to her? Did he resent her faithlessness? Or would he look at her and …?

She was engaged to Sir Godfrey, she reminded herself sternly, cutting off her reverie and forcing herself to catch her fiancé's eye with a smile.

When they arrived, Sir Godfrey led Charissa and Penelope down front again. Charissa noticed every once in a while his eyes darted suspiciously about the sanctuary. She glanced, too, when she hoped he wouldn't notice, but she didn't see Will until the very last minute. He and his unknown companion were up in the second floor balcony on the far side of the room, well-positioned not only to see the pulpit, but also to look down upon Charissa herself. Filled with an uninvited but wholly pleasurable sense of excitement, she sat down quickly and busied herself looking up the opening song in the hymnal.

The first preacher delivered a fine message on the love found in friendship, exemplified by David and Jonathan. During the interval afterwards, Sir Godfrey hovered over Charissa protectively, but Will and his friend did not come anywhere near them. Later, Reverend Dr. Seymour spoke eloquently and passionately on the love of God shown in the discipline of His children. Most men would have used this topic to put fear into the hearts of their listeners, but Reverend Dr. Seymour painted the picture of a loving Father who will settle for nothing less than the very highest good for His beloved sons and daughters.

After the preaching had concluded, Sir Godfrey led Charissa and Penelope back up the aisle. Will and Barnabas, also heading for the door, were waiting for an opening to join the press of people moving outside, and the five of them saw each other at exactly the same time.

Sir Godfrey let go of Charissa's arm. "Wait outside for me," he ordered. He pushed his way to where Will and Barnabas stood and spoke a few words Charissa couldn't hear, following which the three men moved backwards against the flow to find a spot devoid of other people.

Penelope, a look of trepidation in her eyes, tried to move Charissa along toward the front door, but Charissa would not go with her. Extricating herself from Penelope's grasp, she propelled herself through the exiting crowd to join the three men.

"…and I warn you—stay away from her!" she heard Sir Godfrey demand heatedly.

"I assure you, you mistake the matter entirely," Will responded, his voice taut. "I had no idea you would be one of the preachers when Mr. Worthington invited me to attend."

Charissa ran up beside Sir Godfrey and caught his arm. "Please, Godfrey," she urged, "this is unnecessary. Come away. Let him be."

Will stared at her, as still as a statue.

Barnabas looked at her, too, then raised his eyes to Sir Godfrey's reddened face. "The lady is correct, sir," he stated. "This is unnecessary. My friend Lord Hartwell and I are here to enjoy the exposition of the Word of God, nothing else."

"And who are you?" Sir Godfrey demanded.

"Mr. Barnabas Worthington." He added with an almost mischievous smile, "An attendee of this convocation—and your brother in Christ."

That took the wind out of Sir Godfrey's sails. "Yes, yes, of course," he allowed, taking a step backward. "I am Sir Godfrey Scrivener, and may I present Miss Charissa Armitage. *My fiancée.*"

Barnabas gave her a courtesy, while Will's eyes travelled to Charissa's throat, where the silver cross gleamed around her neck. "May I offer you my best wishes, Miss Armitage," Will said evenly, bowing his head.

Sir Godfrey tugged her away. "Come, my love. It is late, and Miss St. Swythin is waiting for us."

Before Charissa could object, he escorted her expeditiously though the door and out to the place where Penelope was standing by a coach. The three of them stepped into it without a word and rode back to Kensington in total silence.

Wednesday morning, the weather—a cold, melancholy drizzle—matched Charissa's state of mind, and as she lay in the bed trying to convince herself to get out of it, she particularly missed the warmth of the dogs curled up against her legs. But she knew it was well past time to start the day, and in spite of her slug-a-bed desires, she rose and dressed for breakfast. She admitted to herself that her lack of enthusiasm stemmed from the fact she would not be attending the convocation that evening, thus missing the opportunity to see Will again. Wistfully, though, she decided it was for the best; she was in London to encourage Sir Godfrey, not distract him with concerns about Lord Hartwell. She made an effort to avoid thoughts of Will by shopping with Mrs. Mainwood and walking briskly with Penelope in Hyde Park.

When evening finally came, Sir Godfrey departed for Grosvenor Chapel alone, and the rest of them headed in the opposite direction, to a stately red-brick townhouse not far from the hotel. The home's exterior matched hundreds of similar dwellings in London's West End, but the décor inside told a different story—it was filled with unusual furniture, paintings, and *objets d'art* from places as diverse as the European continent, India, South Africa, and the West Indies.

The house's owners—General and Mrs. Rutledge—greeted the group in the drawing room. The General was a trim, sharp-eyed man in his early fifties. His left cheek was scarred from nose to ear, and he walked with a pronounced limp. These battle wounds made him appear fierce at first glance, but his amiable manners quickly won over everyone. His wife, a plump, richly dressed woman, welcomed her guests warmly.

To even out the company, the Rutledges had invited two army officers to join them, Captain Aldwin and Major Purvis. By happy coincidence, the Mainwoods were acquainted with Captain Aldwin, although he served in the infantry and not in the cavalry, as had the Colonel and his son Samuel.

When everyone went into the dining room, General and Mrs. Rutledge, of course, took their seats at either end of the table, while Charissa was placed to the General's left. On her other side was Captain Aldwin, a ruddy-cheeked man in his forties with a receding hairline and hearty laugh. Across from her sat Mrs. Mainwood, at whose right hand was Major Purvis, a tall, thin soldier sporting an unusually bushy mustache. Both of them looked the part, carrying themselves as men who had earned the right to wear their dashing uniforms.

Since all the men were army officers—except Edgar, who promptly faded into the background and stayed there—the conversation consisted of exciting or humorous stories about military life. The men tailored their narratives to suit female company and did not speak much about actual fighting. Charissa appreciated their discretion; she understood any true description of war would be disturbing. Nonetheless, she learned a great deal from them—and from Mrs. Rutledge—about what it was like to live in extreme climates, struggle with foreign customs, and eat strange food.

At one point, Major Purvis addressed Captain Aldwin, referencing a specific battle. "It occurs to me, Aldwin," he said as he helped himself to a generous slice of beef, "I've always wanted to ask you about that chap at Vimeiro."

Charissa looked sharply across the table at the major. "Vimeiro?" she repeated.

"Yes, Miss Armitage. A British victory in Portugal two years ago," Major Purvis explained. Then he returned his attention to Captain Aldwin. "You know the man I'm referring to. The piper, the one who continued to play in the midst of the fighting. Awfully brave fellow, eh?"

Captain Aldwin nodded. "Yes, you mean Piper George Clark of the 71st Highlanders. Wounded in combat, yet sat on a rock and kept playing to encourage his fellow soldiers. Good man. I wasn't anywhere close to him, though. Didn't hear it myself."

"I had wondered whether you were nearby or not. Did you know that some Scottish society recently presented him with a set of silver bagpipes for his valor?"

"I wasn't aware of that. He earned such an honor, I'd say. He was one of many fine men who fought there that day, such as Captain Samuel Mainwood." Captain Aldwin inclined his head respectfully toward Colonel and Mrs. Mainwood. "We had a well-deserved victory—and we would have gone on to completely decimate the French if General Wellesley had had his way!"

Charissa listened with heightened interest. It was surely fascinating that Captain Aldwin, like Samuel Mainwood, was a veteran of that particular battle—but far more important to her was the memory of someone who had *not* survived it.

Without a second thought, she set down the glass she had just raised to her lips. "Captain Aldwin," she stated, turning to him, "may I ask you a question about the battle?"

He looked at her in surprise. "Certainly, Miss Armitage."

"I've been told about the courage of the men who fought there—an illustrious group which I now understand includes you, Captain," she said. "And Colonel and Mrs. Mainwood's son, of course, who was commended for his bravery. But I know of someone else—an infantry officer who, sadly, perished in the conflict. The Honorable Lieutenant Edward Devreux. Were you acquainted with him?" Out of the corner of her eye, Charissa saw Helen lean forward with interest.

Captain Aldwin nodded. "I know of him, although I was not in his brigade. He was killed in action, I'm afraid. But his sacrifice allowed us to capture two French cannon."

"He was the Earl of Hartwell's second son," General Rutledge said. "I remember meeting him once. A quiet sort, but not at all soft or weak."

"Yes, he was a pious man like his father—although not, I've heard, like his elder brother, the notorious Lord Disborough," Captain Aldwin mused.

"But his brother is the Earl of Hartwell now, and he has apparently reformed himself," Mrs. Rutledge commented. "In fact, lately the talk is the earl has become something of an evangelical."

"Fancy that," Major Purvis said in a shocked tone.

Mrs. Mainwood took a sip of wine. "I do hope it is true. I rather liked him when he was Mr. Lyon."

Although Mrs. Rutledge naturally did not comprehend Mrs. Mainwood's mysterious reference to Mr. Lyon, the general's wife reassured the group that the gossip had been confirmed by several of Lord Hartwell's former friends.

"How very unusual," Captain Aldwin remarked. "In any event, I recall the soldiers loved his brother, Lieutenant Devreux. Especially one sergeant in particular who served with him—the one who lost an arm at Vimeiro. Deeply loyal to the lieutenant. His name was, hmm, ah yes, I remember, Sergeant Mundy. He is a pensioner now at the Royal Hospital Chelsea."

"Mundy. I've heard of him. Courageous fellow indeed," agreed Colonel Mainwood.

"Speaking of sergeants, I am reminded of a man in my regiment named Sergeant Platt." Major Purvis finally jumped into the discussion and turned it away from weightier topics, launching into an amusing tale about a popular soldier who'd had an affinity for onions and bit into them the way other people ate apples.

Thus the conversation moved on, but Charissa did not hear a word of it. Despite her sincere attempts that day to dislodge Will from her thoughts, now she couldn't stop thinking about his brother. Her mind flew back to what Captain Aldwin had said about Edward Devreux—that he'd had a reputation as a godly man, and that his fellow soldiers highly esteemed him, even though he'd been in the army only a short time before he was killed.

Especially, she was intrigued by Sergeant Mundy, who'd been close to Edward and served him loyally. Charissa knew soldiers developed deep bonds serving together in war, even men of different classes and backgrounds. If the sergeant had been with Edward in the days leading up to his death, perhaps he could offer insight into Edward's state of mind at the time. And, more specifically, she wondered if the sergeant knew anything that might help Will deal with his brother's death. She wanted to discover something that could reveal a purpose in his brother's military service—especially something that might allow Will to forgive himself, or at least not despise himself so severely.

Throughout the rest of the evening, although she moved with the rest of the company into the drawing room to play cards, Charissa paid scant attention to hearts, diamonds, clubs, and spades. Instead, she devised a plan. She had only one day left in London, but she would be free to do as she wished. She decided she would ask Captain Aldwin, the veteran of Vimeiro, to take her to the Royal Hospital Chelsea to help her find Sergeant Mundy, if possible. There, she would ask the sergeant if he had any information about Edward that might be a comfort to Will.

It was a far-fetched scheme, but the more she considered it, the more determined she became to carry it out.

She worked out all the details in her head. She knew she couldn't go alone with the captain, but she could always count on Penelope, and so, at a point in the evening when everyone else was otherwise occupied, she took her friend aside and convinced her to accompany her to Chelsea the next day.

Bolstered by Penelope's acquiescence, Charissa privately proposed the excursion to Captain Aldwin. She gave him a simple explanation of her purpose, and to her surprise and delight, he readily agreed, being familiar with Sergeant Murphy by reputation if not by sight. He explained he had obligations in the morning, but he would be able to meet her and Penelope at midday. Fortunately, the Royal Hospital—a home for old or infirm military pensioners—wasn't far from Kensington, just a few miles southeast toward the Thames River. The captain assured her she would be back in plenty of time to hear Sir Godfrey's sermon that evening.

And if, for the rest of the night, Charissa's heart sang more than she thought it had any right to, and if she danced with Will in her dreams, she kept such sentiments strictly to herself.

Chapter 27

The imposing Royal Hospital Chelsea testified to the respect and concern the British people felt for their battle-scarred troops. Neither Charissa nor Penelope had been there before, or even to the Ranelagh Gardens which lay between the hospital complex and the Thames River. As Captain Aldwin assisted the two women out of the hackney early Thursday afternoon, they paused, staring in amazement at the colossal, U-shaped edifice.

"It's enormous!" Penelope exclaimed.

"So it is. It was designed by Sir Christopher Wren one hundred and fifty years ago, specifically with veterans in mind," the captain informed her. "For example, he designed the stairs to be very wide and shallow, so elderly and feeble men can easily navigate them."

"Amazing," Charissa replied sincerely, and Penelope concurred.

The neo-classical building rose four stories into the sky, and a long, wide path led to a columned portico through which they would enter. Once they finally made it to the steps and up into the building, Captain Aldwin waylaid the first official-looking person he saw, introduced himself, and asked about Sergeant Mundy. The orderly, who had his arms wrapped precariously around a stack of boxes, replied as best he was able. "Don't rightly know him, sir, but he's probably on the lawn out back. Go search for him there."

"But we don't know what he looks like," Captain Aldwin objected.

"No? Well, let me find someone who can guide you. Hallo there!"

he called out to an old veteran stumping down the hall with a cane. "Do you know Sergeant Thomas Mundy?"

The elderly soldier paused. "Aye," he said cautiously.

"You can help the captain and these ladies find him outside," the orderly said. "Thanks awfully." And he whisked himself away without further ado.

The veteran's mouth twisted into a smile. "Well, I can't take ye fast, but I can take ye," he offered. "I know where he likes to sit."

Captain Aldwin thanked him and introduced himself once again. "And these are Miss Armitage and Miss St. Swythin," he finished.

The veteran saluted the officer and did his best to give the ladies a courtesy. "I'm Lance Corporal Jeremiah Jenkins. Pleased to meet ye." He led them haltingly toward the tall back door which opened onto a white, four-columned portico identical to the one through which they had entered. "We'd best be on our way, then."

"Thank you for assisting us," Charissa said, following him out, with Captain Aldwin and Penelope at her side.

"Happy to oblige, Miss." Corporal Jenkins took the steps very carefully, refusing Captain Aldwin's offer of help. He turned his face toward Charissa once he'd made it to the bottom. "I must say, I'm surprised Tom is getting so many visitors today," he commented.

An unwelcome thought passed through Charissa's mind, and she exchanged a look with Penelope. "He's had other visitors today?"

"Aye. Downright odd, I think it. T'aint been nobody looked him up in a long time, and now it's been twice the same day. Not that that's a bad thing, o' course," he amended quickly.

The four of them headed slowly down a gravel walkway, where extensive wings—appropriately called Long Wards—stretched out on either side of them. Since it was such a nice autumn day, many men strolled about the courtyard, while others sat on benches or chairs. They were of all ages, some having been grievously wounded.

But Charissa was not focused on them, as much as she admired their sacrifice. She turned to Corporal Jenkins. "Who came to see the sergeant this morning?" she asked him.

"Don't know their names, but 'twere a gentleman and a lady. She weren't as pretty as ye are, miss. Bit of a sauce box, too, if ye ask me."

Looking away, Charissa frowned. She suspected that the couple had been none other than that inveterate schemer Helen and her accomplice Edgar, snooping around in the hopes of doing who-knew-what in an effort to insinuate themselves into Will's good graces. After all, they had been at the dinner party last night and had heard the conversation about Edward Devreux and Sergeant Mundy. Charissa was tempted to ask more about the two visitors, but she decided that she would be better served by sticking to her own business.

So she smiled at Corporal Jenkins, and said, "Never mind about them, then. But, to answer your previous question, no, I'm not Sergeant Mundy's relative. However, I do want to ask him a few important questions I believe only he can answer."

The corporal grinned back at her. "I like an honest answer. And I'm happy to help a fellow soldier," he said proudly, nodding at the captain.

At last, after they had walked almost the whole length of the Long Wards at a snail's pace and had snaked through several groups of residents, they approached a man Charissa supposed must be Sergeant Mundy. He looked about sixty years old, though he could have been younger in spite of his weather-beaten face. He had his right sleeve pinned up onto his chest, and he was sitting in an uncomfortable-looking chair with his eyes closed.

"Sergeant," said Corporal Jenkins loudly, "ye have callers. This time 'tis an officer and two gracious ladies. Cap'n Aldwin, Miss Armitage, and Miss St. Swythin."

The soldier's eyes flew open, and he jumped to his feet. He stared at them, a shade of confusion passing over his face before it disappeared. "Sergeant Thomas Mundy, at your service," he said, with a bow to Charissa and Penelope, and a left-handed salute to the captain.

The corporal departed, heading back to the building, and the sergeant asked his callers if they wished to take a turn about the grounds, to which they agreed. "And to what do I owe the honor of your visit?" he asked as they strolled in the direction of the Ranelagh Gardens and the Thames.

"First of all," Captain Aldwin said soberly, "I wish to express my appreciation for your service to our King and country. I—like you, Sergeant Mundy—am a veteran of the Peninsular War, and I cannot thank you enough for the sacrifice you've made to save the world from the threat of so evil an overlord as Napoleon Bonaparte."

Sergeant Mundy's expression deepened. "It'll take much more than anything I've given to stop that madman."

"With the commitment of us all, it will be done, God willing," the captain asserted.

"God willing," Sergeant Mundy echoed fervently.

He and the captain launched into a discussion of their military experiences, although once again they kept unpleasantness to a minimum out of consideration for the women present. Soon Captain Aldwin mentioned that they had both fought in the Battle of Vimeiro on the twenty-first of August, 1808. After they had compared memories for a while, the captain remarked, "If I remember aright, Sergeant, you were with Lieutenant Edward Devreux when he was killed."

For the first time in the conversation, the sergeant hesitated. "Aye." He gave Penelope a quick glance.

"If you are able to speak of him," the captain said respectfully, " that is the reason we sought you out today. Miss Armitage wishes to ask you a few questions."

The sergeant's eyes narrowed. "Just what, exactly, is this all about?"

Seeing his wariness, Charissa realized that if it had been Helen who had accosted him earlier in the day, it had certainly been an uncomfortable visit, causing him to suspect her own motives now. She forced herself to swallow her irritation with the interfering Helen and to concentrate on making her own case to Sergeant Mundy.

"The purpose of my visit today is simple," she said earnestly. "I've come to see you because I'm concerned for the Earl of Hartwell, Lieutenant Devreux's brother. He is a friend of mine."

The sergeant's expression didn't change. "Oh?"

"Lord Hartwell feels responsible for his brother's death." She described the final, devastating argument Will and Edward had had and explained how Edward had joined the army soon afterwards. "Lord Hartwell regrets his unkind words—*profoundly* regrets them."

"I see." The sergeant's eyes had softened, but he offered no other thoughts.

"And so," Charissa concluded a bit desperately, "I was

thinking—hoping—that since you knew Lieutenant Devreux, you might have some knowledge about his brother's final days, something that could ease Lord Hartwell's pain—because if you did, you could possibly...." Her voice faltered.

Sergeant Murphy stopped walking and turned to face her. "I could possibly what?"

She looked him full in the face. "You could send Lord Hartwell a message. Tell him something good about his brother's time in the army, something that might help him come to terms with the young man's death."

"But," the sergeant pointed out, "even if I had a story to comfort Lord Disborough—I mean, Hartwell— why should I care about him? Isn't he just a toff who doesn't give a fig for anything except his own fun? Maybe a little guilt for someone like him isn't a bad thing."

She had a ready response. "I understand why you think poorly of Lord Hartwell, but I must assure you it is no longer the case. I am aware he has an unsavory past, but he has changed! He has repented of his former life and is trying to make amends for it. I, too, doubted his sincerity at first, but I was wrong."

The sergeant snorted skeptically. "He's turned over a new leaf, has he?"

"Yes," Charissa declared without hesitation. "He is a new man."

"Miss Armitage is speaking the truth, sir," put in Penelope.

"And it is not only these women who will testify to Lord Hartwell's reformation," added Captain Aldwin. "His religious conversion has not gone unnoticed by many of the *beau monde*."

The sergeant pursed his lips. "A new man, you say? Religious conversion? And the swells are gossiping about it?" He shook his head. "Mercy me, I never would have thought it. But I want to hear you say the words one more time, Miss." He fixed Charissa with an intimidating stare.

Undaunted, she met his challenge. "Lord Hartwell has come to faith in Christ, sir. I've seen convincing evidence of it, and I believe it with my whole heart!"

"Well, then." Sergeant Mundy's face relaxed suddenly, his stern eyes softening. "I'm thinking that there is indeed something I can do for you."

"Truly? Oh, thank you, Sergeant Mundy. Thank you!" Charissa clapped her hands together in genuine gratitude.

He gave her a grin, made an about-face, and started to walk purposefully back toward the building. He moved along much more swiftly than had the old corporal. "Come along!" he called over his shoulder.

Charissa, Penelope, and Captain Aldwin glanced at each other in surprise and hurried to follow him.

"To be perfectly aboveboard, Miss Armitage," the sergeant remarked as Charissa fell into step beside him, "I wasn't too keen on your request at first. Especially since your friend is named Miss St. Swythin. I wasn't sure what you were going to ask of me."

"Let me guess. You were wary of Miss *Penelope* St. Swythin because you have already encountered Miss *Helen* St. Swythin and her cousin Mr. Edgar Duddridge. You might be interested to know I believe those two are attempting to use Lord Hartwell's brother's memory to—well, to swindle him somehow."

"Aye! You're right. This morning a Miss St. Swythin did come to visit me, asking about Lieutenant Devreux like you have. Except she was nothing like you or your friend. She said she was Lord Hartwell's betrothed, which I thought right away was a sham, and she hounded me for some trophy, some memory—anything that had to do with Lieutenant Devreux. But I'm no fat wit."

"You are a perceptive man, Sergeant Mundy. Helen is Penelope's sister, but you're correct; they are nothing alike," Charissa stated emphatically

Sergeant Mundy shook his head in disgust. "The first Miss St. Swythin is a bamboozler all right. Like I said, she was pressing me hard for something as had to do with Lieutenant Devreux." He looked back at Penelope. "A regular shrew, she was."

"But I take it you gave her nothing?" Penelope asked.

"That's right. Or, well, that's almost right." Sergeant Mundy's face split in a boyish grin. "Actually, I did hand over something—I gave her an old epaulette. It was gold braid, with a star. And if she thought it belonged to the lieutenant, well, that weren't my fault."

Captain Aldwin snorted at this last statement, although the women weren't sure what to make of the sergeant's tale.

"But what if Lord Hartwell is deceived by this epaulette his brother supposedly wore?" Charissa asked worriedly.

"If he's half as clever a man as rumor has it, he won't be hoodwinked," the sergeant said confidently.

"I can't imagine he would be fooled," Captain Aldwin agreed.

Charissa supposed the sergeant and the captain couldn't both be wrong. After all, she knew next to nothing about military insignia, and apparently neither did Helen. But Will probably did. "I'll take your word for it," she conceded.

By now, they had reached the portico, but before he mounted the stairs, Sergeant Mundy stopped. "Now," he said, "I'm going to tell you what I aim to do for his lordship. I don't need to write him a letter."

"No?" Charissa said, puzzled. "Why not?"

"Well, you see, it's this way. I remember Lieutenant Devreux as clear as if he was standing right in front of me. Oh yes, he was the best of men! Finer than the whole lot of those other officers—begging your pardon, Captain, I don't mean you, as you weren't in our brigade. But Lieutenant Devreux was a man of honor for certain!"

The sergeant grew somber as he recalled a long-ago conversation. "The night before he died, the lieutenant gave me something—and he told me I should get it to his brother if he didn't survive the battle that was coming. Don't know why he thought I'd survive and he wouldn't— maybe the Lord revealed something to him. But anyway, he told me in no uncertain terms not to hand it over until his brother was ready. When I asked what he meant by ready, he said it was when his brother had come to faith in Christ. Given what I knew about his lordship, I never thought that would happen. But now I've met you, and I know what must be done, what Lieutenant Devereux would want. You're to take what he gave me to Lord Hartwell, Miss Armitage. He's *ready.*"

Charissa couldn't speak for a moment. Whatever it was that the sergeant was proposing, it seemed to be far more than she could have possibly imagined or hoped for. "What is it Lieutenant Devreux gave you?" she inquired.

"Let me tell you. The truth is that sometimes it was a real bad situation down there in Portugal. You recall, Captain," Sergeant Mundy said soberly. "Lots of men acting like wild beasts, doing things you could never tell a lady about. But Lieutenant Devreux was different. He talked about God to me and to as many of the men as would pay him mind. He'd read to us out of the Bible—things about Christ and about believing in Him. And, well, to make a long story short, I was one of the poor sinners who listened."

"You're saying he led you to faith?" Penelope asked, fascinated.

"Aye," the soldier testified, "he did. And that night, the day before he got taken up to heaven, he gave me his New Testament. That's what I have for Lord Hartwell—his brother's New Testament."

"I can't think of anything that would mean more to him," Charissa said softly. Penelope quietly reached over and took Charissa's hand in hers.

The sergeant nodded. "You wait here, and I'll go up to my berth to get it. I'll just be a minute," he advised, running rapidly up the steps and into the building.

Charissa, Penelope, and Captain Aldwin waited patiently for him to return, and he reappeared shortly, carrying with him a small, leather-bound New Testament. It had stains and scrapes as though it had been through not just a single battle but a lifetime of war. "Open the cover and look inside," he instructed Charissa as he pressed it into her willing fingers.

The inside pages were creased and worn, too, but on the frontispiece she could easily read the name inscribed there: *the Hon. Edward Devreux.*

Sergeant Mundy watched her closely and was pleased with what he read in her face as she gazed at the book she held. "Godspeed, Miss," he told her gently. "Godspeed."

When Charissa and Penelope arrived back at the Queen Anne Hotel, they bade Captain Aldwin goodbye, thanking him for his kindness. They went directly upstairs and, after a brief but warm embrace, each went silently into her own room. Food would be ready for the Mainwood party in about an hour—earlier than usual—because all of them were attending the lecture series tonight to hear Sir Godfrey read his sermon. Tomorrow morning, as planned, they would be leaving for Staffordshire.

However, no matter how tired she felt, Charissa had something of vital importance to accomplish before she could go downstairs. She had to write Will a note explaining the gift she would give him tonight at the convocation—assuming, of course, he would be there. She had been composing the letter in her head for the entire coach ride home from Chelsea, and she knew exactly what she wanted to say.

She sat down on her bed and took Lieutenant Devreux's New Testament out of her reticule, holding it reverently. Truly, she thought, the prayers Edward had lifted before the Lord on Will's behalf had been answered.

She opened the battered volume carefully, observing that the Gospel of John was especially well-worn. After she turned all the way the end of Revelation and was about to close up the book, she happened to notice an odd little pocket fashioned out of thick paper and glued to the inside back cover. Tucked into the pocket was a single sheet of paper, folded up neatly.

She withdrew it and saw that it was a letter, written with confident, flowing penmanship.

Dear Will,

I hope this letter finds you well and in good spirits, my brother. I wish I had more time to write of the many things I have in my heart to tell you, but the words below must, alas, suffice. You see, tomorrow I am being sent into battle, and I feel compelled by the Holy Spirit to write to you tonight. I know in the past you have scoffed at such things, and yet I am also certain that someday you will understand.

Specifically, I feel I must tell you why it was God called me here. Yes, it was His will that led me to join the army. I had been sensing His direction for some time—and resisting Him—but at last I capitulated. And now I know why.

Although I have been in Portugal only a short time, already enduring the miseries and horrors that inevitably accompany war, I have become our unit's unofficial chaplain—someone the men have chosen to come to for spiritual comfort and insight. I have wept with them, prayed with them, laughed with them, and led not a few of them to a saving relationship with Jesus Christ, who stands even in the battlefield with arms outstretched, ready to receive those who cast themselves upon His grace and mercy.

I shall never regret my decision to be a part of the army. There are souls now destined for heaven who may never have arrived in that safe haven had it not been for the Lord's sending a witness—even one so unworthy as I—to this severe place.

I look forward to the day when you, too, will have made the choice to dwell in the New Jerusalem, where there is love and light and joy forevermore. When we see each other again, we shall speak of these things and know that God is good.

I am, always, your loving brother,
Edward

Chapter 28

The afternoon's events at Hartwell House, however, had proceeded in a decidedly less sanguine manner.

While Barnabas attended the convocation during the day, Will was been left to his own devices. He had ridden in the park during the early morning hours, galloping ferociously until he had been yelled at by several irate gentleman, and afterwards, upon his return home, he had written his stepmother a letter. But all the while, he was thinking about Charissa.

The knowledge that she was lost to him maddened him, and because it was Sir Godfrey—that spiritual snob—who was to marry her, he was infuriated all the more.

But what, Will speculated, did she think of himself? He was gratified that she had tried to call off Sir Godfrey's verbal attack the second night of the convocation, although from what she'd said, he didn't know whether or not she believed his conversion was real. And although he attempted to convince himself her opinion shouldn't matter, the effort failed spectacularly. He couldn't deny in his heart that it mattered enormously. Furthermore, not seeing her last night had underscored the persistent loneliness he felt without her.

He was not doing well.

Because it had previously helped him settle his mind, he went to the study to resume work on her portrait. But soon he was interrupted; the butler announced visitors, the same couple who had called two days prior—Helen St. Swythin and Edgar Duddridge.

Will grimaced, but again curiosity won out over distaste for their company. He deliberately left them waiting for fifteen minutes, then joined them in the drawing room.

Edgar was dozing in a chair with his mouth partly open, while Helen was gazing at the painting of Lieutenant Devreux with her back to the door. She whirled around when she heard Will enter. She was wearing the same new gown she had donned for her previous visit, and he could see that she was holding an object wrapped in a cloth. Her cheeks were flushed and her eyes bright. "Lord Hartwell," she greeted him, "I am so happy to see you!"

"Good day, Miss St. Swythin," he said, unable to return her sentiment.

"I must tell you I have been carrying the thought of your brave brother in my heart ever since I first laid eyes on his likeness. I couldn't let go of my admiration for him and of my sympathy for your grief. Indeed, I felt compelled by God Himself to make a journey out to the Royal Hospital Chelsea. There I sought out a brave soldier, Sergeant Mundy, in order to learn what I could about your brother's death. The sergeant was with your brother in his final hours, and he knew him intimately. For my only goal, dearest Lord Hartwell, has been to ease your pain," she insisted, her voice wavering with emotion.

Will looked warily at the article in her hands. "What is that?"

Helen held it out to him triumphantly as she crossed the room. "This," she declared, "belonged to your brother. I have accepted it as a gift from his comrades-in-arms, to bring you solace—and to prove that I love you!"

Afraid she would throw herself into his arms, Will took the package from her and moved away. He unwrapped it carefully and saw she had given him an object made out of gold braid; it was an infantry officer's epaulette.

He examined it for a few seconds. "I thank you for your kind attention," he said, turning back to her, "but this cannot be from my brother's uniform. You may take it back."

Helen blinked. "No, it is his, I assure you."

"I'm sorry, your assumption is false. My brother was a company officer—a lieutenant—but this is the epaulette of a field officer. You can tell by the insignia." He raised it to show her the badge. "It is a star, which indicates the rank of major." When she did not move to take it from him, he threw the epaulette down onto a chair. "That did not belong to him."

"No," Helen repeated stubbornly, the pitch of her voice rising. "You must be mistaken. I have it on the very best authority this is his."

"It is the wrong insignia," Will countered coldly. "Obviously."

Deathly white, Helen's face contorted as she opened her mouth to argue with him—until a memory struck her with both the speed and the sting of a whip's lash. In her mind's eye, she saw Major Purvis' uniform from the night before. He had worn a star on his shoulder, which meant the epaulette she had worked so hard to acquire could not have been Lieutenant Devreux's.

Helen groaned, her fingernails pressing into her flesh as she clenched her fists. How had her artist's eye missed such a definitive detail? She had been too overcome with the cleverness of her scheme, too careless. Be that as it may, she knew instantly her best-laid plan had just collapsed spectacularly into a heap of ruins.

"I have been played for a fool," she hissed. Turning to Edgar, who was still slumbering peacefully, she slapped him on the shoulder. "Why did you not tell me this?" she screeched.

"Whaaa?" he called out, unaware of what had happened.

"Oh, you are worthless!" she shrieked.

Will had been backing up steadily, anxious to avoid her histrionics, and in no time managed to exit through the open doorway. Seeing one of the footman at the other end of the hall, he walked swiftly toward the servant, intending to have his callers shown to the door. But to his amazement, Helen flew out into the hallway in search of him.

"William, please stop!" she called out, succeeding in grabbing his coat.

He faced her, angered by her presumption. "You overstep your bounds, Miss St. Swythin."

"But don't you remember *this?*" She held up her left hand. "You must remember—you *must!* It's the ring you gave me!"

His face contorted with incredulity. "I gave you?" It was the serpent ring she had shown him at Charissa's birthday party.

"The symbol of eternal love! You bestowed it upon me!"

"Your memory deceives you. I gave you no gift at Silvercrosse Hall."

"Not at Silvercrosse—in London! And not this year. It was five years ago. You came to my rescue and entrusted to me this secret promise of love. When God brought you to me again in Staffordshire, I tried to remind you of the ring and all that it means."

Now Will was certain Helen was completely insane. Out of the corner of his eye he saw the door to his study. As fast as he could, he opened it and tried to escape inside the room, but she pushed all her weight into the door and stumbled in after him.

"Darling William!" she exclaimed, "My own true love, don't leave me. I know you remember me! The Lord has destined us to be husband and wife! You must believe…" But whatever she was about to say was lost forever when she saw the exquisite portrait of Charissa sitting on its easel by the window.

She froze.

"Get out!" ordered Will, motioning to the stunned footman, who stood agape at the open doorway. The servant recovered himself, walked up to Helen, and rested his hand under her elbow, thinking she would come quietly. But he had never before reckoned with someone quite like Helen St. Swythin.

If she had been pallid before, now her face grew red and blotched with fury. She shook her arm out of the footman's grasp and pointed an accusing finger at Will. "You… still… love… *her!*" she screamed at the top of her lungs.

She reached out to grab something—anything—to throw at the painting. However, both Will and the footman acted quickly to restrain her, preventing her from wreaking her vengeance on the portrait, although she struggled and raged against them. Will noticed Edgar skulking uselessly in the hallway and with a loud voice ordered him to assist in Helen's removal from the premises.

It took all three men to wrestle her into the hall. She was small in stature, but she made up for her lack of height with kicking and screaming.

Only when Will threatened to slap her did she stop flailing, but she dissolved into a tempest of tears, clutching at Will in wild desperation.

"God has called *me* to be your wife!" she cried. "You are to be *my* husband!"

Will detached himself from her in disgust. Moving away from her as fast as he could, he ordered Edgar and the footman to finish the job of hauling her outside the house. Leaving them to it, he pounded up the stairs to his room. As he went, he could hear her wails of grief even after she, along with Edgar, had been ushered unceremoniously out onto the street.

Feeling unclean, Will ordered a bath. He sat in the hot water until it was cool, playing the ridiculous scene over and over again in his mind. Helen's obsession with him unnerved him—and he hated the disgraceful uproar she had raised in his own home, no less. He might have even felt sorry for her had she behaved in a ladylike manner, but her reprehensible tantrum was beyond the pale.

Ah well, he thought with a rueful smile as he began to calm down at last, what an interesting and outrageous tale he would have to tell Barnabas at dinner.

As Charissa rode in the carriage to Grosvenor Chapel, she fingered the reticule resting unobtrusively on her lap. It had never held a greater treasure, she believed, than the tattered New Testament now hidden within it. Her hands covered the bag protectively as everyone spoke enthusiastically about the evening ahead of them—everyone, that is, except Sir Godfrey, who was unusually quiet.

Absent from their party were Helen and Edgar. Helen had arrived back at the hotel early that afternoon without her cousin and in a baleful mood. Mrs. Mainwood informed Penelope and Charissa that Helen had retired to her room, refusing to come out for any reason. When Penelope knocked on the door, Helen rudely resisted her sister's efforts to engage her. So the rest of them left her alone, unwilling to be the recipients of her abuse.

Unbeknownst to the others, of course, Penelope and Charissa understood Helen's anger. They guessed she had presented Will with the epaulette and that he had recognized it was not his brother's—just as Sergeant Mundy and Captain Aldwin had predicted. Will had repudiated Helen's gift and, therefore, rejected Helen herself. Thus

Helen's dream of finding love and honor as the Countess of Hartwell had been decisively shattered.

But now, as the coach clattered through the streets on the way to Mayfair, Charissa was not concerned about Helen.

Once they arrived, Charissa and Penelope guided Colonel and Mrs. Mainwood to the second row pew, while Sir Godfrey joined the Reverend Dr. Seymour in the robing room. Penelope watched him go and gave Charissa an encouraging nod as the four of them took their seats.

Charissa felt her face grow warm. She turned away from her companions and looked over her shoulder, scanning the sanctuary with spurious nonchalance. Sure enough, she identified Will and his friend Mr. Worthington up in the balcony almost at once. He was looking away, but she saw him move to examine the crowd below. She quickly lowered her gaze to the program in her hands, forcing herself to read the words: *Introductory Address/Simon, Do You Love Me? A Sermon on the Restorative Love of God/Sir Godfrey Scrivener of Silvercrosse Hall.*

After the opening hymn, Sir Godfrey mounted the steps to the pulpit and stared out over the congregation. He spread out his papers in front of him, cleared his throat, and began to speak. At first, his voice sounded tight and slightly high-pitched, but he soon relaxed and began to speak clearly and powerfully. It was an excellent sermon, and although she was at the front of the Chapel, Charissa could tell from the people around her that his message was being well-received. If only both she and Sir Godfrey had been able to put that message into practice the night of the Murrington assembly, extending to Will the same grace that Jesus had given Simon Peter.

When Sir Godfrey had concluded his discourse and the congregation had begun chatting during the interval, he came down to the pew where the Murrington party was seated. Charissa congratulated him first, and her pride shone in her eyes. He had truly done well.

As the others began to praise him and even strangers circled around him, adding their voices to the hubbub, Charissa picked up her reticule and slipped away, heading for the balcony. She found Will easily. He was standing by a window, speaking with his friend and another man. Her heart in her throat, she walked over to the little group.

"Good evening, Lord Hartwell, Mr. Worthington." She looked up at Will, hoping her voice wouldn't tremble. "Would you mind, sir, if I had a word with you?"

Barnabas drew the other man away, without even asking Will's permission, while Will affected an outward calm he most certainly did not feel. "How may I help you, Miss Armitage?"

"I have something for you, but the tale of how it came into my hands is too long to be told now, so I have written it all in a letter." She reached into the bag and pulled out the New Testament, wondering if he would recognize it, but as she showed it to him, she gathered by his expression he had never seen it before. "My letter is tucked underneath the front cover," she explained, "but there is another letter you will want to read folded into a small pocket inside the back cover."

"Thank you," he said politely, holding out his hand.

Charissa gave him the book, but as she did so, his fingers brushed hers, and her heart thumped so violently she thought he would hear it. "I must return to my friends now," she stated in a rush, pulling her hand back. She swiveled to walk away, but she couldn't help herself—she whirled around again and looked him in the eyes. "God bless you, Will!" she said fiercely. "May He bless you always." Then she ran back to the stairs and fled down them with rapid steps.

Will watched her go without a word.

"Charissa, haven't you eaten yet? Penelope, where are those gloves I loaned you? Helen! Where are you? Why haven't you finished packing? We are supposed to be leaving now!" Mrs. Mainwood fussed about their rooms like an overwrought hen, trying to put everything in order and mostly accomplishing the opposite of her intentions. Plainly, they would not be leaving London as early in the day as Colonel Mainwood had hoped.

Penelope came out into the hall holding a book. "Oh dear. Mrs. Mainwood, I've forgotten to return this novel to Hookham's. And I believe Helen still has one or two borrowed books as well."

"For goodness sakes," Mrs. Mainwood grumbled. "You're grown women, the both of you!" Muttering other things Penelope was glad she couldn't hear, Mrs. Mainwood strutted into Helen's room. "Helen!

Where are you?" But the younger Miss St. Swythin was nowhere to be found.

Mrs. Mainwood flashed her eyes about the room. Helen did seemed to have finished packing, since only a shawl lay on the bed with a borrowed novel sitting beside it. Grousing that Helen had probably conveniently planned to avoid returning the book, Mrs. Mainwood snatched it up. On her way out, she saw another stack of reading material in Helen's still-open trunk. Making an irritated noise, she bustled over and examined the books' covers. One of them was a text on botany—a Hookham's loan, Mrs. Mainwood concluded—and underneath it was another fancy volume looking like it belonged to the library as well. She scooped them both up and closed the trunk with a bang. As she went out into the hall, she instructed a waiting servant to take the trunk to the carriage, and she took the books down to hotel's front desk herself. "Please deliver these to Hookham's Circulating Library in Mayfair," she ordered the employee.

"Yes, madam," he replied. "I'll see it's done straightaway."

At last, over half an hour later, all the baggage had been loaded onto the Mainwood's coach. "Where is Helen?" Colonel Mainwood inquired impatiently as the group stood outside the hotel.

Charissa and Penelope exchanged a look, but before there was serious trouble, Helen appeared around the corner of the hotel building, holding her hat on her head and clutching a package. "I know I'm late," she said defensively, "but I had to pick up some special paintbrushes I ordered. The shop sent me a message this morning that they were ready."

Penelope handed her sister her shawl. "Yes, it was better to get them now than to have them sent to Murrington," she agreed, although she wished her sister had thought to inform them of her errand. "Come, let's get into the carriage."

"You're not late, you're right on time," Charissa added in an attempt to calm the troubled waters.

Helen ignored her. "What about my book from Hookham's? I hope you didn't pack it," she said to Penelope accusingly.

"No, Helen," Mrs. Mainwood replied crisply. "I've sent all our books back—including that rather large one on plants you checked out."

Helen's mouth fell open when she realized which book Mrs. Mainwood meant. "What have you done? That book wasn't from Hookham's—it belongs to Lord Hartwell!" She glared at Charissa.

"From Lord Hartwell? How in the world...?" began Mrs. Mainwood.

But Penelope interrupted her briskly. "And you were taking his property with you back to Staffordshire?" she asked her sister disapprovingly.

"I was going to send it back when I was finished with it," Helen retorted.

"Please, ladies, get into the carriage!" Colonel Mainwood ordered firmly, putting a stop to the budding argument. "And do join them, Sir Godfrey, if you would be so kind. As you all settle yourselves, I'll go back inside the hotel and dash off a note to Lord Hartwell to inform him that his book has been sent to the library. I'll also notify Hookham's of the mistake. Then we shall please depart, so that we may at least get a few miles down the road before sundown!"

Everyone did as the Colonel had commanded. It didn't take him long to write the two messages about Lord Hartwell's book, and soon the group from Murrington were finally on their way home.

229

Chapter 29

Will stayed up late after the convocation ended, alone in the quiet of his room apart from any distractions. Beside him on his bed's coverlet lay the worn New Testament.

After a moment of silence and a few deep breaths, he picked up the volume and turned to the frontispiece. He noticed Charissa's letter, but he set it aside because an inscription at the top of the printed page caught his eye. His throat constricted when he recognized it—his brother's signature.

So this book of Scripture had belonged to Edward. He stared at it for a long time, feeling a connection with his brother for the first time since he'd received news of his death.

Then he remembered what Charissa had said about a second letter, and he quickly flipped to the back of the testament. It didn't taken him long to discover the pocket with its precious contents. He took out the note and read it hungrily several times over, trying to process the final things his brother had wanted to communicate to him.

Finally, he set down the paper and allowed the tears that had been pricking his eyes and blurring his vision to flow freely. He'd always assumed it was the vicious quarrel they'd had that had pushed his brother into the army, but now it turned out Edward had been following a divine call.

Edward's death had *not* been Will's fault.

But how had his brother known to answer the one question that had haunted him for two years? The answer was clear—Edward himself explained that he'd been prompted by the Holy Spirit to put pen to paper. The letter had even been kept providentially hidden until exactly the right time, when Will would be able to come to terms with his brother's choice. He closed his eyes, realizing with the amazement of newfound faith that even in the midst of evil and its resultant pain, God was still on His throne.

A heartbeat later, however—in spite of Will's discovery of God's sovereign care—he felt a surge of resentment. Why would the Lord consign such a godly young man to the grave when he still had so much to give? Edward could have influenced so many people for good. It didn't seem fair—if anyone should have been stricken with an early death, it was Will himself!

But the Lord had not chosen to work that way. And Will had to admit that he was tired of the bitterness that had eaten away at him since his brother's passing. As he pondered the words Edward had written, he realized he had no desire to be locked in an endless, futile struggle with the Almighty over what had happened in the past. He had been angry with himself and angry at God for a very long time. But here was proof the situation was not as he had perceived it; he had completely misunderstood his brother.

How he wished he could tell Edward that now he did understand— that he was proud of him—that he thought him strong and noble and worthy of honor. He wept again as he mourned the loss of the companionship they could have shared.

But it would never be, not in this life. Will would simply have to lay his grief and disappointment at God's feet in surrender.

So he did. And as he prayed, he sensed that he was not now—nor ever again would be—alone.

At last, he put away the New Testament with Edward's note and picked up Charissa's letter. Her words affected him in a different but nonetheless powerful way.

She explained what she had heard at the Rutledge's dinner party and described her visit with Sergeant Mundy. Will smiled when he thought of her venturing out to the Royal Hospital Chelsea to seek the truth. But she had also closed her missive with a heartfelt apology:

> *Before I conclude this letter* (she wrote), *I must humbly and sincerely ask for your forgiveness. I behaved wretchedly toward you the night of the assembly. Yes, I was hurt and I felt betrayed, but there was no excuse not to listen to your side of the story. You had shared so much of your heart with me I should have had no doubt at all that "Viscount Disborough" was as dead as a doornail. I cannot express how much joy it gives me to know you are truly following the Lord Jesus Christ. May the Lord bless you and keep you all the days of your life.*
>
> *Always your friend,*
> *Charissa Armitage*

Always your friend. Will sighed. Edward was lost to him until eternity—he accepted that—but he continued to rebel against the idea that Charissa was alive and yet beyond his reach. Grimacing, he put her letter on the night table beside the bed and lay down to try to get some rest before the sun came up. But he could not forget her face as he had last seen it, and when he finally fell asleep, he dreamed not of Edward but of Charissa, laughing as he chased her beside Ferne Brook and caught her up into his arms.

Will slept late the next day, not rising until afternoon. He and Barnabas entertained themselves at Tattersall's, admiring the horses for sale and discussing which of them would be best for Barnabas to purchase. They went to a concert in the evening, and Will fell into bed exhausted, glad he had managed to keep Charissa out of his thoughts, more or less.

After he awoke the following morning, dressed, and wandered downstairs, he discovered Barnabas had been unexpectedly called out for the day, and Will missed his companionship. He would have liked to ride with his friend or undertake some other vigorous exercise. As it was, though, he stayed at the house. He avoided the study, not quite able to face Charissa's portrait at the moment, and so went into the library to find a book to read. As he was staring at the shelves without success, a footman entered.

"A message came for you yesterday morning whilst you were still abed, m'lord," the servant said, handing the paper to him, "but I fear you didn't see it on the tray."

"How careless of me," Will said, thanking the man and opening it. It was the note from Colonel Mainwood advising him the book he had lent to Helen St. Swythin had been accidentally returned to the circulating library. He shrugged and threw the letter onto the table. Maybe he would send a servant to pick it up next week. Or never. He didn't really care.

When Barnabas returned to Hartwell House for the evening meal, Will told him the story of Edward's New Testament. After they had thoroughly discussed Edward's letter and its implications, Will explained how Charissa had found Sergeant Mundy in Chelsea.

"Miss Armitage is a remarkable woman," Barnabas commented. "She reminds me of Susannah—not in appearance, but in spirit."

Will smiled faintly. "When I met Susannah, she reminded me of Charissa."

That night Will slept soundly, but he was awakened in the wee hours of the morning by a dream he couldn't remember. It hadn't been a nightmare exactly, but he woke with a sense of urgency he couldn't explain. However, he put the strange feeling out of his mind and fell back asleep, and by the time he had taken a morning ride in the park and sought out breakfast, the unease had dissipated.

After the meal, as he and Barnabas sat in the morning room reading the newspaper, a package arrived for Will from Hookham's. Will unwrapped the box, expecting to find Stevenson's *Illustrated Botany of the British Isles*, but he was surprised to discover another book packed with it—an expensively bound volume with no writing on the outside.

Gazing at it curiously, Will was certain it hadn't come from his own library. Yet he also knew he'd come across something like it in the recent past, and, after a moment spent searching his memory, he recalled where and when. At Silvercrosse Hall during Charissa's birthday party, Helen had given Charissa a book strikingly similar to this one. He opened the front cover and, sure enough, he saw Helen's name inscribed on the first page with fanciful flourishes and surrounded by flowering vines.

He grimaced. The book did indeed belong to none other than the bane of his existence, Helen St. Swythin. The library must have sent it along with the other tome by unhappy accident, and he supposed with a longsuffering sigh he'd have to send it back to her.

He flipped idly to the middle of the book and noticed it was a diary, decorated with drawings. Nothing out of the ordinary, or so he thought. But all at once he caught sight of his own (former) name—*Viscount Disborough*. Given her infatuation with him, he wasn't surprised to be mentioned, though it seemed odd that she referred to him as a viscount since she only knew him as the Earl of Hartwell.

Curious, he read the whole sentence: *I wanted to hear news of Viscount Disborough,* she'd written. His brow furrowed. What news? When? Why? But he had no opportunity to examine the diary further to find out; Barnabas distracted him by asking his opinion about an article concerning the ongoing Peninsular War.

Will closed the volume, put it atop his botany text on a side table, and conversed with his friend for a while. After they had exhausted the topic at hand, Barnabas returned to his paper and Will, sitting back on the settee and crossing his arms, looked over at the diary again. What irony, he thought, that he should have in his possession mad Helen's journal.

He stared at the fancy leather cover. If his name had been included in anyone else's personal papers, he wouldn't have thought anything of it, but, after all, this was Helen St. Swythin. The woman had stubbornly demonstrated a wild and distasteful infatuation with him. Did she have a compelling reason to choose *him* as her obsession, he wondered, or was it merely a coincidence?

And—particularly disconcerting—during that awful scene a few days ago, she had again insisted that God Himself had ordained their marriage. How doggedly did she believe this prophecy? Just how far-reaching were her plans to see it fulfilled?

He grunted and stood up, intending to find some sort of distraction, but his attention was once more arrested by the diary sitting innocently on the table where he'd placed it.

The thought of Helen's infatuation continued to bother him: Helen St. Swythin was nothing if not persistent. She was undoubtedly the most tenacious human being he'd ever met. He wanted to believe that she'd finally abandoned her fascination with him. But—on the other hand—it was entirely conceivable that she might at this very moment be conjuring up a new scheme to ensnare him.

Will did not trust her even now.

He sat down on the settee and drummed his fingers on the fabric. He could find out the answers to his questions, he mused—he could open the diary and see for himself. His conscience troubled him briefly, but the power of Helen's delusion finally compelled him to take advantage of the opportunity serendipitously afforded him. He resolved to examine what she had written in her journal, hoping to discover the truth. He regretted violating her privacy, but he also believed that forewarned was forearmed.

He picked up the volume and, setting it on his lap, turned to the page where her neat yet extravagant script began. He noted at once that the diary commenced in May 1805. There, just as he anticipated, Helen had indeed laid out the details of precisely why she had fixed her heart on him.

Helen's Journal

May 17, 1805
London

> *My life has changed forever. Yesterday I thought I was nothing, an afterthought, a wallflower destined to wilt unnoticed. But today God has revealed to me my destiny!* I shall marry a viscount! *And not just any viscount, mind you, but William Devreux, Viscount Disborough, who shall upon the death of his father become the Earl of Hartwell. I shall be a countess, cherished and adored. It shall be I— and not Penelope or even Hector—who restores our family's fortunes and honor.*
>
> *How do I know this, dear reader? How can I be sure God has revealed this to me? Just listen to my tale of divinely ordained circumstances, and see if you do not agree!*

Last night, I attended a ball—just one more stupid event in which stupid ladies and stupid gentlemen engage in disgusting flirtation and stupid conversation. The only gentleman to ask me to dance was Mr. Rigdon Pugsbottom who is at least one hundred and ten years old with little piggy eyes and bad breath. I was sick of it all, and in a fit of righteous indignation I started—foolishly, I admit—to try to walk home by myself. I had only gone a block or two when I was set upon by a pair of ruffians, and I was afraid. But who should come to my rescue but a rakishly handsome gentleman. I could tell he was in his cups, but he managed to vanquish my foes all the same. He asked me why a lovely lady like myself was out alone at such a late hour, and I began to weep, falling into his arms.

As I poured out my heart to him, he admonished me to dry my tears. Then he reached into his pocket, which had jewelry inside it, and pressed a ring into the palm of my hand. It was in the shape of a serpent with its tail in its mouth—a symbol of everlasting love! He put me in a hackney, paid for it, and sent me home.

And who was this man, you ask? He was none other than the notorious Viscount Disborough. How many ladies have swooned over him, I cannot count, but now, as you see, he is mine! My own William! He has placed upon my finger an enduring promise. He has forged a secret bond between us. Oh yes, his deed is something that God Almighty has ordained. This came from the Lord; it is wondrous in our sight.

Will was astounded—Helen had not been making up the bit about the ring! The incident must have occurred more or less the way she had recorded it, but he recalled nothing. More than likely he had been drinking heavily and had won someone else's possessions in a game of chance. Not having the presence of mind to push Helen away as she had clung to him, he had probably given her the ring just to shut her up. He certainly had not given a thought to any possible significance of the gift, if he had even known what it was when he handed it to her. But how quickly she had added romantic significance to it; in her mind he had literally placed the ring upon her finger with ulterior motives.

This incidental meeting was the whole reason she had set her marital sights on him. It had been ridiculous right from the beginning, but instead of fading with time, as do most infatuations, Helen's grew worse.

Will scanned the next fifty or so pages. Over the ensuing five years, he learned, she had fantasized ceaselessly about him and tried to learn everything she could about his life, convinced God would bring them together in the future. This, he noted uncomfortably, was the context for the sentence that had piqued his curiosity.

He started to read closely again when he arrived at her spring 1810 entries. He soon noted that she had indeed dreamed of his arrival at Silvercrosse Hall before the fact, as she had claimed. But it wasn't because of any prophetic gift. It was because he was often the subject of her dreams.

And, of course, she had recognized him at once in the Silvercrosse Hall drawing room. She had been thrilled by his miraculous appearance there, convinced that the Almighty's long-awaited plan to unite them was finally underway. She'd played along with his charade, and, displaying admirable patience, had not revealed herself to him all at once. Instead, she had subtly encouraged him to remember their encounter of five years ago.

First, she had shown him the ring, thinking he would understand its meaning and realize she was the woman he had rescued that night— the one who had loved him loyally ever since. It had disappointed her when he had not shown any recollection of either her or the ring, but she had not lost hope. Instead, she had attempted to jog his memory in other ways, such as showing him her painting of the London cityscape, which she had created to canonize the exact street corner where their first meeting had taken place. Yet nothing had worked.

Instead, she had watched him fall in love with Charissa.

Nevertheless, she had a breathtaking capacity to interpret events to her own advantage, never doubting her ultimate goal would be achieved. In spite of her escalating jealousy, she had persevered in her campaign to push Charissa towards Sir Godfrey and draw Will to herself, confident her plan was God's plan.

Will paused for a moment and rubbed his eyes. He had never suspected any of this, although of course he had seen from the beginning that Helen was attracted to him. Over the years many women had been, but none of them had ever been as batty as this. It was hard for him to fathom.

He resumed reading and soon noticed a disturbing trend. Helen's envy of Charissa had turned into disapproval, then rapidly deteriorated into dislike. There were more and more short, sharp sentences such as: *Charissa thinks she deserves his love, but she is shallow and vain*! Or, *How can he stand her insipid sweetness? Her fawning over him is revolting.*

Before long came a revealing entry Helen had written the day after the Mainwoods' party in Murrington, when she had thrown herself at him, and he had rejected her.

Helen's Journal

June 8, 1810
Wisteria Cottage

> *I wrote last night of the terrible anguish I am suffering, all because Lord Hartwell has succumbed to Charissa's wiles. She is a witch who claims to be a Christian but is in fact doing everything in her power to thwart the purposes of the Almighty!*
>
> *I must separate my William from Charissa at all costs, even if it mean he leaves Murrington.*
>
> *As I lay awake last night, I agonized over how to accomplish this without seeming to be the agent of their parting, but this morning I am once again confident, for I have been given an inspired plan of action.*
>
> *Do you remember my cousin Mr. Edgar Duddridge? Oh, I know he is very stupid, but he also has not a sixpence to scratch with. His poverty makes him amenable to any course of action which will refill his pockets—and I shall promise*

to do so once I am Lady Hartwell. But that is not the only reason I am convinced he will help me. You see, dear diary, not only is Edgar in danger of bankruptcy, but I also happen to know he absolutely HATES Lord Hartwell, who has won large sums of money from him several times in the past. Thus I shall enlist my dear cousin!

Here is my plan: I shall invent a pretext for Edgar to come to Murrington, since Penny will never agree to ask him to Wisteria Cottage, more's the pity. I think I'll invite myself to visit his widowed sister Agnes in Oxfordshire (even though she is a terrible bore), and he can escort me to her home via the mail coach. He shall arrive conveniently in time for the assembly in a couple of weeks and unmask Lord Hartwell in front of the entire village. He will enjoy that little act of revenge, I am certain. Sir Godfrey will be outraged, to be sure, and Charissa will fall apart like the pitiful creature she is. But no one, especially William himself, will suspect me!

After the dust settles and when the time is right, I will travel to London to find my William!

So it had all been an outlandish plot; the unveiling of Will's identity had been part of a hidden plan to destroy his relationship with Charissa. He seethed inwardly, thinking again how none of them had suspected Helen of anything other than an unrealistic but innocent attachment to him. How wrong they had been.

He no longer felt the slightest shred of guilt for intruding upon Helen's private thoughts. Flipping forward to the final diary entries, Will discovered the journal was completely up to date. He was not surprised to read that she had attempted the epaulette incident after learning about Sergeant Mundy at the same party Charissa had attended. Helen had written violently of her pain when it became clear Will did not love her, having thrown her ignominiously out of his house.

But the most troubling words he found were scrawled on the last page, where Helen's controlled, artistic handwriting disintegrated into an angry, blotchy mess. Her last entry exposed the climax of the trend he had noticed earlier—her animosity toward Charissa had developed into a stark, raw loathing.

Helen's Journal

November 1, 1810
London

> *I hate her, I hate her, I hate her, I hate her, I hate her.*
> *She is stealing from me what is MY RIGHT, what I have cherished, sacrificed for, and lived for these past five years. Faithless trollop! She is engaged to marry another, and yet she twines her tendrils around the man who is mine. Like ivy around an oak tree, she encircles my beloved and holds him fast.*
> *Marriage to Sir Godfrey is not enough to stop her. Her very existence sows wickedness! She is poisonous black bryony in the garden of a sweet English rose, a funeral bell sucking the life from an evergreen.*
> *The way forward is obvious. Like a weed or a toadstool, she must be completely REMOVED.* By the roots.

Removed? By the roots? Whatever Helen meant by *poisonous black bryony* or *funeral bell*, it didn't sound good. Will glared at the words, sickened by Helen's bitter hatred.

His eye moved to the illustration beside the rancorous paragraphs. Unlike the written words, Helen had drawn the picture with noticeable care—mushrooms at the foot of a pine tree.

The sense of unease that had been hanging over him like a cloud intensified. As he pondered the significance of what he had seen, out of the corner of his eye he caught a glimpse of the *Illustrated Botany of the British Isles*. Impulsively he grabbed the text, and when he opened it, he found a pink lace ribbon hidden between two pages. A pair of detailed illustrations met his gaze: one mushroom depicted on the left page and another on the right, both listed under the category *Midsummer Through Late Autumn*. The caption read:

Shown at left is the Brown Stew Mushroom, enjoyed by the particularly refined connoisseur. An observant searcher will find this colorful little beauty growing in abundance on tree stumps. But beware—do not mistake it for the Funeral Bell Mushroom, depicted on the opposite page. This appealing yet toxic fungus is rightly named, for it is as deadly as its more famous cousin, the Death Cap Mushroom. Alas, there is very little to distinguish between the Brown Stew and the Funeral Bell. Thus great care should be exercised when gathering the Brown Stew for food.

Will saw at once that the sketch in the diary mirrored the drawing on the right-hand page of the botany book, and his stomach turned. Consumed by her hatred for Charissa, Helen had compared her rival to a lethal mushroom found in late autumn, one that resembled an edible variety. The symbolism was plain: Helen considered Charissa a hypocrite, comparable to a destructive toadstool, itself worthy of annihilation.

Her very existence sows destruction, Helen had written, and a deadly plant must be *removed by the roots*.

Will choked. Could Helen be planning to solve her problems by...?

No! He forced himself to take a deep breath. He was jumping to ludicrous conclusions, he argued, telling himself to be reasonable. Helen St. Swythin, however hurt and angry, would not *poison* Charissa—the very idea was patently absurd. And yet...

"Barney!" Will exclaimed, jumping to his feet. "I have to ride to Staffordshire straightaway!"

Barnabas looked up in surprise. "Staffordshire?"

"Yes." Will's mind insisted that he should *go now*. "Are you willing to stay here by yourself until I return?"

"I'm able to do that," Barnabas answered, concern wrinkling his forehead. "My business is keeping me in London a while longer. I'm grateful for your hospitality, but what's wrong? May I assist you in any way?"

As briefly as possible, Will explained his concern. "I know it sounds bizarre," he finished, feeling idiotic, "but I am compelled to make the journey." Was he as delusional as Helen herself? He hoped not.

He expected Barnabas to try to talk him out of travelling north, but to his surprise his friend agreed he should take his inner alarm seriously. "This warning may or may not be of the Lord," Barnabas told him, "but it seems right to me that you should err on the side of obedience rather than passivity."

Will needed no more encouragement. "I shall leave within the hour and take the reins myself," he declared. He knew he could outride even the best of his carriages and maintain the pace for not merely hours, but days.

Chapter 30

It was a grueling trip, although Will changed horses frequently so as not to tire them severely. But his compulsion to keep moving was unrelenting. He only stopped when he could no longer see the road, and he was off again at first light. It often crossed his mind that he was going to make a complete fool of himself, but he refused to give in to self-doubt. Better to appear ridiculous than neglect to warn Charissa of the danger lurking in a deceitful friend.

He arrived at Silvercrosse Hall in the late afternoon; the sun was low in the sky at the end of a cold day. The familiar, tawny-stoned Elizabethan house brought back memories of the happy days he had spent here, but now, unfortunately, he knew he was no longer welcome.

Nevertheless he galloped his horse down the drive and, when he reached the house, he pulled firmly on the reins. Grabbing Helen's journal out of the saddlebag, he leapt off his mount and sprinted up to the front door, although he hardly knew why such speed was necessary. But he was soon to find out.

He rapped sharply on the door, and Jack the footman answered it. The servant stared in consternation when he saw who it was. "Mr. Lyon! I mean, Lord…"

"Hartwell. Lord Hartwell," Will said briskly, stepping uninvited into the front hall. "It's important that I speak with Sir Godfrey and Miss Armitage." He had to see them together for propriety's sake.

"Sir Godfrey is in his study. I'll inform him you're here," Jack replied.

Before the servant had taken a step, however, two white, fluffy balls of fur streaked into the front hall. Commodore and Sprite had recognized Will's voice, and they rushed toward him, jumping up on him with joyous enthusiasm. Will bent down and rubbed their heads, moved by their exuberance.

As Jack circled around the dogs to notify Sir Godfrey of Will's arrival, Will stressed, "It is imperative I speak with Miss Armitage as well as Sir Godfrey. Where is she?"

"Miss Armitage is in the kitchen," Jack told him. "If you'll wait here, I'll speak with Sir Godfrey and be back shortly."

"Why is she in the kitchen?" Will demanded. Below stairs was Mrs. Harper's sphere and not a place Charissa visited frequently.

Jack stared at him, noticeably apprehensive. "Miss St. Swythin invited her to go for a walk, and they chose to return to the kitchen."

"*Which* Miss St. Swythin?"

"Miss Helen."

Will felt a frisson of fear. "What were they doing on their walk?"

"Whatever it is ladies do when they're out alone together. Talk, I guess."

"But why are they in the kitchen?" Will tried not to sound threatening. "Please tell me. It's important."

Jack was baffled by the question, but he said with a shrug, "I heard Miss Armitage say Miss St. Swythin wanted to forage for mushrooms, so I suppose they're…."

"*No!*" Will shouted before he had even heard the end of the sentence. He took off running down the hall, heading for the stairs which led down to the vast old Tudor kitchen, but found his way blocked by an irate Sir Godfrey.

"*What is the meaning of this?*" Sir Godfrey yelled, putting out a hand and jerking Will's arm. Helen's journal crashed to the floor. "How dare you invade my home! Jack, help me!" Jack obeyed, and together they seized Will, pushing him roughly against the wall.

The dogs barked furiously, adding to the confusion. "Quiet!" Sir Godfrey yelled, angry that they seemed to be defending Will rather than cornering him.

"Sir Godfrey," Will said, deciding to talk rather than fight his way out and forcing himself to sound as rational as possible. "Forgive this intrusion, but I have good reason to believe that Charissa is in immediate danger. Please let me go!"

"Danger?" scoffed Sir Godfrey. "At Silvercrosse Hall? You are mad. The only danger to her at the moment is you."

"I am not mad," Will countered, "and her life could very well be at stake, but certainly not from me. If you will be so good as to unhand me, I will show you evidence. I fear we have not a moment to lose."

After a brief hesitation, Sir Godfrey nodded at Jack, and they both released Will. Jack moved to block the ancient oak door which led to the kitchen stairs, but Will turned in the opposite direction, picking up Helen's diary and opening to the last entry.

"Helen St. Swythin is still obsessed with me, and she believes Charissa is an insurmountable obstacle to gaining my affections," he explained, handing the book to Sir Godfrey. "This is Helen's personal journal, which I acquired by what can only be described as an act of divine providence. *Read this.*" He pointed at the words and picture which had provoked him to action, and Sir Godfrey looked at them impatiently.

Moments later, however, as Sir Godfrey's expression turned from one of annoyance to one of shock, Will saw Charissa's cousin was beginning to understand the situation. "So I take it you know what a funeral bell is?" Will asked heatedly. "It's a deadly mushroom. And that's what they're eating. Mushrooms! *Right now!*"

Sir Godfrey's mouth dropped open, and Jack looked at his master questioningly. Seizing the opportunity, Will thrust the unsuspecting Jack out of the way and barreled down the stairs into the rooms below, shouting, "Charissa! Charissa! Where are you?"

Sir Godfrey followed, with the dogs barking again at his heels, and although Jack had no idea what was happening, he came, too. It took a few seconds for them all to pass through several thick-walled storerooms, but finally they reached the kitchen, which boasted an enormous fireplace and held a number of tables, both large and small. Mrs. Harper was rolling dough out on one of them, while a couple of scullery maids stood nearby, one chopping vegetables and the other whipping something in a bowl. Another young woman Will didn't recognize, clearly not a kitchen servant, was wielding a pestle to grind dried herbs into a powder.

Charissa and Helen sat on a bench at one of the larger tables at the far end of the room close to the brightly burning fireplace, where they had been sorting the booty from their excursion in the woods. Sitting beside Charissa on the table was a bowl filled with some cut-up raw mushrooms; she was holding a fork in midair when Will, Sir Godfrey, and Jack burst into the room.

"I thought I heard Sprite and Commodore…" she began, but she completely forgot whatever it was she had been planning to say. She could only gasp, "Lord Hartwell!"

The rest of the women gaped at the men. Helen's eyes widened, while Mrs. Harper bobbed an uncertain curtsey.

"Stop, Miss Armitage!" Will bellowed. "Don't eat anything!"

Charissa put her fork down, completely confused, her gaze going from Will to Sir Godfrey and back again to Will. "I've just tasted some of the mushrooms Helen and I picked this afternoon. But… Lord Hartwell, what are you doing here?"

"What have you eaten? How many?" Will demanded, almost sick with fear. He reached the table where they were sitting and attempted to seize the bowl, but Helen, jumping to her feet, snatched it out of his hands.

"They're just harmless little mushrooms," Helen stated, keeping the table between them. "Why are you here, Lord Hartwell? When did you arrive? Why are you acting strangely?"

Ignoring her questions, he reached for the bowl, but she shifted it further away from him. "We've been sampling tasty mushrooms," she repeated. "They're almost gone."

"You eat one," commanded Will, narrowing his eyes. "Now. From the bowl."

She looked at him quizzically, carefully fished one out of the crockery, and ate it. "Mm," she said.

Will glanced at Sir Godfrey, who was frowning doubtfully. "Let me see that," Will ordered Helen, holding out his hand.

"Of course," she replied. But as she moved around the table towards him, she tripped over one of the large uneven flagstones which constituted the ancient floor. The bowl went flying out of her hands, its contents spilling directly into the hottest part of the fire. "Oh dear!" she cried out as the remaining mushrooms blazed up and turned quickly to ash.

Horror-struck, Will believed she had destroyed them on purpose, and it was all he could do to restrain himself from wrapping his hands around her throat and choking her to death. But he only asked fiercely, "What is the antidote for funeral bells?"

"Funeral bells?" Helen cocked her head to one side.

"Don't play the fool with me. Funeral bells. Poisonous mushrooms. What is the antidote?"

"Surely you don't think…"

"What is the antidote?!"

"There is none," said Helen, sounding worried now. "But we've picked only edible mushrooms. I can tell a brown stew from a funeral bell—I'm confident of that. We'll be fine." She smiled at Will. "But I'm touched you would be so concerned for me."

Now exasperated, Sir Godfrey spoke up. "Lord Hartwell, I think you should come back upstairs with me."

Helen glanced over at Sir Godfrey for the first time and noticed what he was carrying. She sucked in a quick breath. "What is that you have, Sir Godfrey?"

He scowled. "It is your diary."

She ran over to him, snatching it out of his hand. "Oh! My *personal* journal! Wherever did you find it? I thought Mrs. Mainwood had sent it to Hookham's. I was livid when I found out, and I wrote them straightaway, but I haven't heard back yet. Did they send it here instead of to Wisteria Cottage? Why would they do that?" The crease between her brows deepened. "Oh, Sir Godfrey, surely you haven't been prying into my *private* thoughts?"

"Of course not," he grumbled guiltily.

While this conversation about Helen's journal was going on, however, Will—still unconvinced of Helen's innocence—saw Sprite nosing around on the floor beside the fireplace where the mushrooms had spilled. The dog had found a piece that hadn't fallen into the flames, but after sniffing it, he let it alone. Will bent down, picked it

247

up off the floor, and examined it thoughtfully. Turning to Charissa, he asked urgently, "How many types of mushrooms were in the bowl?"

"Helen put in several kinds," she replied, still trying to wrap her mind around the fact that Will was standing in her kitchen yelling about poisonous mushrooms.

"She knows enough to eat only the edible ones herself," Will muttered under his breath. Turning to Helen, he brandished the surviving piece. "Which variety is this?"

She stared at it. "I don't know. It's too small for me to tell."

"Is it a funeral bell?"

"Of course not. I doubt it's even a brown stew. Why are you obsessed with funeral bells? I would not make such a mistake."

"I agree," he said coldly. "You would not."

She gasped as she moved closer to him, grabbing his free hand and attempting to entwine her fingers with his. "Lord Hartwell, I…"

Will spun away from her and brusquely disentangled his hand from hers. "Mrs. Harper, do you know enough about mushrooms to identify this one?"

"No, no, I don't, Mr. Lyon, I mean, Lord Hartwell."

"Excuse me," broke in an unfamiliar voice, "but I may be able to tell you what it is."

Every eye in the room turned toward the young woman sitting alone at the small table. It was Nancy Roberts, who had made herself indispensible looking after Aunt Caroline. "My gran knows all about herbs and plants and such," Nancy reminded them, "and she's been teaching me. I'll take a look at it, if you please."

Will gave the mushroom to Nancy. After examining it carefully, she sighed. "I'm sorry, but I can't say for certain. Helen is right, it's too small to know for sure. It may be a brown stew, but it could also be a funeral bell. They look very much alike."

"It *could* be a funeral bell?" repeated Will tensely.

"It could be," Nancy affirmed.

"That's ridiculous!" blurted out Helen.

Sir Godfrey glared at her. "Silence!"

"If it *is* a funeral bell, what should we do for Miss Armitage?" Will asked Nancy. "What are the symptoms of poisoning? How fast do they occur? What is the antidote?"

"I already told you, there's no antidote," Helen interrupted again, cradling her journal.

Nancy shook her head. "That's the common understanding, to be sure, but my gran knows what to do."

"Charissa looks fine to me," Helen told Will imploringly. "She is as well as I am. No harm has been done."

Will turned to Charissa. "How *do* you feel?"

"Fine," she replied hesitantly, putting a hand over her stomach.

"But mushroom poisoning symptoms don't show up right away," Nancy told them anxiously. "They appear after a few hours."

"Since there is a chance Miss Armitage has ingested a deadly mushroom, what treatment would your gran recommend for her?" Will demanded.

"First," Nancy said confidently, "she should drink salt water to vomit up whatever's left of the funeral bell in her stomach. But she shouldn't take too long doing that because she's got to take milk thistle extract as soon as possible."

"Then we shall waste no time," Will stated decisively. "Do you have milk thistle extract, Mrs. Harper?"

"Yes. I'll get it." The cook sprang into action. "Lucy," she ordered one of the scullery maids, "you mix salt water."

"Use lots of salt," Nancy advised the girl.

"Ugh," commented the scullery maid, scrambling to obey.

Will turned his attention back to Charissa herself, who was still seated at the table, now looking pale. "Will you do these things, sweetheart? Drink the salt water and take the extract?" he asked, not caring who heard him. He knelt down in front of her and grasped her hands. "Just in case you have swallowed something deadly."

"But I don't understand why you think we picked funeral bells," Charissa repeated, holding on to his hands, still baffled by his presence. "Why do you think Helen would make such a mistake? Why are you even here in Staffordshire?"

"I will explain later, when there is time. I promise. But for now, will you trust me to see you through this unpleasant ordeal?" he requested soberly.

She bit her lip and took a deep breath before answering. "Yes, if you truly believe this is necessary, I will trust you."

"Good," he said encouragingly, although inside he was terrified.

"But stay with me, Will!" she pleaded, squeezing his hands. "Please, stay with me."

"I'll be right here every second." He freed one of his hands from hers and, reaching up, stroked her hair gently.

They had both completely forgotten about Sir Godfrey, who stood against the wall behind them. Yet Charissa's fiancé didn't say a word.

Helen, however, was watching it all disdainfully, and she didn't hesitate to speak her mind. "I'll not drink anything, because I know neither of us are in any danger," she sniffed. "But, Charissa, if you feel you must put yourself through such unpleasantness to impress Lord Hartwell, be my guest."

Charissa stared at her in disbelief. "How can you imagine that what I'm about to do would impress anyone? What could be more humiliating? But Helen," she went on, her tone softening, "I wish you would at least drink the milk thistle extract. I would be devastated if something happened to you!"

Helen's face was unreadable. "I'll be all right," she muttered. "And so will you."

Everyone ignored Helen's reassurances, however. With poorly disguised revulsion, Lucy the scullery maid handed Will a cup of water, viscous with salt. "Get me a large bowl and some clean rags," he directed the girl as he gazed at the thick, nauseating liquid. She scurried away, and he in turn gave the cup to Charissa.

"Cheers!" Charissa said in an attempt at humor as she raised the cup and drank down every last drop of the disgusting beverage.

Chapter 31

"I can't bear to watch this!" Helen proclaimed. She marched toward the doorway, but as she passed Sir Godfrey, he put his hand out and stopped her. "I wish to speak with you," he said.

"Now?" she asked with considerable frustration.

"Of course not. Once Charissa is out of danger."

"She's not *in* any danger," Helen repeated, rolling her eyes.

Sir Godfrey lowered his voice. "I know you despise her."

She glared at him. "You lied. You *were* reading my journal." She clutched it to her chest again. "Why did Hookham's send it to *you?*"

He sidestepped the question. "We will speak of these things later. Wait for me in the drawing room." He looked past her, his heart aching as he watched Charissa's face reflect her rapidly increasing discomfort.

Helen lifted an eyebrow. "I can only hope it will be worth the wait, and it might be, *if* you gird your loins and act like a man. *You* are the master of Silvercrosse Hall. Charissa is *your* fiancée! Go take care of her and dismiss Lord Hartwell. Send *him* up to the drawing room—if you have the courage to, that is!" With that parting shot, she stalked away and came as close as a lady could to stomping up the stairs.

Sir Godfrey looked daggers after her and noticed Jack lurking in the closest storeroom. "Is there anything I can do, sir?" the footman asked uncomfortably, shifting from one foot to the other.

"Go upstairs and keep a sharp eye on Miss St. Swythin." Under his breath Sir Godfrey added, "I wish her sister were here."

Although he had meant to keep that sentiment to himself, Jack heard him. "Should I instruct one of the grooms to bring Miss Penelope St. Swythin to Silvercrosse Hall?" the servant asked.

Sir Godfrey blinked. "Er… yes. Well done. That is an excellent suggestion." The thought of Penelope's serene wisdom gave Sir Godfrey an unexpected, although fleeting, sense of comfort.

After Jack departed, Sir Godfrey turned his attention back to Charissa. Will had dismissed the servants, and she was leaning over the bowl with Will supporting her. Sir Godfrey flushed with resentment at the intimacy of the scene, and Helen's insults rang in his ears. Oh yes, he desperately wanted to run over to Charissa and push Lord Hartwell out of the way, with enough force to send the man sprawling onto the floor. To take Hartwell's place was his right; Charissa was *his* betrothed!

And yet he did not do it. He stayed where he was—worrying for her and yearning to help—but he did not move in or assert his authority. And the reason why he did not do so was simple: in the space of the last few minutes he had seen with sharp and agonizing clarity the truth of the matter, and it stunned him almost more than it hurt him.

In this potentially life or death crisis, Charissa did not want him with her. She wanted Hartwell.

And thus it was Will who held her the entire time. As awful as it was for both men to watch Charissa's body contort and to hear her groan so violently, it was Will who stroked her brow and whispered encouraging words into her ear. It was Will who, when it was all over, handed her a damp cloth to wipe her face. And afterward, it was into Will's embrace that she allowed herself to collapse, and it was he who wrapped his strong arms around her protectively.

Sir Godfrey hung back, painfully conscious that he had been demoted to the role of mere spectator.

Thinking of no one else but Will, Charissa nestled close to him. "How dreadfully unladylike this is," she managed to comment.

"Don't worry," he said, trying to console her. "I've had quite a bit of experience handling this sort of thing."

"With *ladies?*"

"Well, no," he answered, kissing the top of her head, "you have me there. I suppose there is a first time for everything. But how do you feel?"

She gave him a crooked smile. "As though I've eaten a pair of month-old socks."

Will laughed. And although the circumstances were about as unromantic as he could imagine, he had never felt more proud of her or more in love with her than at that moment.

Nancy now reentered the room and gave Charissa the milk thistle extract Mrs. Harper had retrieved. "Here Miss Armitage," she instructed, pouring the liquid into a large spoon and holding it out. "A funeral bell's poison is just like a death cap's, and this extract worked a miracle on my gran's favorite hog when he got into death caps two years ago. Afterwards he was right as rain."

In spite of the gravity of the situation, Charissa exchanged an amused glance with Will as she carefully took the spoon; she had never had a pig as a role model before. She swallowed the extract obediently, then accepted a glass of pure water from Nancy and sipped it.

"Yes, make sure you drink enough fresh water, but just a little bit at a time," Nancy advised her. "You'll want to take a spoonful of the extract every few hours for a whole day. Maybe a little more if you develop other symptoms. You know what those are?"

The symptoms of acute food poisoning were violent and ugly, even more so than what she had just experienced. Suddenly feeling exhausted and overwhelmed, Charissa nodded, tears welling up in her eyes in spite of her determination to be brave. She put the glass down and rolled her face back into Will's chest, murmuring, "Please stay with me."

In answer to her plea, Will stood, sweeping her right up into his arms. "I'll carry you to your room now, where you can rest."

He looked over at Sir Godfrey, whose face was partly hidden in the shadows, and their eyes met. "Miss Roberts and I will watch over her," Will said. "I'll see to it she takes the milk thistle extract. If she develops any further symptoms, Miss Roberts will attend her."

Will was well aware it was not his place to be with Charissa in this crisis—and it wasn't even remotely proper—but Sir Godfrey did not object and made no move to stop him. The master of Silvercrosse Hall merely stepped aside and allowed Will to carry Charissa through the storerooms and up the two long flights of stairs to her room.

Will laid Charissa carefully down on the bed. Nancy followed them inside the room and after her came the two dogs, who sprang onto the coverlet and curled up beside Charissa.

"They always seem to know when anyone isn't feeling well," Charissa murmured, reaching out a hand to stroke Sprite's fur. Commodore had his eyes fixed on the doorway, guarding the room from any possible intruders.

"They were a comfort to me when I was bedridden," Will recalled. He gazed down at Charissa and stroked her hair again.

Nancy observed his tender gesture. "Begging your pardon, Miss Armitage," she said hesitantly, "I'm sorry to interrupt, but I ought to check on Miss Scrivener. I was preparing her afternoon cordial when your situation arose, and of course I had to see to your needs. But now young Sarah's been in with Miss Scrivener for far too long."

"I agree that you ought to relieve Sarah and see to Aunt Caroline," Charissa said.

"Will you be all right, Miss Armitage?" Nancy asked, glancing at Will nervously.

Charissa brushed back the strands of her hair that had slipped out of their pins. "Oh, yes."

"I'll stay with Miss Armitage," Will told Nancy firmly. "But in order that no one may gossip, I'll leave the door open."

Nancy nodded her head respectfully. "Very well, sir. Thank you, sir."

After she had disappeared down the hall, Will brought a chair over to Charissa's bedside and sat down. "I recall when our roles were reversed not so long ago," he said, "and it was I who lay near death in this house. You prayed for me."

She remembered that pivotal day. "I was unaware you heard me. I thought you had fallen back into unconsciousness."

"Ah, but I was listening. Although I confess that, at the time, I didn't want you to pray because I didn't understand why you would do such a thing."

"You wanted me to stop because you thought you were unworthy of God's grace."

"And so I am," Will observed, "but He gave it to me anyway."

Charissa smiled. Will had changed profoundly since they had first met—what a long way he had come! Then her reflections jumped forward to the last time she had seen him, and she wondered if he had found his brother's letter in the worn New Testament.

Apparently his thoughts were moving in the same direction because he said suddenly, "And speaking of God's miraculous acts, I must thank you, Charissa, for delivering Edward's last message to me. If you had not listened to the Lord's voice and obeyed His command, I would never have known the truth about God's will for Edward's life."

Charissa saw the tenderness in his eyes, heard the sincerity in his voice—and her heart melted. "It's because I love you, Will," she said out loud before she thought.

His whole being felt strangely light and happy when he heard her speak those powerful words, but he was so astonished by her assertion that he didn't know how to respond. Instead, he simply bowed his head and prayed, asking God in simple words to heal her.

Charissa couldn't help but think how extraordinary it was that the man praying for her was the same angry stranger who, not long ago, had feared an eternity in hell.

When he had finished his supplication, Will leaned back in his chair. "How are you feeling now?" he asked again, trying not to sound anxious.

"My stomach is still a bit queasy, but I don't know if it's the salt water or the mushrooms," she told him honestly.

"We'll just have to wait and see," he admitted. "Why don't you try to sleep now? I'll keep watch over you."

But she was more interested in the explanation he had promised for his presence at Silvercrosse Hall. "For one thing, Will," she stated, pushing herself up onto her elbows, "you just burst into the kitchen out of nowhere. Were you traveling near here? I thought you were in London. And why in the world did you think that I might have eaten a funeral bell mushroom? For that matter, how did you know we had mushrooms at all? Why were you so unkind to Helen? It's not as though she did anything on purpose."

"That's just it," Will said grimly. "It was no accident Helen invited you to gather mushrooms with her. In fact, I think she arranged everything specifically in order to poison you."

"*What?* Why would she do that?" Charissa exclaimed. "That's absurd. No, I cannot believe it."

"I'm aware it sounds ludicrous, but I could not have lived with myself if Helen had harmed you in some way and I had not warned you of her treachery."

"*Her treachery?*"

"She detests you, sweetheart. She is not your friend."

"Why do you say that?"

"Because not only is she in love with me, as we all guessed, but she also believes God has destined her to be my wife. Apparently, marrying me is her *idée fixe*, her obsession."

This was something Charissa could not deny, and she told him about Helen's practice signatures discarded in the wastepaper basket in London.

Will grunted. "She's been infatuated with me for years, well before I came to Murrington. Evidently I met her once, but I don't recall it."

"But if she knew you, she must have pretended not to recognize you last spring."

"Correct. She chose not to reveal my true identity."

"So when did the two of you first meet? If you don't remember it, how do you know about it? How do you know any of this?"

"I came across her diary. It was an act of providence, or, as Barnabas would say, a matter of God's perfect timing."

"I know Helen keeps a journal—she has often mentioned it—but how did *you* find it?"

Will described how it had come into his possession and confessed his decision to read it in order to protect himself from Helen's volatile behavior. He spelled out how she had become infatuated with him, including her conviction that he was hers by divine fiat.

At first, as she listened to Will's story, Charissa pitied Helen's unrequited love for Will. "It's a tragic case of misplaced affection, to be sure," she agreed, "but I just can't believe Helen would be as angry at me as you imply. For one thing, I've always tried to be kind to her."

"On the contrary, you are her competition. In fact, her diary confirms she's identified you as the lone stumbling block to securing my passionate, exclusive, and lifelong devotion. She considers you her one-and-only obstacle, no matter whom you marry."

Having experienced firsthand Helen's single-minded determination to have her own way, Charissa could no longer doubt Will's story. At last she understood; Helen really did hate her enough to dispose of her. Fear and anger gripped her simultaneously. "If I did eat funeral bells, I may truly die!" she exclaimed, furious at her friend's betrayal.

Tight with anxiety he refused to show, Will scooted over onto the side of the bed and took her right up into his arms. "Hush, sweetheart," he soothed her, nuzzling her hair with his lips. "The danger is real, I confess, yet I cannot believe the Lord has led me here too late to save you. He went to great trouble to prompt me to ride north." God willing, he spoke the truth.

"Yes, perhaps you are right." Comforted, she melted against him.

Although he would have preferred to keep her in his embrace, he laid her back down onto the bed. "Why don't you just sleep now?" he suggested again.

She did feel worn out after her ordeal, she realized. "You will stay here with me?"

"I will," he promised. "I'm not going anywhere."

"Dearest Will," she whispered, resting her head on the pillow and closing her eyes. He pulled a blanket up over her, even though she was still fully dressed.

She fell asleep quickly, and he slid back onto his chair, noticing that the late afternoon shadows had deepened into dusky twilight. He rose, lit a candle, and stoked up the fire, for the evening was sure to be cold. After he had created a good blaze, he returned to his watch over Charissa. *Please God*, he prayed silently, *let this vigil be a calm and quiet one.*

Chapter 32

Meanwhile, downstairs Sir Godfrey had retreated to the library. He wanted to wait until Penelope arrived before he confronted Helen with Will's allegations. He would have liked to read more of the journal itself, but Helen had it with her, and, given its explosive contents, she was unlikely to relinquish it without making an unpleasant scene.

Unable to sit quietly, he ended up standing by the window, watching for Penelope's arrival. He wanted to go upstairs to check on Charissa, but the feeling that he was an interloper in his own home, while it angered him, also held him back. She must be doing well, he knew, because if she were not, he would be told.

In about three-quarters of an hour, although it seemed like a year to Sir Godfrey, he heard the carriage he had sent for Penelope clatter down the drive. Instantly, he flew out of the house and onto the front steps in order to meet her before Helen realized she had come.

"Sir Godfrey!" Penelope cried as the rig came to a stop. "Whatever has happened? How is Charissa?"

Sir Godfrey helped her out of the carriage and held onto her arm, preventing her from continuing up to the front door. "Charissa seems to be well for now. But Penelope," he said heavily, "I need your assistance."

He told her everything, and after she had listened without interruption, they went into the drawing room. Penelope had been dispirited by Sir Godfrey's strange tale, but not as skeptical as he thought she'd be, and he knew he'd been right to send for her.

"Helen," Penelope said, holding her hands out to her sister as Sir Godfrey shut the drawing room door.

"Penny!" groused Helen. She remained seated, her expression sullen. "What are you doing here? I'm all right. *Everyone's* fine. Except I've been in here all by myself for ages," she complained, glaring at Sir Godfrey, who glared back.

Penelope sat down beside her sister, who, she noticed, had the journal in her lap. "Sir Godfrey tells me you are still in love with Lord Hartwell. Is that true?"

Helen fiddled unconsciously with the serpent ring on the fourth finger of her right hand. "Penny," she declared solemnly, "the Lord told me years ago I would marry William Devreux, Viscount Disborough who is now the Earl of Hartwell. You must believe me!"

"It seems unlikely," Penelope replied gently. "Lord Hartwell is a peer. You are merely a gentleman's daughter with no fortune." She did not add that Helen—even if she had had remarkable physical beauty—was nevertheless, at age twenty-seven, considered by the *beau monde* to be past her prime.

"The difference in our stations is no real impediment," countered Helen. "And he has plenty of money. The greatest hindrance to my happiness is *Charissa!* She's trying to steal my William—right out from under my nose!"

"But Charissa is engaged to Sir Godfrey. I can't imagine…"

Helen cut her off. "If her betrothed would play the part of the hero instead of the coward, it would help."

"Now see here!" Sir Godfrey bristled. "You wrote in your diary you would *remove* Charissa *by the roots* whether I marry her or not."

Helen turned to him with a snarl. "You *have* read my journal! How dare you violate my privacy in such an outrageous manner?!"

"I've only read the last page of your pathetic screed!" he snapped back. "It was Hartwell who found the book and showed it to me. What else do you think prompted him to come all the way to Silvercrosse Hall? It is *he* who has read the whole miserable lot of it!"

Helen's face crumpled. *"What?"*

"That's right," Sir Godfrey said unsympathetically. "I was planning to explain it to you tactfully, but you have forced my hand. Hartwell knows everything, and he rejects it all. Every single dimwitted word!"

"Oh!" she gasped in horror. Clutching the diary to her chest she rushed out of the room, sobbing.

Penelope moved after her sister, but Sir Godfrey restrained her. "Let Helen go," he advised. "She'll need time to accept the truth."

Penelope sighed, regret in her eyes. "I'm sorry," she said helplessly.

"So am I," he replied, gazing over her shoulder out the window.

Upstairs, Charissa slowly came to consciousness after a comfortable nap; it had been an hour since she had drifted off to sleep. She sat up, threw off her coverlet, and thought how grubby it felt to sleep in clothes. Looking at the chair beside the bed, she saw Will sprawled out on it, fast asleep and snoring ever so lightly. He must have been exhausted after his breakneck journey north, poor thing.

Then she realized with surprise that she herself felt perfectly fine. No nausea, no cramping, no headache—nothing that resembled food poisoning. Was it because the milk thistle extract was working, or because she had never needed it in the first place? Or was her recovery a bona fide miracle? No matter what the truth, she breathed a prayer of thanks.

She turned her attention back to Will, and her heart beat faster, as it always seemed to do when he was near. He had raced to her side when he believed her to be in danger! A freakish series of circumstances had led him back to Silvercrosse, but how grateful she was he had put two and two together and had made the journey in such haste. Most men would never have risked appearing ridiculous by bringing what seemed to be—on the surface—a wild accusation against a lady.

A mixture of emotions washed over Charissa as she thought about Helen. How dreadful it was to contemplate that someone she'd considered a friend hated her enough to kill her. Although Will's contention Helen had poisoned her would probably never be proved, Charissa could not escape the fact he might very well be correct. She shuddered, unable to think of anything she had done that would merit the loathing Helen had for her. It was not her fault Will had no romantic interest in Helen. Sadly, Helen had either brought her woes upon herself or made them much worse by her poor choices.

Charissa felt aggrieved and yet sorry for the whole situation, too. She had always considered Helen an interesting person, but unfortunately the woman had chosen to waste her sharp mind and lively imagination on futile and selfish fantasies. Although to be fair, Charissa could understand how she had fallen in love with Will. Surely many women had—Charissa herself included!

Charissa wrapped her arms around her knees and looked at Will again, feeling a rush of warmth when she considered again how he had come to rescue her. And how he had carried her up the stairs in his arms. And how she had told him she loved him... but, goodness!—*what was she thinking?*

She was engaged to marry another man.

And yet—in spite of the fact Will had not said he loved her, too—he had held her as though she belonged to him.

What did it all mean?

Her mind in a whirl, she rose, careful not to wake him. She lit another candle, smoothed out her wrinkled gown, and went to the washstand to freshen up. Afterwards, she stepped in front of the mirror over her dresser and took the remaining pins out of her disheveled hair. She shook out the long tresses, and as she brushed them, they fell over her shoulders in loose curls. With no maid present to assist her, she pulled them back and tied them with a ribbon.

She turned around and saw Will staring at her. "Pretty," he said.

She blushed. "You're awake."

"How do you feel?" he asked for the third time.

"Completely well." She beamed at him. "No dreadful symptoms of any kind. Although I *am* getting hungry."

"Not for mushrooms, I hope."

"No!" she agreed fervently. "Toast and tea will suffice. I'll have some sent up. Would you like something to eat as well?"

"Yes, thank you." He stood, and—in order to distract himself from thinking about how attractive she looked—he went over to the fire and stoked it up again.

Charissa had said she would call for a servant, but as she watched

Will stir the embers into crackling flames, she found she didn't want to end the moment alone with him. Not yet.

When Will was done with the poker, he set it back down and straightened up. Gazing across the room at Charissa, he was amazed at how natural, how comfortable, it felt to be close to her. She was so beautiful.

Their eyes locked and they began to move toward one another, but suddenly—bang!—the door to the bedroom flew the rest of the way open, loudly hitting the wall.

Having escaped the drawing room, Helen stormed in, her eyes wild and her breathing a series of frenzied gasps.

"Helen!" Charissa stumbled guiltily back from Will. Both the dogs, who had been stretched lazily on the bed, let out a few startled yips.

Will sprang into action, thrusting his body in front of Charissa's in an instinctive attempt to shield her. *"Get out!"* he bellowed at Helen. The dogs growled as he spoke, their bodies twitching in readiness to protect their mistress.

But Charissa was not Helen's target. "William, dearest William," she blurted out, "you cannot deny the truth any more. Sir Godfrey just told me you've read my journal, and I was so embarrassed to think of it, but now—oh, William—I realize you must finally understand the truth! You know you pledged yourself to me that day in London so long ago, and you must keep to your vow. God has brought you to Murrington to honor it!" She raised up her right hand and her ring gleamed in the firelight. "I love you! I have always loved you! Who else would be so faithful, so loyal always? Certainly not *her!*" Helen glowered at Charissa. "She rejected you, but I *never* will!"

Well past the end of his patience, Will pulled no punches. "Miss St. Swythin, I do not remember the encounter you claim we had years ago, and I most assuredly have never loved you. Neither do I do love you now—or even like you at all—and you may be utterly certain that I *never* want to look upon your face again. Do I make myself clear?"

Helen stood stiffly, staring mutely at him and trying to make sense of his response. But as the meaning of his hard speech dawned on her, she drooped visibly. Her pale face contorted in misery, while her trembling hands still clung to her journal.

"Helen," Charissa said softly, coming up beside Will. "Let go of that book. You've allowed those thoughts to become like Holy Scripture to you, but they're not the words of God. They're your own ideas, and—as real as they seem—they've deceived you and caused you to focus on your own dreams instead of God's plans for you. Don't let them distract you from the truth any longer. Let them go."

"No," Helen replied dully, her fingers curling around the diary.

"We've all done the same thing to a lesser or greater extent," Charissa tried again. "We've all stubbornly followed our own understanding and insisted upon our own way. But you can repent and begin a new life. We all have. I have, Will has."

No light appeared in Helen's eyes as she listened to Charissa's speech, and when Charissa referred to Will by his first name, something inside Helen snapped.

"I hate you, Charissa Armitage!" she shrieked. *"I hate you, hate you, hate you!"* And on the final "hate you!" she hurled the journal straight at Charissa's head.

Charissa leapt out of the way at the same time as Will pulled her toward himself. Thus the book missed her entirely, flew across the room, and ended up right on top of the logs in the roaring fireplace.

"Noooooo!" Helen screamed piteously. *"No!"*

She ran to the hearth, but Charissa reached out and stopped her. "Let it burn, Helen!" she ordered, seeing an opportunity for Helen to be delivered from her bondage to the past.

Helen struggled ferociously and managed to writhe out of Charissa's grasp, but Will caught her and forcibly prevented her from rescuing the diary. "No!" she wailed as the pages curled up and crumbled into the charred relics of a woman scorned. "My journal, my journal!"

Charissa heard footsteps in the hall, and looked up to see Sir Godfrey run into the room, followed by Penelope and, from the other direction, Nancy and Jack. "What is going on here?" Sir Godfrey roared. "What is this screaming?"

"Penny, Charissa destroyed my journal!" Helen sagged into Will's arms, but he quickly pushed her into her sister's embrace.

Charissa explained to the others what had happened. Sir Godfrey shook his head as he listened. Penelope looked not at all like her usual self as she held her distraught sister.

After Charissa finished the story, Sir Godfrey stared at the weeping Helen and glanced back at Will and Charissa for a second or two. Noticing Charissa's undone hair, he whirled around and lashed out at Nancy. "And where were you during all this commotion, Miss Roberts? Why did you leave Miss Armitage alone with Hartwell?"

Alarmed, Nancy replied, "I was with your aunt, sir. She needed me. I was planning to check on Miss Armitage as soon as I could."

"Don't be cross with her, Godfrey!" Charissa retorted. "She has been very solicitous of me, but she can't be in two places at once."

Will set his mouth in a hard line. "I have acted with the utmost propriety, sir, and I deeply resent any implication otherwise!" Involuntarily, his fists clenched.

"Sir Godfrey," Penelope interrupted urgently, as she held the shuddering Helen, "this is neither the time nor the place for such a discussion! We must focus instead on how best to help my sister."

Her remonstration had the desired effect upon Sir Godfrey. "You are correct, Penelope," he conceded, after taking a moment to consider her words. "Your clear thinking does you credit in these ridiculous and regrettable circumstances."

Turning to addressing the anxious Nancy, he said, "Miss Roberts, I do understand you have a responsibility to my aunt. You are free to return to her." Relieved to have been given permission to depart, Nancy fled from the room. "Jack," Sir Godfrey went on, "escort Miss Helen back to the drawing room for now. Miss St. Swythin will come down for her shortly."

Jack took Helen by the arm and was pleasantly surprised she made no objection to his guidance. He led her downstairs and left her there, where she collapsed on a chair, her emotions spent. Utterly alone, she stared desolately at the embers of the drawing room fire, as silent and white as a ghost.

Chapter 33

In Charissa's room, however, the discussion continued.

"Has Sir Godfrey informed you of why I came to Silvercrosse Hall today, Miss St. Swythin?" Will asked Penelope. When she answered in the affirmative, he said regretfully, "I'm sorry to be the bearer of such unpleasant accusations against your sister, but it was all spelled out in her diary."

The four of them glanced at what was left of the journal smoldering in the fireplace.

"Sir Godfrey himself read the last page," Will added, "so you know I am not inventing the story." He looked at Sir Godfrey, half expecting to be contradicted, but the older man merely nodded wearily.

"Tell Penelope about the botany book," Charissa prompted Will.

"Ah yes," he said, and he related how he had found the feminine bookmark on the funeral bell mushroom page. Sir Godfrey hadn't heard that detail before, and he crossed his arms in disgust. Penelope gazed at Will unhappily.

"Now you understand why I came to Silvercrosse at once," Will stated. "I had uncovered a serious threat to Charissa's life. But even beyond that, I had a deep-seated agitation I couldn't disregard. It was a sense of imminent danger. I can't explain it rationally, but it was completely real to me. I asked my friend Mr. Barnabas Worthington his opinion on the matter, and he advised me to trust my intuition and give the results of my actions to God. So I rode with all haste—and frankly, it cannot be mere chance I arrived when I did. It is no coincidence!"

"You did the right thing, Lord Hartwell. But I wish I had recognized the depth of Helen's delusion myself. I should have seen it," Penelope said sadly.

Sir Godfrey grunted irritably. "How could you have seen it? She hid her inner life from us all."

"So what is to be done with her?" Penelope sighed.

"I am the local magistrate," Sir Godfrey reminded them briskly, "and I see no point in bringing the law into this. However, even if Helen did not attempt poisoning, she plainly considers Charissa an enemy."

"I concur," said Will. "Helen is unstable and therefore dangerous."

"I don't suppose reason would have any effect upon her?" Charissa asked bleakly.

Penelope shook her head. "I doubt it. She has rarely shown the ability to accept unpleasant realities."

"That's a nice way of putting it," Will remarked dryly.

"Personally, I think Helen should be separated from Charissa." Sir Godfrey said. "But what is the best way to accomplish that?"

"Is there anywhere else Helen could go to live permanently?" Will inquired. "With some distant cousin somewhere?"

"No," said Penelope flatly, "unless she went to India to join Hector and his new wife. I wish that were possible."

Charissa looked over at Penelope. "Halfway around the world wouldn't be a bad thing."

"Why can't she go?" asked Will. Sending the woman to another continent seemed like a splendid idea.

"I have no money with which to pay her way," Penelope answered honestly.

Well, of course, Will thought. He ought to have remembered the St. Swythins' reduced circumstances. But, happily, what was an obstacle for them was no problem for him. "Then I'll underwrite her journey myself."

"Oh no, Lord Hartwell, I simply couldn't allow…" Penelope began, but Will cut her off.

"Oh yes, Miss St. Swythin, you *will* allow me do this. I shall pay for her passage." He eyed Penelope decisively. "For Charissa's sake."

Penelope opened her mouth to object but found she could not. "You are a good man, Lord Hartwell."

"And I can sweeten the pot," Charissa offered, thrilled with the proposal. "I'll give Helen money for some of the expenses she'll encounter once she arrives."

"Excellent," Will declared. "It is settled. To India Helen shall go!"

Sir Godfrey looked tired, but he could find no fault with their plan. "Very well. It is an appropriate solution."

Now that Helen's fate had been decided, Penelope walked over and put her arms around her friend. "Oh Charissa, I'm so glad you are well."

"So far I feel fine," Charissa admitted, "although Miss Roberts has told me I must continue to take the milk thistle extract. I only ate a few of the mushrooms anyway." She smiled sheepishly. "And they are long gone."

"Poor darling," Penelope said warmly.

Now that their makeshift conference had concluded, Penelope took the pale, spiritless Helen home to Wisteria Cottage. She then returned to Silvercrosse Hall to spend the night watching over Charissa. After the four them suffered through an awkward and mostly silent dinner, Will withdrew to his old room, and Penelope went up to Charissa's bedchamber. However, Sir Godfrey asked Charissa to meet him in the library before she retired. Between the two of them, there was a pressing issue needing to be addressed.

Charissa's normally cheerful countenance was grave as she entered the familiar room. Sir Godfrey sat behind his desk, stiff and unsmiling.

"Please have a seat," he instructed her formally.

She did so without a word.

He pursed his lips. "Charissa, over the last few hours, you have made your feelings quite clear to me. And to the rest of the household."

She stared down at the desk, unable to meet his eyes. "Lord Hartwell saved my life."

"That is one possible interpretation of today's events," Sir Godfrey said. "Obviously, it is what you want to believe."

She remained silent, unsure of how to reply.

"You promised you would marry me," he continued, "and yet you have thrown yourself into another man's arms and sought his comfort instead of mine. What do you have to say for yourself?"

Charissa heard the pain in his voice, and her eyes swam with tears. She despised herself for hurting him. She desperately wanted to reassure him of her love and tell him she eagerly anticipated the day she would become his wife—but she could not do so, because it was not true.

Sir Godfrey waited, but she did not speak.

"If you have nothing to say, I trust I speak for us both when I declare our engagement dissolved," Sir Godfrey stated finally, his voice brittle. "Goodnight, Charissa."

"Godfrey, I never wished to…."

"I said *goodnight*."

Without looking at him, she rose and quit the library without another word, her silken slippers making almost no noise as she went.

Sir Godfrey sat rigidly, his elbows resting on the desktop, but when she had gone he put his head down in his hands. He knew whatever he might say to Charissa would make no difference, because the truth was incontrovertible.

Her heart belonged to William Devreux, Earl of Hartwell, and it had ever since the day he had first come to Silvercrosse Hall.

Charissa returned to her room and found Penelope waiting there, already dressed for bed. Although Charissa was glad her friend was going to stay with her in case she became ill, the last thing she wanted to do was discuss the day's events.

Penelope handed her a bottle and spoon. "It's time for you to take your milk thistle extract now."

"Yes, thank you," replied Charissa, pouring a dose of the liquid for herself and swallowing it.

Penelope adjusted her sleeping cap and climbed into the warm bed, which could easily hold them both. "When Helen and I were young, we shared a room," she recalled. "I always liked the warmth of another body under the covers with me, especially in the wintertime. Tonight you and I will be like sisters."

"I would have liked a sister—an ally and confidante." *But just not tonight*, Charissa added to herself as she pulled on her nightgown.

"Helen was never that," Penelope admitted. "That is why both you and I need each other." She glanced over at Charissa. "Do you want to talk?"

Brushing out her hair in front of the looking glass, Charissa saw Penelope's earnest face reflected from across the room. "Not really." When her friend looked disappointed, she said, "Not yet, anyway."

"I thought you wanted a confidante."

"We'll speak in the morning. For now I just want to sleep. Give myself time to sort through it all. You understand."

"Very well." Penelope lay her head down on the pillow. After a short silence, she said, "He loves you, you know."

"Who?"

"Lord Hartwell."

Charissa hoped so with all her heart. But he still hadn't said the words. "Good night, Penny," she said firmly.

"Good night, Charissa." Penelope gave up and rolled over onto her side.

As Charissa set down the brush and turned to extinguish the candle on the dresser, she saw her silver cross necklace lying on a lace doily, gleaming in the soft light. She had not worn it today. She picked it up and let it rest in the palm of her hand, a unique and beautiful treasure. But at the same time she realized it did not—should not—belong to her, for she was not, and never would be, the mistress of Silvercrosse Hall.

She opened a drawer, put the necklace inside, and blew out the light.

When Will opened his eyes, he stared at the frosty diamond-paned window, confused for a second about where he was. Then he remembered everything and threw off the blanket, anxious to know how Charissa had fared through the night. Surely he would have been notified if anything were amiss, but, cynically, he suspected Sir Godfrey would take pleasure in keeping her away from him.

He had to find out how she was. It was early, but someone would be up; someone would know her condition. He observed that a maid had been in to build up the fire, but he didn't bother to call a servant to help him dress—it would take too long. However, as he buttoned his shirt in haste, he glanced out of the window, and what he saw brought his worries to an abrupt end. Out on the pale, sparkling lawn stood a figure wrapped in a warm cape, accompanied by two white dogs.

Charissa.

He finished dressing quickly and made his way out of the house. He caught up to her on one of the gravel paths, where she was sitting on a bench with her eyes closed.

He paused, not wanting to disturb her. But the dogs welcomed him with their characteristic enthusiasm, and she was aware someone had come. She opened her eyes and saw him.

"Will," she said, her cheeks rosy and her breath a cool, silvery cloud.

Feeling no need for words, he walked over to her and extended his hand. She put her fingers on his palm and stood up, beginning to say something, but he pressed the index finger of his other hand onto her lips. Then, pulling her sharply to him, he kissed her fiercely.

When he knew he had to stop or he would go beyond the bounds of honor, he cradled her head on his chest. He heard her murmur his name again, and he stroked her hair softly.

After a few seconds—during which he gathered his courage—he remarked, seemingly randomly, "I know you appreciate Silvercrosse Hall, Charissa, but Ashbourne Park is picturesque, too. The library is full of all kinds of books. There's a magnificent prospect from upstairs looking out over a waterfall, and beyond it, a folly or two. A ruined Greek Temple of Love, that sort of thing. Great inspiration for novels, I suppose." He was babbling, he realized. "I have lots of dogs, too, and there's room for Mr. Pettmee and Commodore to run and play to their heart's content."

The meaning of his words was not lost on Charissa, and she looked up at him hopefully. "Just what are you intimating, Lord Hartwell?" she asked.

"I was thinking maybe, well… perhaps you might… you might want to come live there." He sounded like a mutton-head, he told himself.

She smiled into his eyes. "I assume you're not suggesting I accept a position as keeper of the canines."

In spite of his nervousness, or perhaps because of it, he smirked. "Confound it, Charissa. Of course not. I'm asking you to be *my wife!*"

Charissa felt a thrill run through her—from her head right down to her toes—and for a moment she was simply too full of joy to respond.

However, Will misunderstood her silence. "Unless you feel honor-bound to keep your word to Sir Godfrey," he said, fear gripping him as he contemplated the unthinkable—her refusal. The silence before she replied was pure torture.

But his trepidation vanished when she said simply, "I am no longer betrothed."

"Then marry *me*, my love," Will insisted. *"Marry me!"*

"Oh yes, Will, yes." She threw back her head and laughed jubilantly. *"Yes!"*

He wanted to kiss her, but instead he lifted her right up off her feet and twirled her around, making her squeal. Then he set her back down on her toes and kissed her anyway. It was a long, satisfying, and exquisitely passionate moment.

When they paused for breath once again, he told her the plans he had been so bold as to map out in his head during the night.

"Today," he advised her, "it seems you must continue with the milk thistle extract in order to make sure you are quite well, my love. But, if you are willing, tomorrow we leave for London, and I am hoping that Miss Penelope St. Swythin will consent to accompany us for propriety's sake."

"You're taking me to London and not Ashbourne Park?"

"We'll go to Ashbourne Park soon enough, but in London I plan to purchase a special license from the archbishop. You see, being a peer does mean some things can be rather more easily accomplished."

Charissa gasped with delight. "A special license! Oh Will, we won't need to have the banns read and wait weeks to be married!"

"That's right, my darling. I confess I can barely stand to wait at all. Therefore, we shall be married the day after we arrive in London. With Miss St. Swythin and Mr. Worthington on hand to be our witnesses. Is that acceptable to you?"

"More than acceptable. It's perfect!"

"A perfect beginning, at any rate. I wish I could promise a perfect middle and perfect ending, but life being what it is…"

"Life being what it is, it is in the Lord's hands. He's brought us this far, my dearest love, and He shall bring us the rest of the way." She stroked his cheek with her hand.

"I am truly amazed. How I love you, Charissa." Savoring the delicious softness of her lips, he allowed himself once more to kiss her lingeringly. He would never deserve such happiness, but he could be supremely grateful for it. *"Amazing grace, how sweet the sound that saved a wretch like me!"*

She smiled; the words of the well-known hymn described her, too. *"I once was lost, but now am found—was blind, but now I see,"* she said, kissing him back.

Regency Glossary

Banns	public announcements of the intention to marry, read in the Anglican church on each of the three Sundays before the wedding (required unless a *special license* was purchased from a bishop or archbishop)
Battledore and shuttlecock	game similar to badminton
Beau monde	fashionable upper class society
Bit of muslin	woman of low morals
Blood and thunder	mixture of port wine and brandy
Come-out	young woman's official entrance into society, signaling her eligibility as a marriage partner
Courtesy	bow of respect (origin of the word *curtsey*)
Courtesy title	lord's lesser title used by his eldest son and heir
Dower house	smaller house on an estate where the widow moved after the death of the owner
Fat wit	foolish person
Four-in-hand	carriage pulled by four horses
Foxed	drunk
Gentleman	upper class man, indicative of good breeding and social standing rather than upright character and behavior
In one's cups	drunk

Jingle-brain	foolish person
Landau	large carriage, the Regency version of a family van
Light-skirt	woman of low morals
Marriage mart	popular term for the season
Mutton-head	foolish person
Nonconformist	describes any of a number of Protestant groups in England which did not conform to the theology and/or practices of the Anglican Church
Royal Hospital Chelsea	retirement home for military veterans designed by Sir Christopher Wren
Sauce box	aggressive, cheeky person
Season (the)	usually the three months after Easter, when most of the upper class were in London; debutantes and eligible bachelors attended social events with the express purpose of finding a spouse
Sent down (from university)	expelled
Special license	marriage license purchased from a bishop or archbishop so that the wedding could take place, without reading the banns
Spencer	short jacket worn over a dress
Swell	slang for gentleman (see definition above)
Tilbury	small, one-horse carriage
Tisane	fragrant, often herbal, tea
Toff	slang for gentleman (see definition above)
Ton	fashionable upper class society
Vauxhall Gardens	popular pleasure gardens in London

About the Author

Educated at Duke University, Yale Divinity School, and Regent University, Dana has always had a love of both Scripture and history. She works as a graphic designer and enjoys traveling with her husband, her daughter, and her parents to interesting destinations. In 2013 she completed a pilgrimage she had long hoped to accomplish—a visit to Chawton Cottage in England, Jane Austen's home!

Made in the USA
Middletown, DE
22 July 2024

57829045R00168